OUTCAST

BY KIRKMAN
& AZACETA

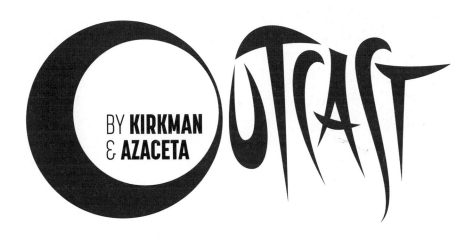

VOLUME 4: UNDER DEVIL'S WING

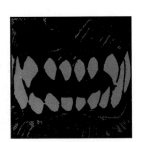

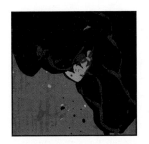

OUTCAST BY KIRKMAN & AZACETA
VOL. 4: UNDER DEVIL'S WING
February 2017
First printing

ISBN: 978-1-5343-0050-7

Published by Image Comics, Inc.

Office of publication: 2701 NW Vaughn St., Ste. 780, Portland, OR 97210.

Printed in the U.S.A.

For information regarding the CPSIA on this printed material call: 203-595-3636 and provide reference # RICH - 724108.

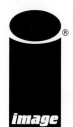

Robert Kirkman
Creator, Writer

Paul Azaceta
Artist

Elizabeth Breitweiser
Colorist

Rus Wooton
Letterer

Paul Azaceta
Elizabeth Breitweiser
Cover

Arielle Basich
Assistant Editor

Sean Mackiewicz
Editor

Rian Hughes
Logo Design

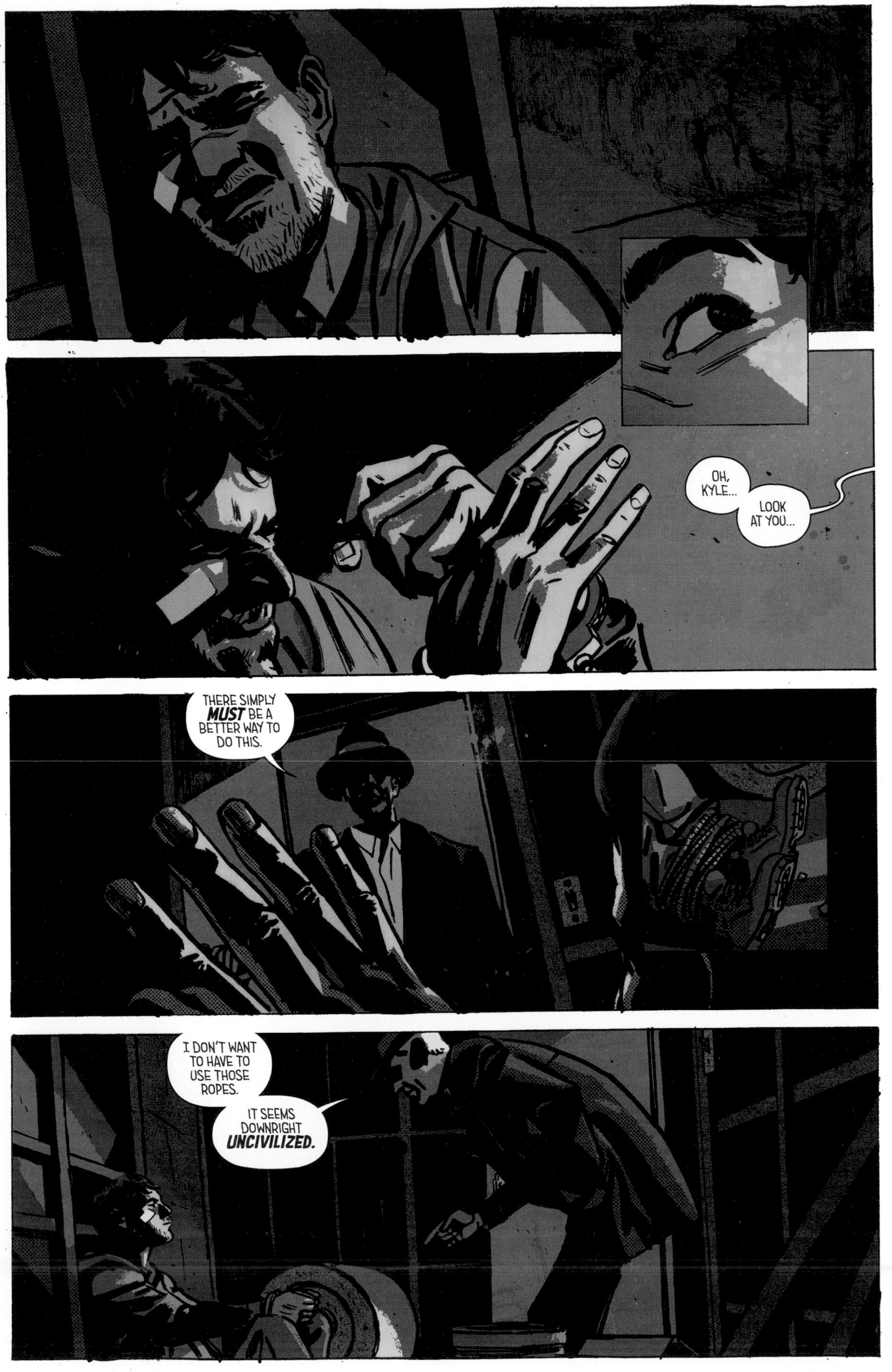
OH, KYLE...
LOOK AT YOU...
THERE SIMPLY **MUST** BE A BETTER WAY TO DO THIS.
I DON'T WANT TO HAVE TO USE THOSE ROPES.
IT SEEMS DOWNRIGHT **UNCIVILIZED.**

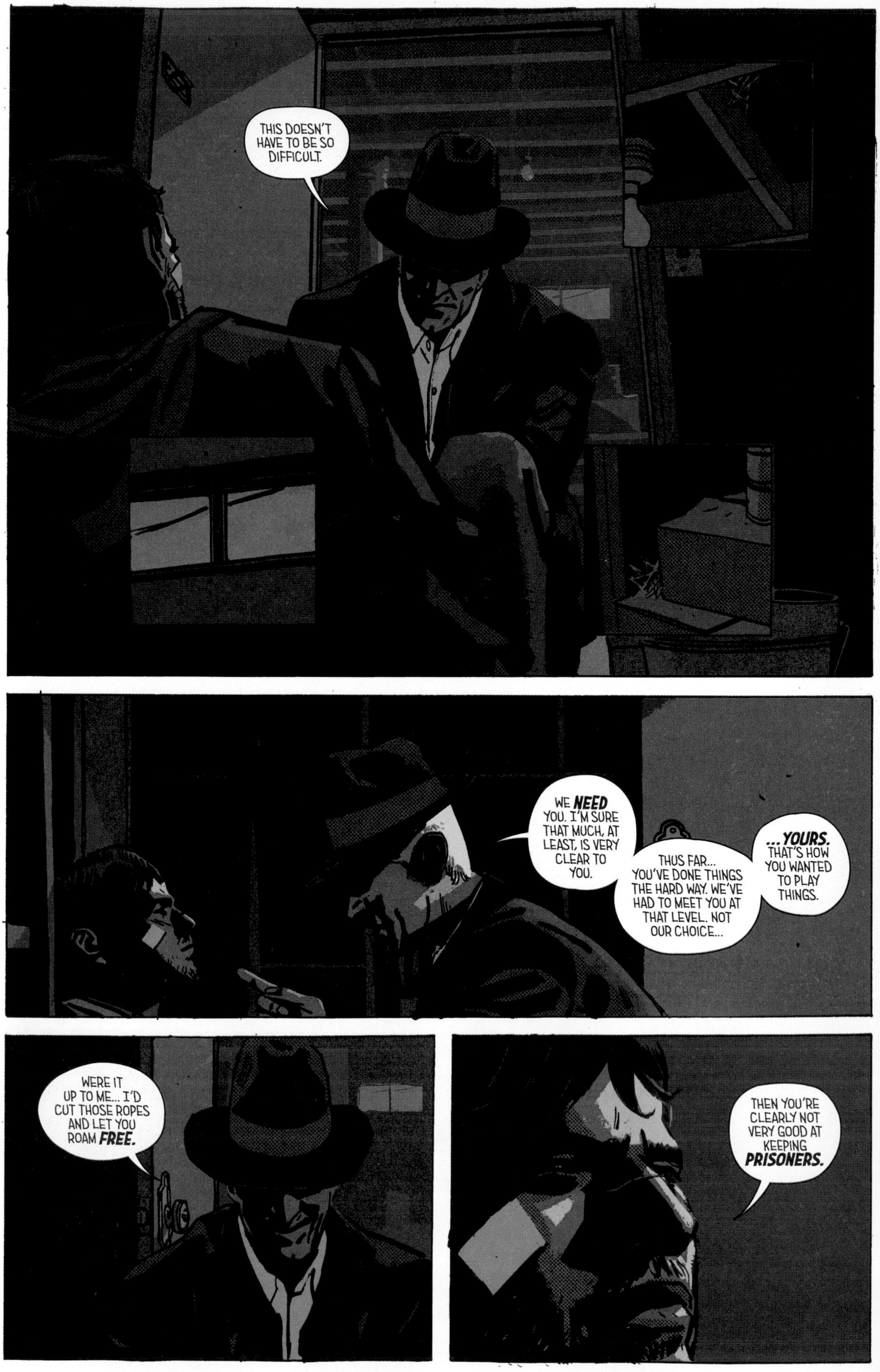
THIS DOESN'T HAVE TO BE SO DIFFICULT.
WE **NEED** YOU. I'M SURE THAT MUCH, AT LEAST, IS VERY CLEAR TO YOU.
THUS FAR... YOU'VE DONE THINGS THE HARD WAY. WE'VE HAD TO MEET YOU AT THAT LEVEL. NOT OUR CHOICE...
...YOURS. THAT'S HOW YOU WANTED TO PLAY THINGS.
WERE IT UP TO ME... I'D CUT THOSE ROPES AND LET YOU ROAM ***FREE.***
THEN YOU'RE CLEARLY NOT VERY GOOD AT KEEPING ***PRISONERS.***

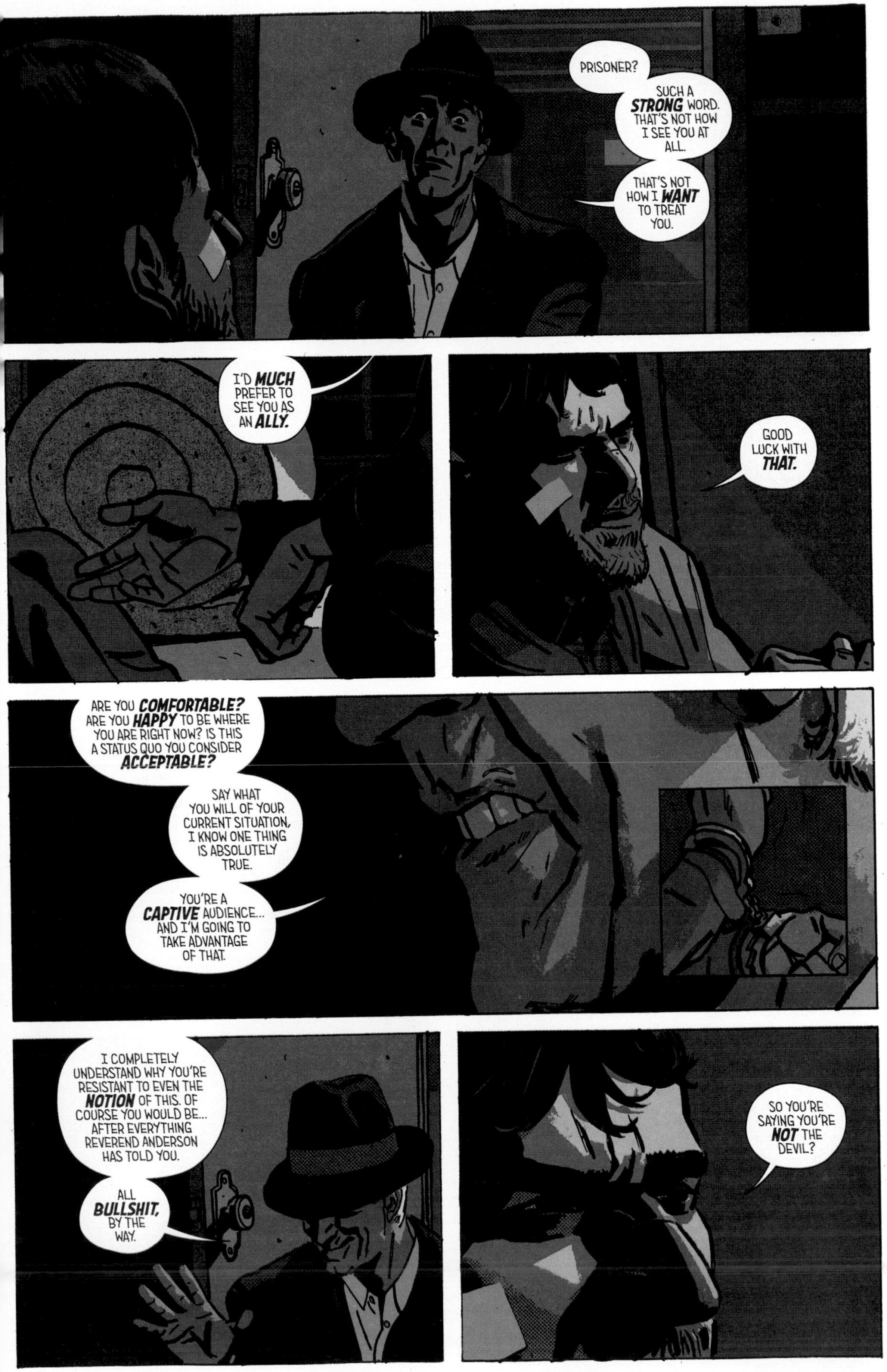
PRISONER?
SUCH A STRONG WORD. THAT'S NOT HOW I SEE YOU AT ALL.
THAT'S NOT HOW I WANT TO TREAT YOU.
I'D MUCH PREFER TO SEE YOU AS AN ALLY.
GOOD LUCK WITH THAT.
ARE YOU COMFORTABLE? ARE YOU HAPPY TO BE WHERE YOU ARE RIGHT NOW? IS THIS A STATUS QUO YOU CONSIDER ACCEPTABLE?
SAY WHAT YOU WILL OF YOUR CURRENT SITUATION, I KNOW ONE THING IS ABSOLUTELY TRUE.
YOU'RE A CAPTIVE AUDIENCE... AND I'M GOING TO TAKE ADVANTAGE OF THAT.
I COMPLETELY UNDERSTAND WHY YOU'RE RESISTANT TO EVEN THE NOTION OF THIS. OF COURSE YOU WOULD BE... AFTER EVERYTHING REVEREND ANDERSON HAS TOLD YOU.
ALL BULLSHIT, BY THE WAY.
SO YOU'RE SAYING YOU'RE NOT THE DEVIL?

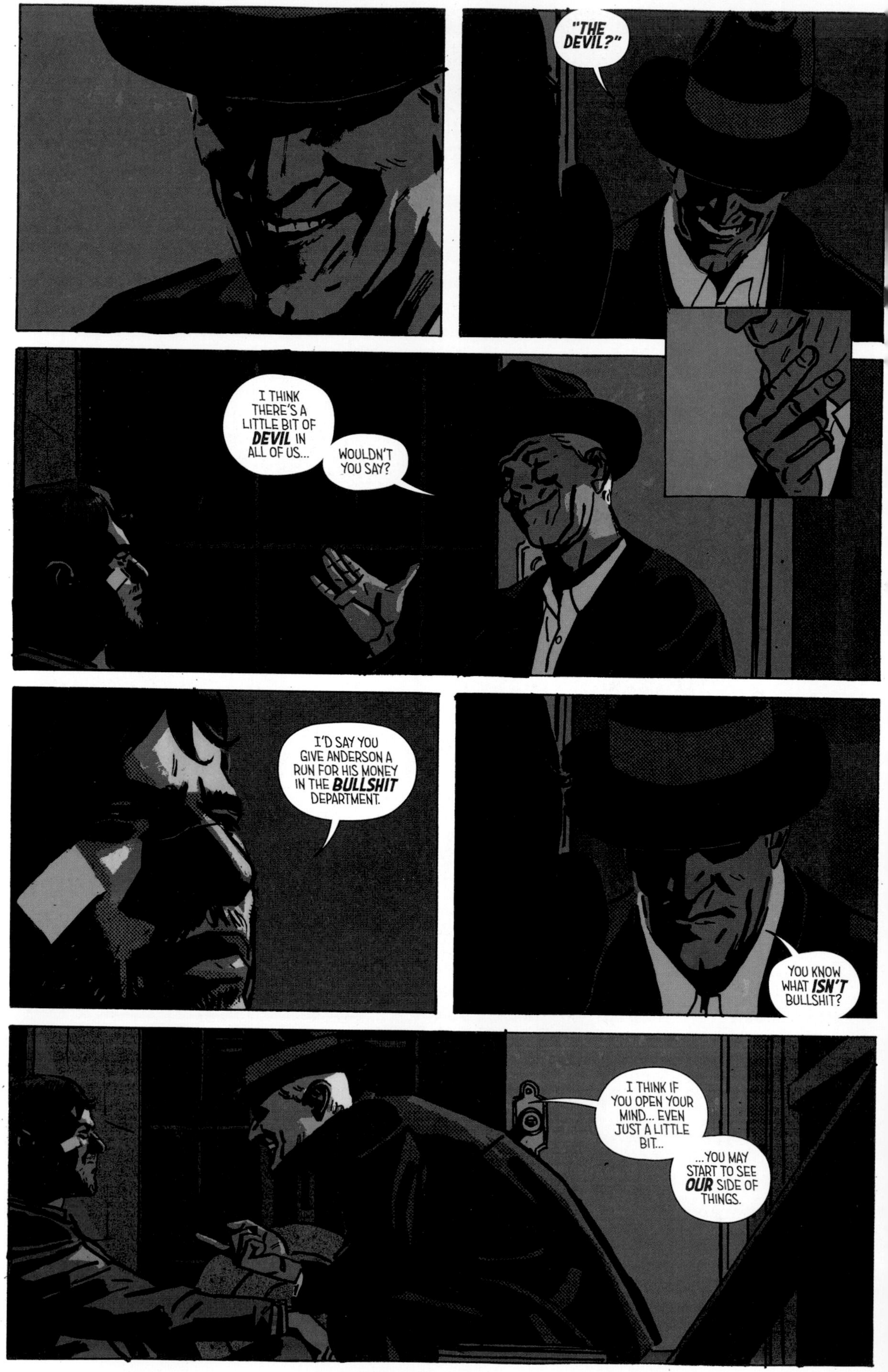

"THE DEVIL?"
I THINK THERE'S A LITTLE BIT OF DEVIL IN ALL OF US...
WOULDN'T YOU SAY?
I'D SAY YOU GIVE ANDERSON A RUN FOR HIS MONEY IN THE BULLSHIT DEPARTMENT.
YOU KNOW WHAT ISN'T BULLSHIT?
I THINK IF YOU OPEN YOUR MIND... EVEN JUST A LITTLE BIT...
...YOU MAY START TO SEE OUR SIDE OF THINGS.

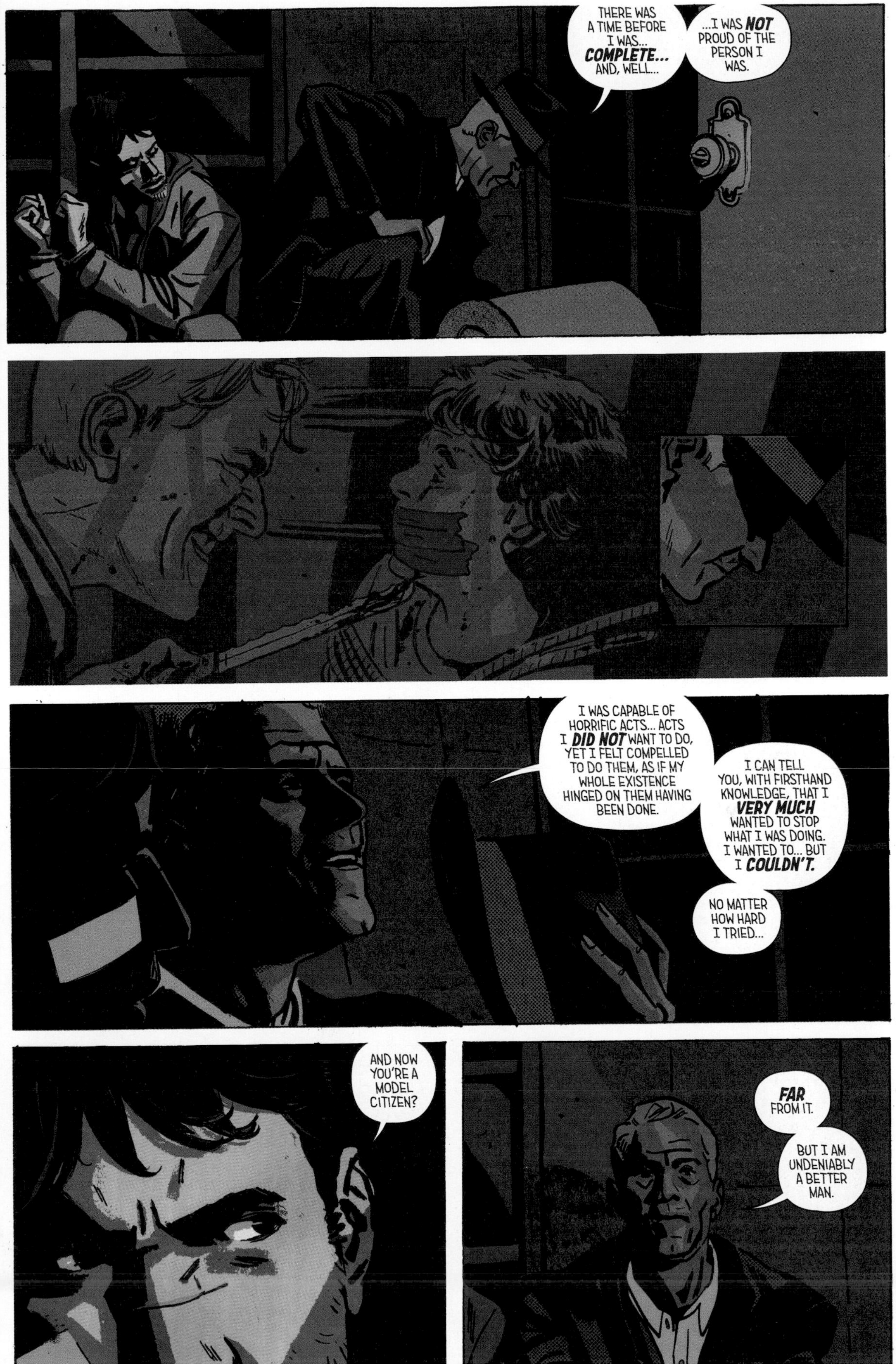
THERE WAS A TIME BEFORE I WAS... COMPLETE... AND, WELL...
...I WAS NOT PROUD OF THE PERSON I WAS.
I WAS CAPABLE OF HORRIFIC ACTS... ACTS I DID NOT WANT TO DO, YET I FELT COMPELLED TO DO THEM, AS IF MY WHOLE EXISTENCE HINGED ON THEM HAVING BEEN DONE.
I CAN TELL YOU, WITH FIRSTHAND KNOWLEDGE, THAT I VERY MUCH WANTED TO STOP WHAT I WAS DOING. I WANTED TO... BUT I COULDN'T.
NO MATTER HOW HARD I TRIED...
AND NOW YOU'RE A MODEL CITIZEN?
FAR FROM IT.
BUT I AM UNDENIABLY A BETTER MAN.

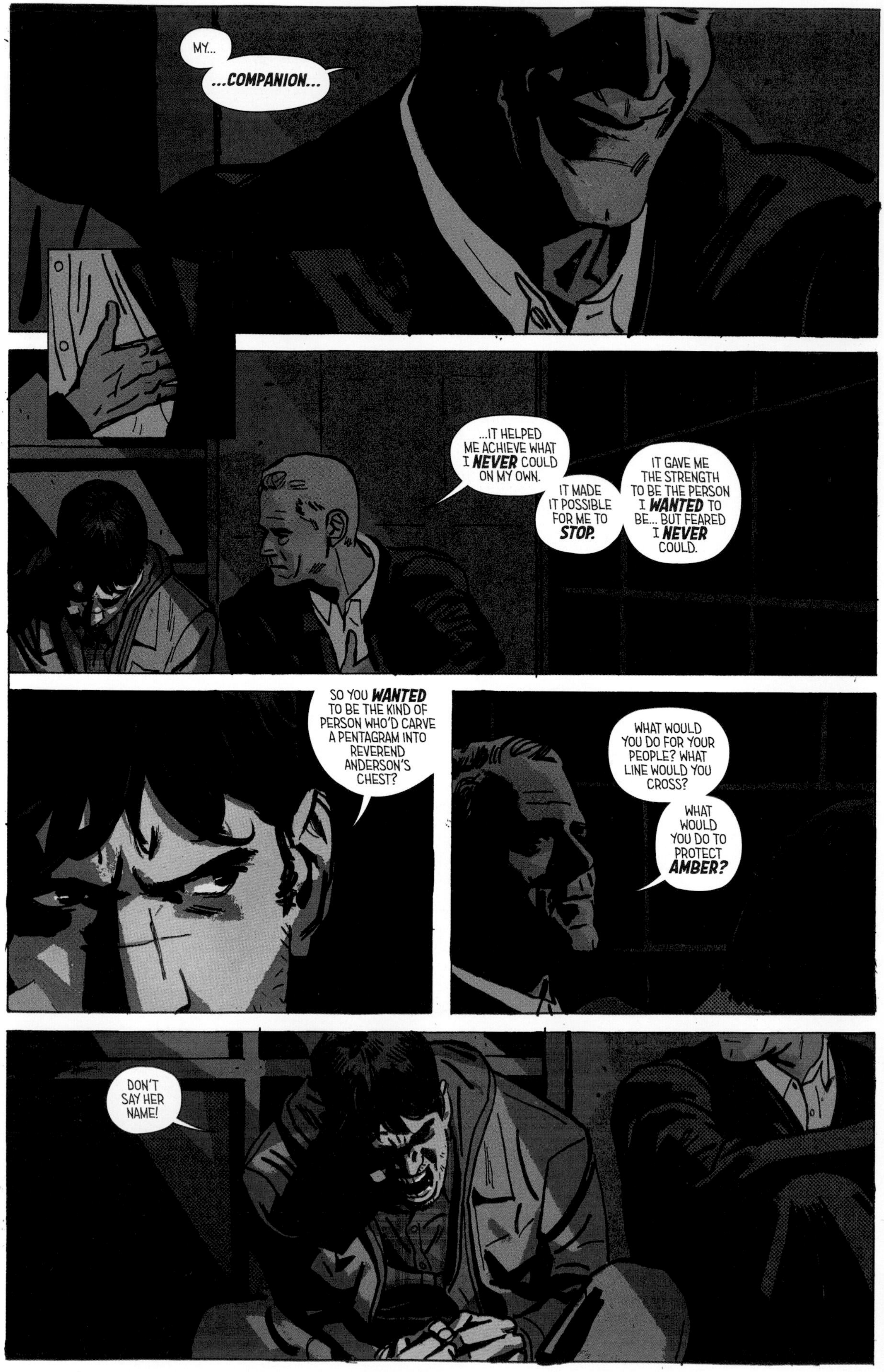

MY...
...COMPANION...
...IT HELPED ME ACHIEVE WHAT I NEVER COULD ON MY OWN.
IT MADE IT POSSIBLE FOR ME TO STOP.
IT GAVE ME THE STRENGTH TO BE THE PERSON I WANTED TO BE... BUT FEARED I NEVER COULD.
SO YOU WANTED TO BE THE KIND OF PERSON WHO'D CARVE A PENTAGRAM INTO REVEREND ANDERSON'S CHEST?
WHAT WOULD YOU DO FOR YOUR PEOPLE? WHAT LINE WOULD YOU CROSS?
WHAT WOULD YOU DO TO PROTECT AMBER?
DON'T SAY HER NAME!

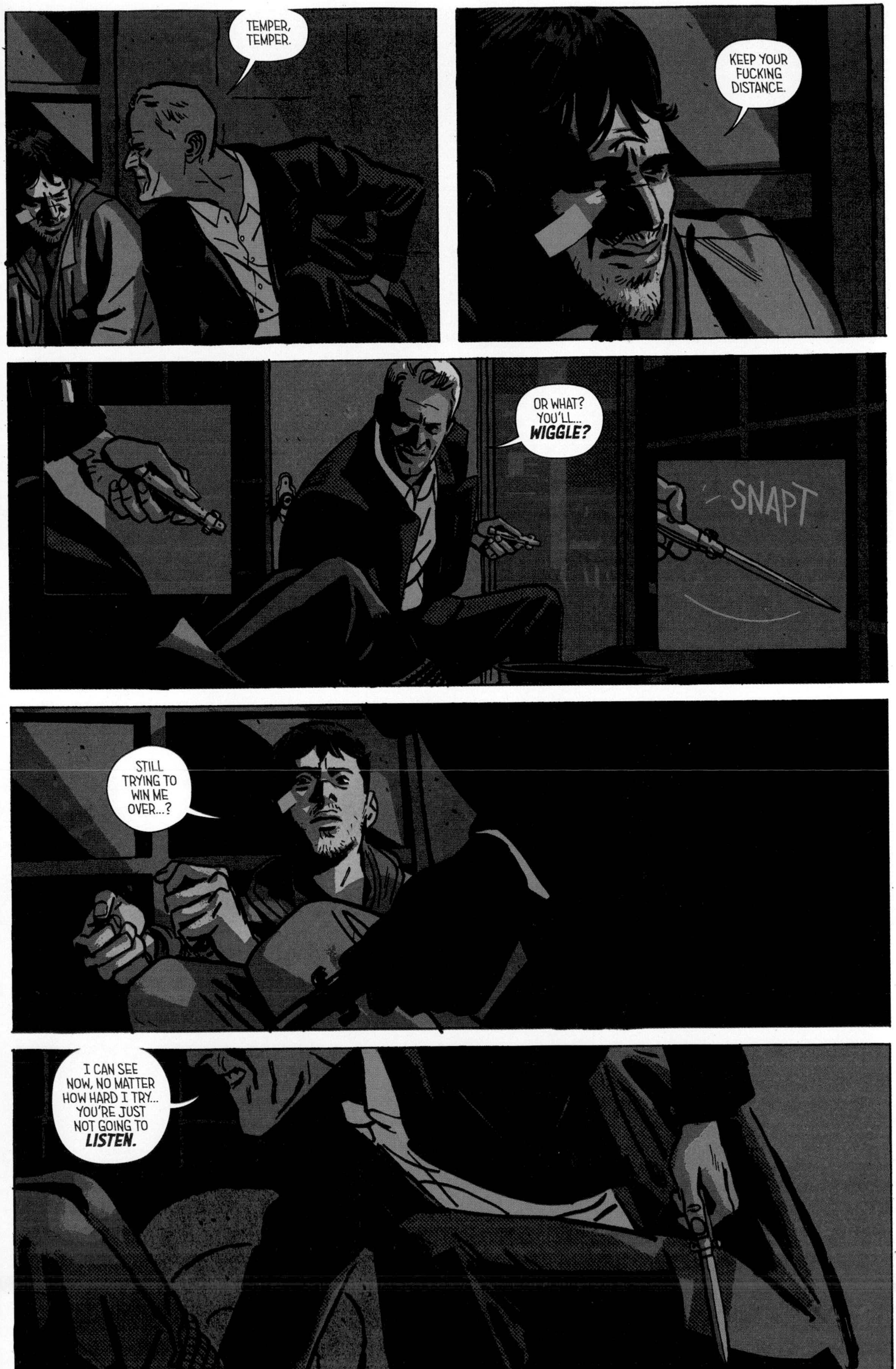
TEMPER, TEMPER.
KEEP YOUR FUCKING DISTANCE.
OR WHAT? YOU'LL... **WIGGLE?**
SNAPT
STILL TRYING TO WIN ME OVER...?
I CAN SEE NOW, NO MATTER HOW HARD I TRY... YOU'RE JUST NOT GOING TO **LISTEN.**

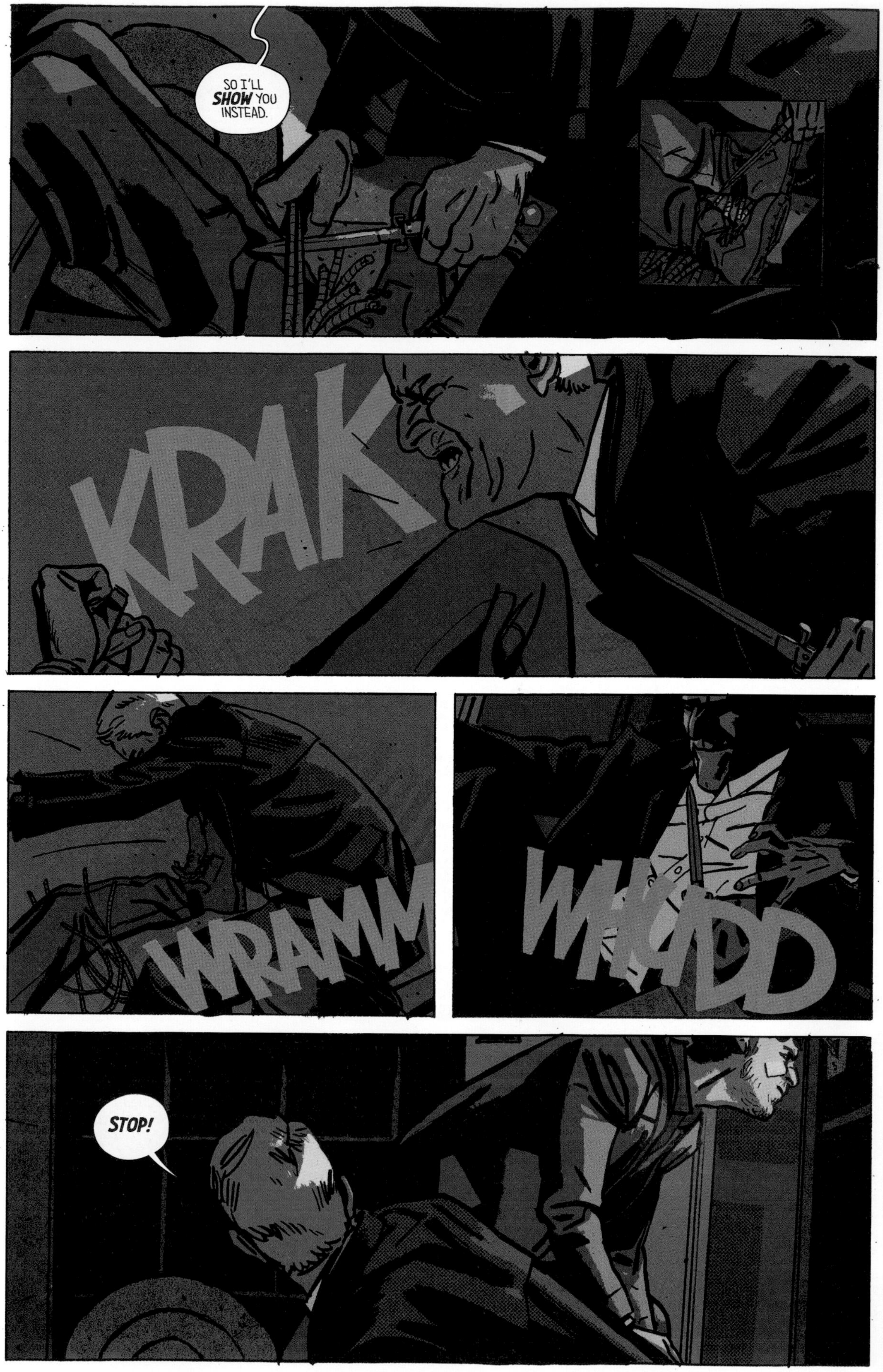
SO I'LL SHOW YOU INSTEAD.
KRAK
WRAMM
WHUDD
STOP!

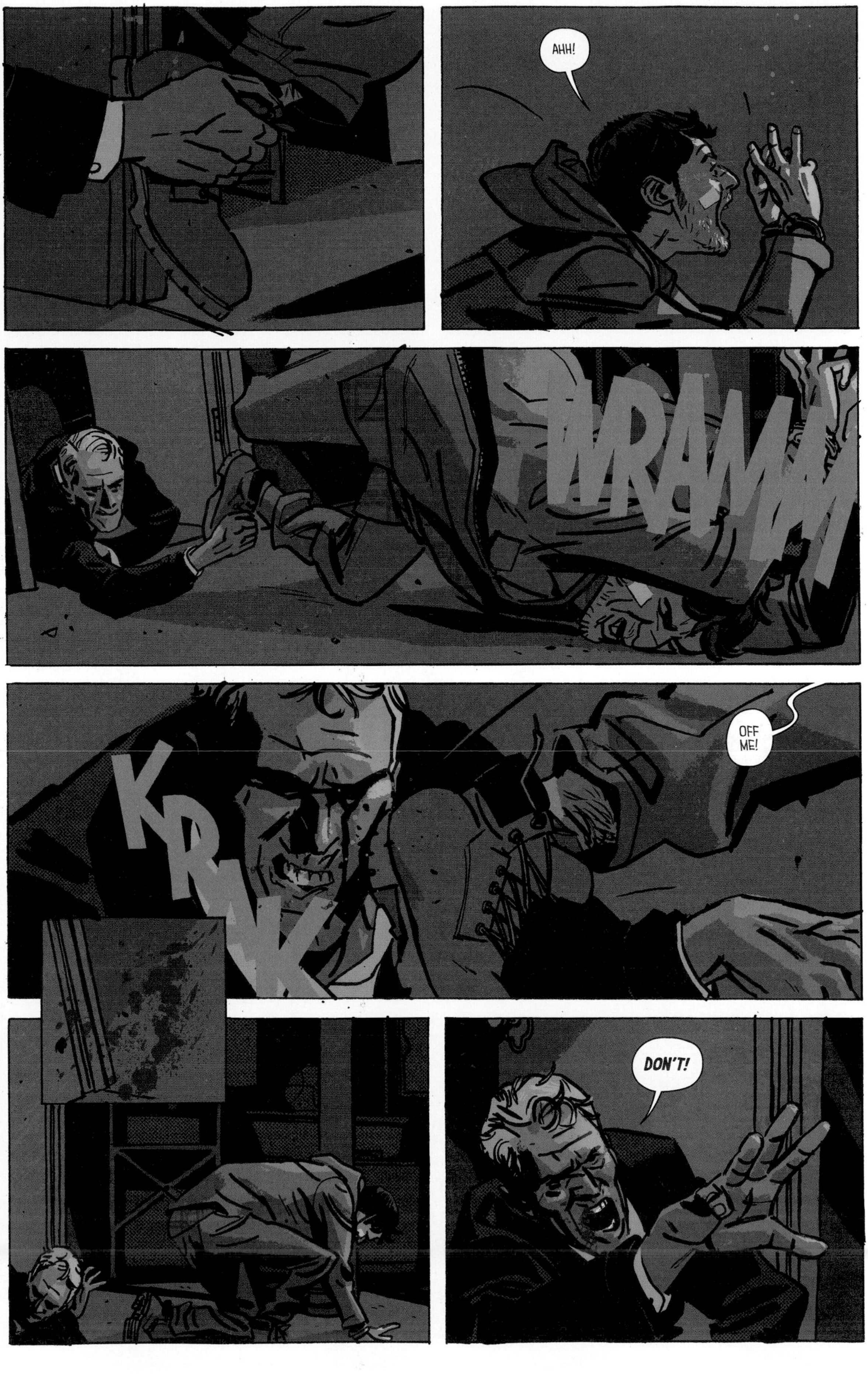
AHH!
THWRAMM
KRAK
OFF ME!
DON'T!

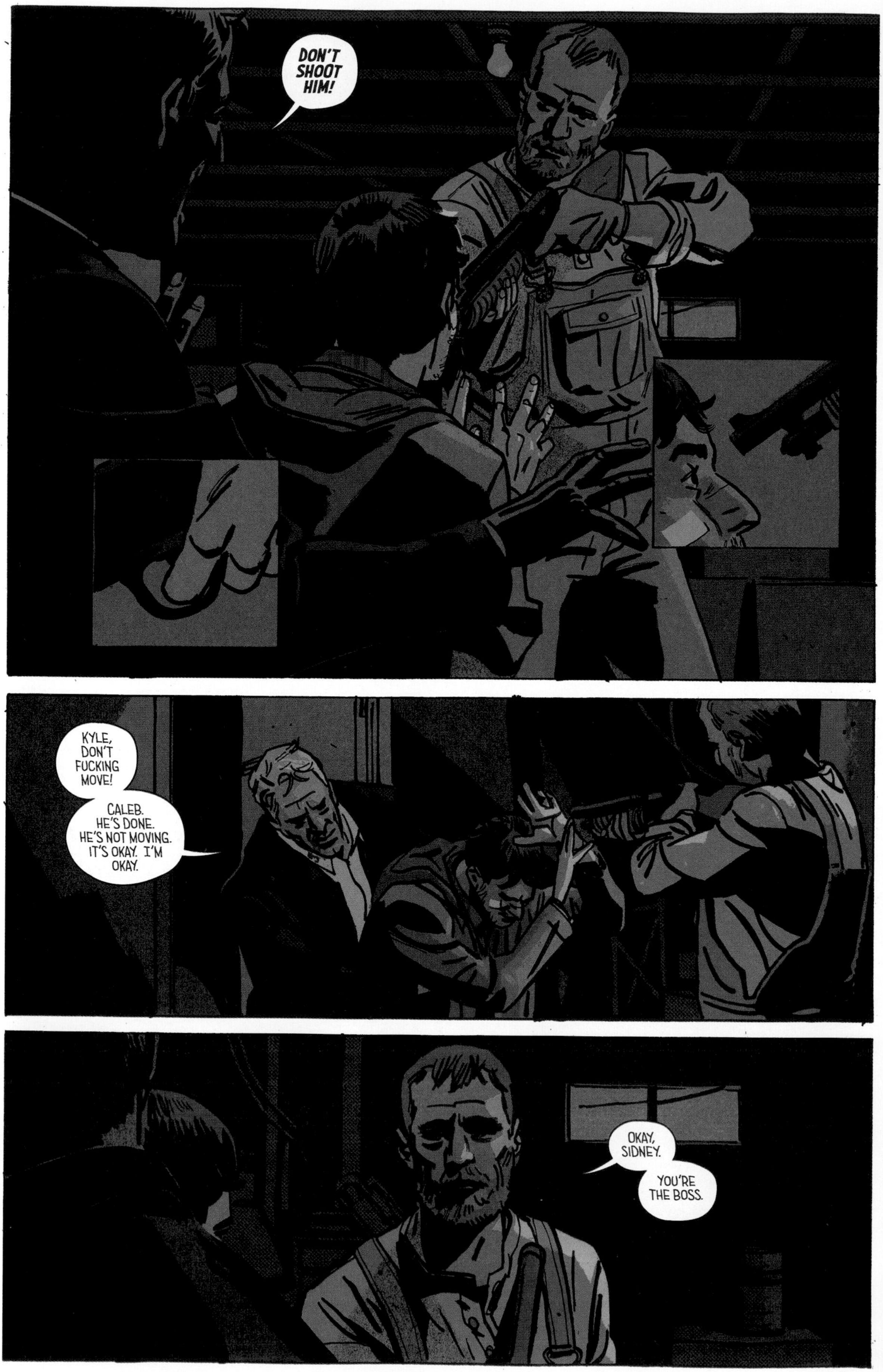
DON'T SHOOT HIM!
KYLE, DON'T FUCKING MOVE!
CALEB. HE'S DONE. HE'S NOT MOVING. IT'S OKAY. I'M OKAY.
OKAY, SIDNEY.
YOU'RE THE BOSS.

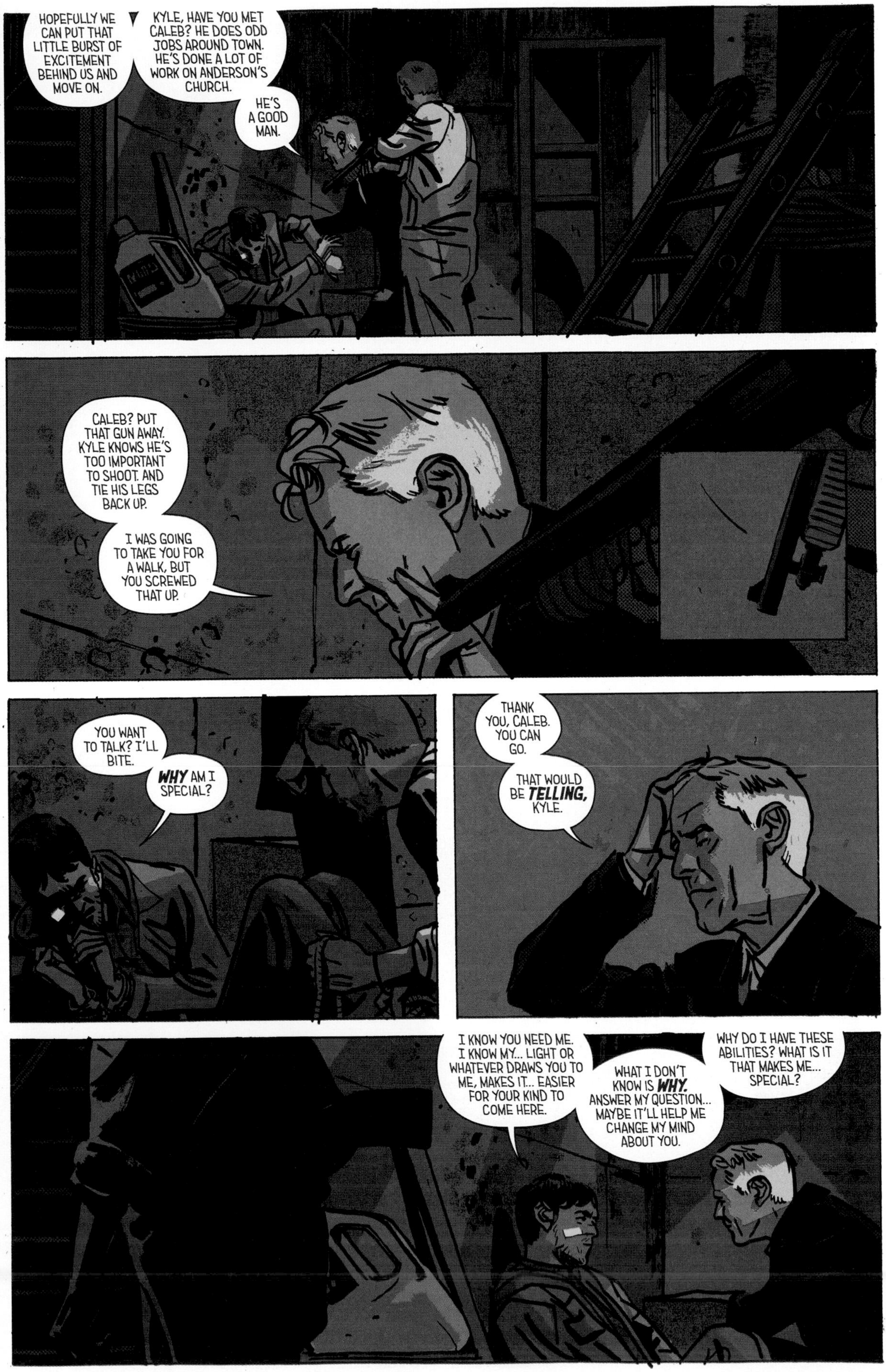
HOPEFULLY WE CAN PUT THAT LITTLE BURST OF EXCITEMENT BEHIND US AND MOVE ON.
KYLE, HAVE YOU MET CALEB? HE DOES ODD JOBS AROUND TOWN. HE'S DONE A LOT OF WORK ON ANDERSON'S CHURCH.
HE'S A GOOD MAN.
CALEB? PUT THAT GUN AWAY. KYLE KNOWS HE'S TOO IMPORTANT TO SHOOT. AND TIE HIS LEGS BACK UP.
I WAS GOING TO TAKE YOU FOR A WALK, BUT YOU SCREWED THAT UP.
YOU WANT TO TALK? I'LL BITE.
WHY AM I SPECIAL?
THANK YOU, CALEB. YOU CAN GO.
THAT WOULD BE ***TELLING,*** KYLE.
I KNOW YOU NEED ME. I KNOW MY... LIGHT OR WHATEVER DRAWS YOU TO ME, MAKES IT... EASIER FOR YOUR KIND TO COME HERE.
WHAT I DON'T KNOW IS **WHY.** ANSWER MY QUESTION... MAYBE IT'LL HELP ME CHANGE MY MIND ABOUT YOU.
WHY DO I HAVE THESE ABILITIES? WHAT IS IT THAT MAKES ME... SPECIAL?

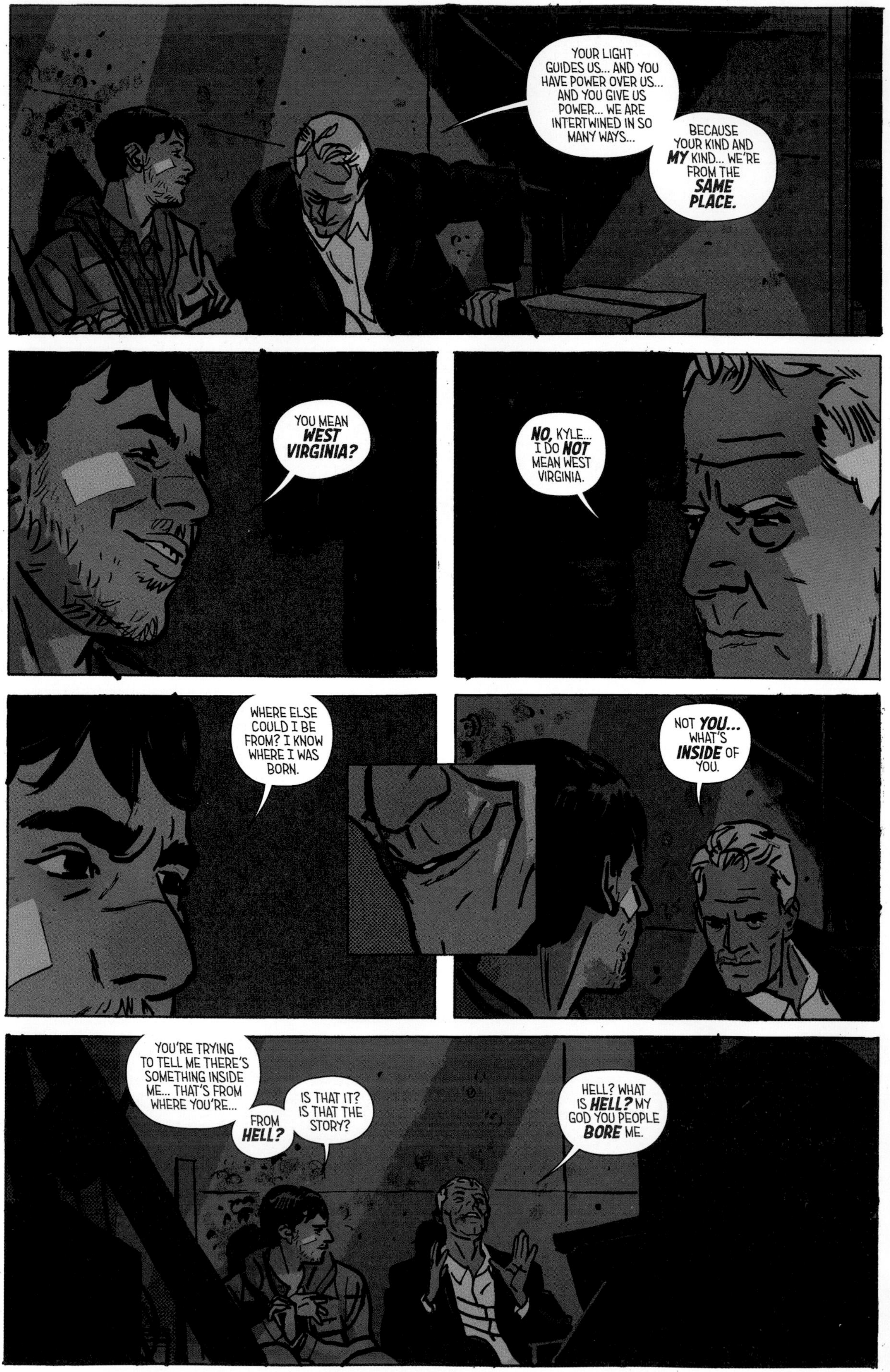
YOUR LIGHT GUIDES US... AND YOU HAVE POWER OVER US... AND YOU GIVE US POWER... WE ARE INTERTWINED IN SO MANY WAYS...
BECAUSE YOUR KIND AND MY KIND... WE'RE FROM THE SAME PLACE.
YOU MEAN WEST VIRGINIA?
NO, KYLE... I DO NOT MEAN WEST VIRGINIA.
WHERE ELSE COULD I BE FROM? I KNOW WHERE I WAS BORN.
NOT YOU... WHAT'S INSIDE OF YOU.
YOU'RE TRYING TO TELL ME THERE'S SOMETHING INSIDE ME... THAT'S FROM WHERE YOU'RE...
FROM HELL?
IS THAT IT? IS THAT THE STORY?
HELL? WHAT IS HELL? MY GOD YOU PEOPLE BORE ME.

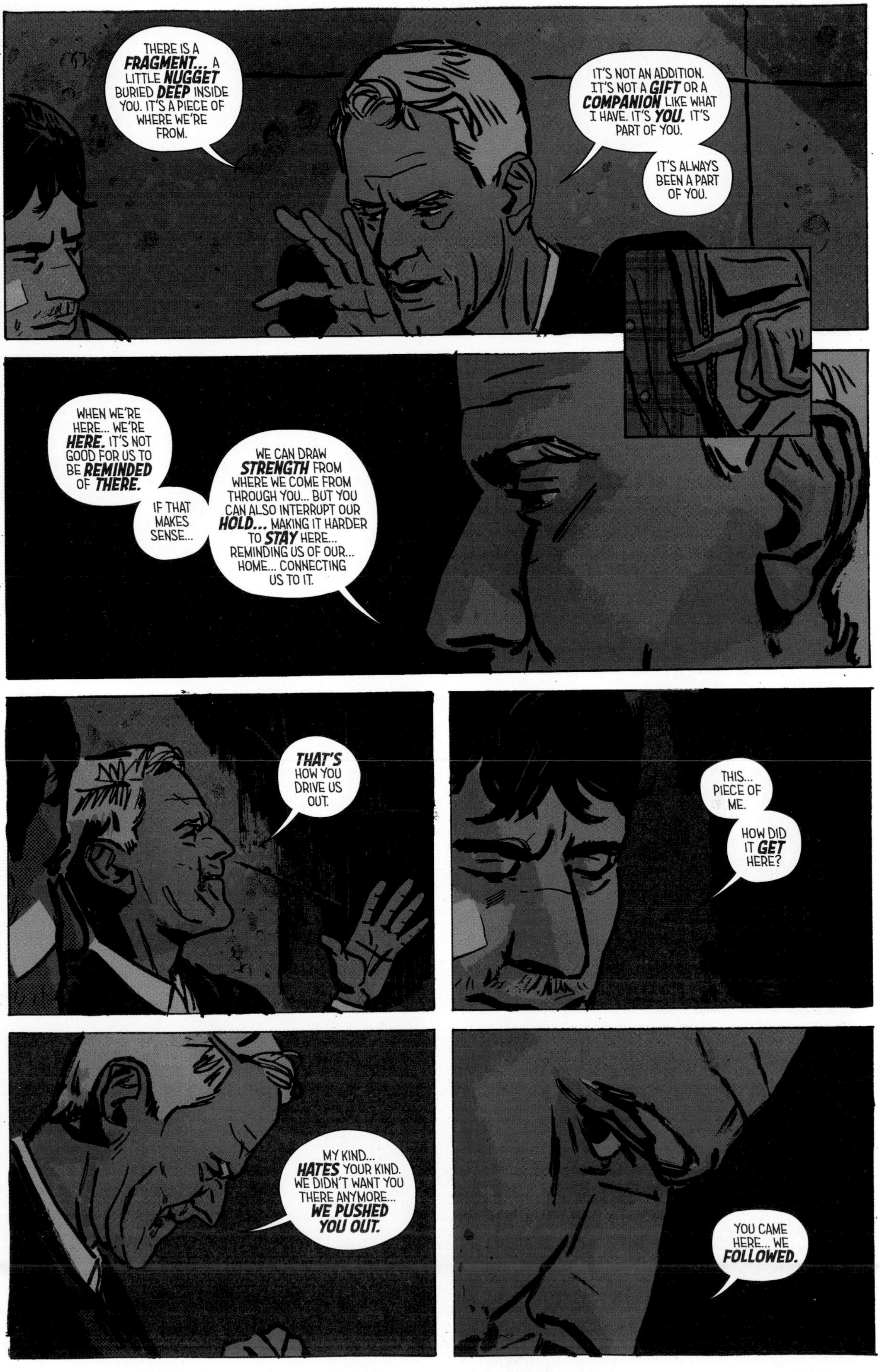
THERE IS A FRAGMENT... A LITTLE NUGGET BURIED DEEP INSIDE YOU. IT'S A PIECE OF WHERE WE'RE FROM.
IT'S NOT AN ADDITION. IT'S NOT A GIFT OR A COMPANION LIKE WHAT I HAVE. IT'S YOU. IT'S PART OF YOU.
IT'S ALWAYS BEEN A PART OF YOU.
WHEN WE'RE HERE... WE'RE HERE. IT'S NOT GOOD FOR US TO BE REMINDED OF THERE.
IF THAT MAKES SENSE...
WE CAN DRAW STRENGTH FROM WHERE WE COME FROM THROUGH YOU... BUT YOU CAN ALSO INTERRUPT OUR HOLD... MAKING IT HARDER TO STAY HERE... REMINDING US OF OUR... HOME... CONNECTING US TO IT.
THAT'S HOW YOU DRIVE US OUT.
THIS... PIECE OF ME.
HOW DID IT GET HERE?
MY KIND... HATES YOUR KIND. WE DIDN'T WANT YOU THERE ANYMORE... WE PUSHED YOU OUT.
YOU CAME HERE... WE FOLLOWED.

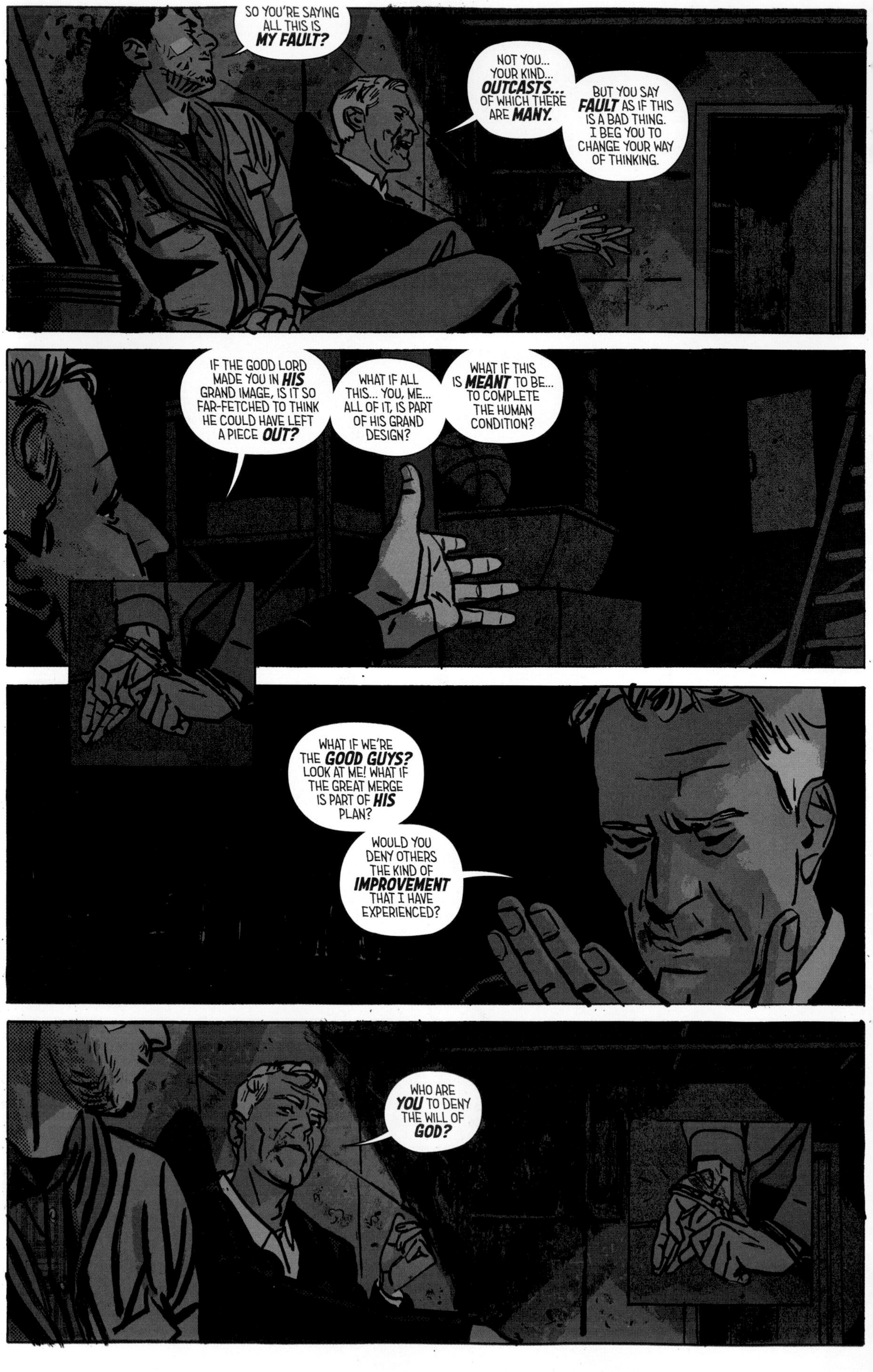
SO YOU'RE SAYING ALL THIS IS MY FAULT?
NOT YOU... YOUR KIND... OUTCASTS... OF WHICH THERE ARE MANY.
BUT YOU SAY FAULT AS IF THIS IS A BAD THING. I BEG YOU TO CHANGE YOUR WAY OF THINKING.
IF THE GOOD LORD MADE YOU IN HIS GRAND IMAGE, IS IT SO FAR-FETCHED TO THINK HE COULD HAVE LEFT A PIECE OUT?
WHAT IF ALL THIS... YOU, ME... ALL OF IT, IS PART OF HIS GRAND DESIGN?
WHAT IF THIS IS MEANT TO BE... TO COMPLETE THE HUMAN CONDITION?
WHAT IF WE'RE THE GOOD GUYS? LOOK AT ME! WHAT IF THE GREAT MERGE IS PART OF HIS PLAN?
WOULD YOU DENY OTHERS THE KIND OF IMPROVEMENT THAT I HAVE EXPERIENCED?
WHO ARE YOU TO DENY THE WILL OF GOD?

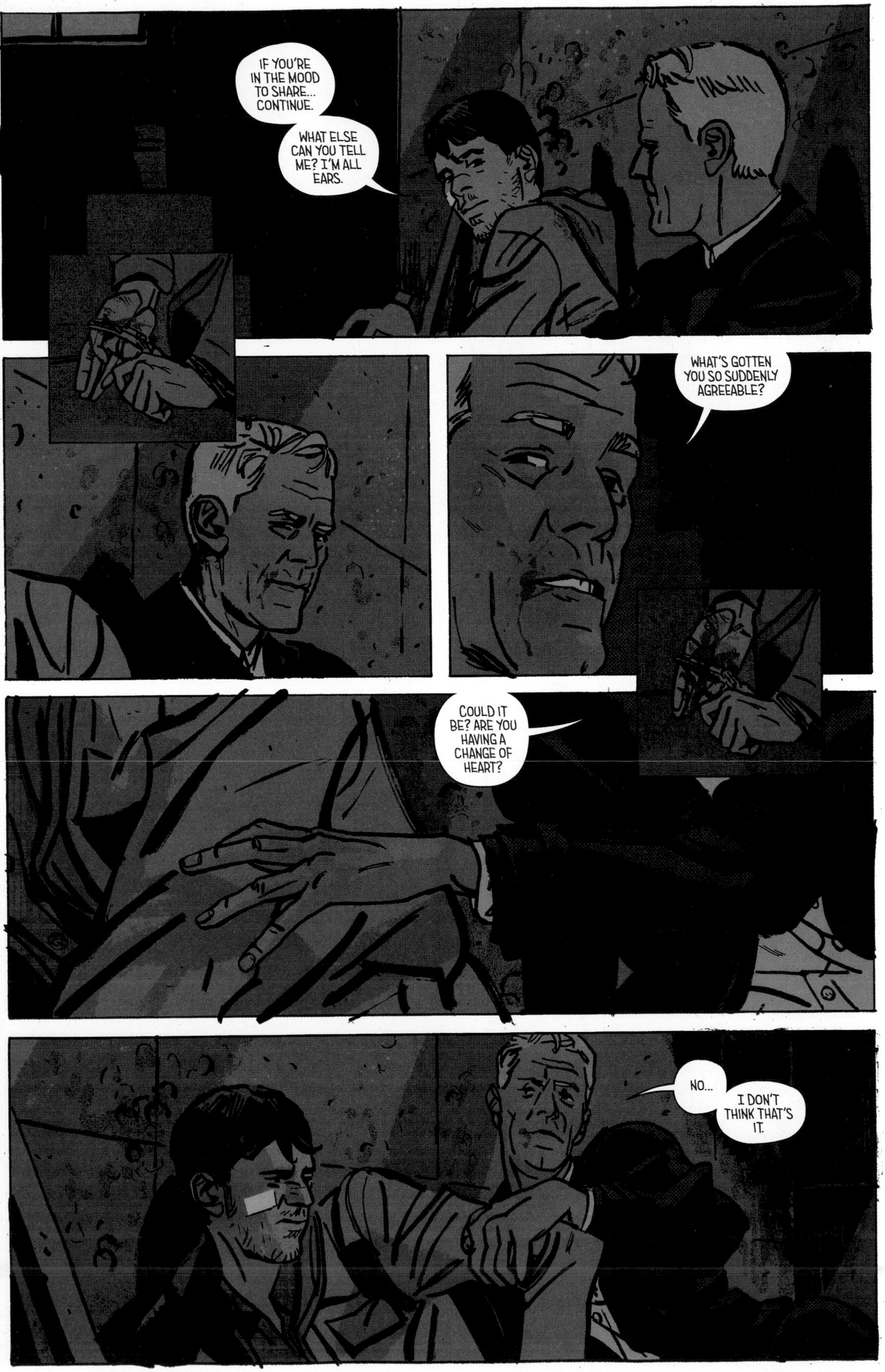
IF YOU'RE IN THE MOOD TO SHARE... CONTINUE.
WHAT ELSE CAN YOU TELL ME? I'M ALL EARS.
WHAT'S GOTTEN YOU SO SUDDENLY AGREEABLE?
COULD IT BE? ARE YOU HAVING A CHANGE OF HEART?
NO...
I DON'T THINK THAT'S IT.

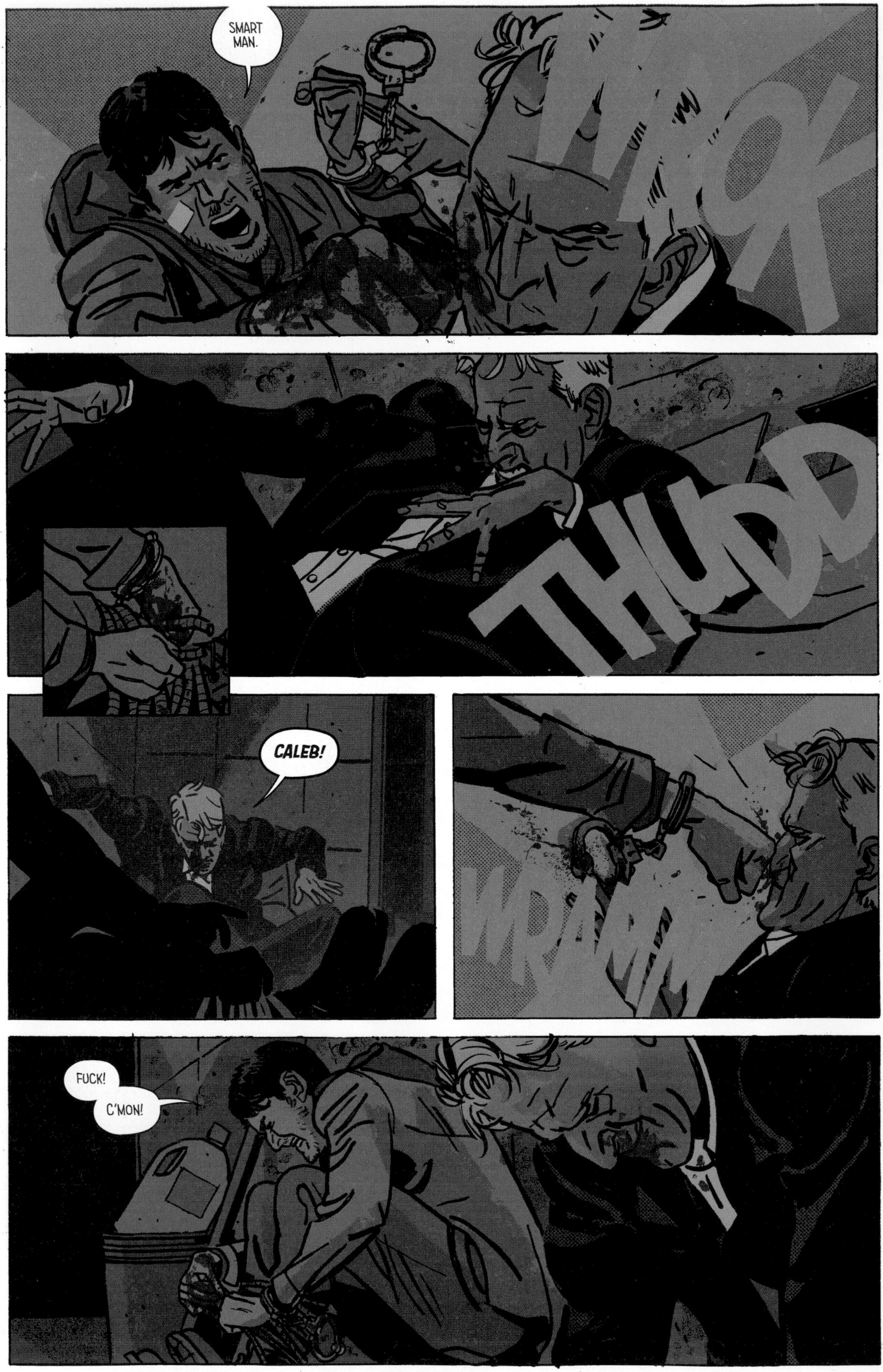
SMART MAN.
WHOK
THUDD
CALEB!
WRAMM
FUCK!
C'MON!

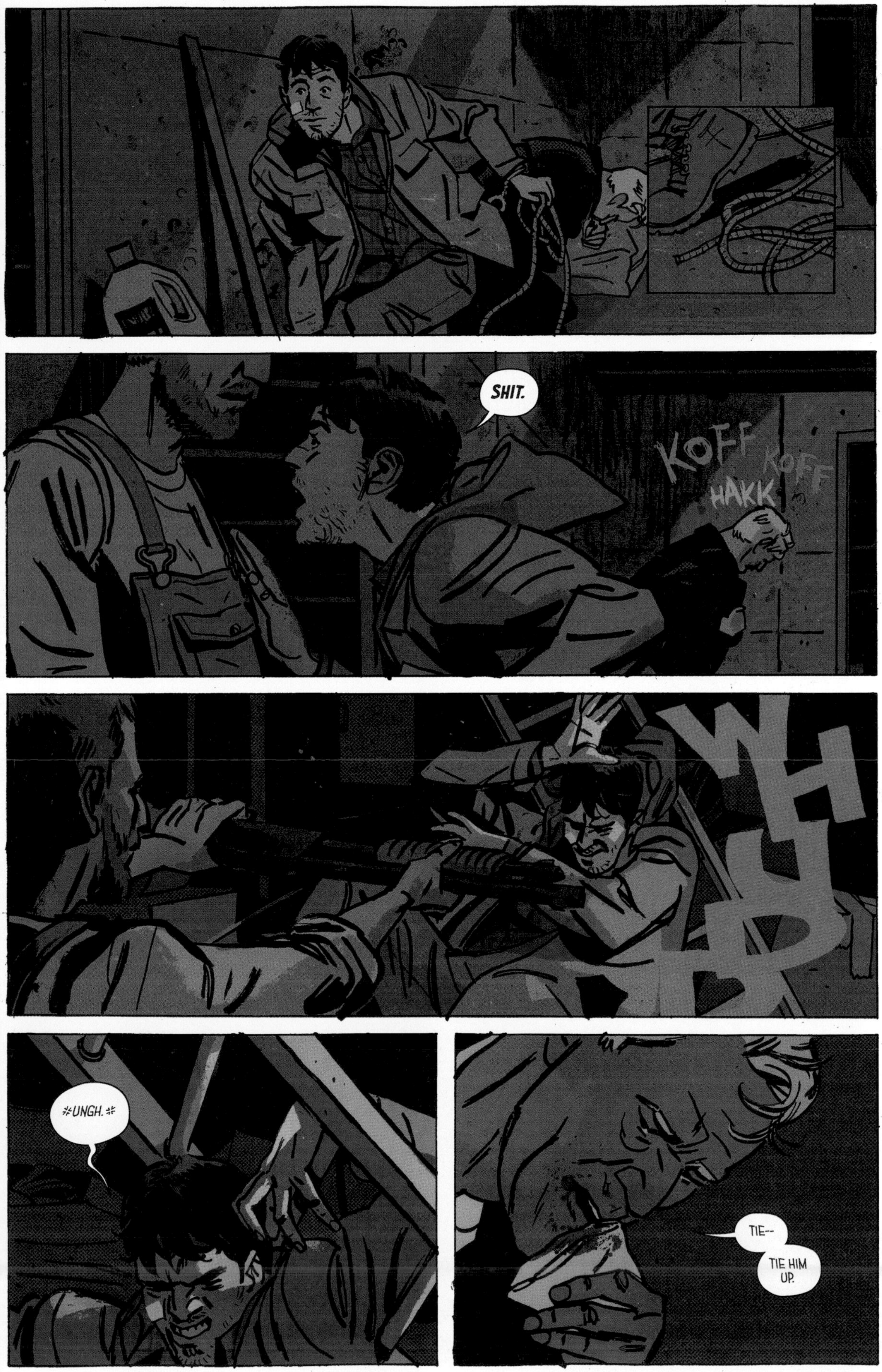
SHIT.
KOFF KOFF
HAKK
WHUD
#UNGH.#
TIE--
TIE HIM UP.

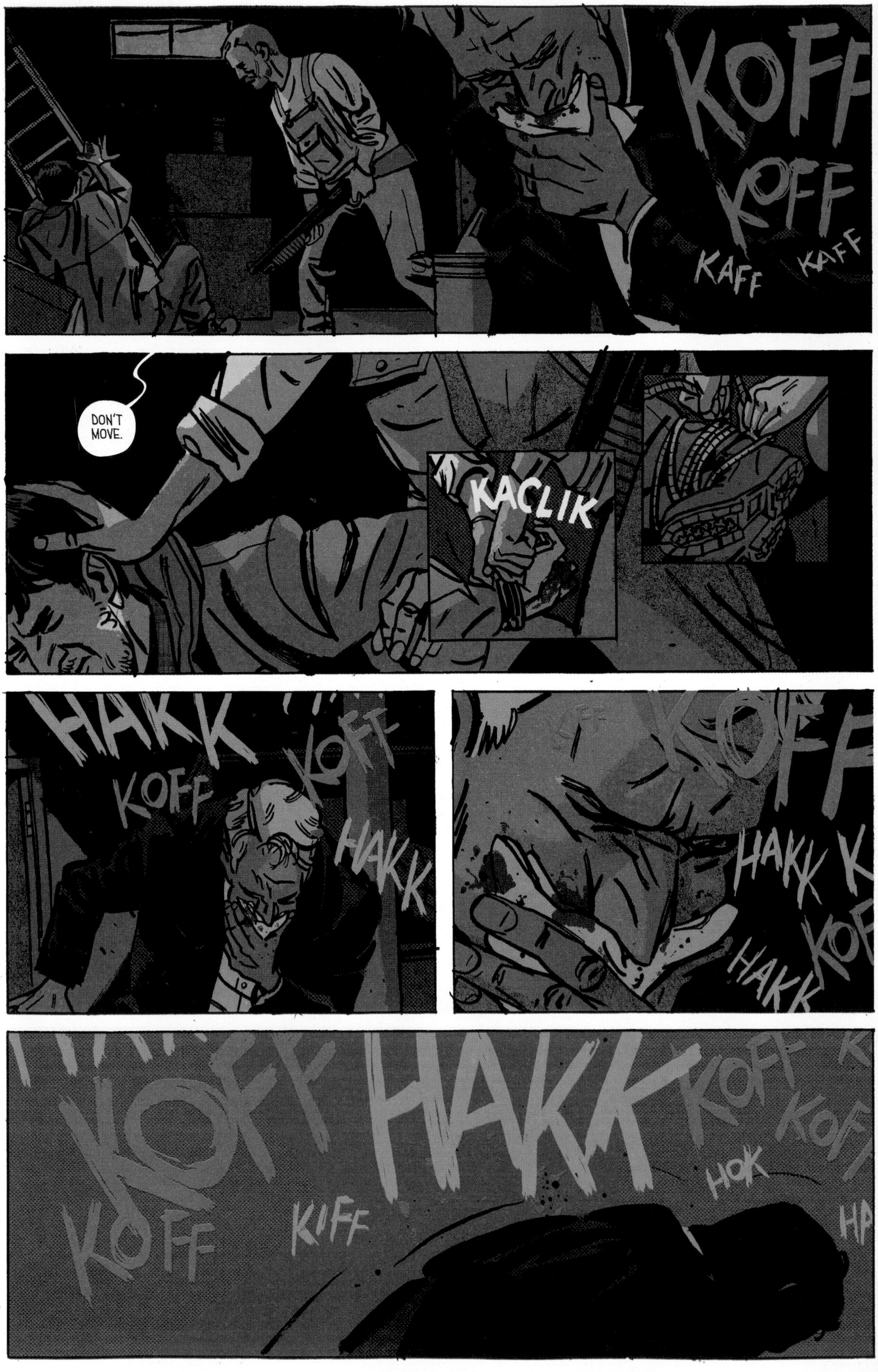
KOFF
KOFF
KAFF
KAFF
DON'T MOVE.
KACLIK
HAKK
KOFF
KOFF
HAKK
KOFF
HAKK K
KOF
HAKK
KOFF
HAKK
KOFF
KOFF
HOK
KOFF
KIFF

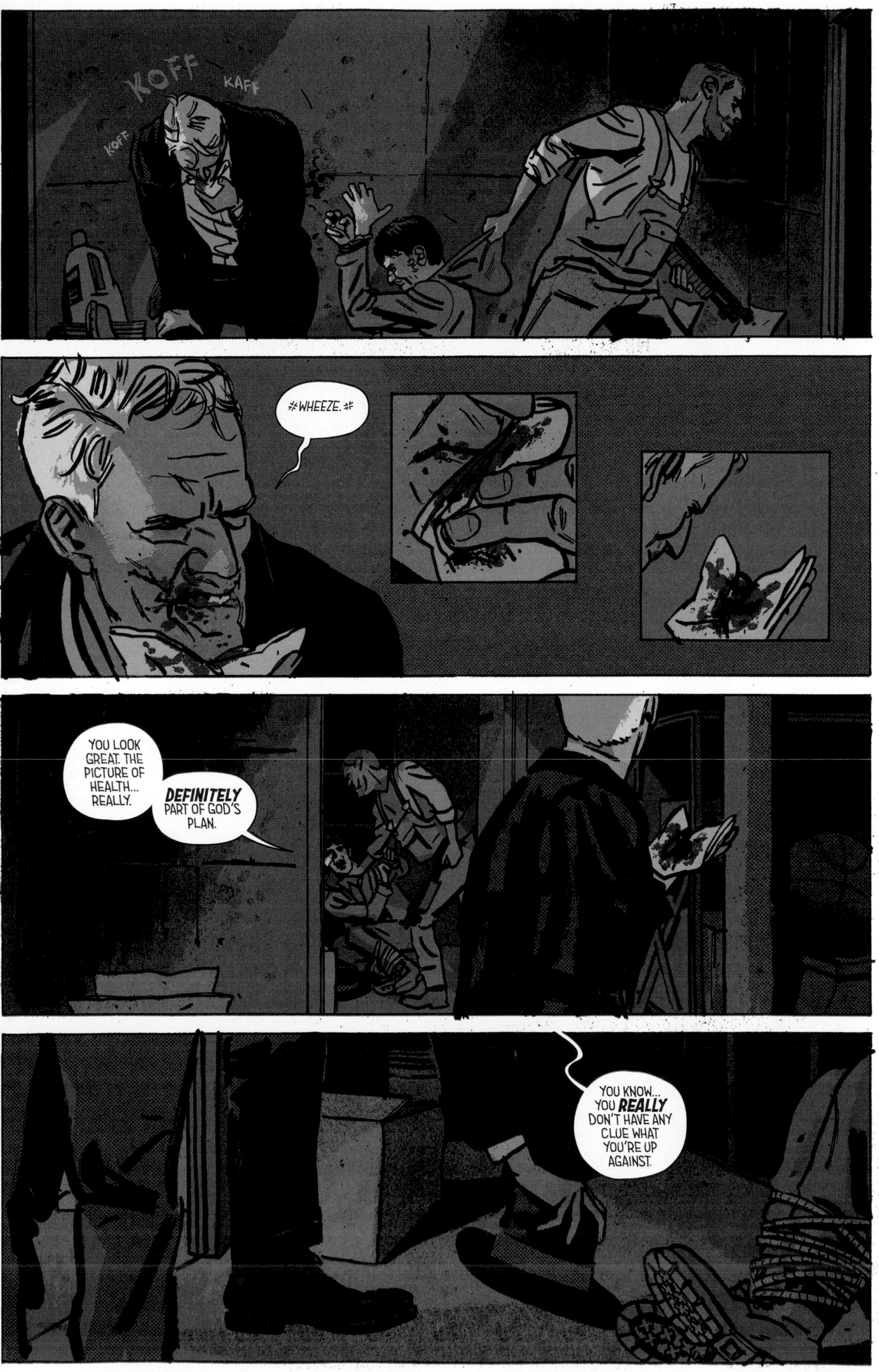
KOFF
KAFF
KOFF
#WHEEZE.#
YOU LOOK GREAT. THE PICTURE OF HEALTH... REALLY.
DEFINITELY PART OF GOD'S PLAN.
YOU KNOW... YOU REALLY DON'T HAVE ANY CLUE WHAT YOU'RE UP AGAINST.

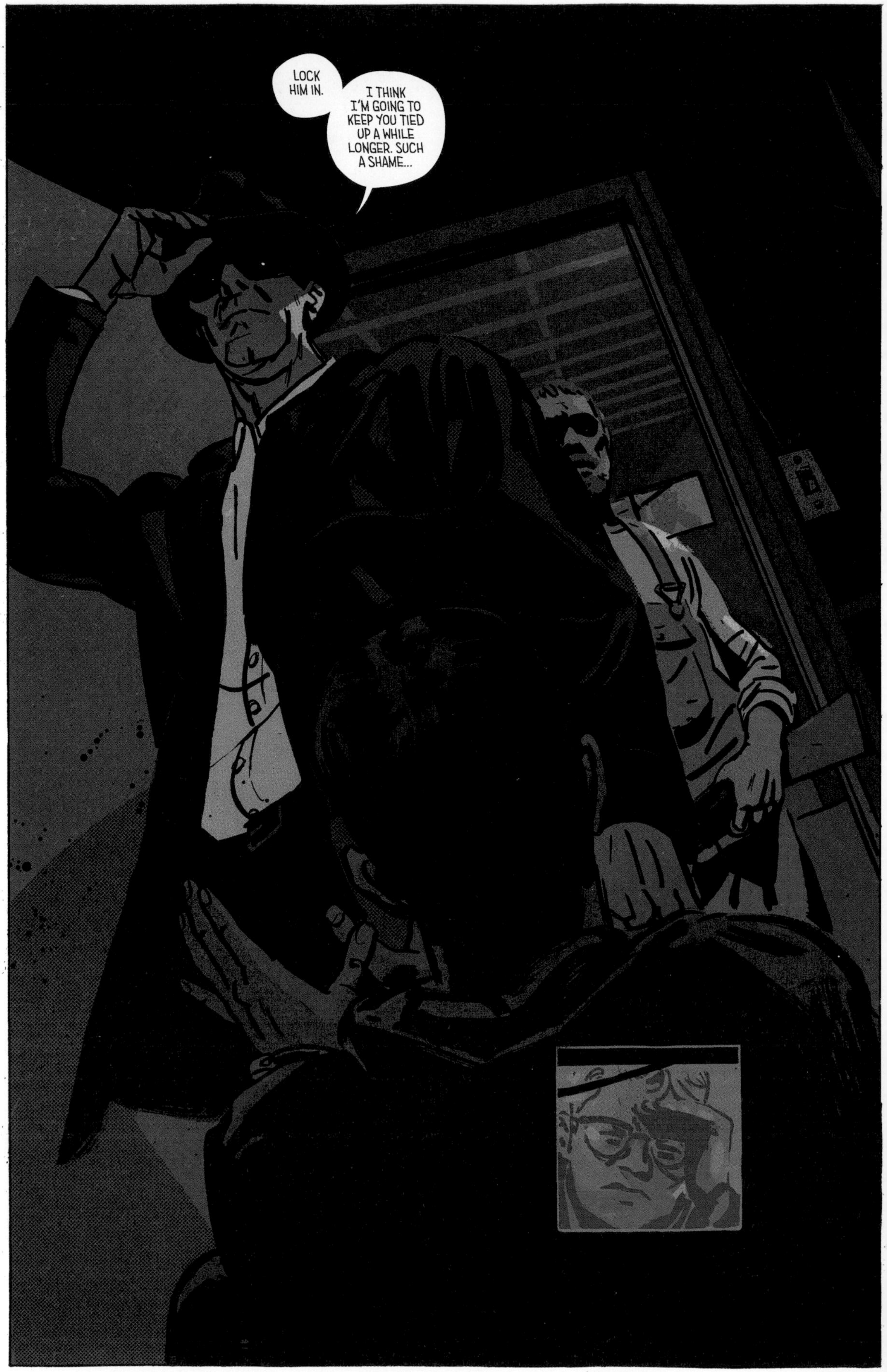
LOCK HIM IN.
I THINK I'M GOING TO KEEP YOU TIED UP A WHILE LONGER. SUCH A SHAME...

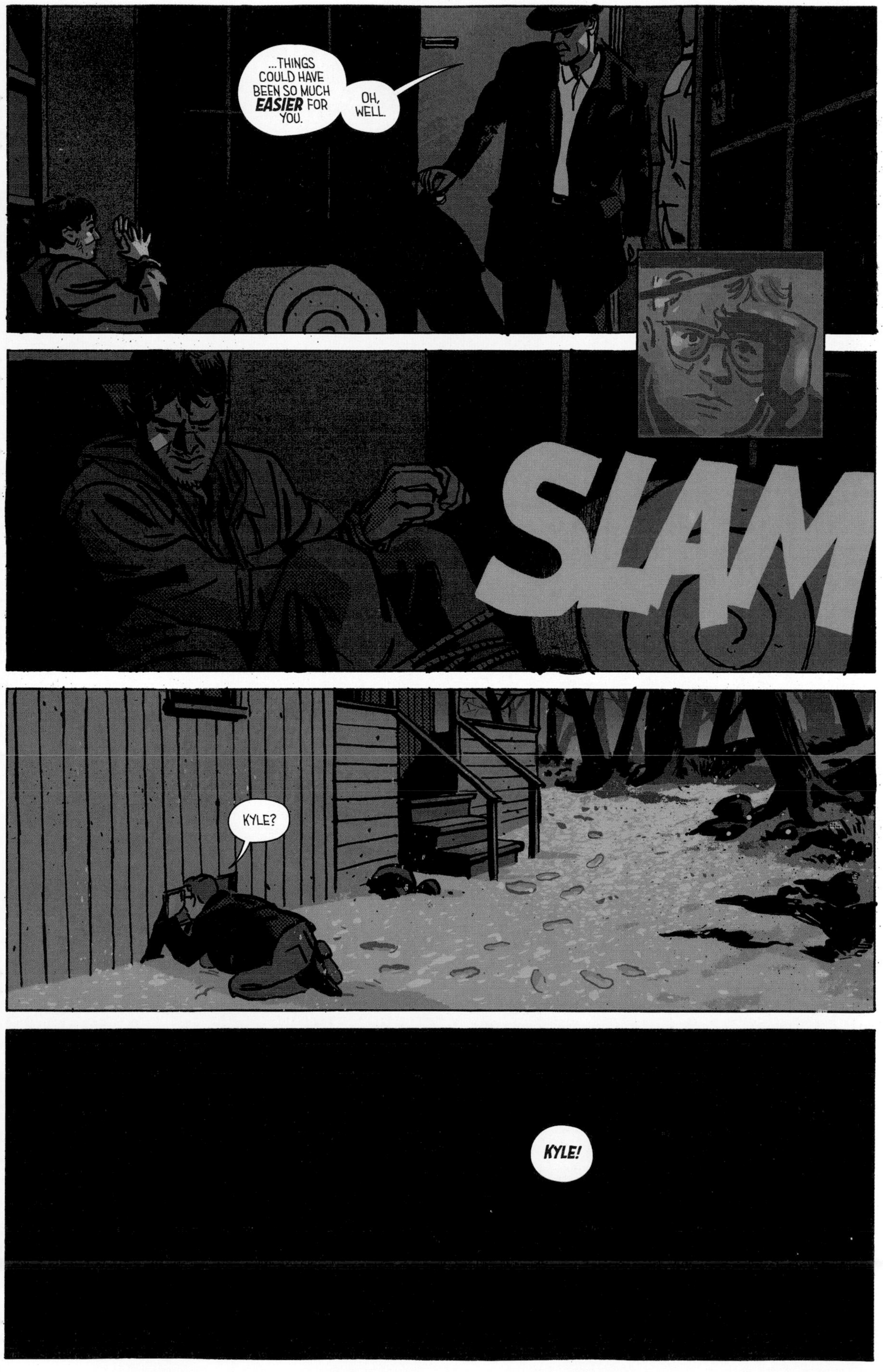
...THINGS COULD HAVE BEEN SO MUCH **EASIER** FOR YOU.
OH, WELL.
SLAM
KYLE?
KYLE!

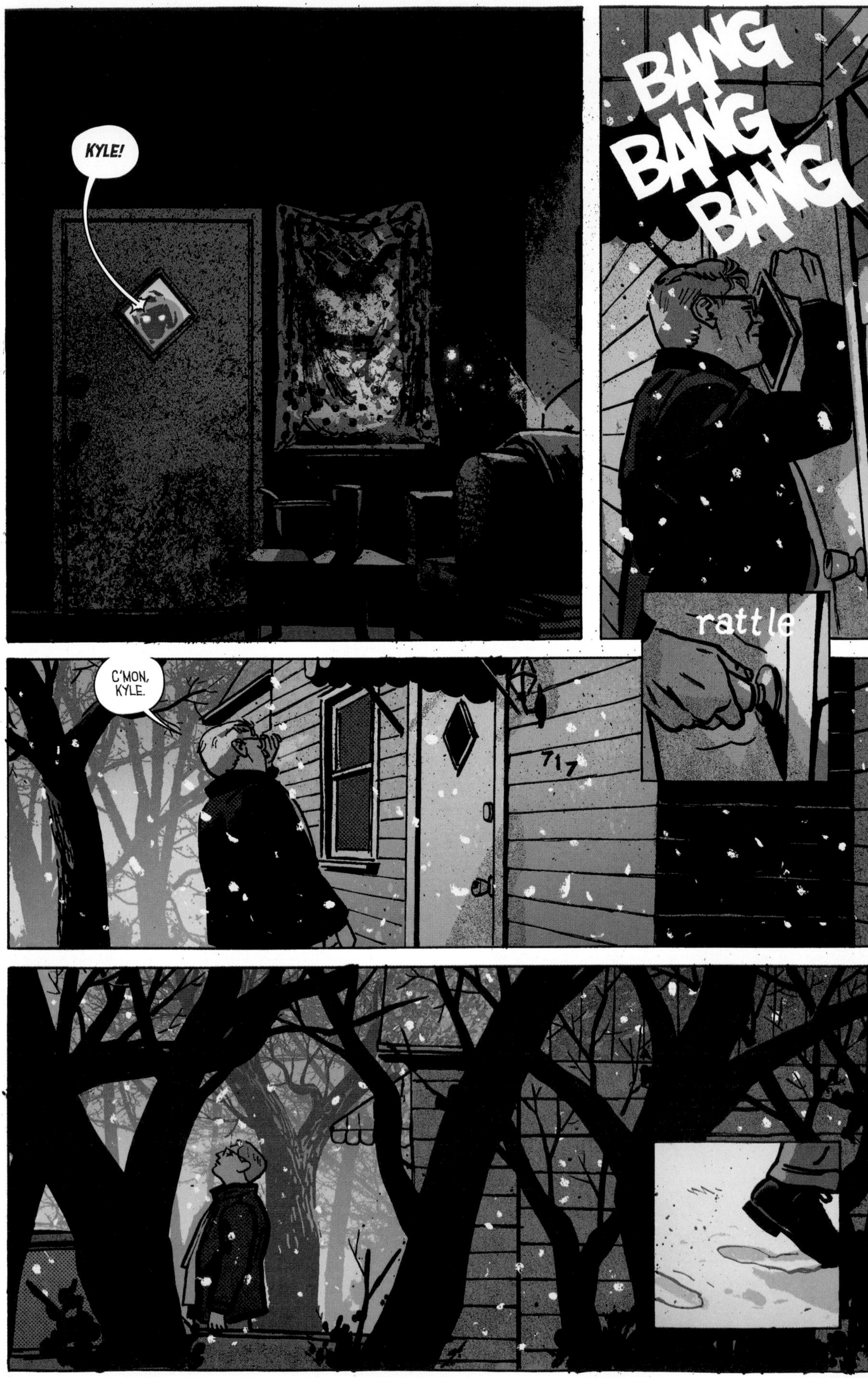
KYLE!
BANG
BANG
BANG
rattle
C'MON, KYLE.
717

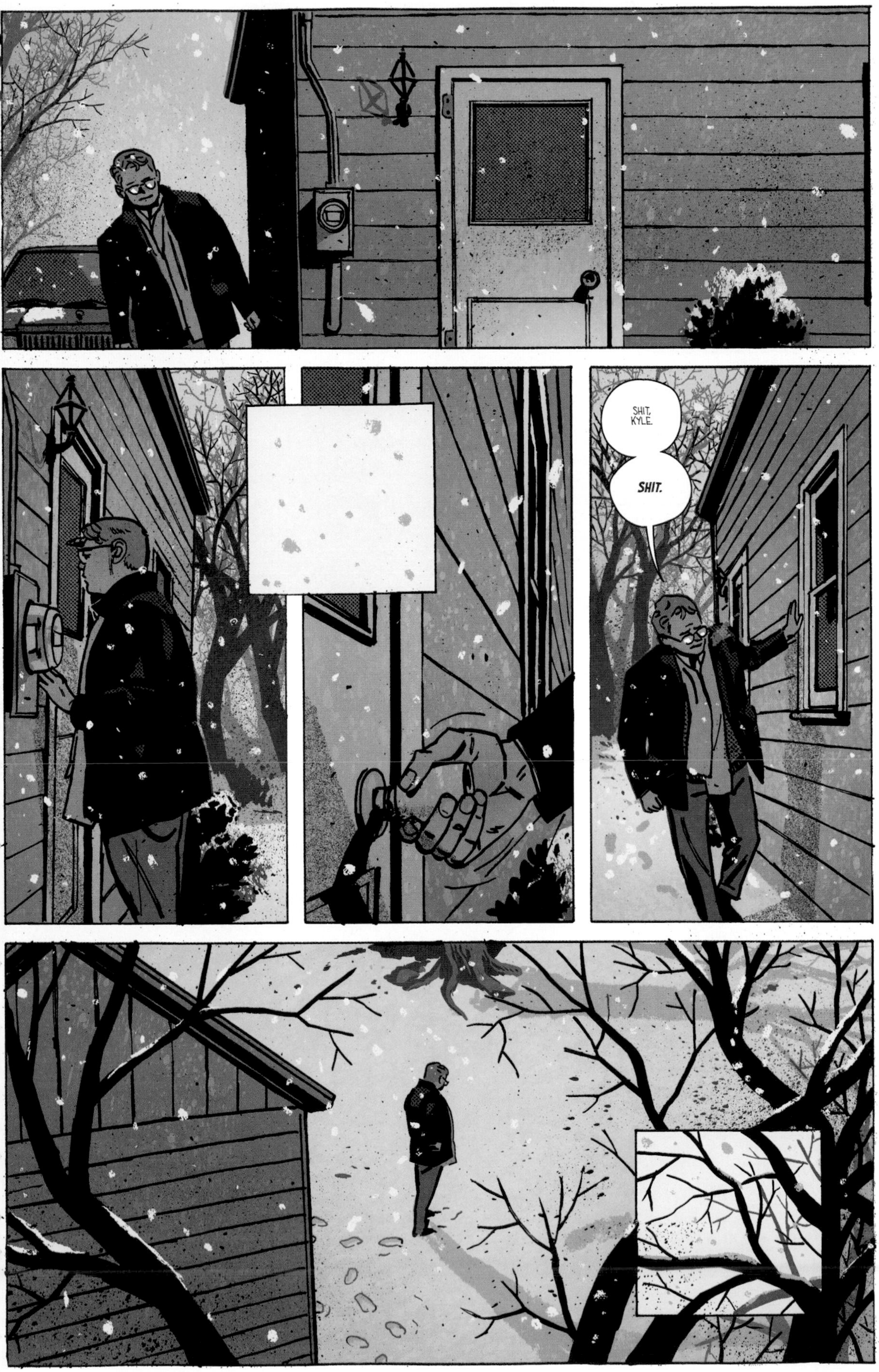
SHIT, KYLE.
SHIT.

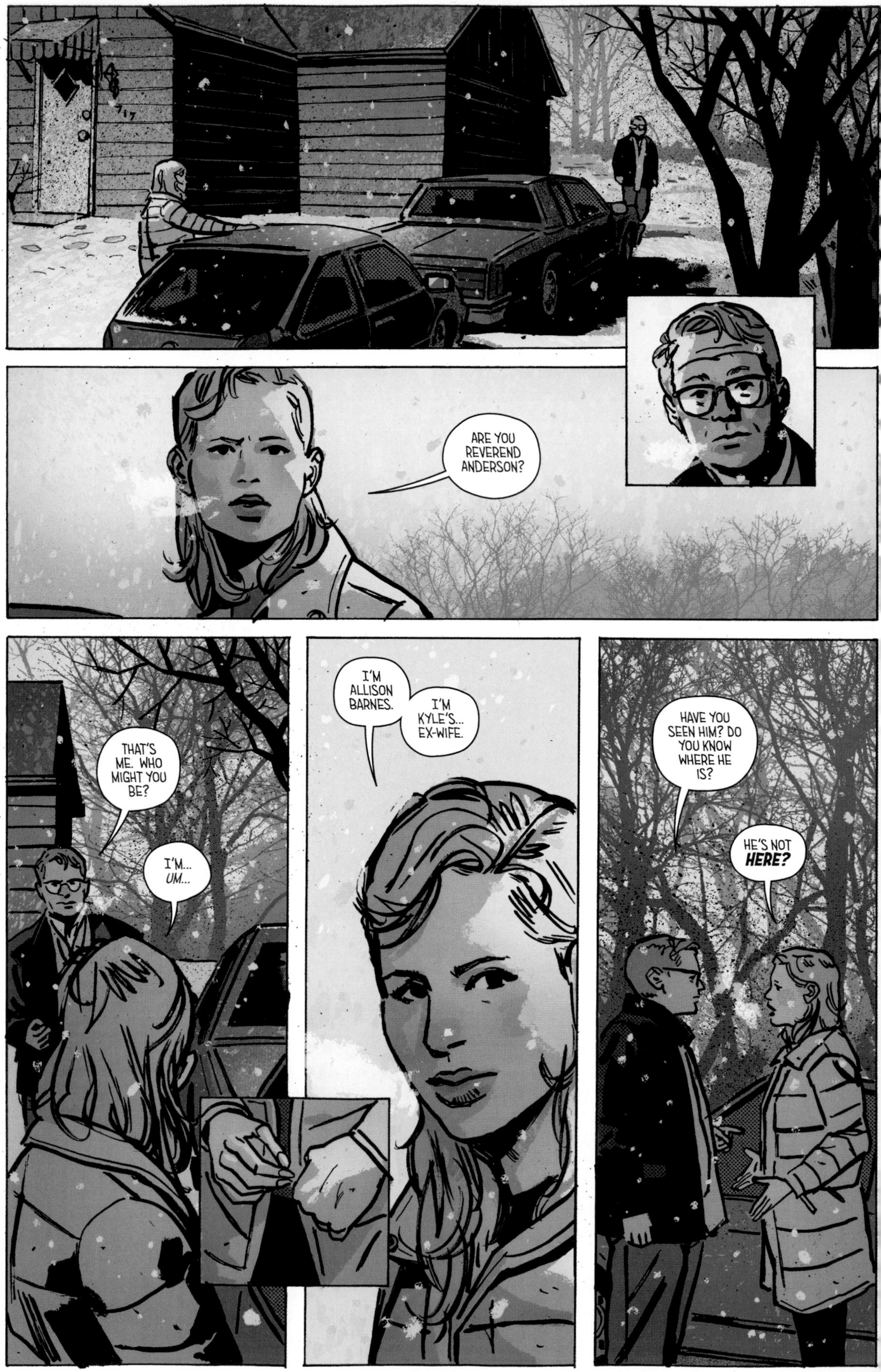

ARE YOU REVEREND ANDERSON?
THAT'S ME. WHO MIGHT YOU BE?
I'M... *UM...*
I'M ALLISON BARNES.
I'M KYLE'S... EX-WIFE.
HAVE YOU SEEN HIM? DO YOU KNOW WHERE HE IS?
HE'S NOT ***HERE?***

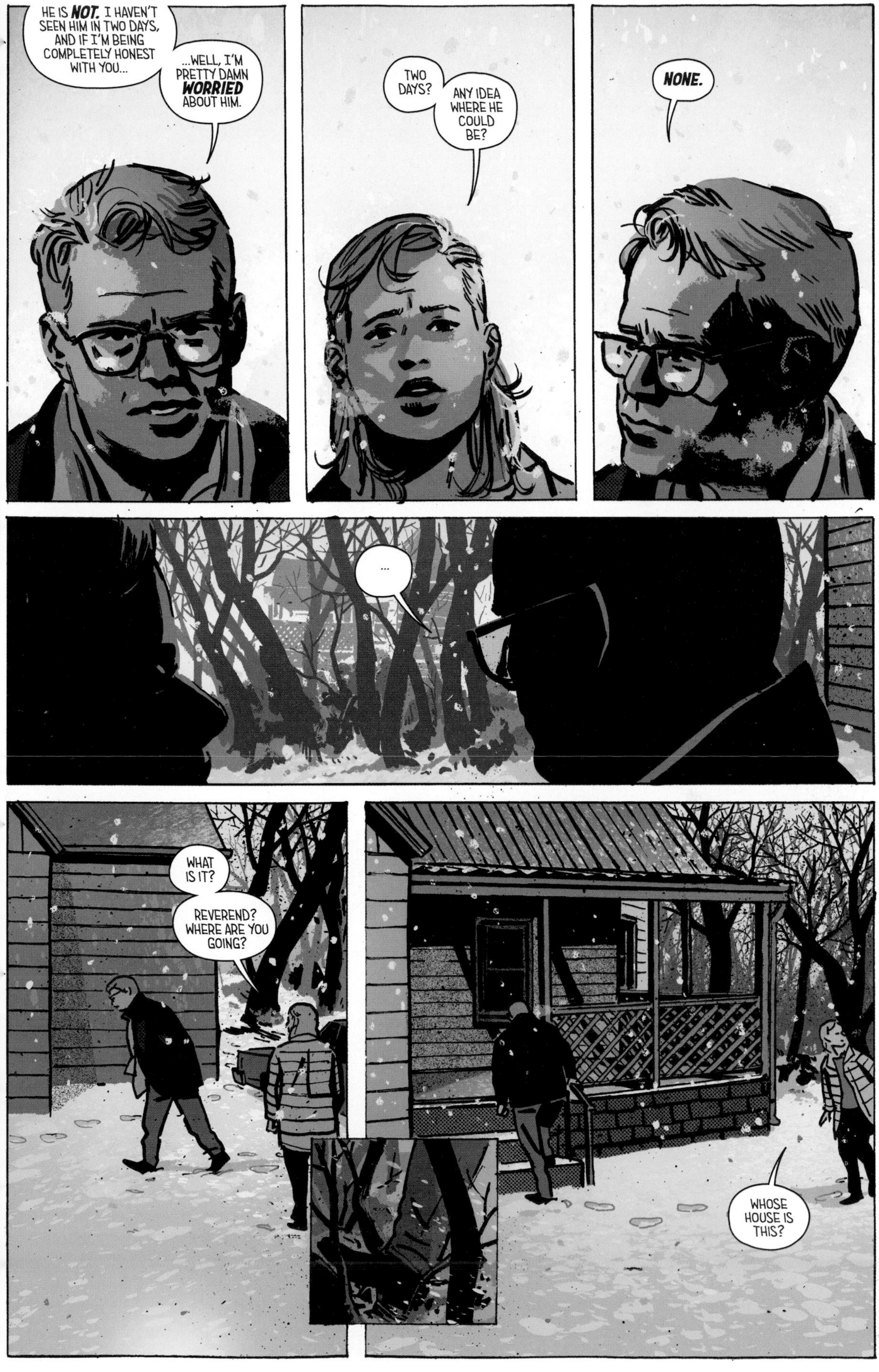

HE IS NOT. I HAVEN'T SEEN HIM IN TWO DAYS, AND IF I'M BEING COMPLETELY HONEST WITH YOU...
...WELL, I'M PRETTY DAMN WORRIED ABOUT HIM.
TWO DAYS?
ANY IDEA WHERE HE COULD BE?
NONE.
...
WHAT IS IT?
REVEREND? WHERE ARE YOU GOING?
WHOSE HOUSE IS THIS?

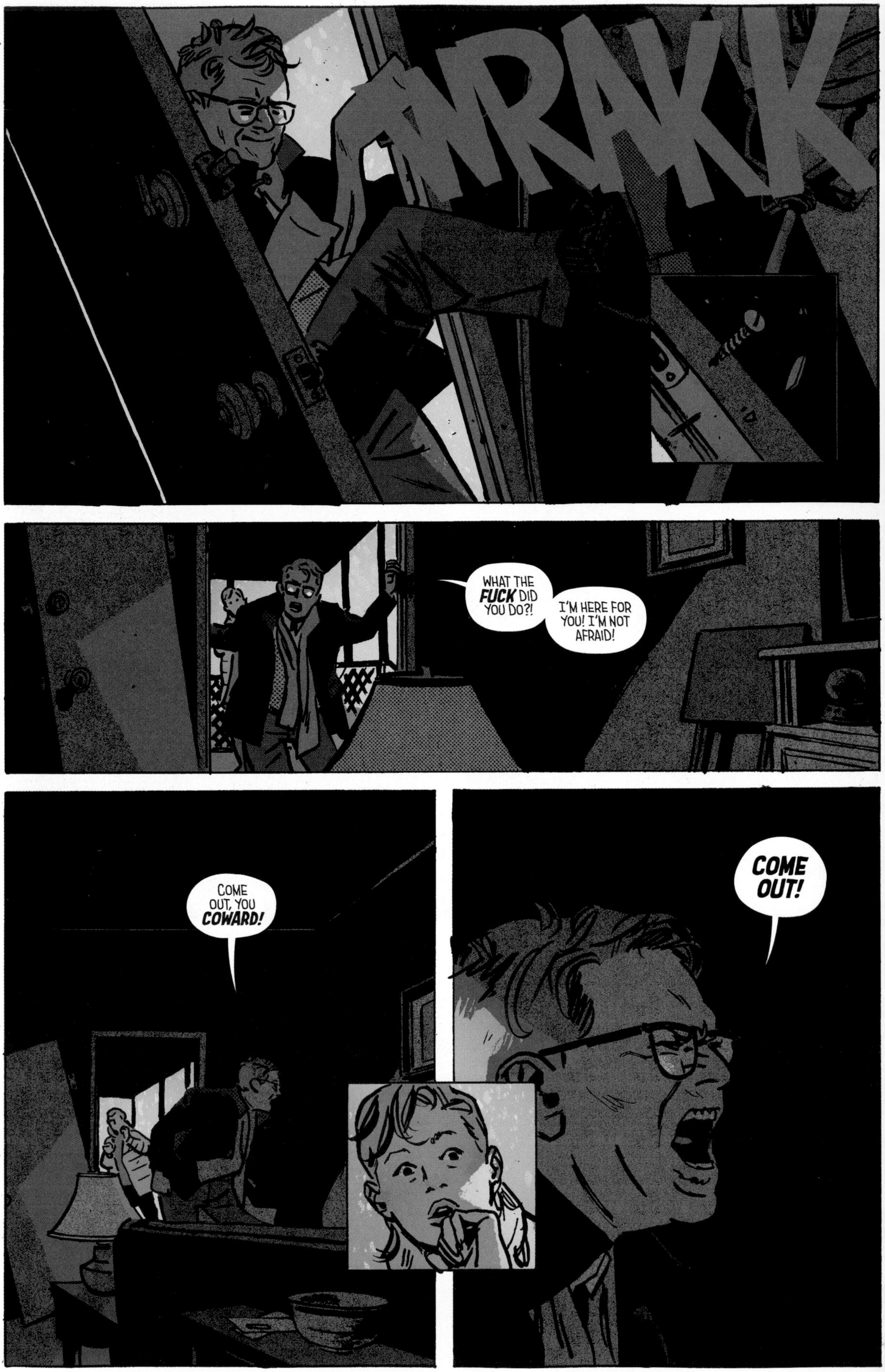
WRAKK
WHAT THE FUCK DID YOU DO?!
I'M HERE FOR YOU! I'M NOT AFRAID!
COME OUT, YOU COWARD!
COME OUT!

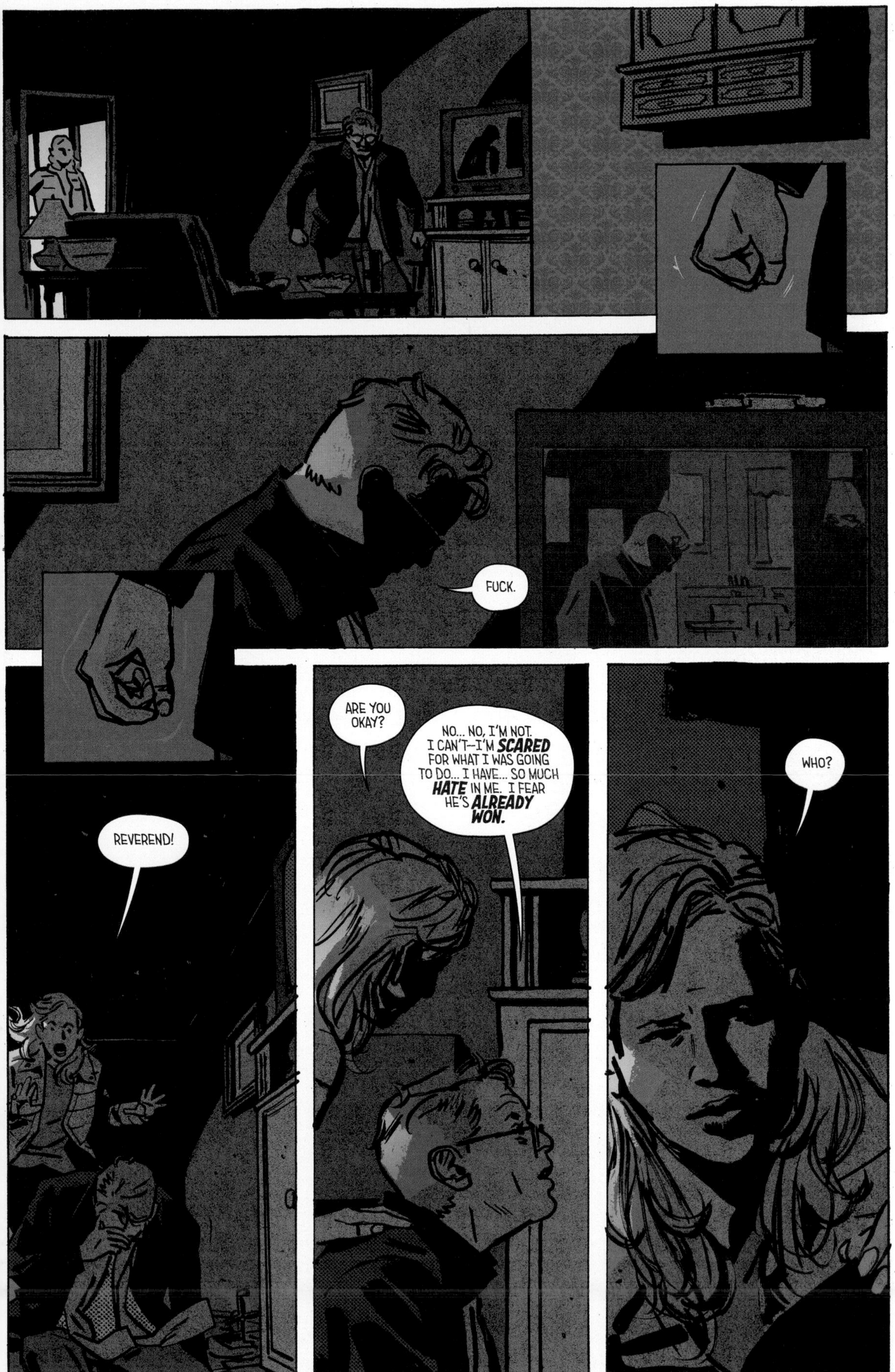
FUCK.
REVEREND!
ARE YOU OKAY?
NO... NO, I'M NOT. I CAN'T--I'M SCARED FOR WHAT I WAS GOING TO DO... I HAVE... SO MUCH HATE IN ME. I FEAR HE'S ALREADY WON.
WHO?

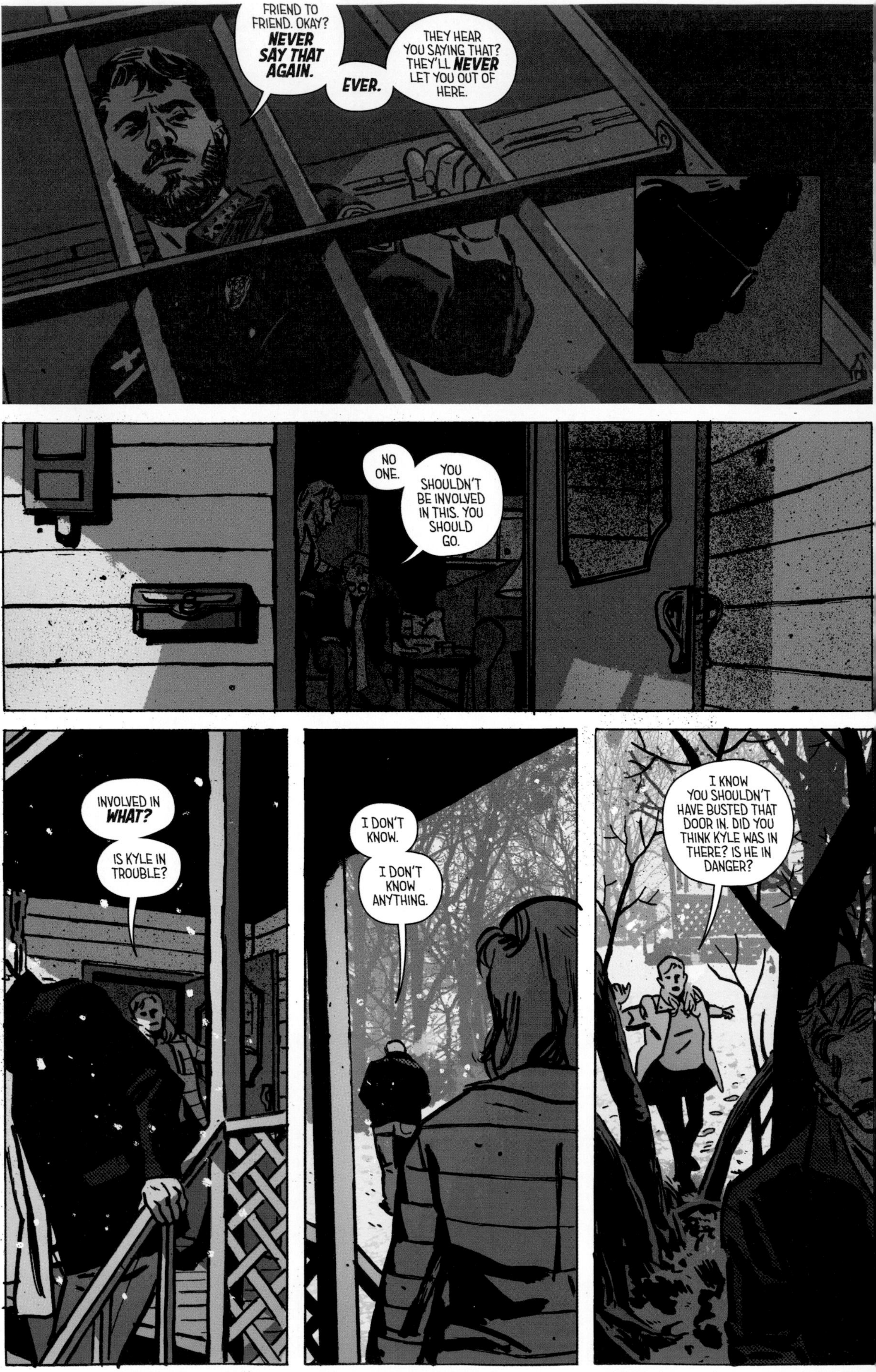
FRIEND TO FRIEND. OKAY? NEVER SAY THAT AGAIN.
EVER.
THEY HEAR YOU SAYING THAT? THEY'LL NEVER LET YOU OUT OF HERE.
NO ONE.
YOU SHOULDN'T BE INVOLVED IN THIS. YOU SHOULD GO.
INVOLVED IN WHAT?
IS KYLE IN TROUBLE?
I DON'T KNOW.
I DON'T KNOW ANYTHING.
I KNOW YOU SHOULDN'T HAVE BUSTED THAT DOOR IN. DID YOU THINK KYLE WAS IN THERE? IS HE IN DANGER?

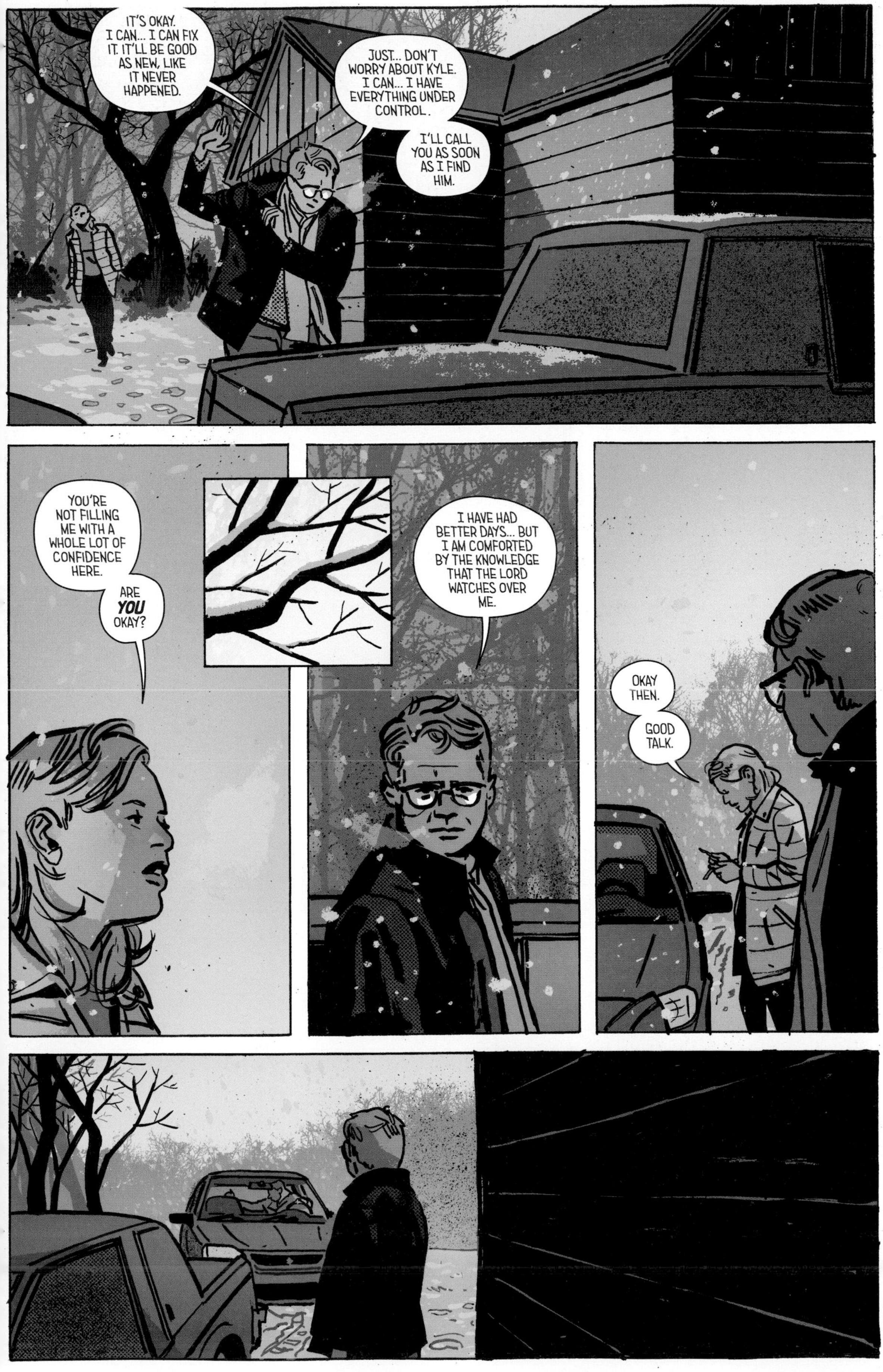
IT'S OKAY. I CAN... I CAN FIX IT. IT'LL BE GOOD AS NEW, LIKE IT NEVER HAPPENED.
JUST... DON'T WORRY ABOUT KYLE. I CAN... I HAVE EVERYTHING UNDER CONTROL.
I'LL CALL YOU AS SOON AS I FIND HIM.
YOU'RE NOT FILLING ME WITH A WHOLE LOT OF CONFIDENCE HERE.
ARE *YOU* OKAY?
I HAVE HAD BETTER DAYS... BUT I AM COMFORTED BY THE KNOWLEDGE THAT THE LORD WATCHES OVER ME.
OKAY THEN.
GOOD TALK.

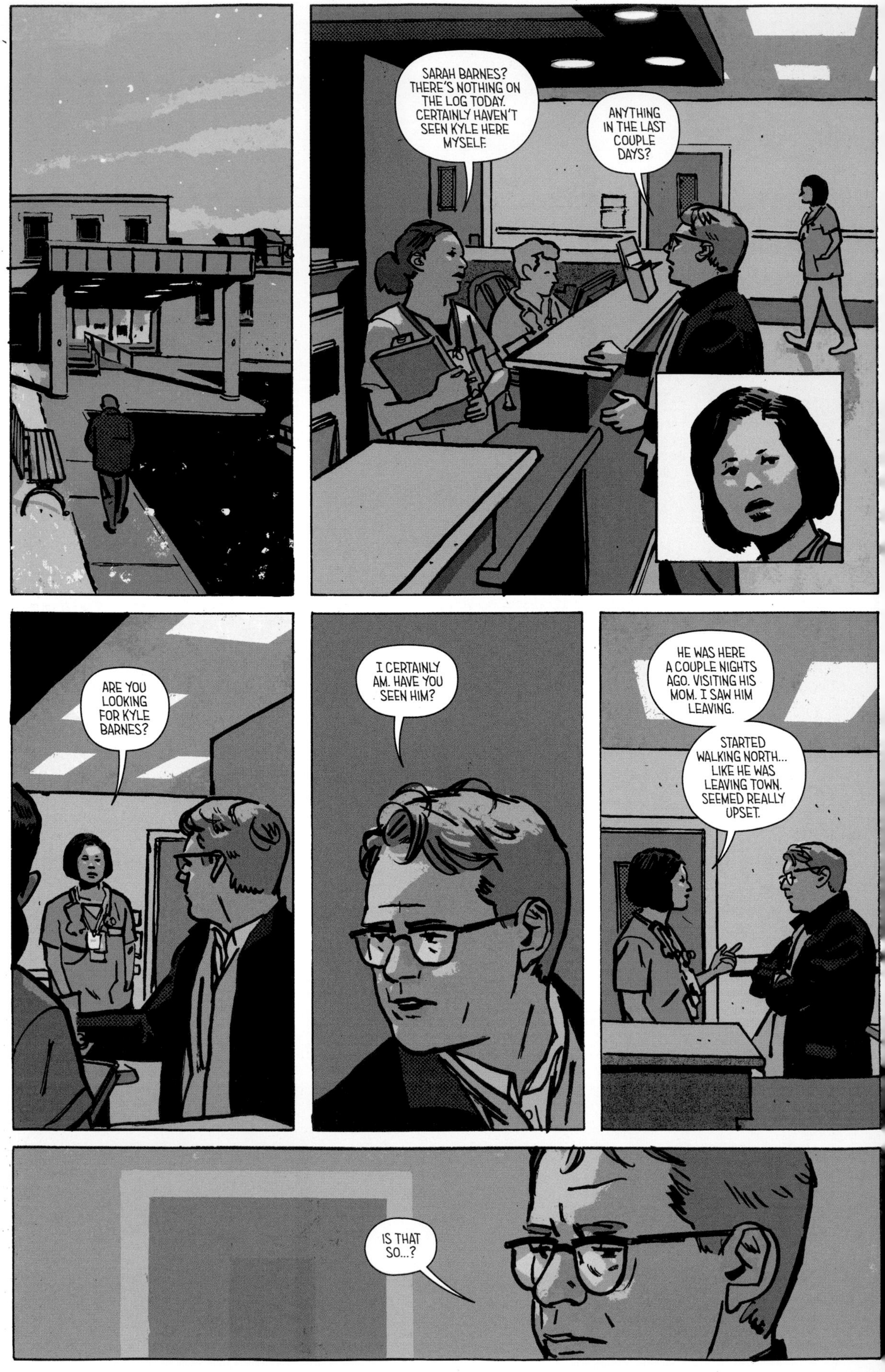
SARAH BARNES? THERE'S NOTHING ON THE LOG TODAY. CERTAINLY HAVEN'T SEEN KYLE HERE MYSELF.
ANYTHING IN THE LAST COUPLE DAYS?
ARE YOU LOOKING FOR KYLE BARNES?
I CERTAINLY AM. HAVE YOU SEEN HIM?
HE WAS HERE A COUPLE NIGHTS AGO. VISITING HIS MOM. I SAW HIM LEAVING.
STARTED WALKING NORTH... LIKE HE WAS LEAVING TOWN. SEEMED REALLY UPSET.
IS THAT SO...?

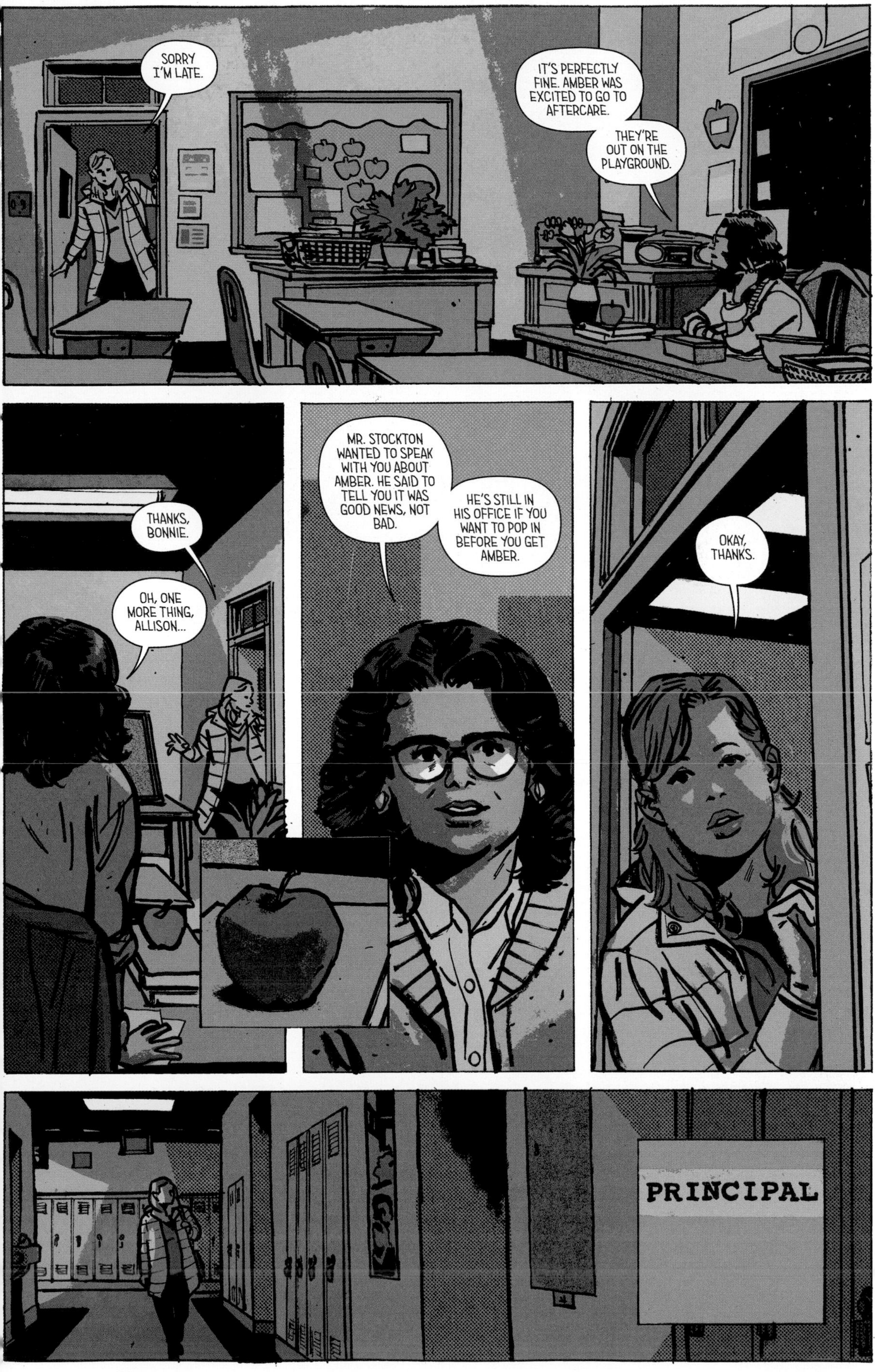
SORRY I'M LATE.
IT'S PERFECTLY FINE. AMBER WAS EXCITED TO GO TO AFTERCARE.
THEY'RE OUT ON THE PLAYGROUND.
THANKS, BONNIE.
OH, ONE MORE THING, ALLISON...
MR. STOCKTON WANTED TO SPEAK WITH YOU ABOUT AMBER. HE SAID TO TELL YOU IT WAS GOOD NEWS, NOT BAD.
HE'S STILL IN HIS OFFICE IF YOU WANT TO POP IN BEFORE YOU GET AMBER.
OKAY, THANKS.
PRINCIPAL

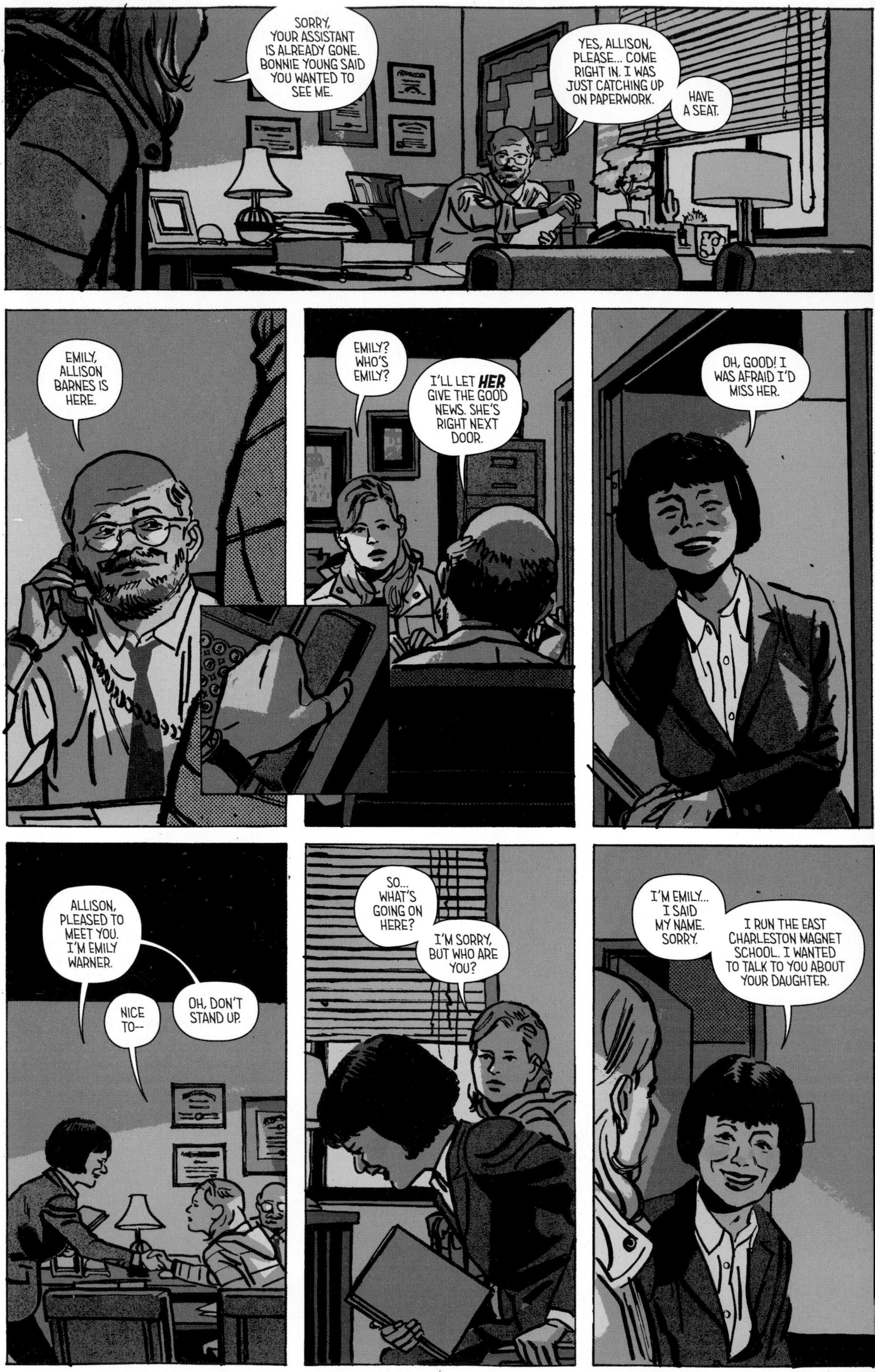
SORRY, YOUR ASSISTANT IS ALREADY GONE. BONNIE YOUNG SAID YOU WANTED TO SEE ME.
YES, ALLISON, PLEASE... COME RIGHT IN. I WAS JUST CATCHING UP ON PAPERWORK.
HAVE A SEAT.
EMILY, ALLISON BARNES IS HERE.
EMILY? WHO'S EMILY?
I'LL LET HER GIVE THE GOOD NEWS. SHE'S RIGHT NEXT DOOR.
OH, GOOD! I WAS AFRAID I'D MISS HER.
ALLISON, PLEASED TO MEET YOU. I'M EMILY WARNER.
NICE TO--
OH, DON'T STAND UP.
SO... WHAT'S GOING ON HERE?
I'M SORRY, BUT WHO ARE YOU?
I'M EMILY... I SAID MY NAME. SORRY.
I RUN THE EAST CHARLESTON MAGNET SCHOOL. I WANTED TO TALK TO YOU ABOUT YOUR DAUGHTER.

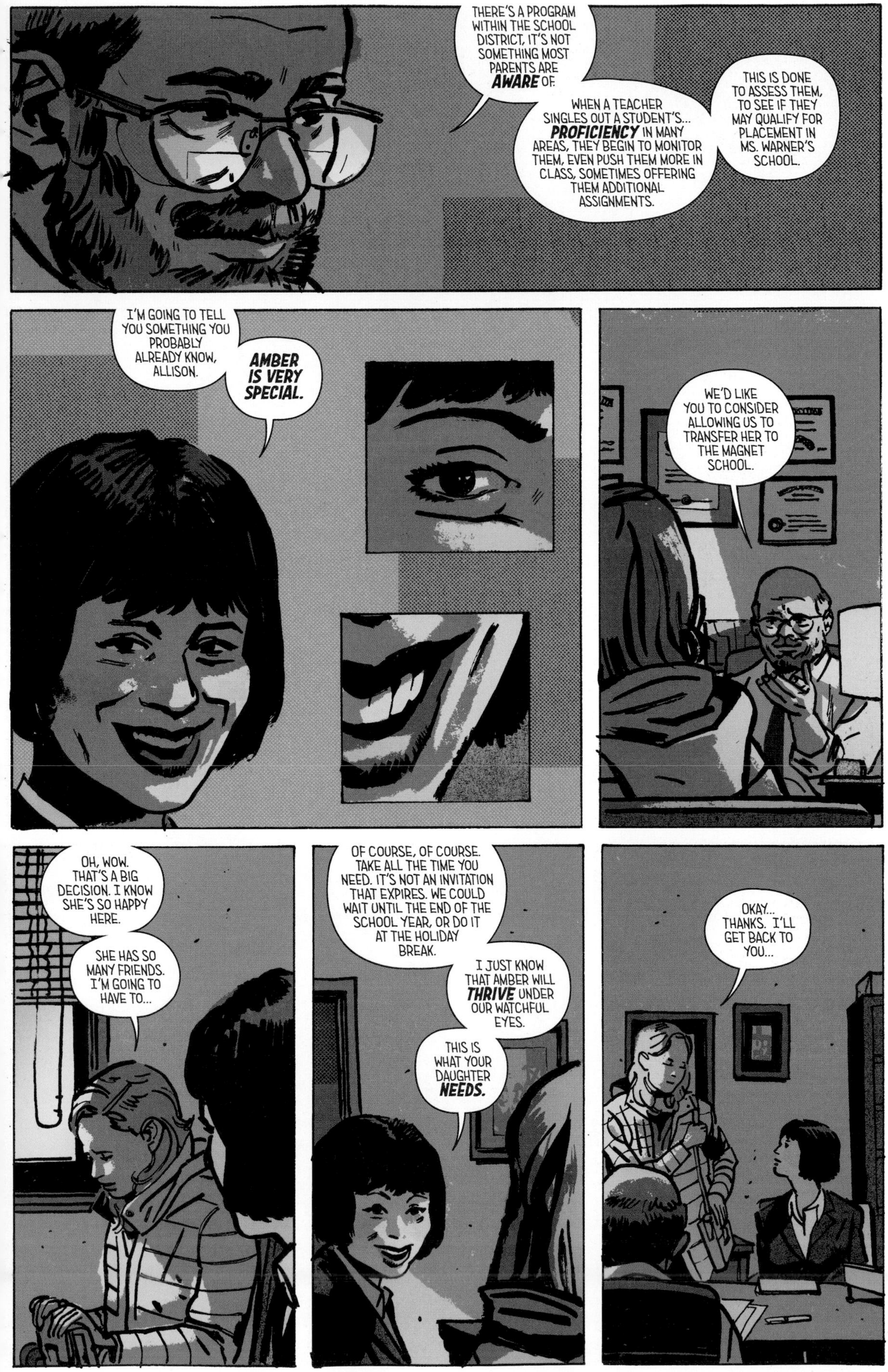
THERE'S A PROGRAM WITHIN THE SCHOOL DISTRICT, IT'S NOT SOMETHING MOST PARENTS ARE AWARE OF.
WHEN A TEACHER SINGLES OUT A STUDENT'S... PROFICIENCY IN MANY AREAS, THEY BEGIN TO MONITOR THEM, EVEN PUSH THEM MORE IN CLASS, SOMETIMES OFFERING THEM ADDITIONAL ASSIGNMENTS.
THIS IS DONE TO ASSESS THEM, TO SEE IF THEY MAY QUALIFY FOR PLACEMENT IN MS. WARNER'S SCHOOL.
I'M GOING TO TELL YOU SOMETHING YOU PROBABLY ALREADY KNOW, ALLISON.
AMBER IS VERY SPECIAL.
WE'D LIKE YOU TO CONSIDER ALLOWING US TO TRANSFER HER TO THE MAGNET SCHOOL.
OH, WOW. THAT'S A BIG DECISION. I KNOW SHE'S SO HAPPY HERE.
SHE HAS SO MANY FRIENDS. I'M GOING TO HAVE TO...
OF COURSE, OF COURSE. TAKE ALL THE TIME YOU NEED. IT'S NOT AN INVITATION THAT EXPIRES. WE COULD WAIT UNTIL THE END OF THE SCHOOL YEAR, OR DO IT AT THE HOLIDAY BREAK.
I JUST KNOW THAT AMBER WILL THRIVE UNDER OUR WATCHFUL EYES.
THIS IS WHAT YOUR DAUGHTER NEEDS.
OKAY... THANKS. I'LL GET BACK TO YOU...

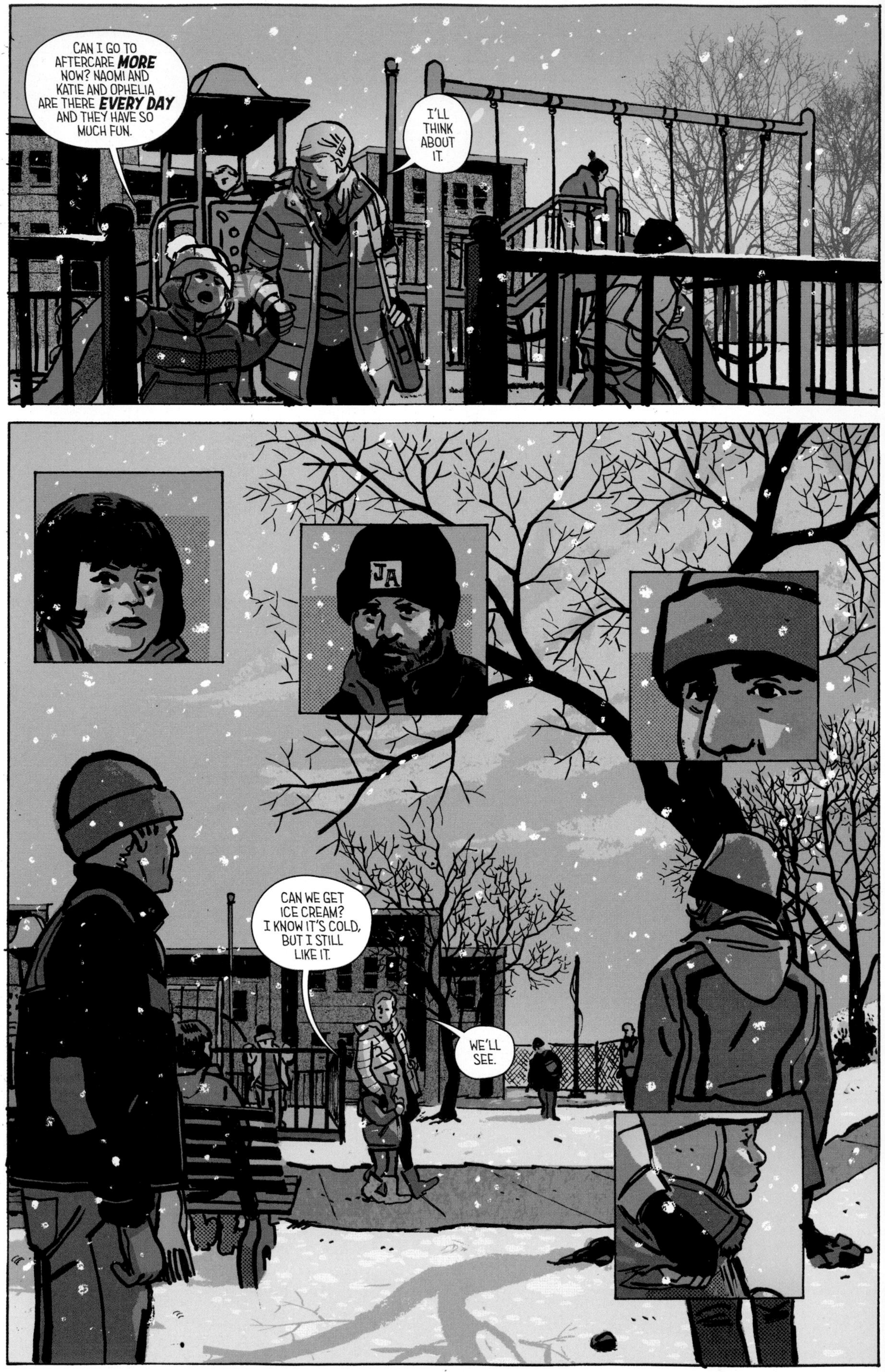
CAN I GO TO AFTERCARE **MORE** NOW? NAOMI AND KATIE AND OPHELIA ARE THERE **EVERY DAY** AND THEY HAVE SO MUCH FUN.
I'LL THINK ABOUT IT.
JA
CAN WE GET ICE CREAM? I KNOW IT'S COLD, BUT I STILL LIKE IT.
WE'LL SEE.

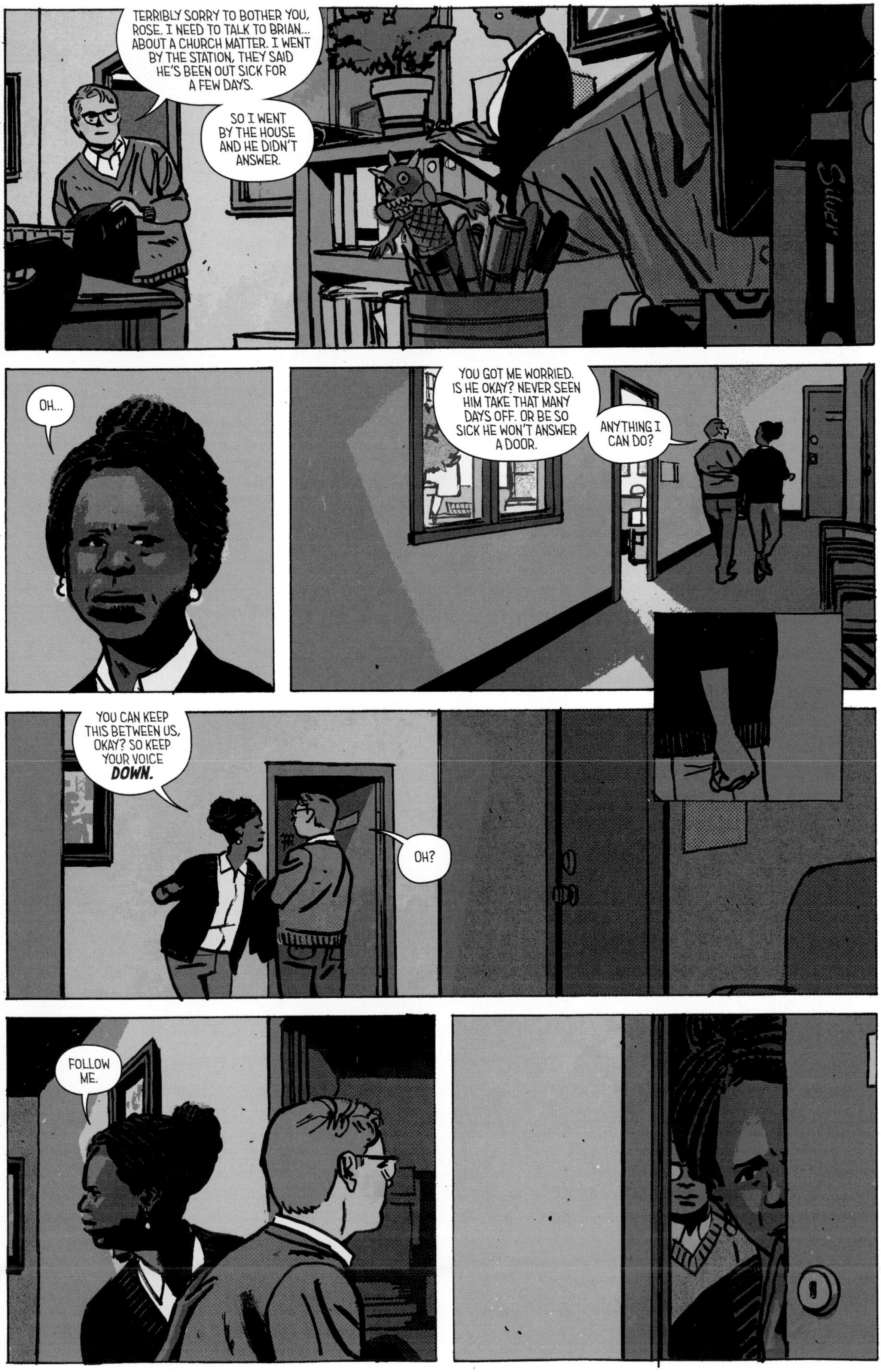
TERRIBLY SORRY TO BOTHER YOU, ROSE. I NEED TO TALK TO BRIAN... ABOUT A CHURCH MATTER. I WENT BY THE STATION, THEY SAID HE'S BEEN OUT SICK FOR A FEW DAYS.
SO I WENT BY THE HOUSE AND HE DIDN'T ANSWER.
OH...
YOU GOT ME WORRIED. IS HE OKAY? NEVER SEEN HIM TAKE THAT MANY DAYS OFF. OR BE SO SICK HE WON'T ANSWER A DOOR.
ANYTHING I CAN DO?
YOU CAN KEEP THIS BETWEEN US, OKAY? SO KEEP YOUR VOICE **DOWN.**
OH?
FOLLOW ME.

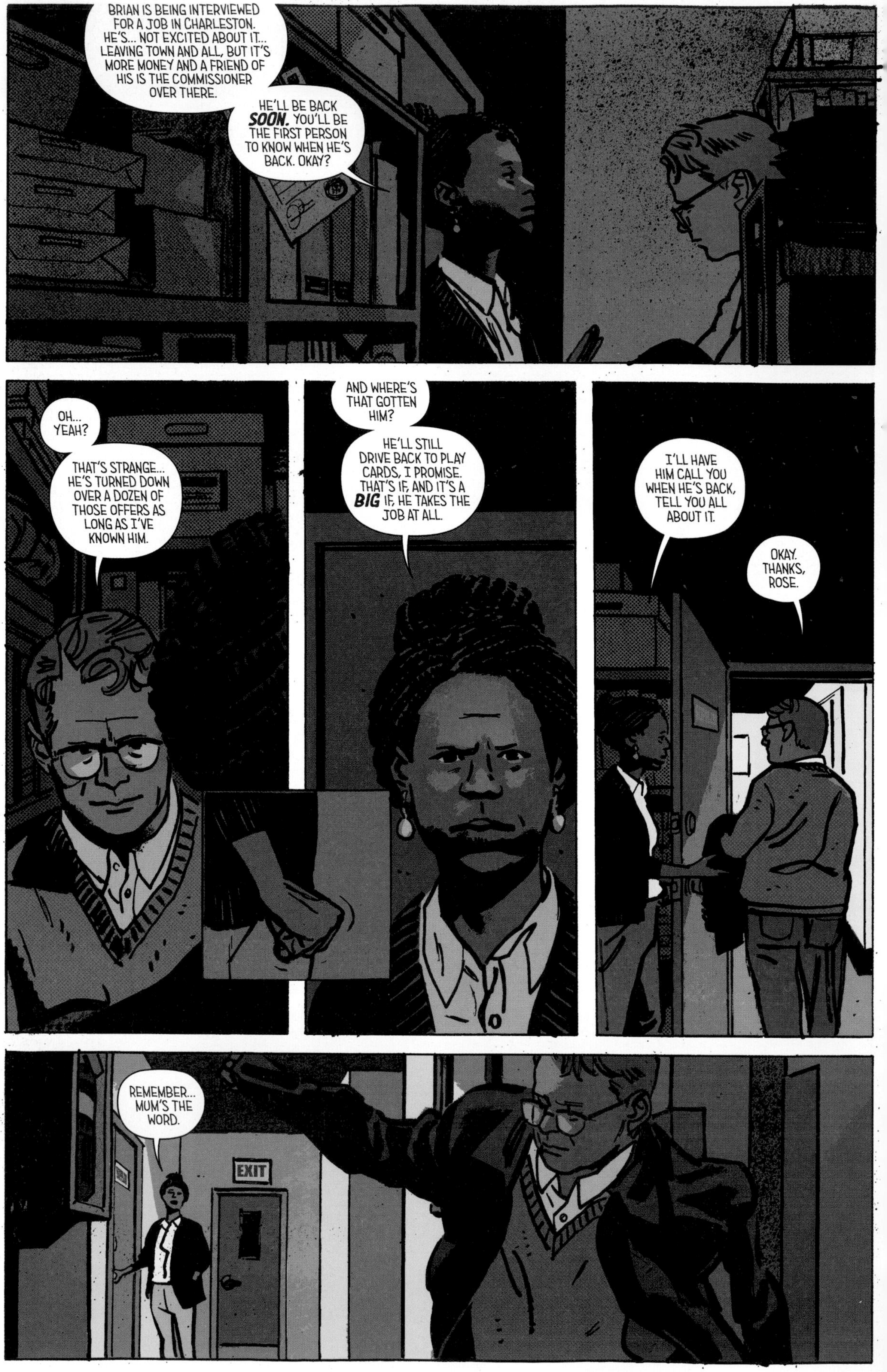
BRIAN IS BEING INTERVIEWED FOR A JOB IN CHARLESTON. HE'S... NOT EXCITED ABOUT IT... LEAVING TOWN AND ALL, BUT IT'S MORE MONEY AND A FRIEND OF HIS IS THE COMMISSIONER OVER THERE.
HE'LL BE BACK **SOON.** YOU'LL BE THE FIRST PERSON TO KNOW WHEN HE'S BACK. OKAY?
OH... YEAH?
THAT'S STRANGE... HE'S TURNED DOWN OVER A DOZEN OF THOSE OFFERS AS LONG AS I'VE KNOWN HIM.
AND WHERE'S THAT GOTTEN HIM?
HE'LL STILL DRIVE BACK TO PLAY CARDS, I PROMISE. THAT'S IF, AND IT'S A **BIG** IF, HE TAKES THE JOB AT ALL.
I'LL HAVE HIM CALL YOU WHEN HE'S BACK, TELL YOU ALL ABOUT IT.
OKAY. THANKS, ROSE.
REMEMBER... MUM'S THE WORD.
EXIT

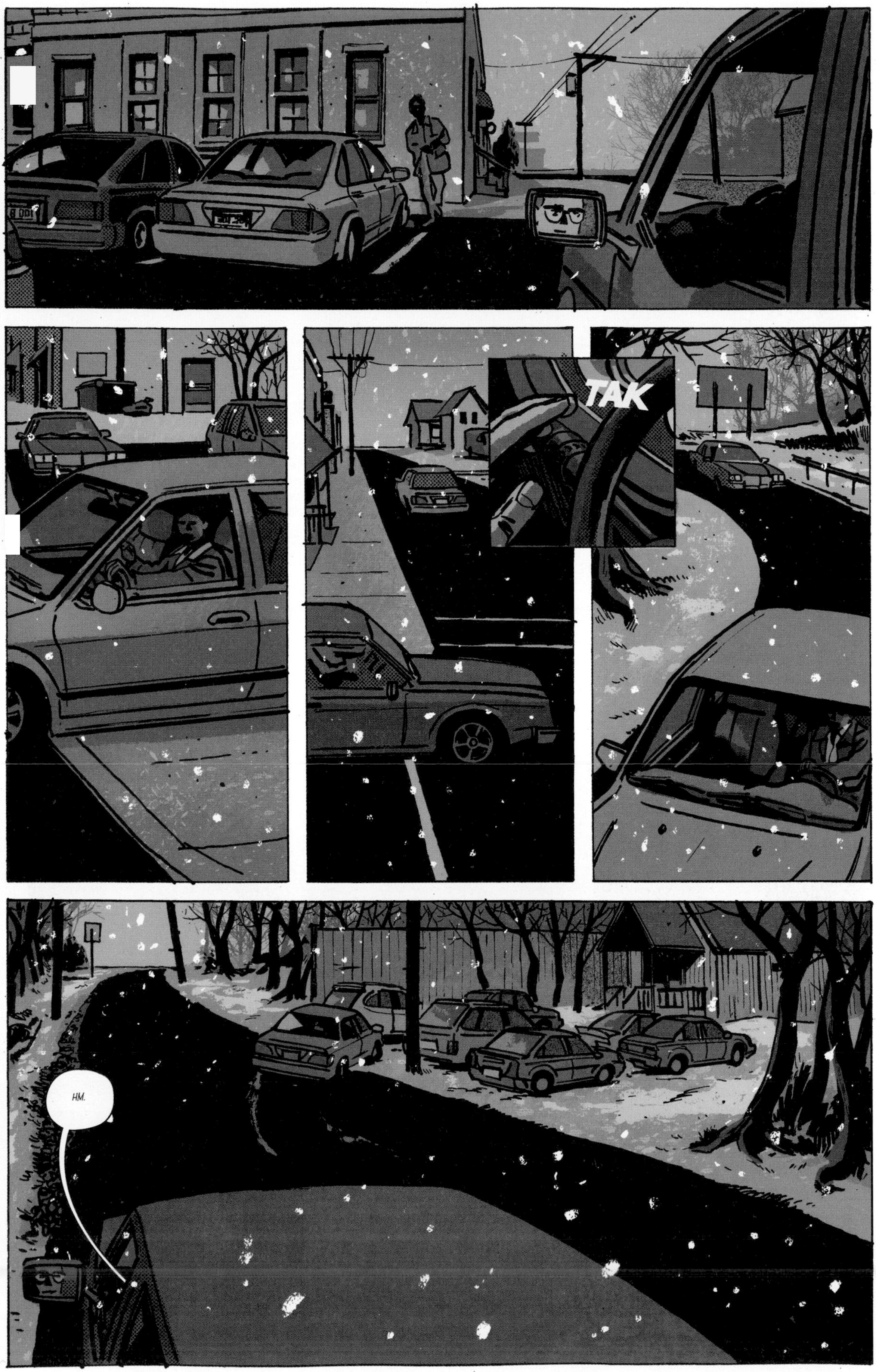
TAK
HM.

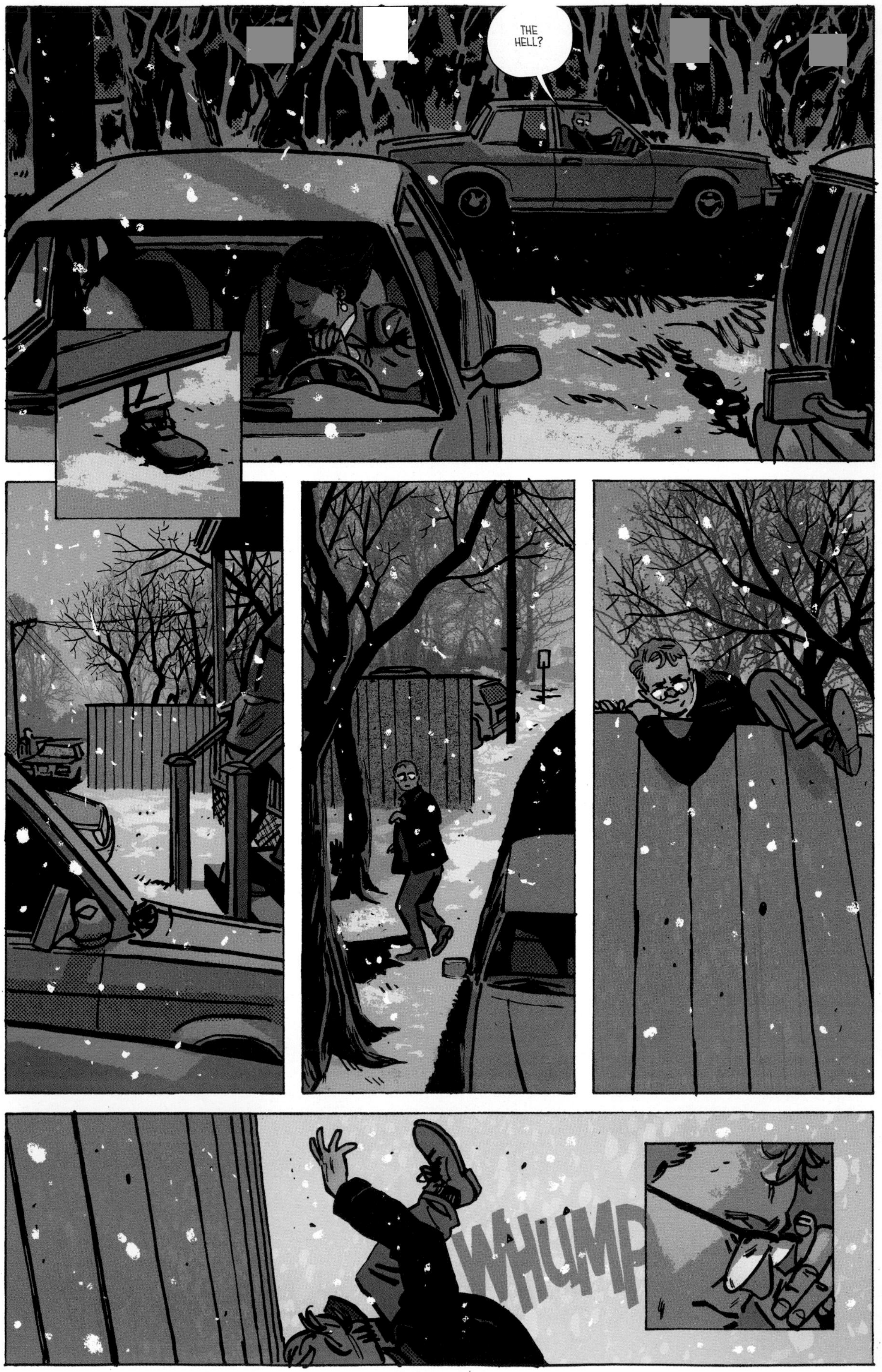
THE HELL?
WHUMP

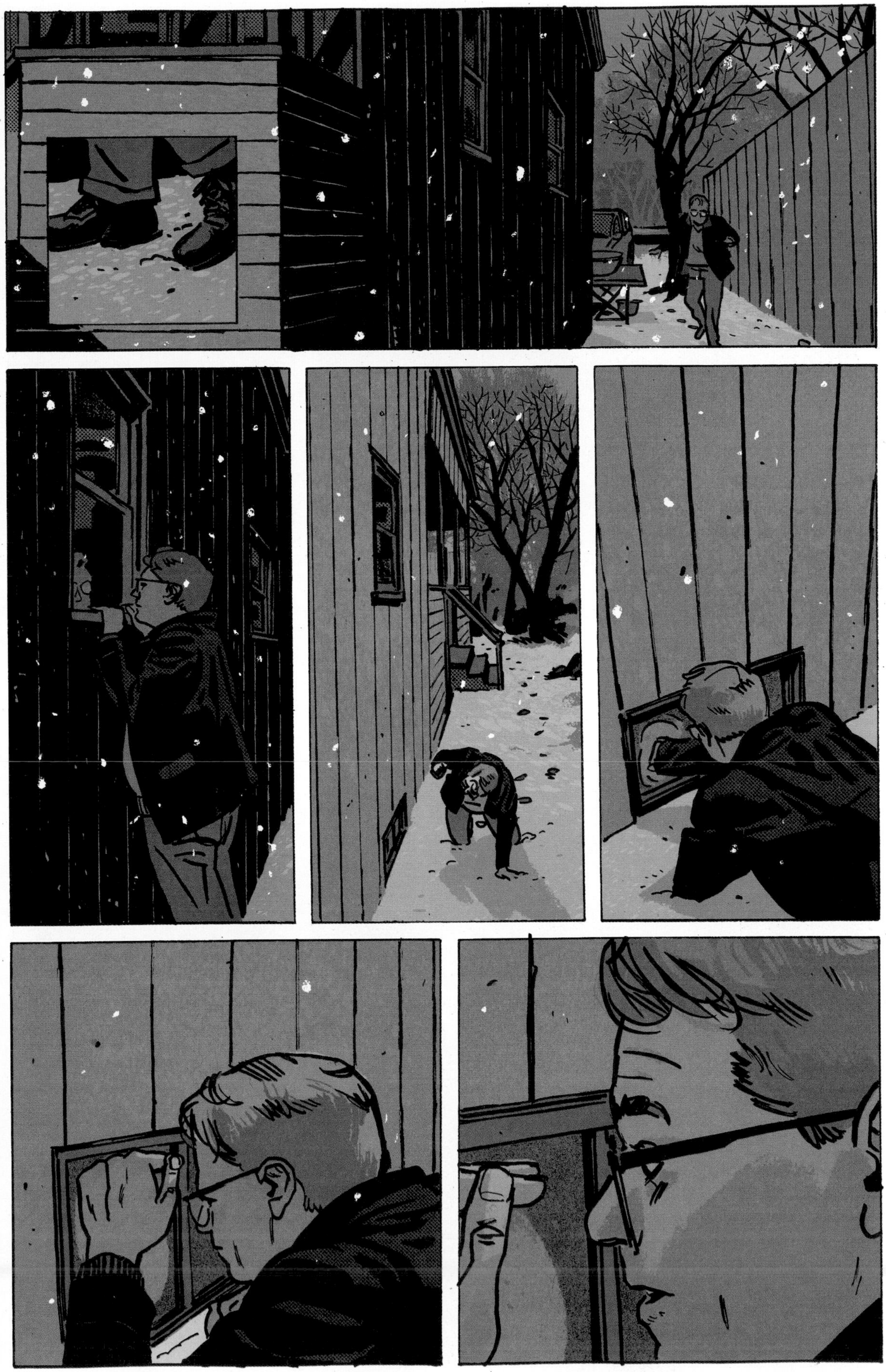

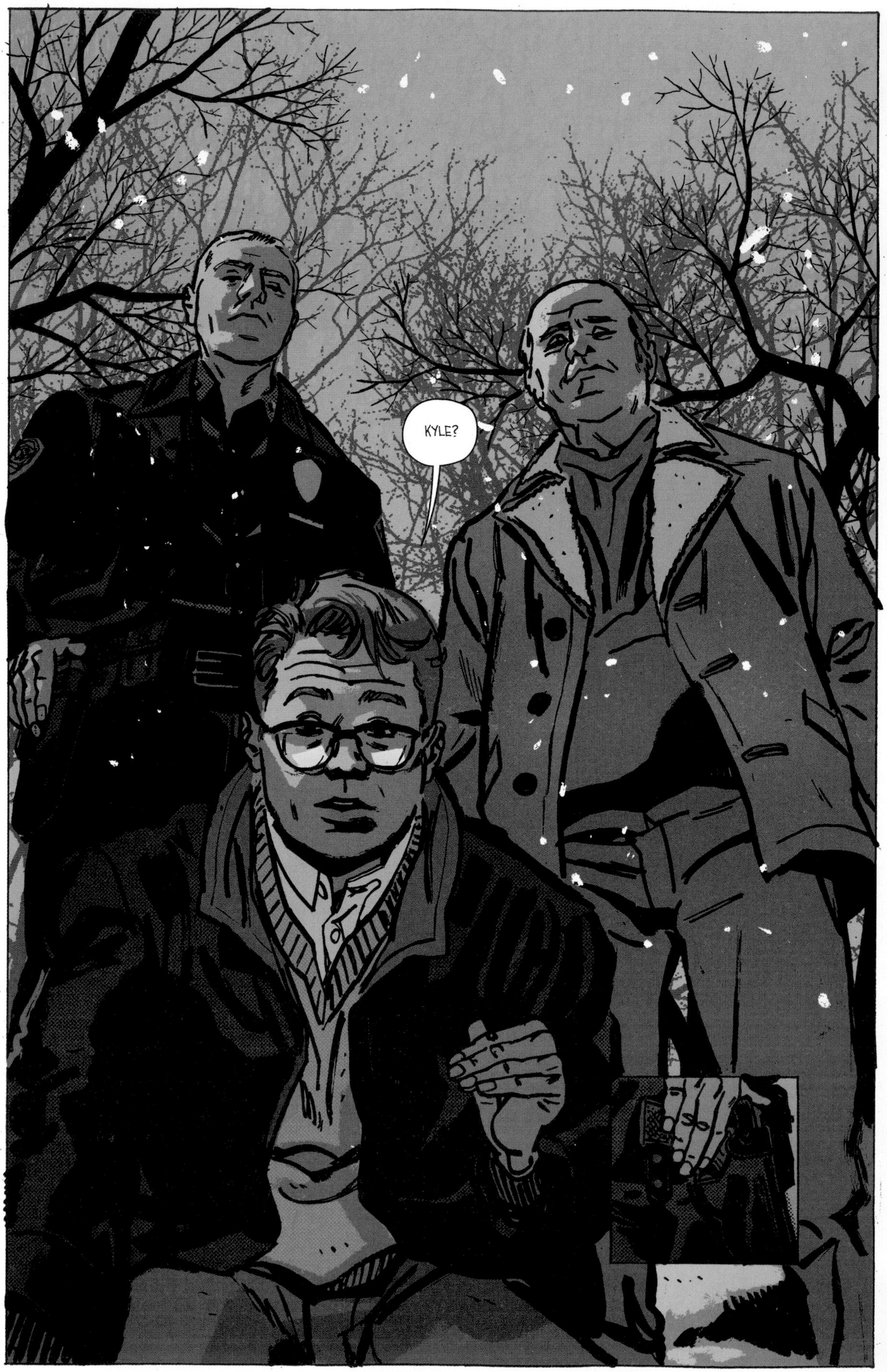
KYLE?

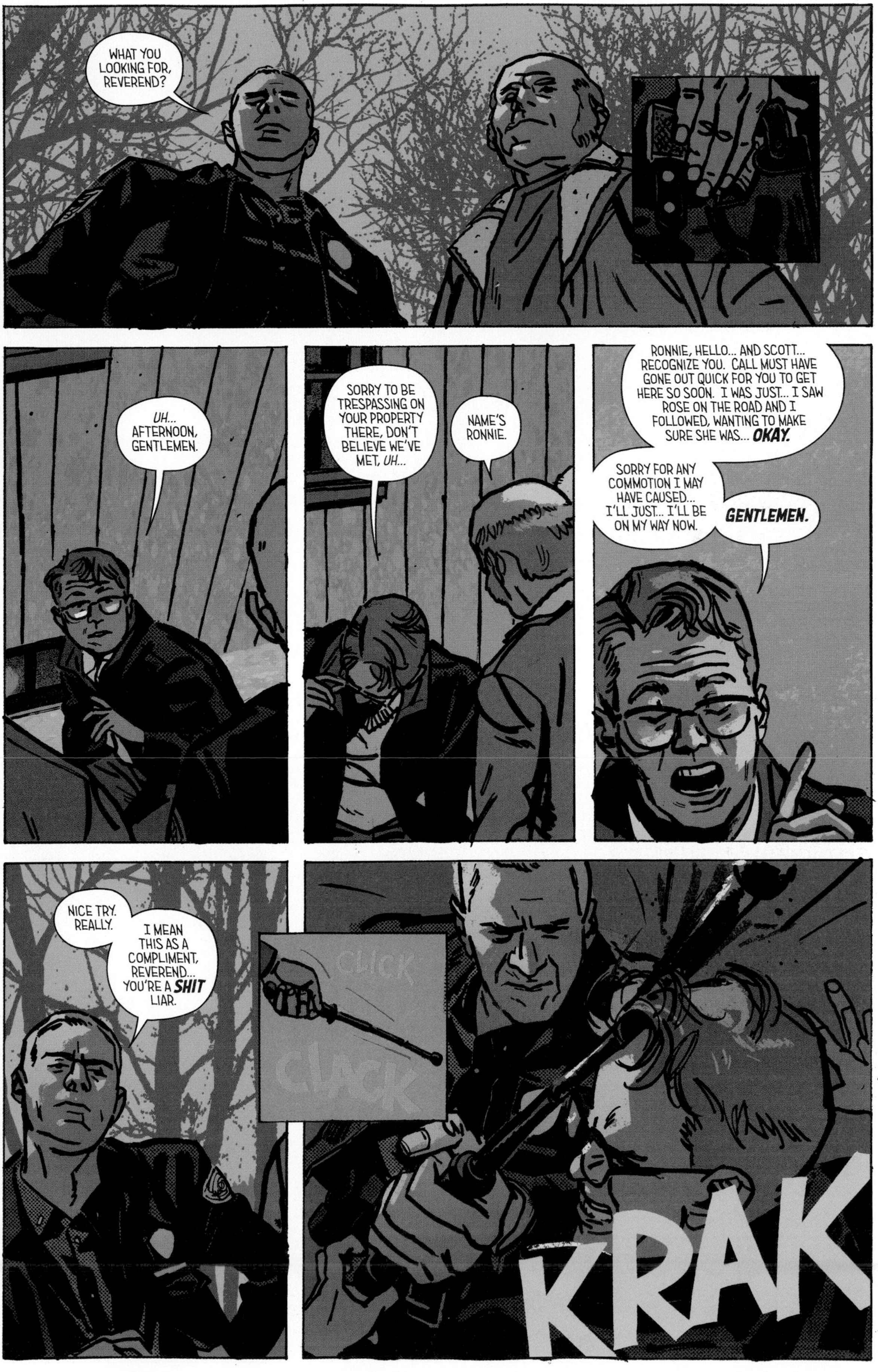
WHAT YOU LOOKING FOR, REVEREND?
UH... AFTERNOON, GENTLEMEN.
SORRY TO BE TRESPASSING ON YOUR PROPERTY THERE, DON'T BELIEVE WE'VE MET, UH...
NAME'S RONNIE.
RONNIE, HELLO... AND SCOTT... RECOGNIZE YOU. CALL MUST HAVE GONE OUT QUICK FOR YOU TO GET HERE SO SOON. I WAS JUST... I SAW ROSE ON THE ROAD AND I FOLLOWED, WANTING TO MAKE SURE SHE WAS... OKAY.
SORRY FOR ANY COMMOTION I MAY HAVE CAUSED... I'LL JUST... I'LL BE ON MY WAY NOW.
GENTLEMEN.
NICE TRY. REALLY.
I MEAN THIS AS A COMPLIMENT, REVEREND... YOU'RE A SHIT LIAR.
CLICK
CLACK
KRAK

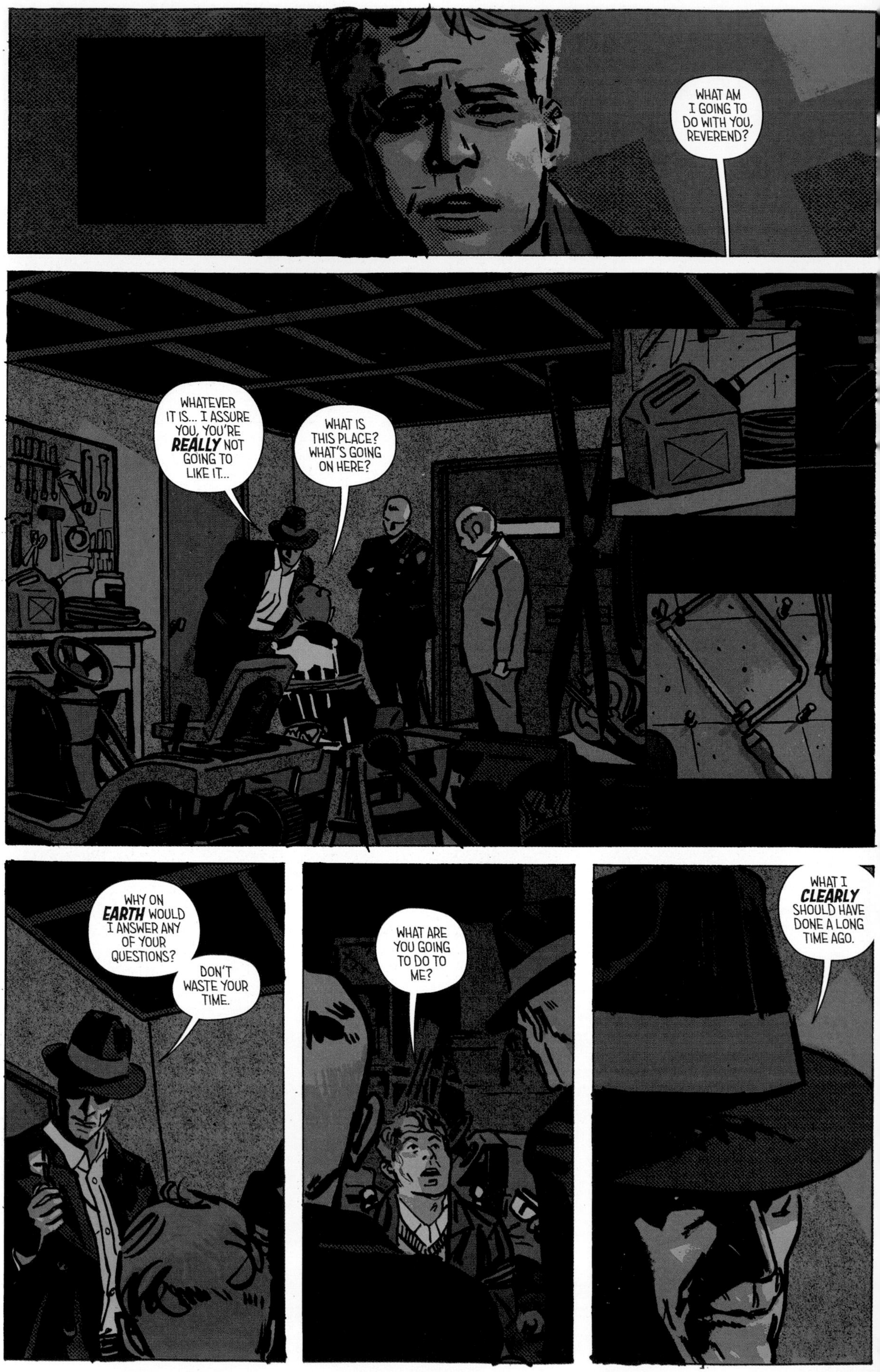
WHAT AM I GOING TO DO WITH YOU, REVEREND?
WHATEVER IT IS... I ASSURE YOU, YOU'RE REALLY NOT GOING TO LIKE IT...
WHAT IS THIS PLACE? WHAT'S GOING ON HERE?
WHY ON EARTH WOULD I ANSWER ANY OF YOUR QUESTIONS?
DON'T WASTE YOUR TIME.
WHAT ARE YOU GOING TO DO TO ME?
WHAT I CLEARLY SHOULD HAVE DONE A LONG TIME AGO.

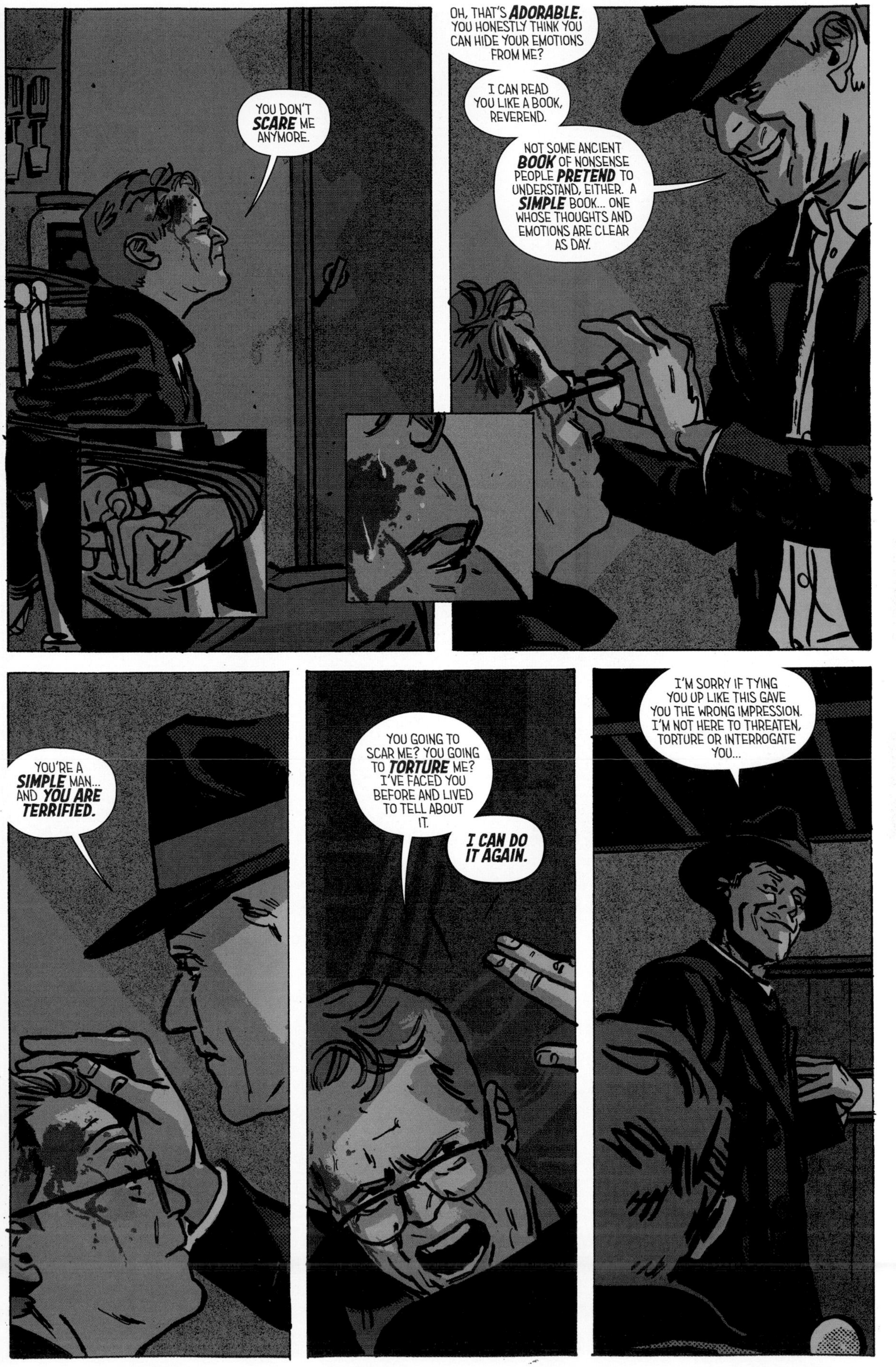
YOU DON'T SCARE ME ANYMORE.
OH, THAT'S ADORABLE. YOU HONESTLY THINK YOU CAN HIDE YOUR EMOTIONS FROM ME?
I CAN READ YOU LIKE A BOOK, REVEREND.
NOT SOME ANCIENT BOOK OF NONSENSE PEOPLE PRETEND TO UNDERSTAND, EITHER. A SIMPLE BOOK... ONE WHOSE THOUGHTS AND EMOTIONS ARE CLEAR AS DAY.
YOU'RE A SIMPLE MAN... AND YOU ARE TERRIFIED.
YOU GOING TO SCAR ME? YOU GOING TO TORTURE ME? I'VE FACED YOU BEFORE AND LIVED TO TELL ABOUT IT.
I CAN DO IT AGAIN.
I'M SORRY IF TYING YOU UP LIKE THIS GAVE YOU THE WRONG IMPRESSION. I'M NOT HERE TO THREATEN, TORTURE OR INTERROGATE YOU...

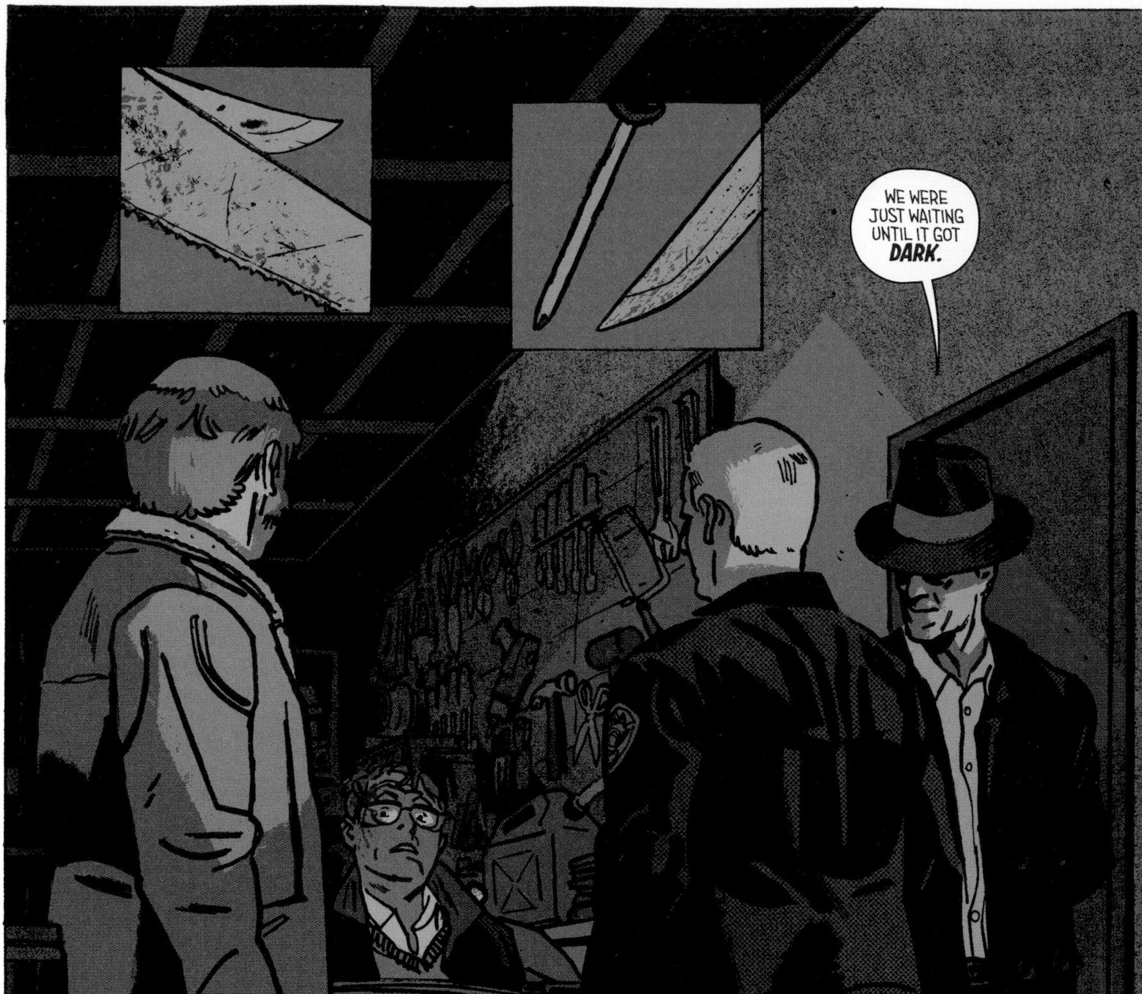
WE WERE JUST WAITING UNTIL IT GOT **DARK.**

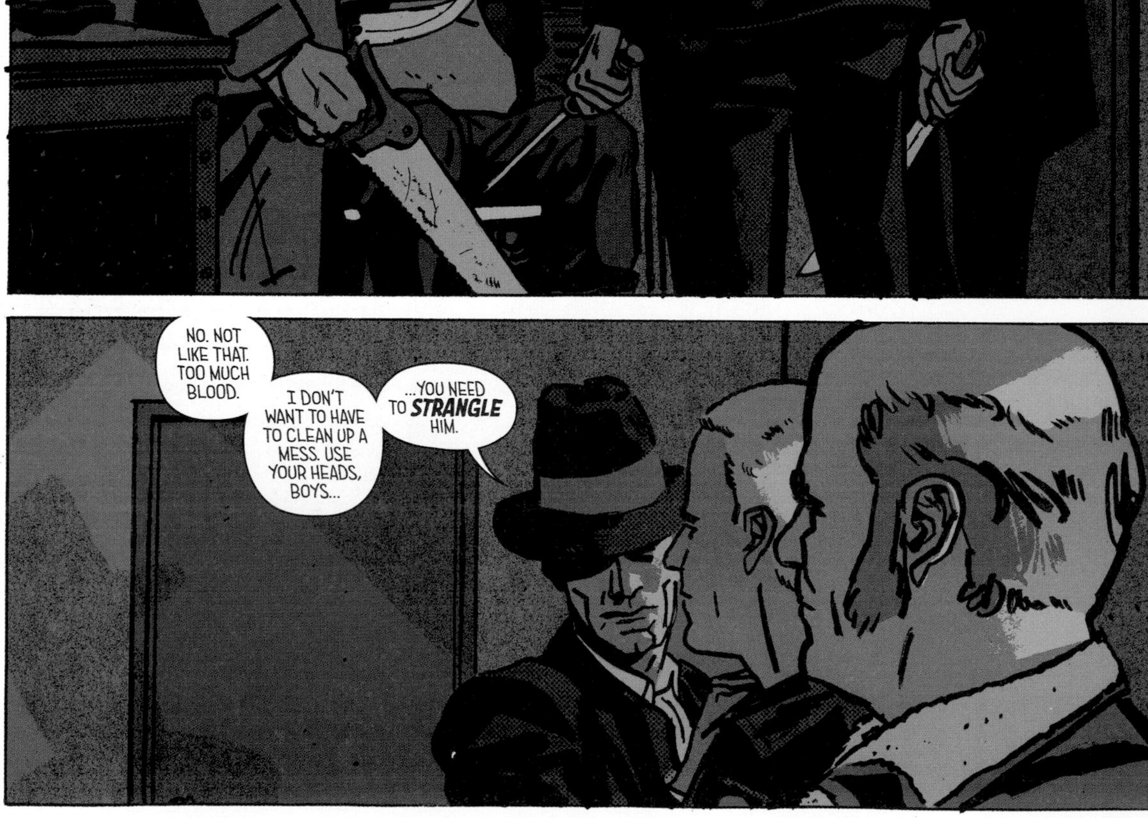
NO. NOT LIKE THAT. TOO MUCH BLOOD.
I DON'T WANT TO HAVE TO CLEAN UP A MESS. USE YOUR HEADS, BOYS...
...YOU NEED TO **STRANGLE** HIM.

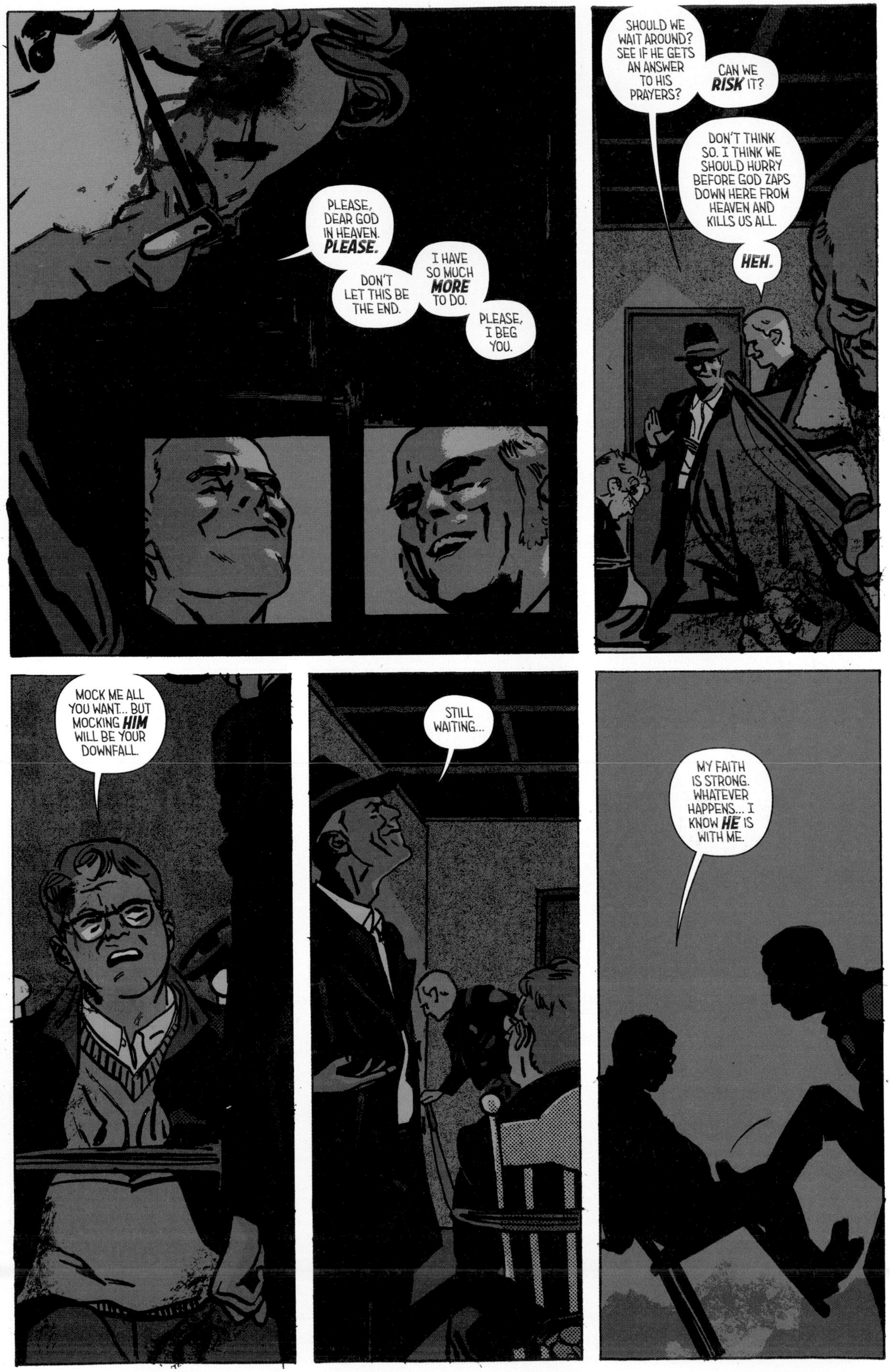
PLEASE, DEAR GOD IN HEAVEN. **PLEASE.**
DON'T LET THIS BE THE END.
I HAVE SO MUCH **MORE** TO DO.
PLEASE, I BEG YOU.
SHOULD WE WAIT AROUND? SEE IF HE GETS AN ANSWER TO HIS PRAYERS?
CAN WE **RISK** IT?
DON'T THINK SO. I THINK WE SHOULD HURRY BEFORE GOD ZAPS DOWN HERE FROM HEAVEN AND KILLS US ALL.
HEH.
MOCK ME ALL YOU WANT... BUT MOCKING **HIM** WILL BE YOUR DOWNFALL.
STILL WAITING...
MY FAITH IS STRONG. WHATEVER HAPPENS... I KNOW **HE** IS WITH ME.

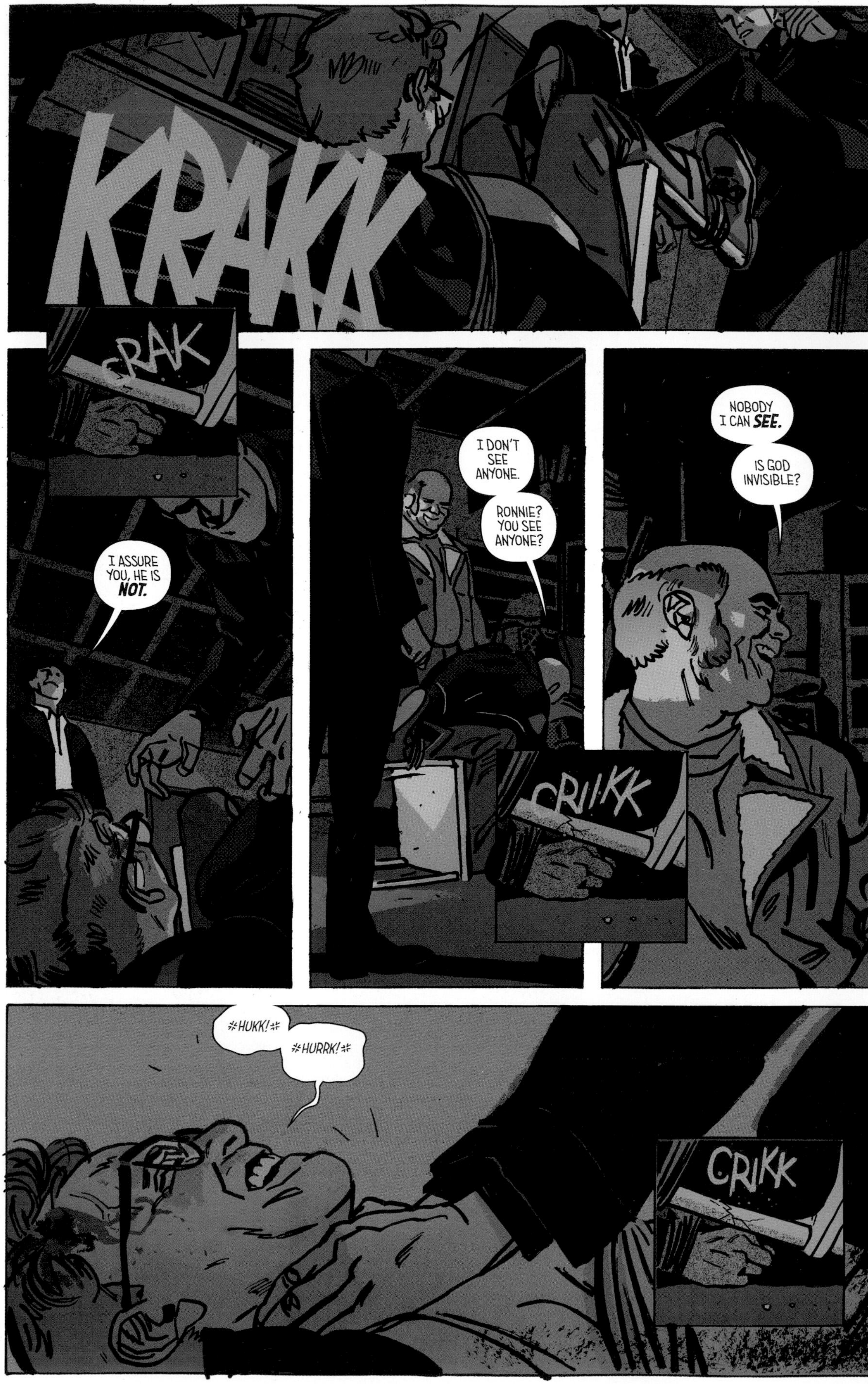
KRAKK
CRAK
I ASSURE YOU, HE IS NOT.
I DON'T SEE ANYONE.
RONNIE? YOU SEE ANYONE?
NOBODY I CAN SEE.
IS GOD INVISIBLE?
CRIIKK
HUKK!
HURRK!
CRIKK

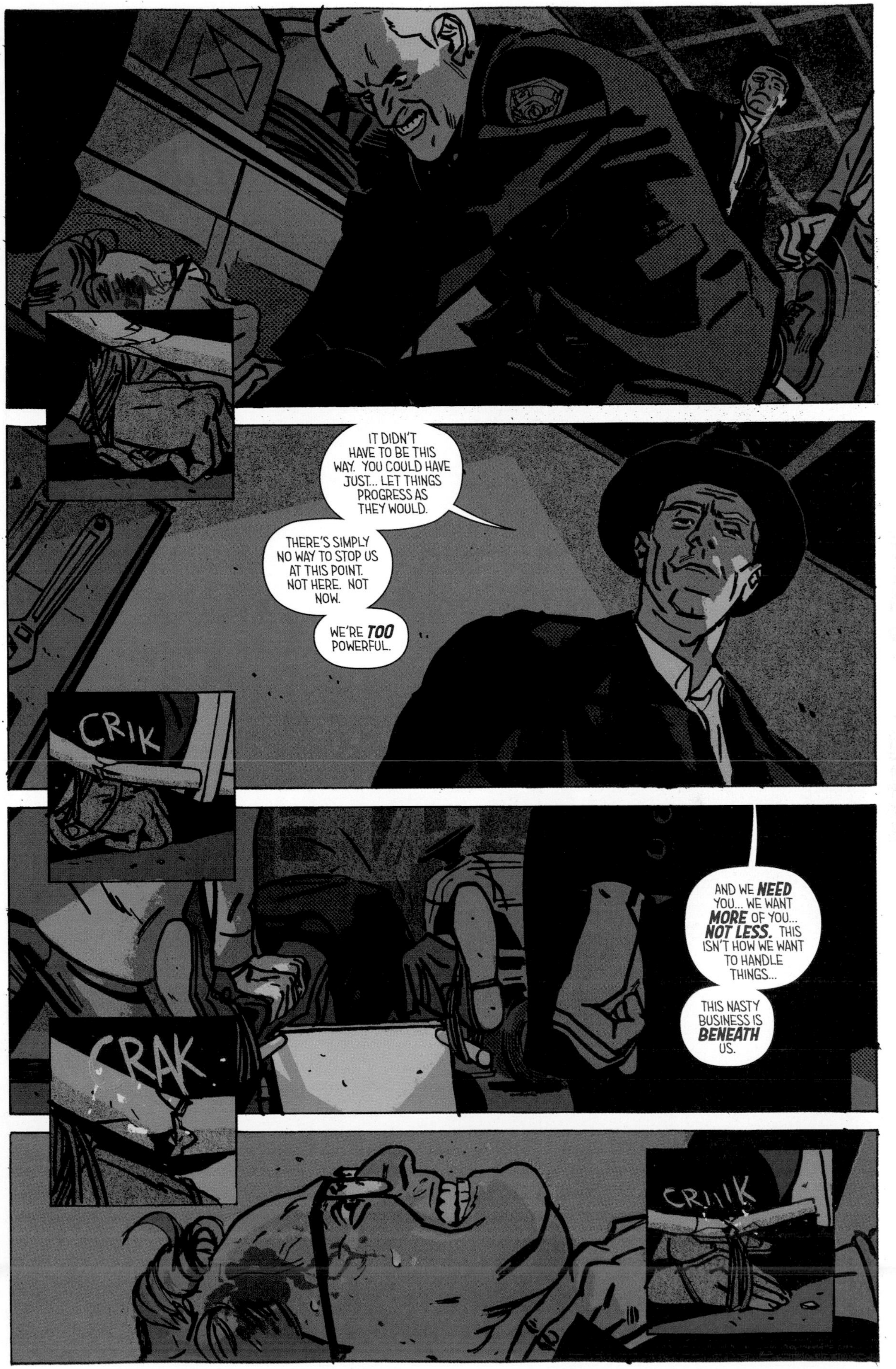

IT DIDN'T HAVE TO BE THIS WAY. YOU COULD HAVE JUST... LET THINGS PROGRESS AS THEY WOULD.
THERE'S SIMPLY NO WAY TO STOP US AT THIS POINT. NOT HERE. NOT NOW.
WE'RE **TOO** POWERFUL.
CRIK
AND WE **NEED** YOU... WE WANT **MORE** OF YOU... **NOT LESS.** THIS ISN'T HOW WE WANT TO HANDLE THINGS...
THIS NASTY BUSINESS IS **BENEATH** US.
CRAK
CRIIIK

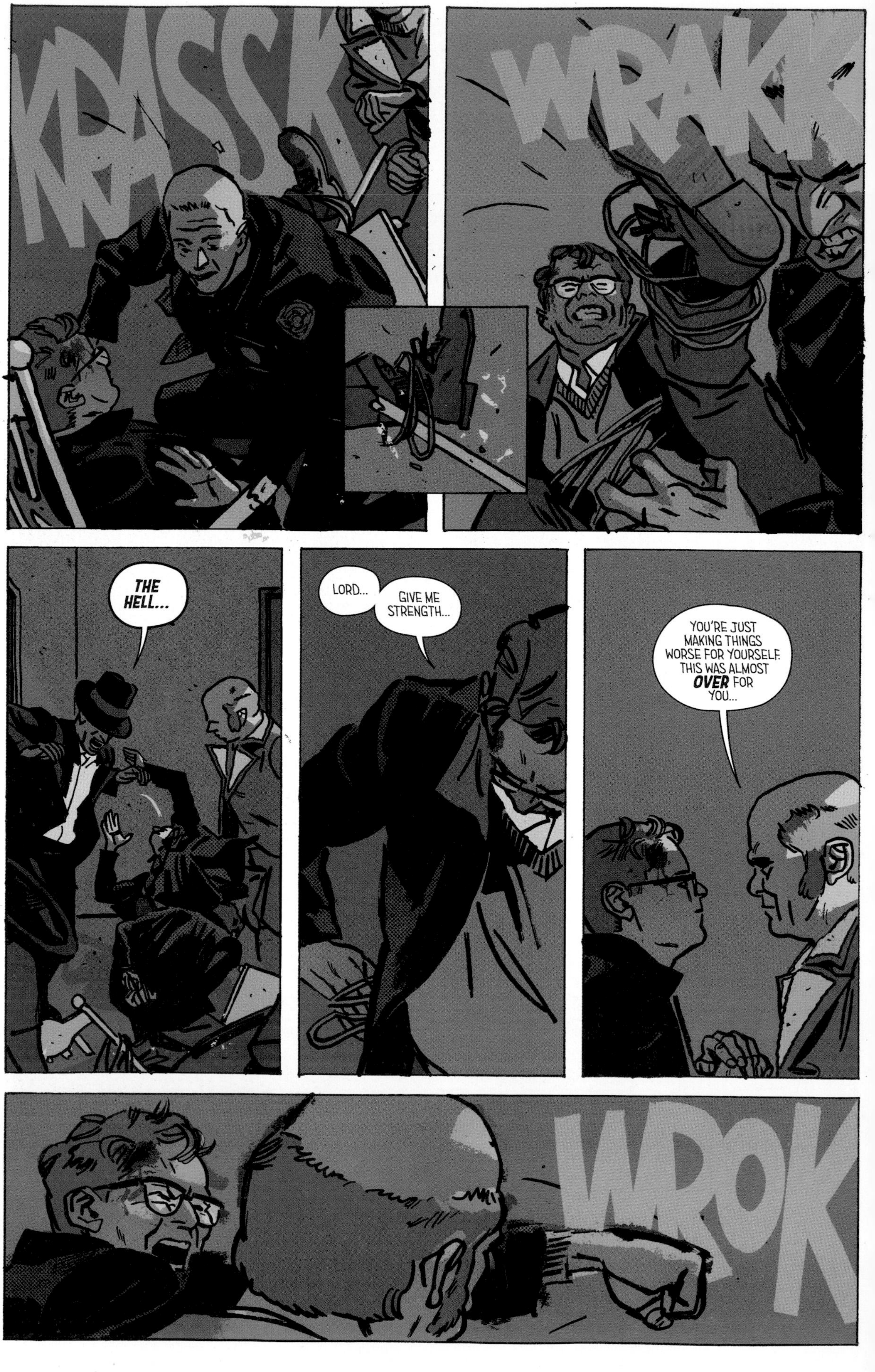
KRASSK
WRAKK
THE HELL...
LORD...
GIVE ME STRENGTH...
YOU'RE JUST MAKING THINGS WORSE FOR YOURSELF. THIS WAS ALMOST OVER FOR YOU...
WROK

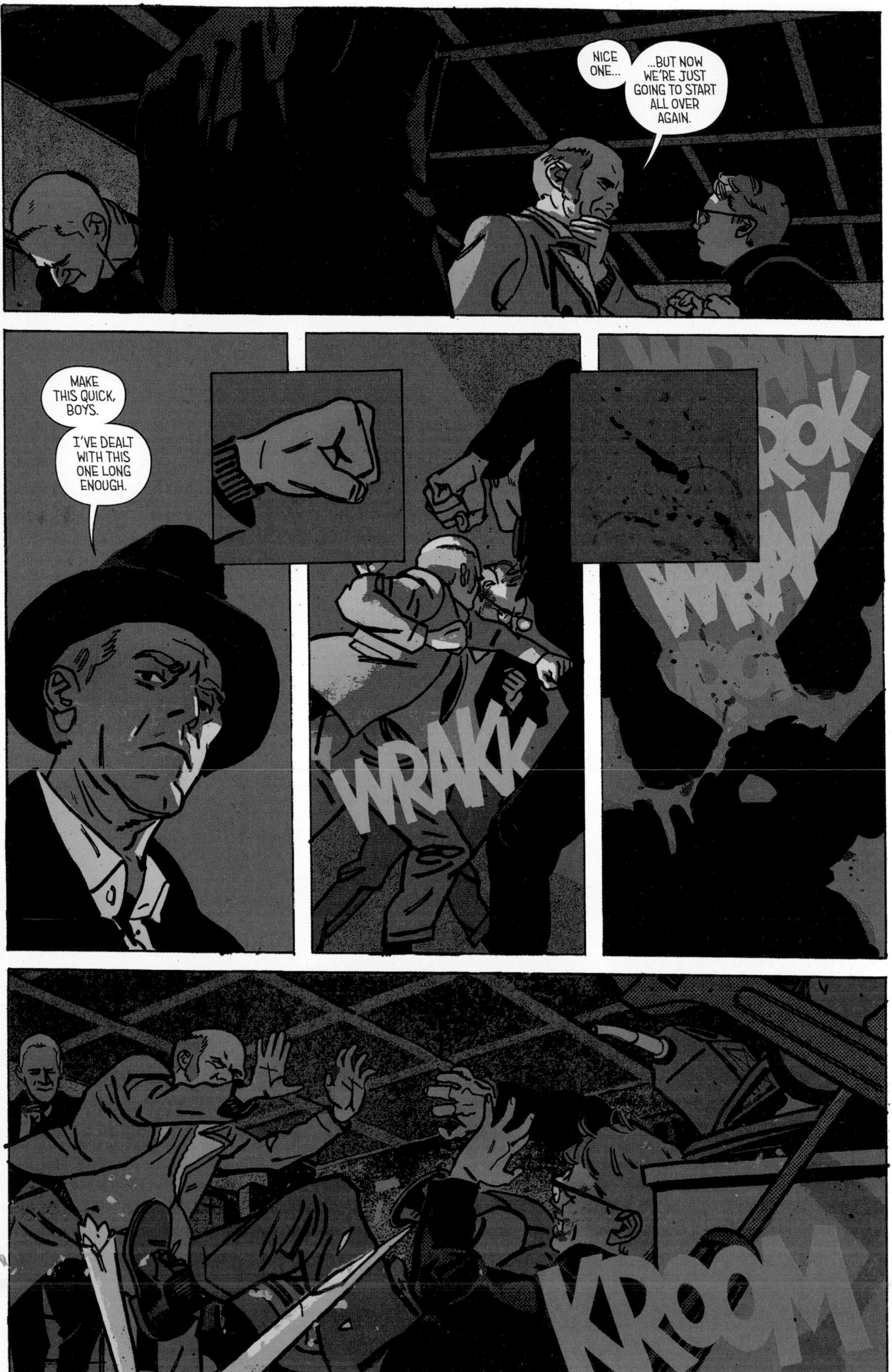
NICE ONE...
...BUT NOW WE'RE JUST GOING TO START ALL OVER AGAIN.
MAKE THIS QUICK, BOYS.
I'VE DEALT WITH THIS ONE LONG ENOUGH.
WRAKK
KROOM

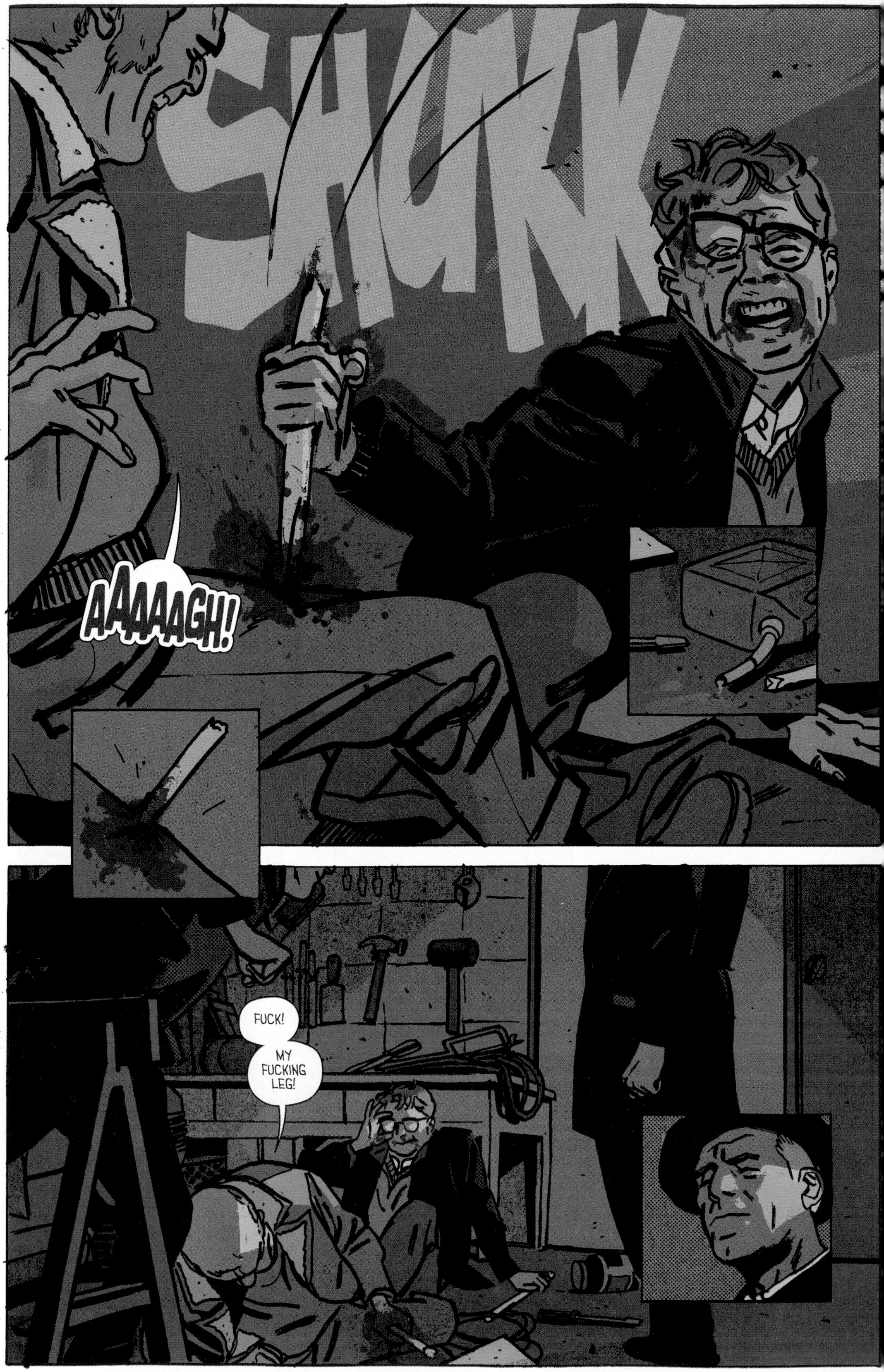
SHUNK
AAAAAGH!
FUCK!
MY FUCKING LEG!

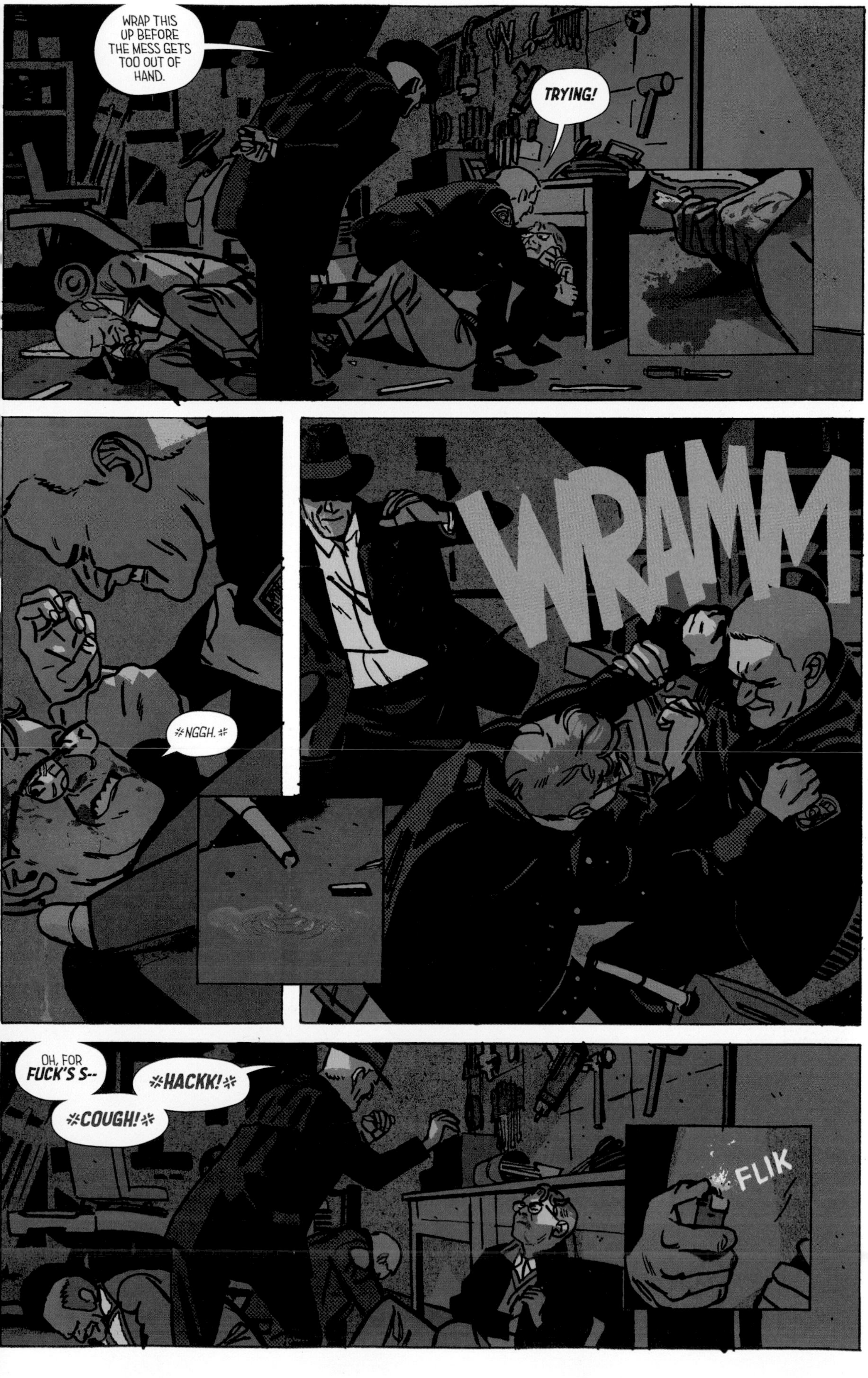
WRAP THIS UP BEFORE THE MESS GETS TOO OUT OF HAND.
TRYING!
NGGH.
WRAMM
OH, FOR FUCK'S S--
HACKK!
COUGH!
FLIK

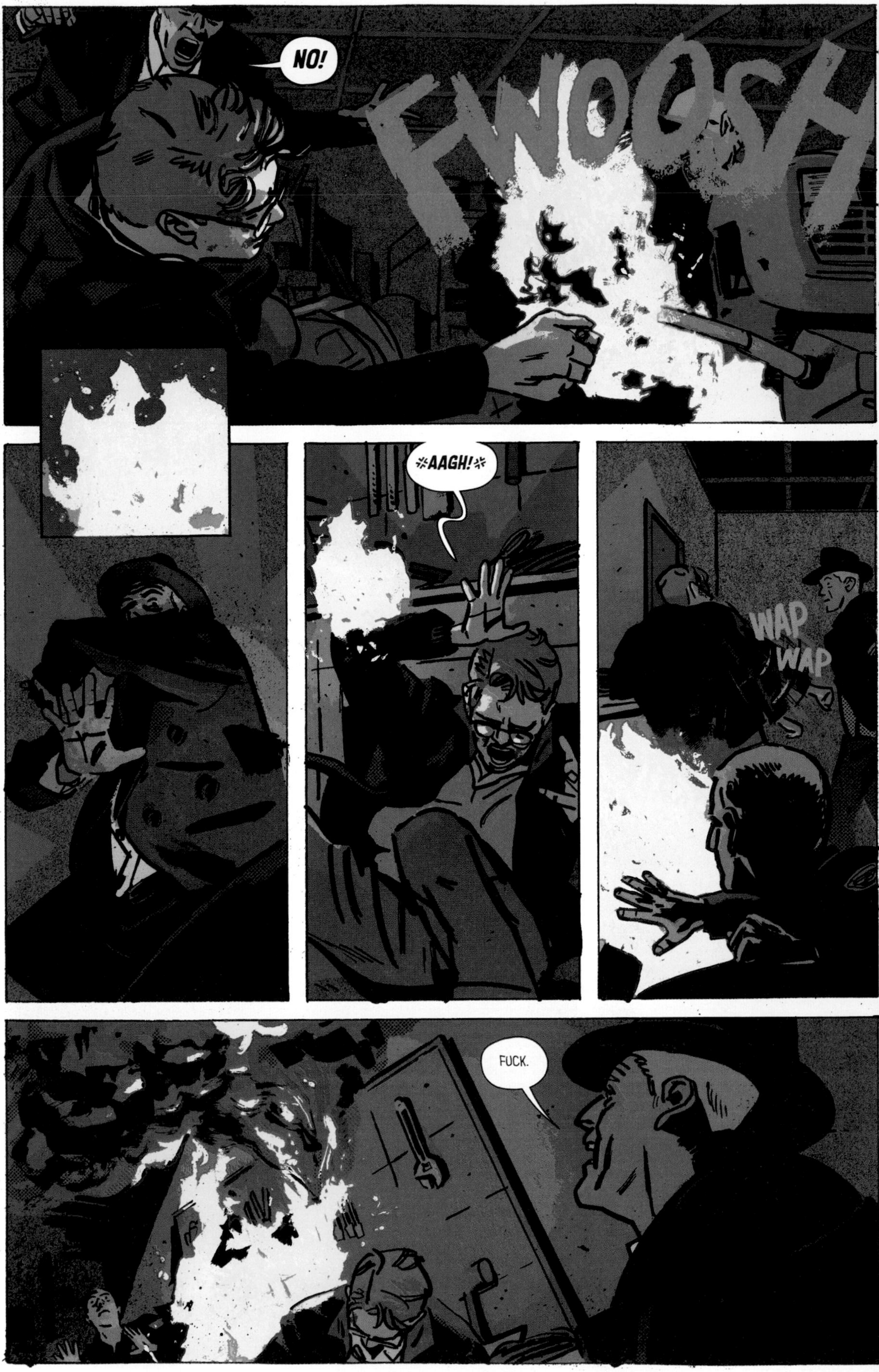
NO!
FWOOSH
AAGH!
WAP
WAP
FUCK.

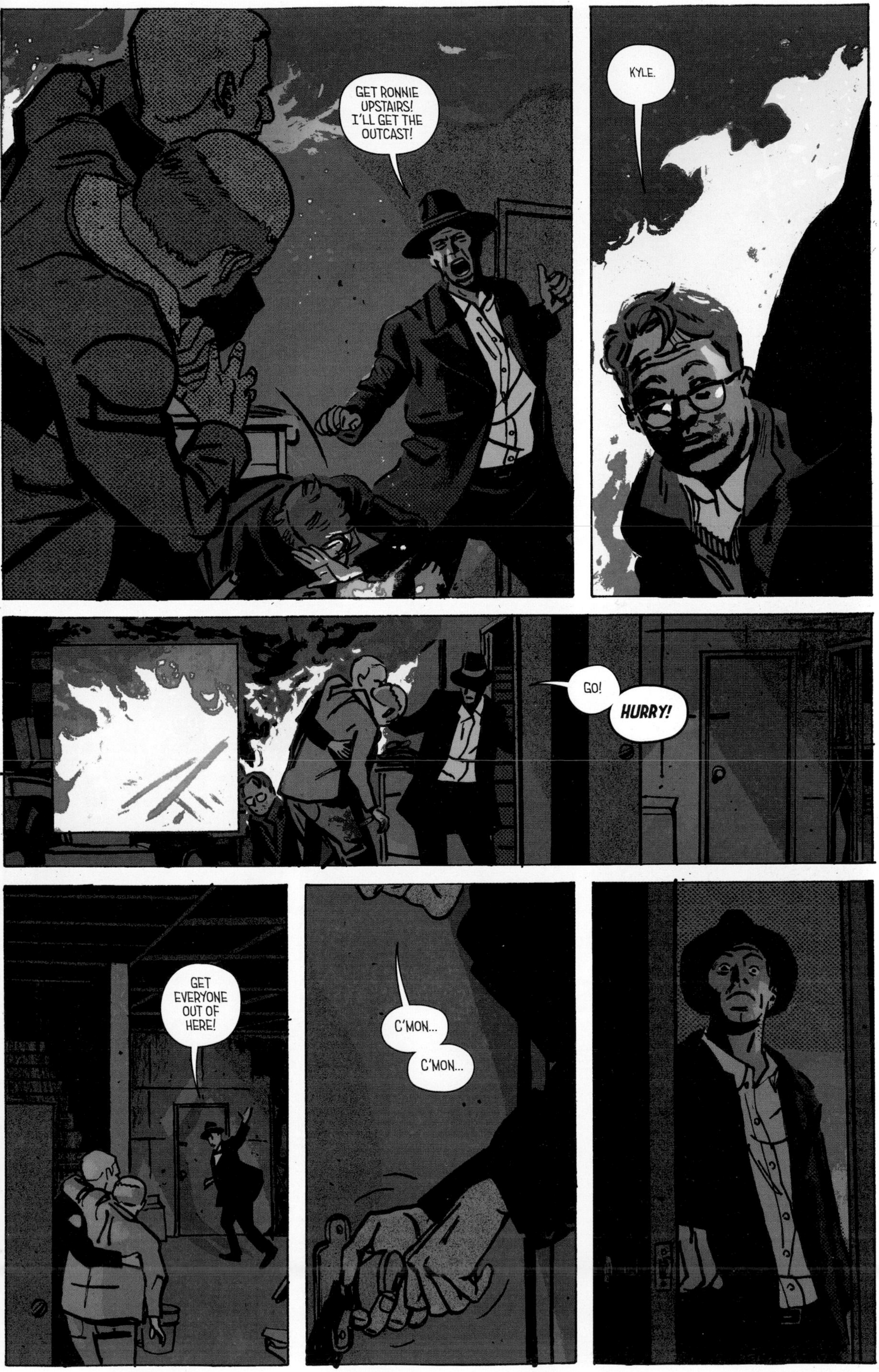

GET RONNIE UPSTAIRS! I'LL GET THE OUTCAST!
KYLE.
GO!
HURRY!
GET EVERYONE OUT OF HERE!
C'MON...
C'MON...

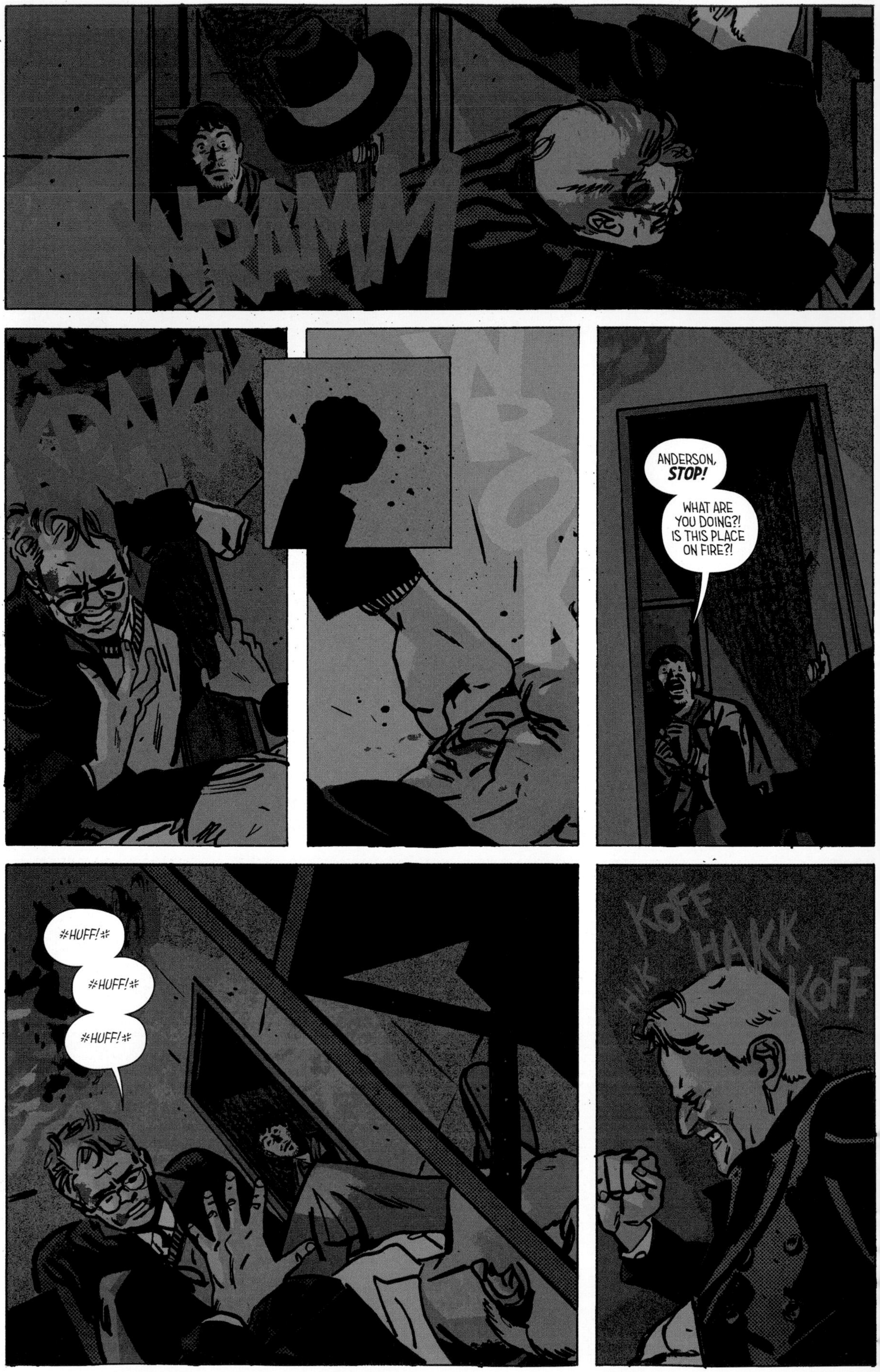
WRAMM
ANDERSON, **STOP!**
WHAT ARE YOU DOING?! IS THIS PLACE ON FIRE?!
#HUFF!#
#HUFF!#
#HUFF!#
KOFF
HAKK
HIK
KOFF

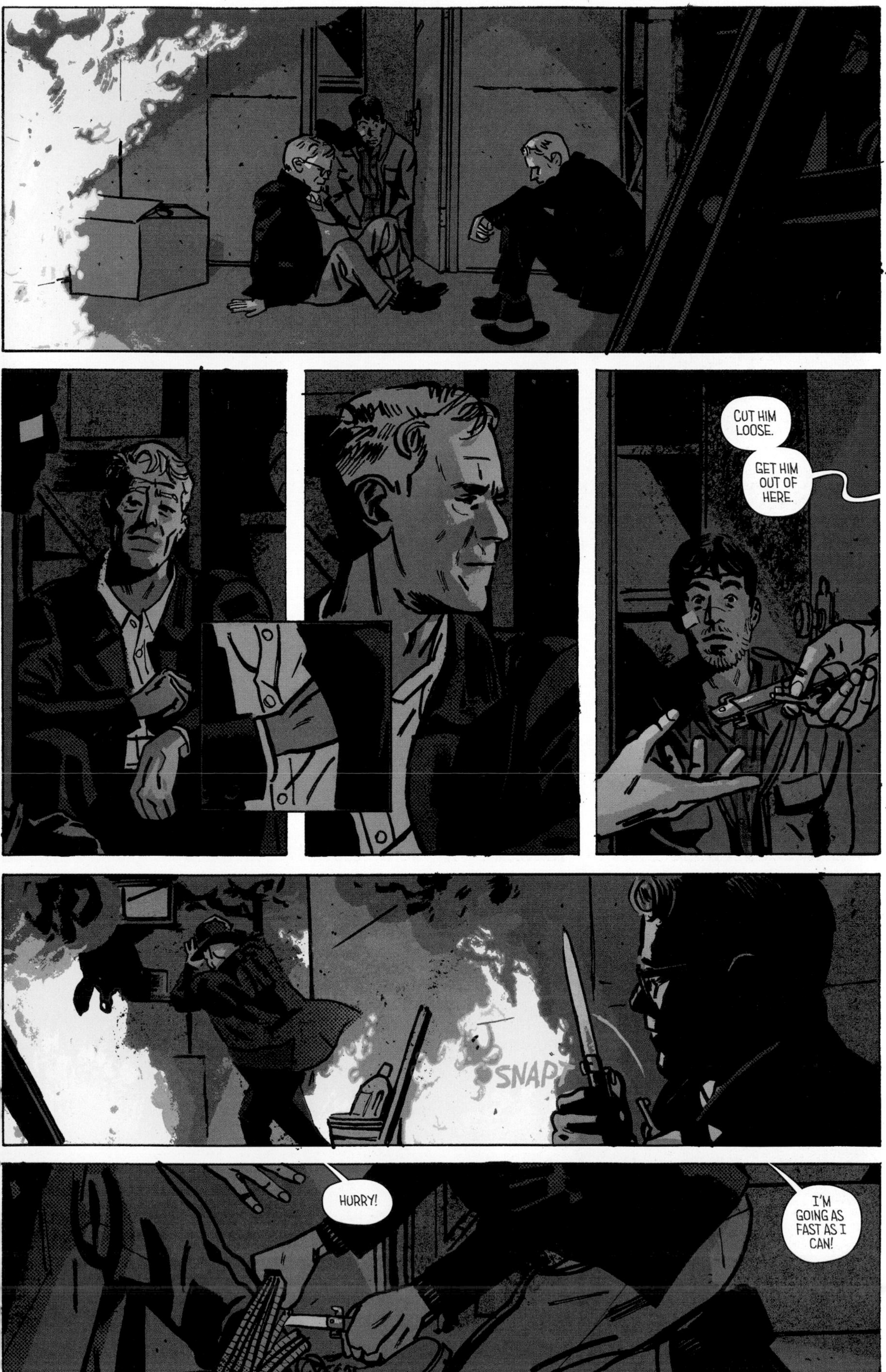
CUT HIM LOOSE.
GET HIM OUT OF HERE.
SNAP!
HURRY!
I'M GOING AS FAST AS I CAN!

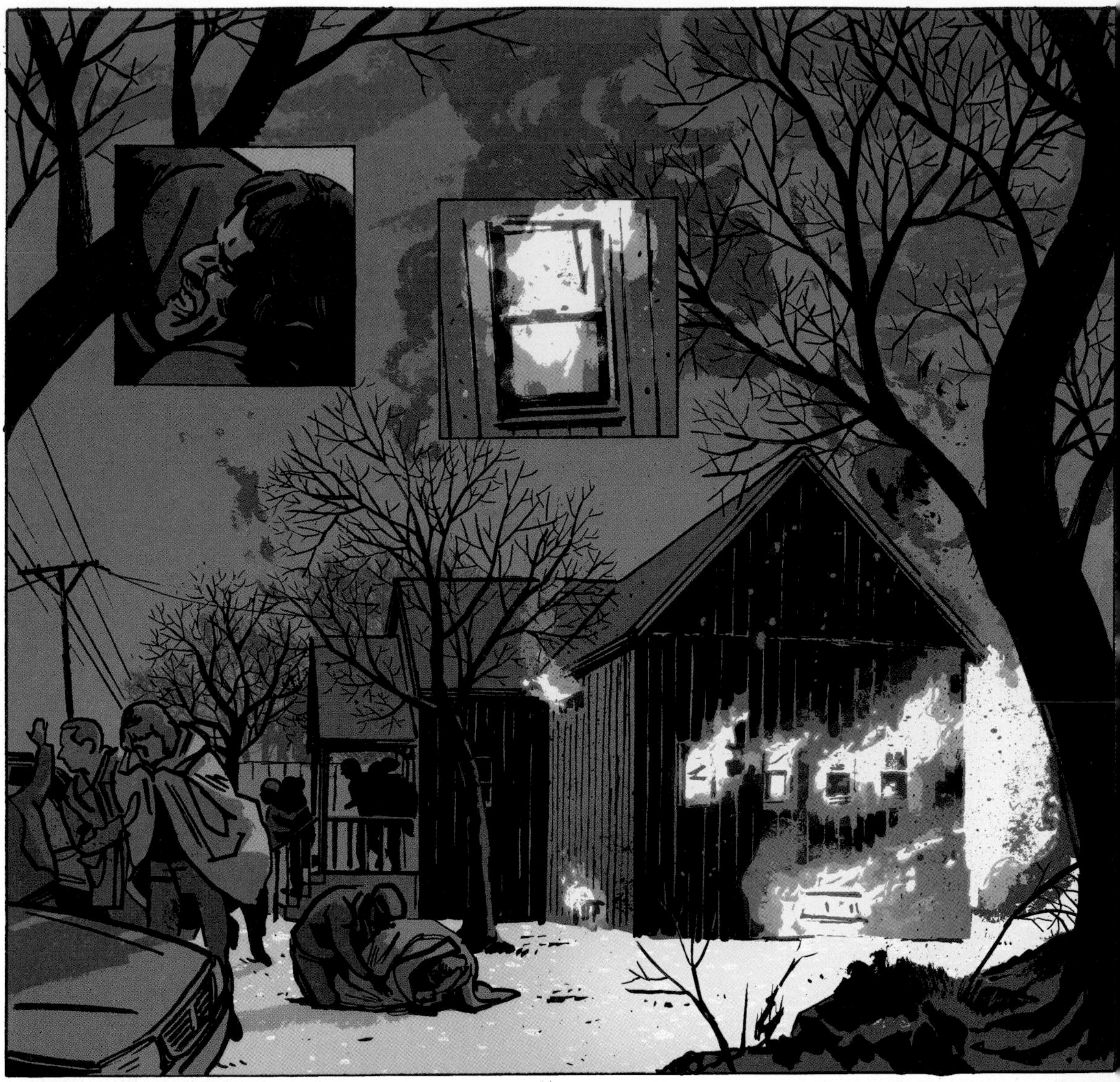

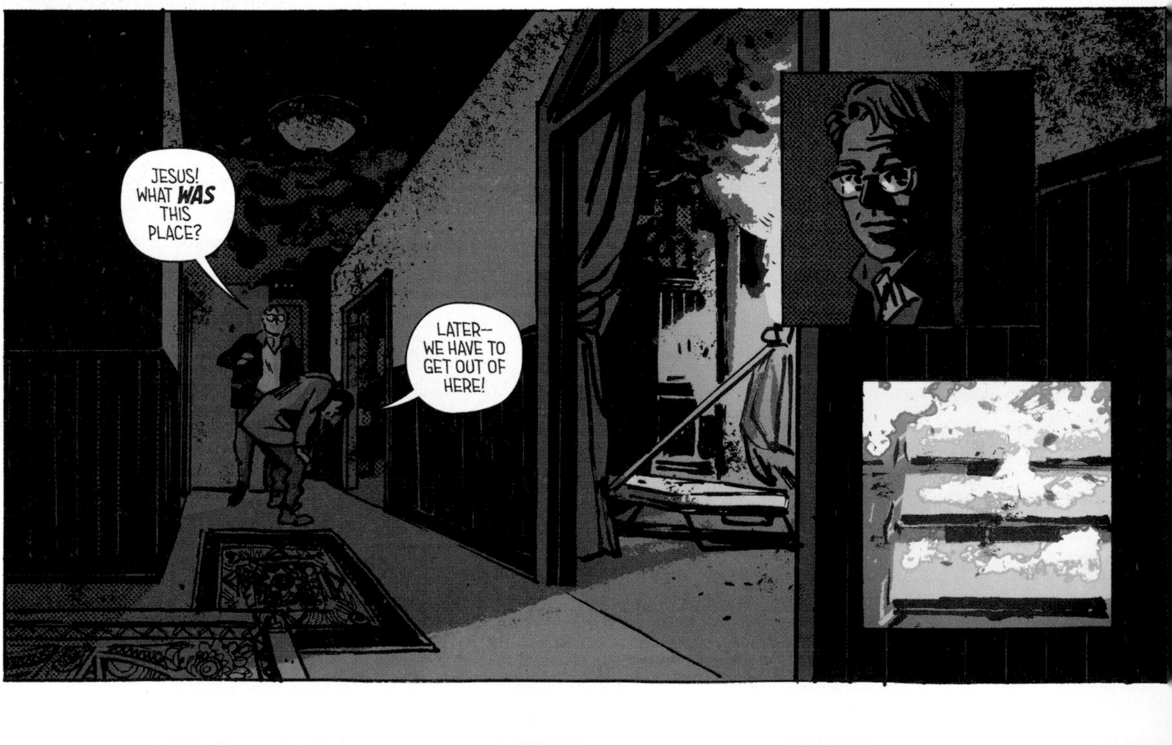
JESUS! WHAT WAS THIS PLACE?
LATER-- WE HAVE TO GET OUT OF HERE!

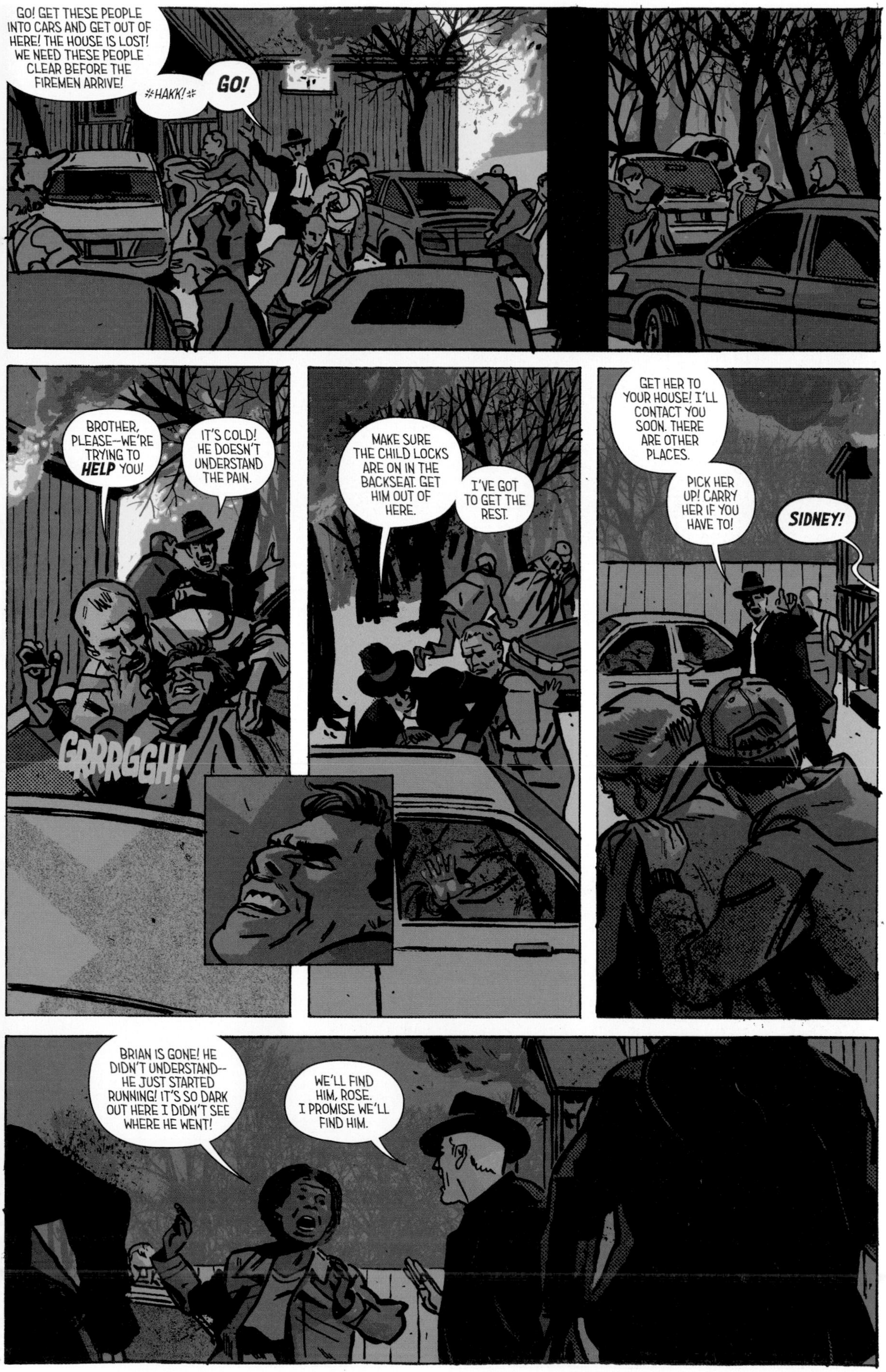
GO! GET THESE PEOPLE INTO CARS AND GET OUT OF HERE! THE HOUSE IS LOST! WE NEED THESE PEOPLE CLEAR BEFORE THE FIREMEN ARRIVE!
HAKK!
GO!
BROTHER, PLEASE--WE'RE TRYING TO **HELP** YOU!
IT'S COLD! HE DOESN'T UNDERSTAND THE PAIN.
GRRRGGH!
MAKE SURE THE CHILD LOCKS ARE ON IN THE BACKSEAT. GET HIM OUT OF HERE.
I'VE GOT TO GET THE REST.
GET HER TO YOUR HOUSE! I'LL CONTACT YOU SOON. THERE ARE OTHER PLACES.
PICK HER UP! CARRY HER IF YOU HAVE TO!
SIDNEY!
BRIAN IS GONE! HE DIDN'T UNDERSTAND-- HE JUST STARTED RUNNING! IT'S SO DARK OUT HERE I DIDN'T SEE WHERE HE WENT!
WE'LL FIND HIM, ROSE. I PROMISE WE'LL FIND HIM.

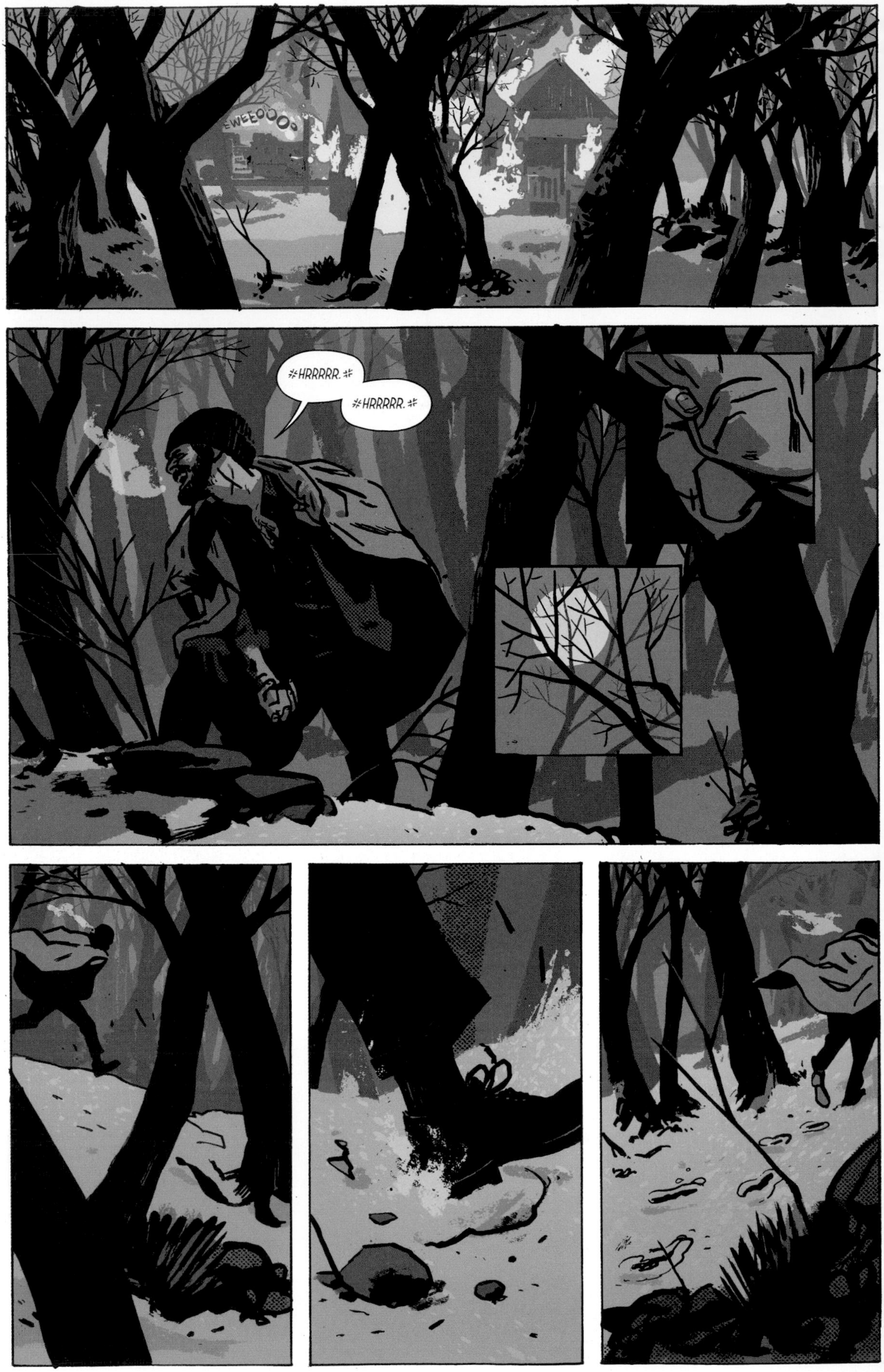
EWEEOOOo
#HRRRRR.#
#HRRRRR.#

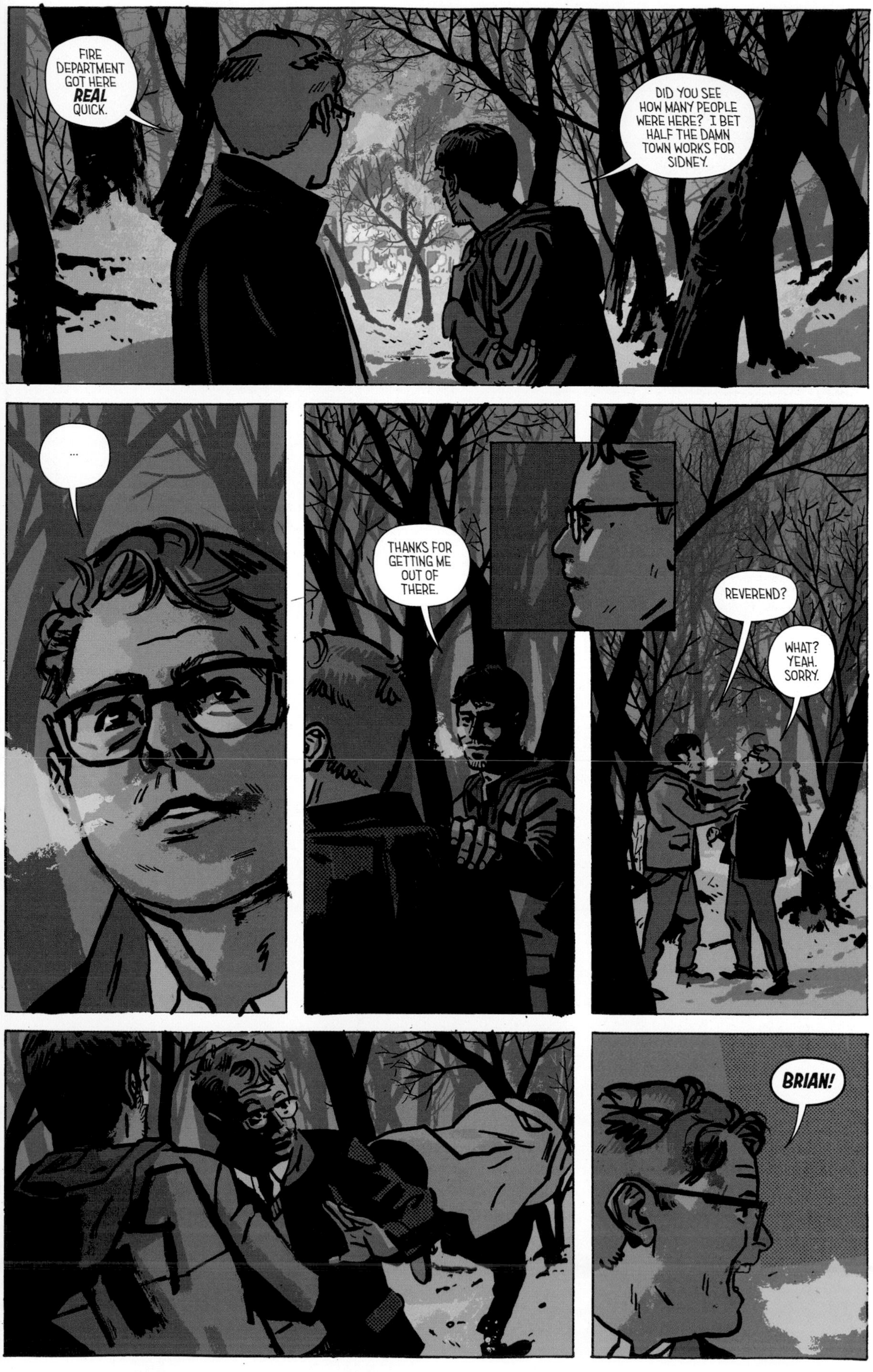
FIRE DEPARTMENT GOT HERE **REAL** QUICK.
DID YOU SEE HOW MANY PEOPLE WERE HERE? I BET HALF THE DAMN TOWN WORKS FOR SIDNEY.
...
THANKS FOR GETTING ME OUT OF THERE.
REVEREND?
WHAT? YEAH. SORRY.
BRIAN!

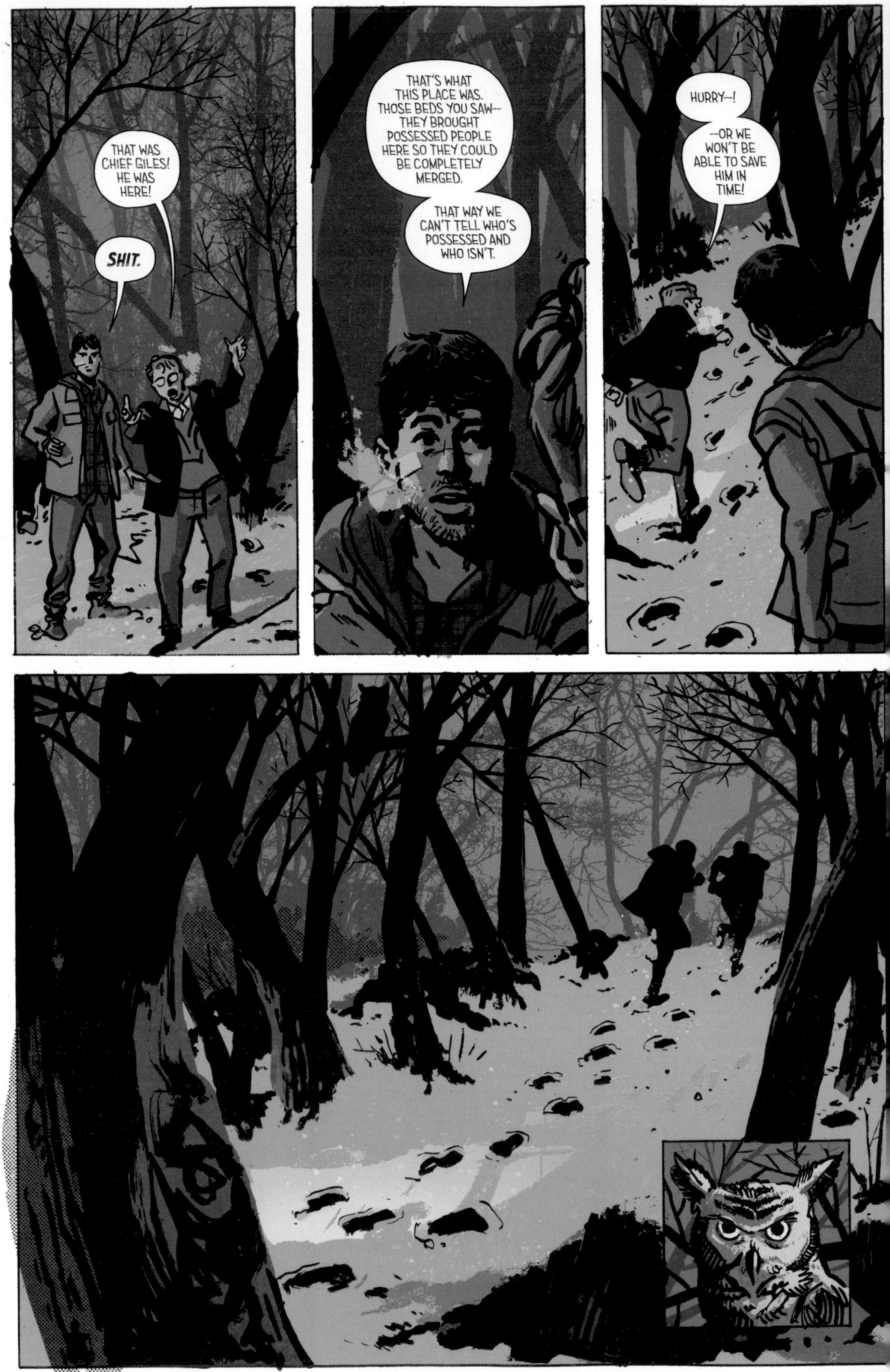
THAT WAS CHIEF GILES! HE WAS HERE!
SHIT.
THAT'S WHAT THIS PLACE WAS. THOSE BEDS YOU SAW-- THEY BROUGHT POSSESSED PEOPLE HERE SO THEY COULD BE COMPLETELY MERGED.
THAT WAY WE CAN'T TELL WHO'S POSSESSED AND WHO ISN'T.
HURRY--!
--OR WE WON'T BE ABLE TO SAVE HIM IN TIME!

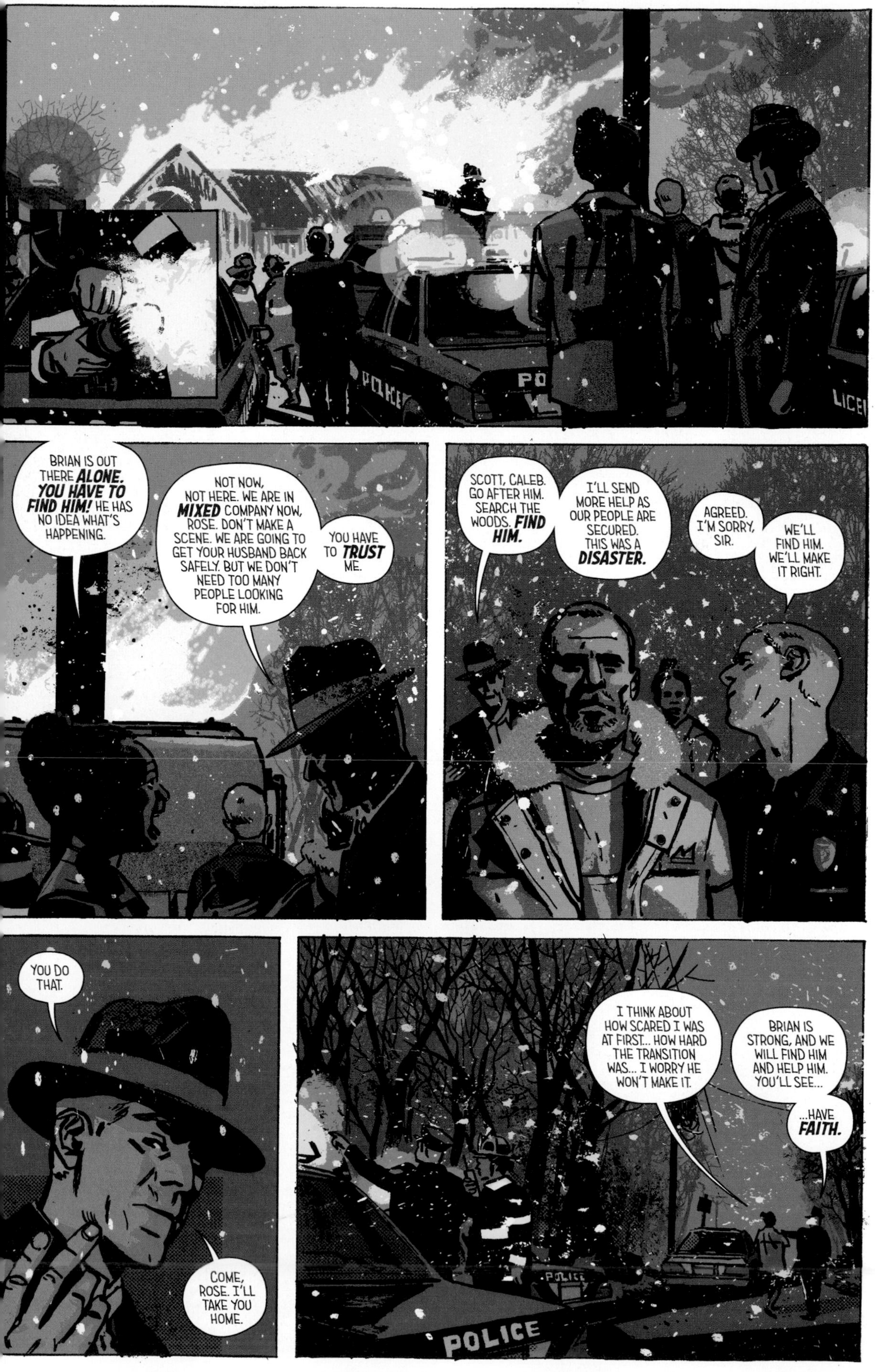
BRIAN IS OUT THERE ALONE. YOU HAVE TO FIND HIM! HE HAS NO IDEA WHAT'S HAPPENING.
NOT NOW, NOT HERE. WE ARE IN MIXED COMPANY NOW, ROSE. DON'T MAKE A SCENE. WE ARE GOING TO GET YOUR HUSBAND BACK SAFELY. BUT WE DON'T NEED TOO MANY PEOPLE LOOKING FOR HIM.
YOU HAVE TO TRUST ME.
SCOTT, CALEB. GO AFTER HIM. SEARCH THE WOODS. FIND HIM.
I'LL SEND MORE HELP AS OUR PEOPLE ARE SECURED. THIS WAS A DISASTER.
AGREED. I'M SORRY, SIR.
WE'LL FIND HIM. WE'LL MAKE IT RIGHT.
YOU DO THAT.
COME, ROSE. I'LL TAKE YOU HOME.
I THINK ABOUT HOW SCARED I WAS AT FIRST... HOW HARD THE TRANSITION WAS... I WORRY HE WON'T MAKE IT.
BRIAN IS STRONG, AND WE WILL FIND HIM AND HELP HIM. YOU'LL SEE...
...HAVE FAITH.
POLICE

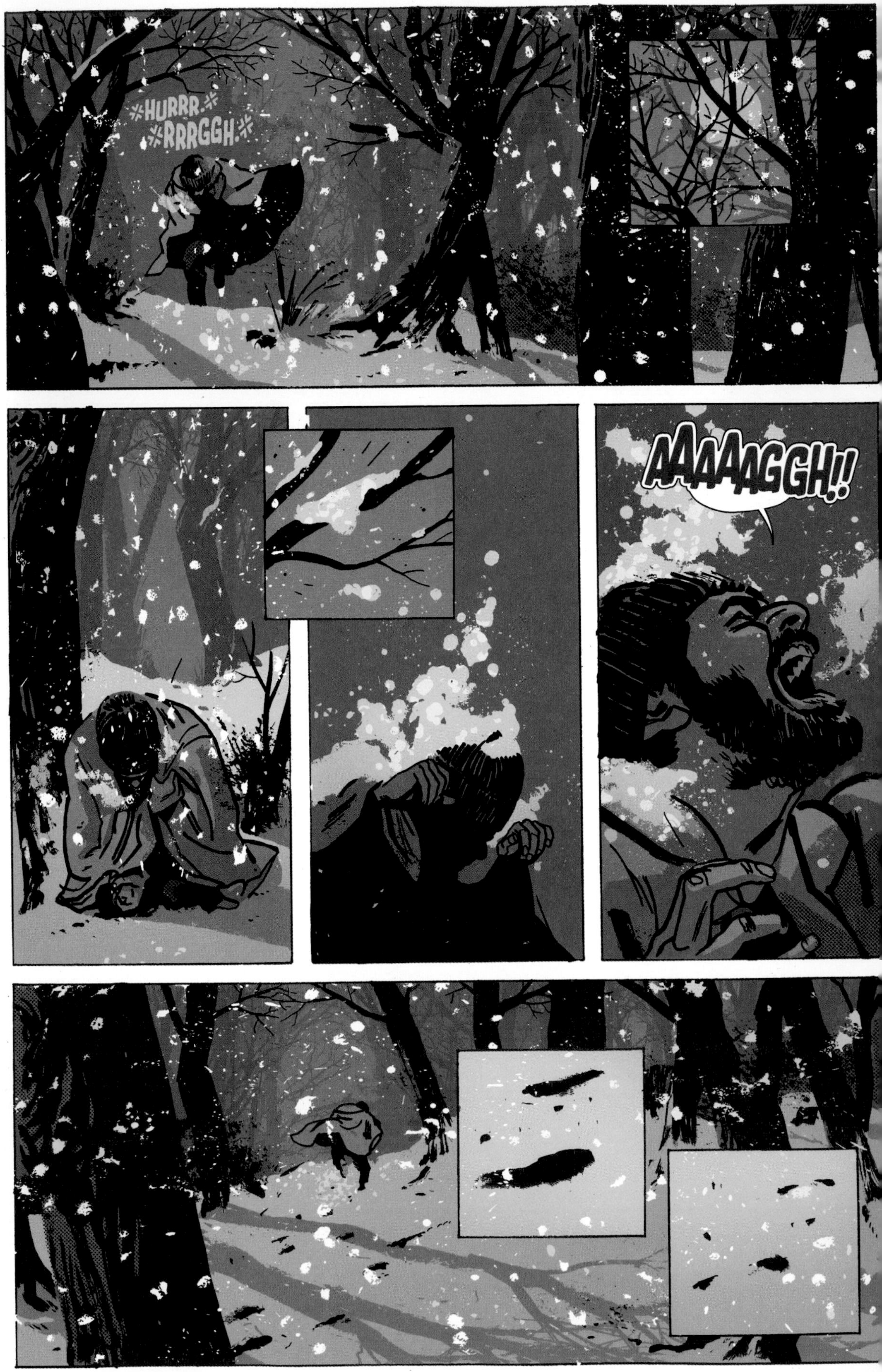
HURRR.
RRRGGH.
AAAAAGGH!!

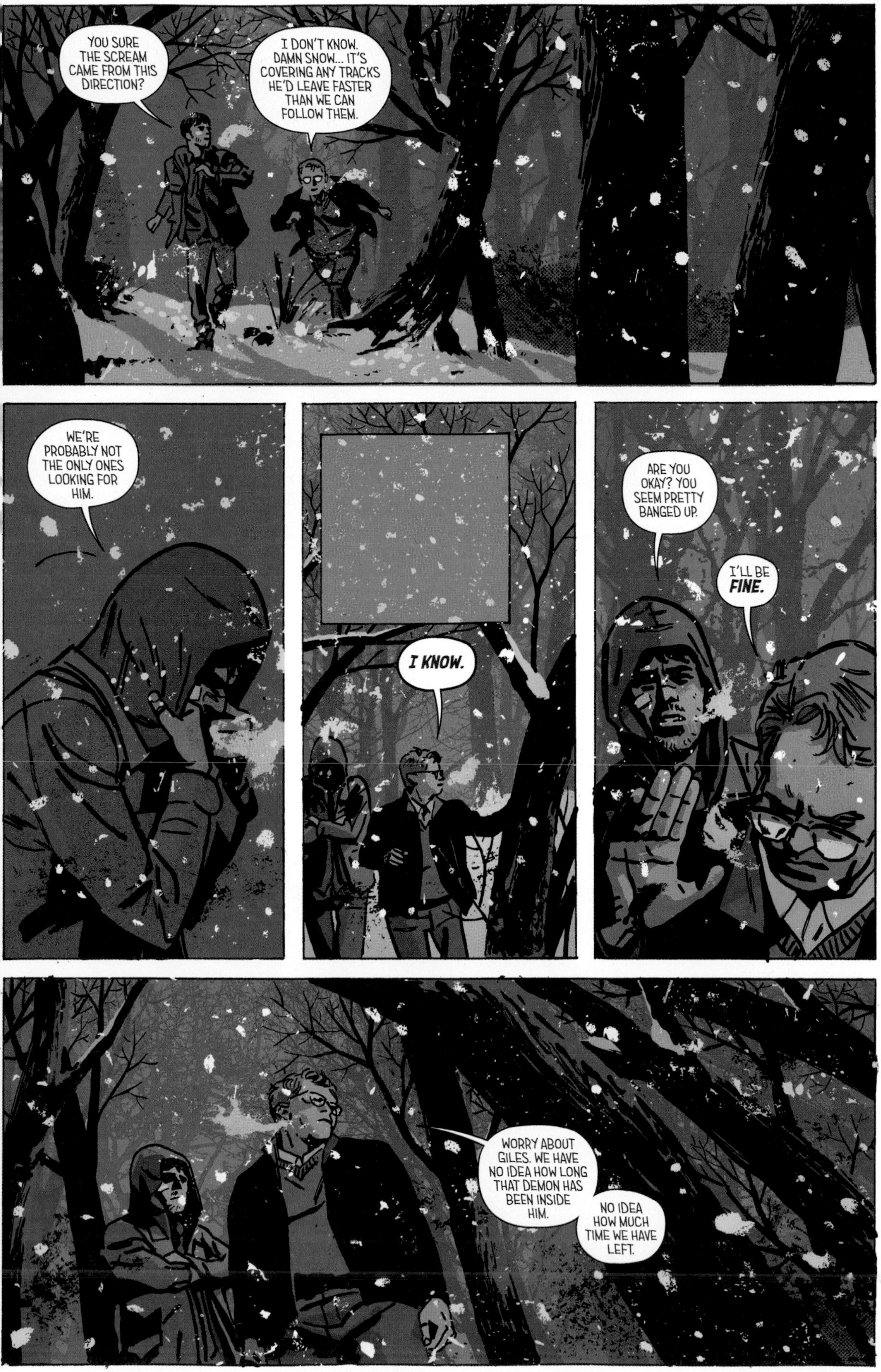
YOU SURE THE SCREAM CAME FROM THIS DIRECTION?
I DON'T KNOW. DAMN SNOW... IT'S COVERING ANY TRACKS HE'D LEAVE FASTER THAN WE CAN FOLLOW THEM.
WE'RE PROBABLY NOT THE ONLY ONES LOOKING FOR HIM.
I KNOW.
ARE YOU OKAY? YOU SEEM PRETTY BANGED UP.
I'LL BE FINE.
WORRY ABOUT GILES. WE HAVE NO IDEA HOW LONG THAT DEMON HAS BEEN INSIDE HIM.
NO IDEA HOW MUCH TIME WE HAVE LEFT.

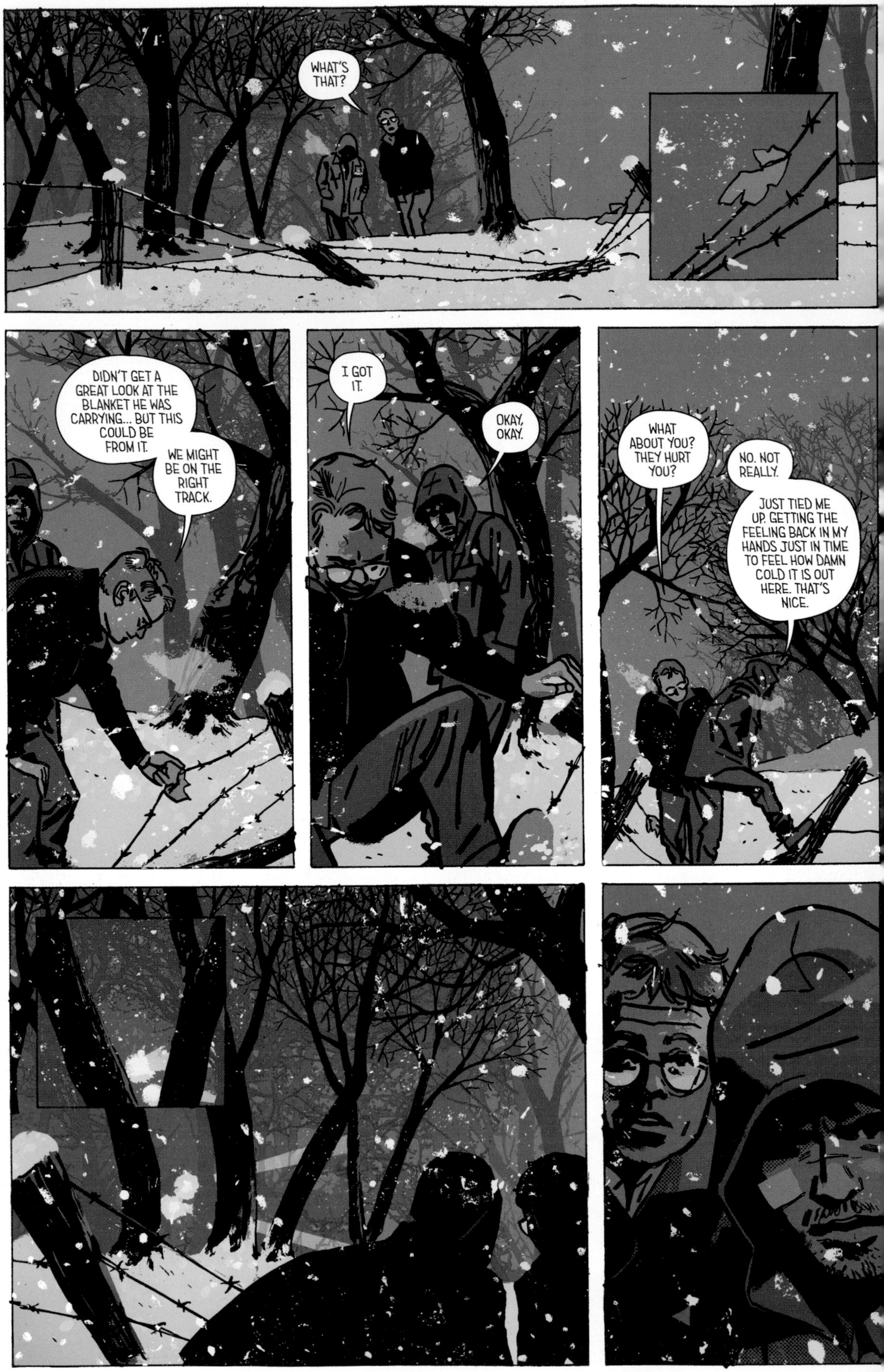
WHAT'S THAT?
DIDN'T GET A GREAT LOOK AT THE BLANKET HE WAS CARRYING... BUT THIS COULD BE FROM IT.
WE MIGHT BE ON THE RIGHT TRACK.
I GOT IT.
OKAY, OKAY.
WHAT ABOUT YOU? THEY HURT YOU?
NO. NOT REALLY.
JUST TIED ME UP. GETTING THE FEELING BACK IN MY HANDS JUST IN TIME TO FEEL HOW DAMN COLD IT IS OUT HERE. THAT'S NICE.

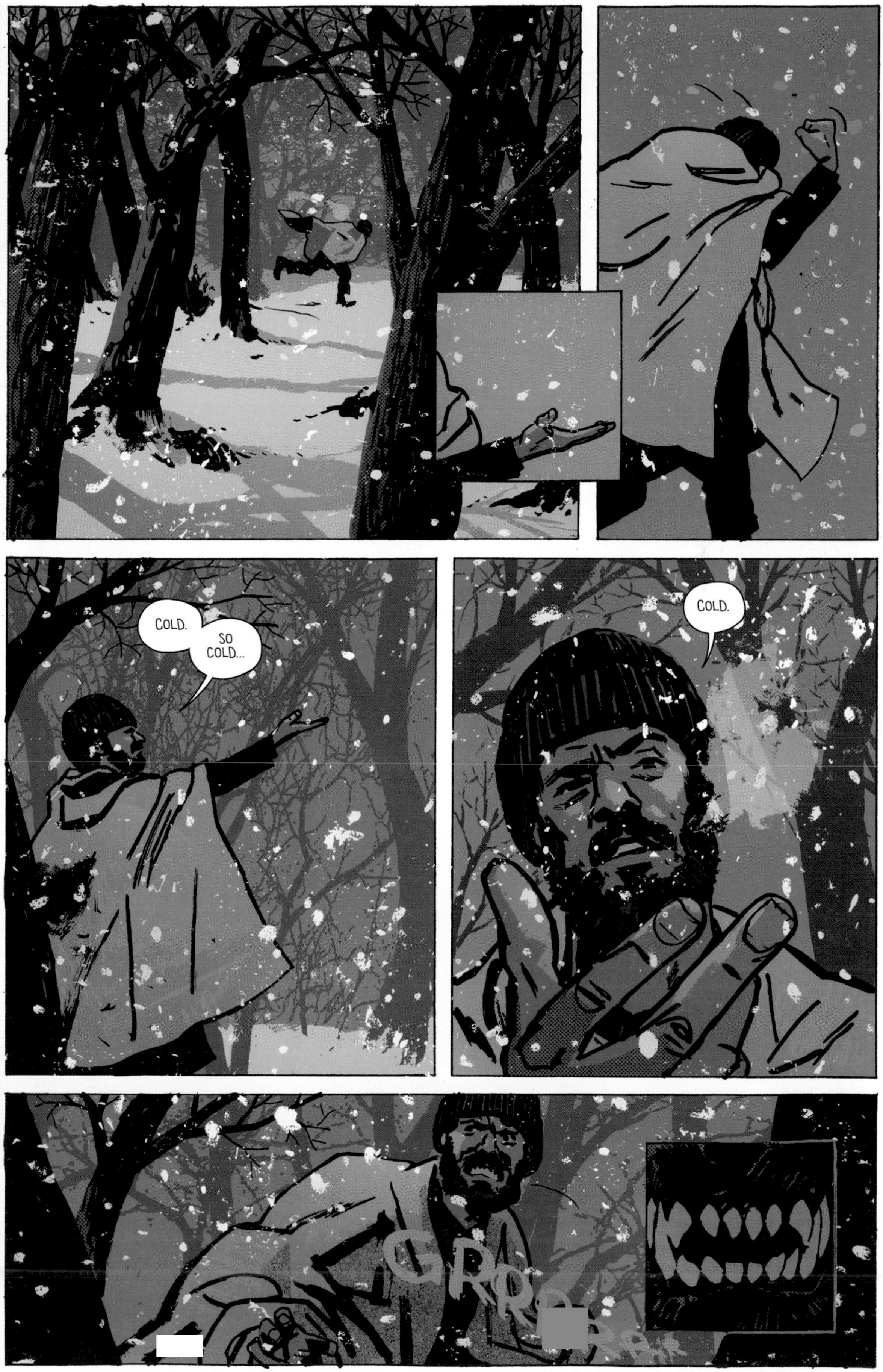
COLD.
SO COLD...
COLD.
GRRRRRR

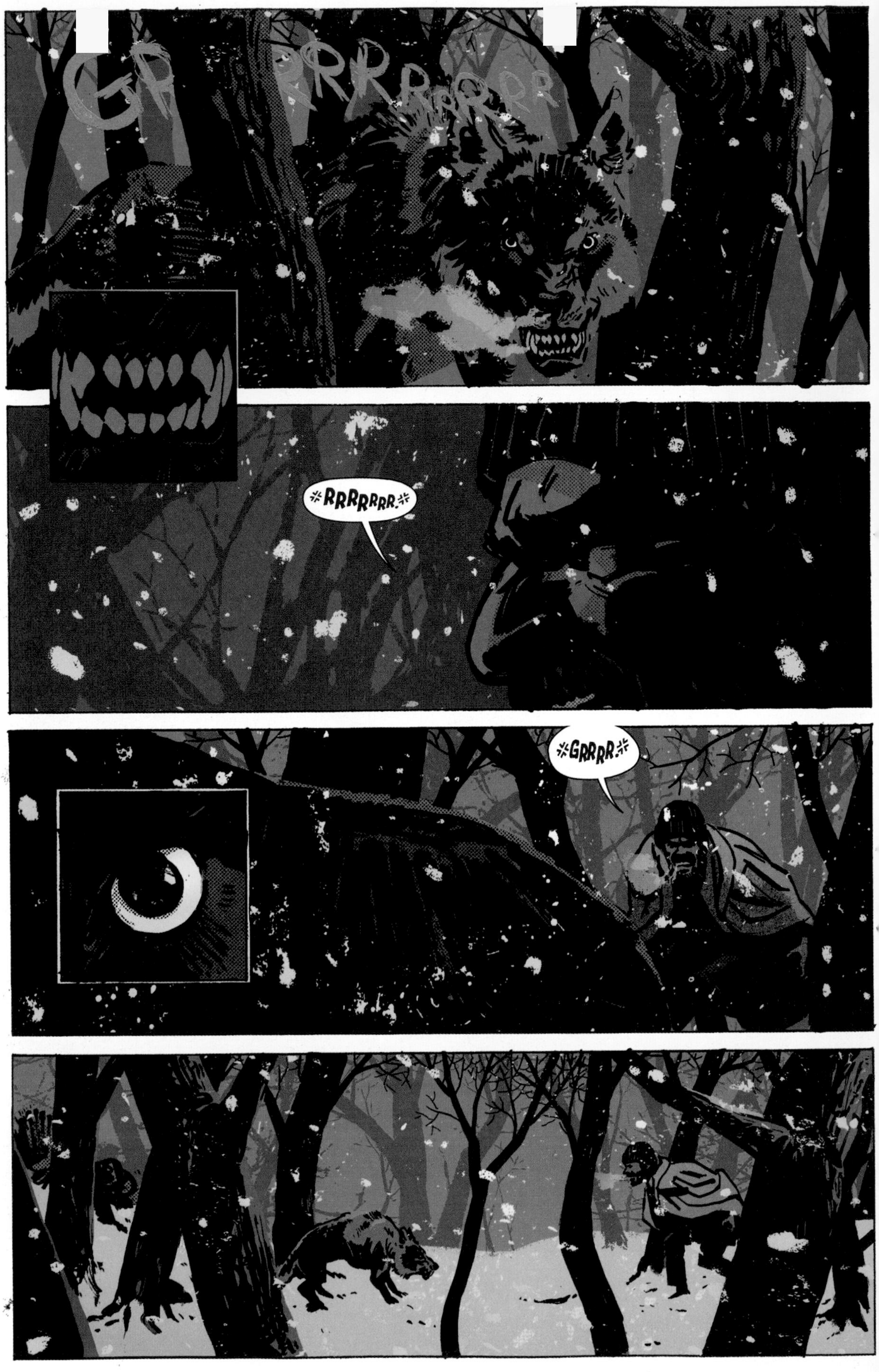
GRRRRRRRRRRR
RRRRRRR.
GRRRR.

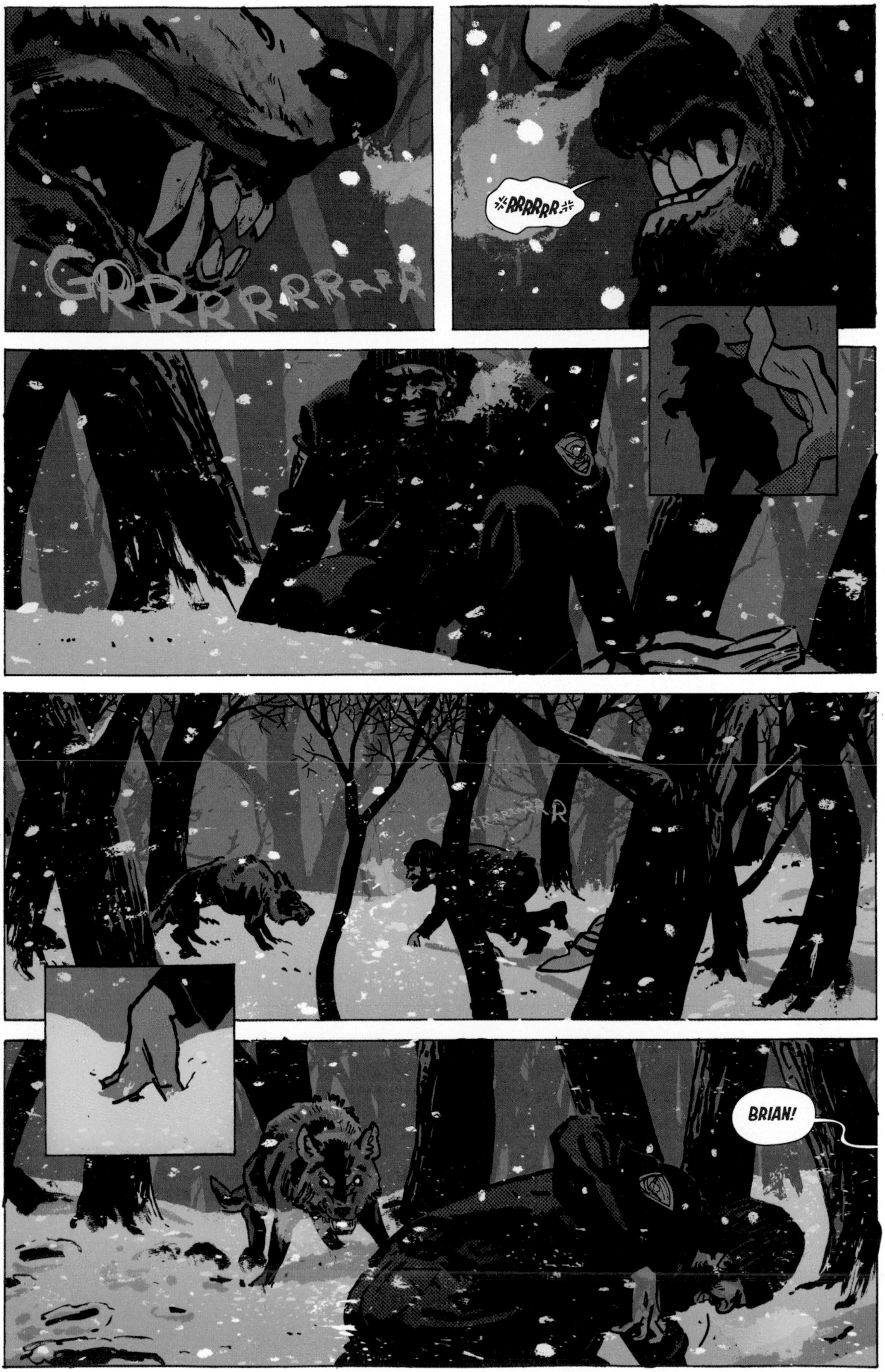
GRRRRRRRR
RRRRRR
GRRRRRRR
BRIAN!

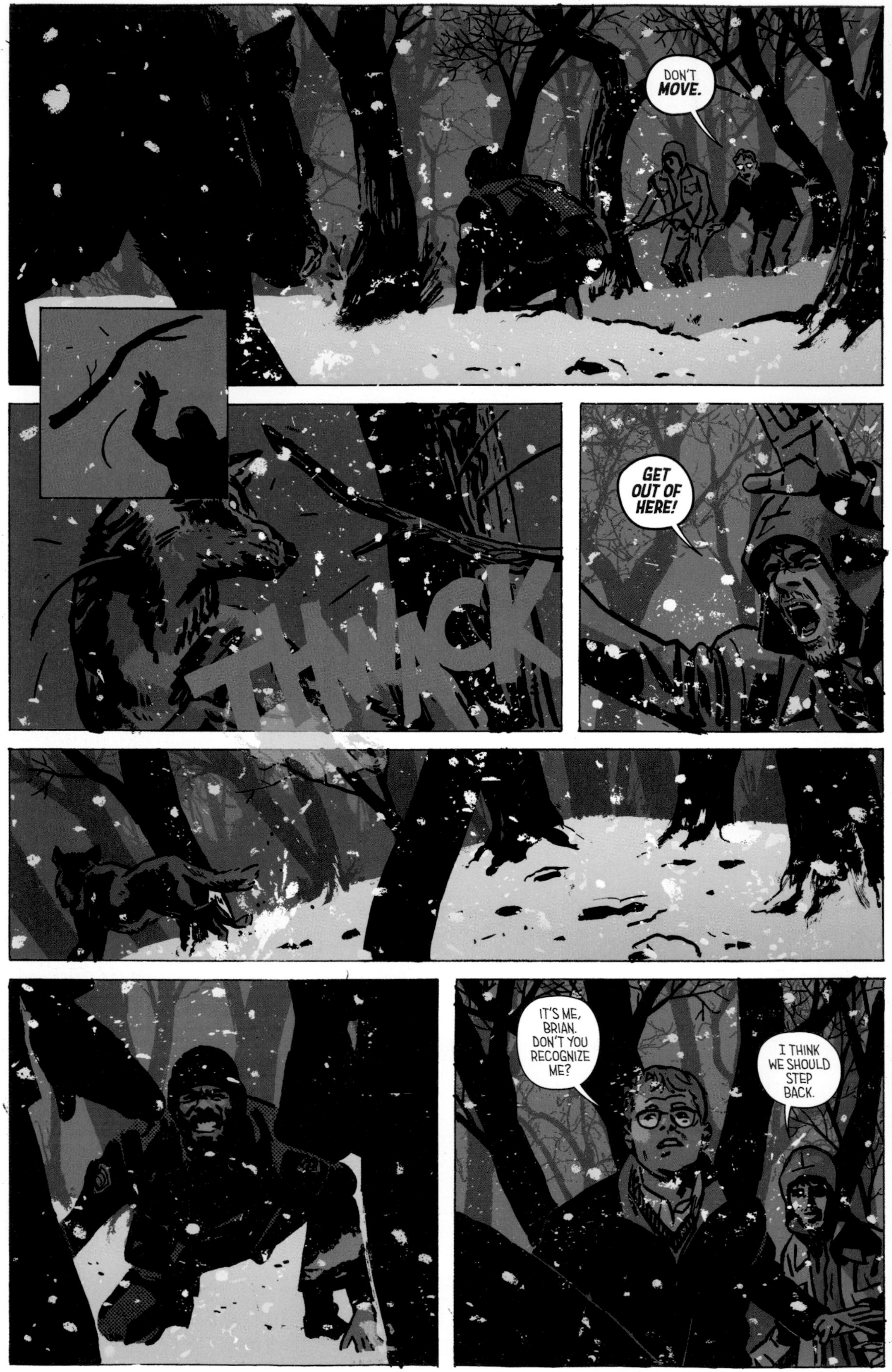
DON'T MOVE.
THWACK
GET OUT OF HERE!
IT'S ME, BRIAN. DON'T YOU RECOGNIZE ME?
I THINK WE SHOULD STEP BACK.

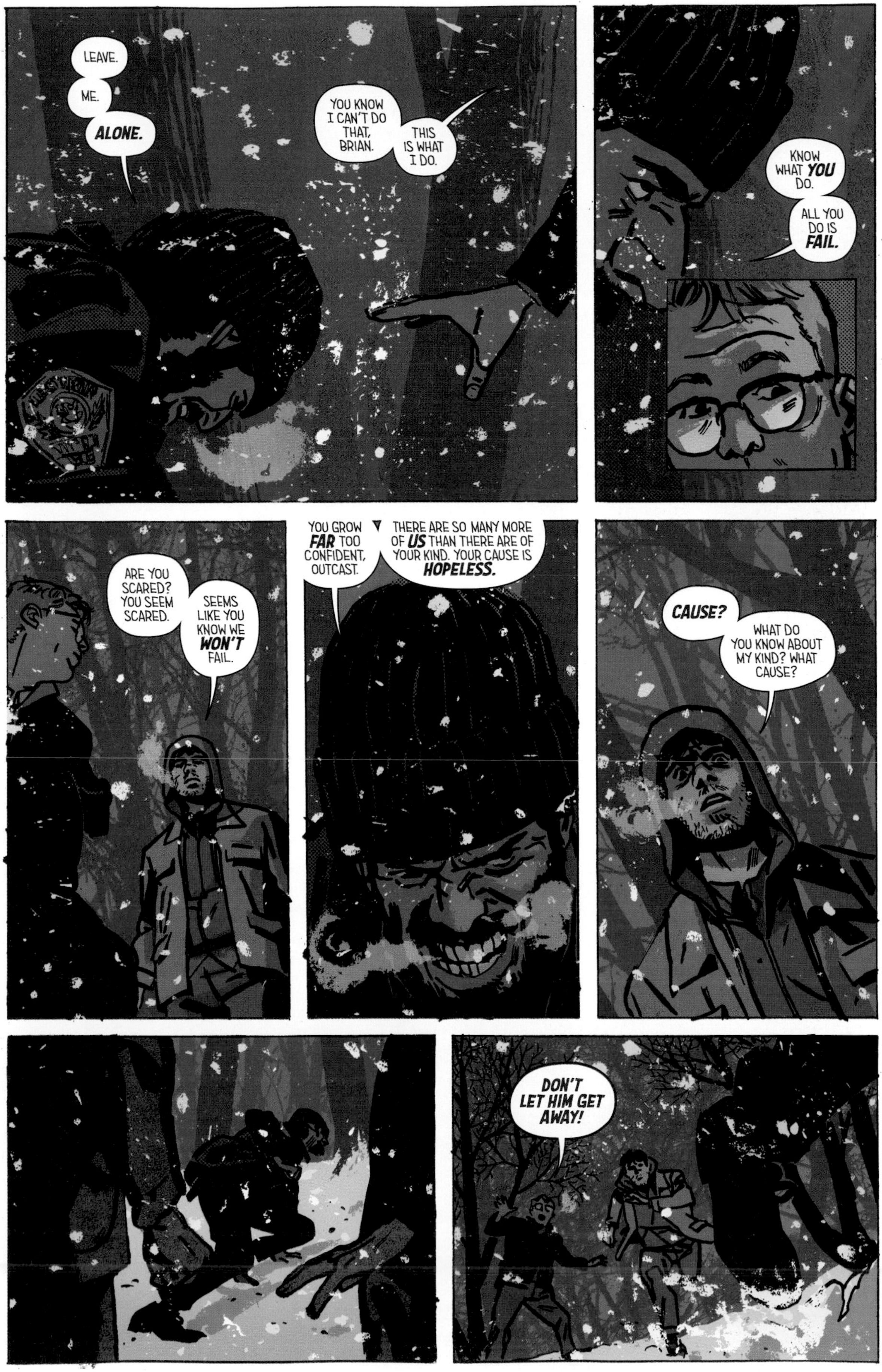
LEAVE.
ME.
ALONE.
YOU KNOW I CAN'T DO THAT, BRIAN.
THIS IS WHAT I DO.
KNOW WHAT YOU DO.
ALL YOU DO IS FAIL.
ARE YOU SCARED? YOU SEEM SCARED.
SEEMS LIKE YOU KNOW WE WON'T FAIL.
YOU GROW FAR TOO CONFIDENT, OUTCAST.
THERE ARE SO MANY MORE OF US THAN THERE ARE OF YOUR KIND. YOUR CAUSE IS HOPELESS.
CAUSE?
WHAT DO YOU KNOW ABOUT MY KIND? WHAT CAUSE?
DON'T LET HIM GET AWAY!

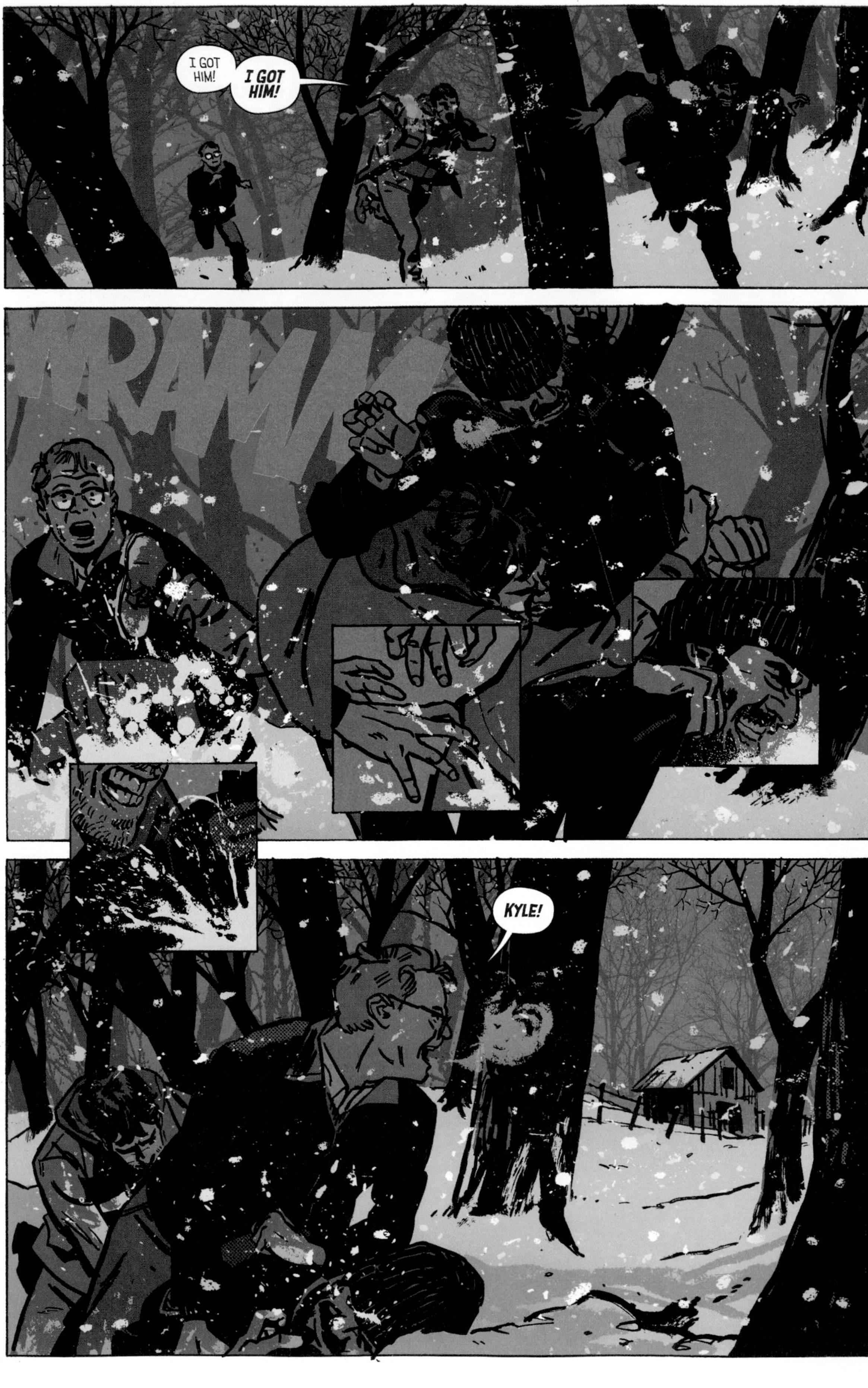
I GOT HIM!
I GOT HIM!
KYLE!

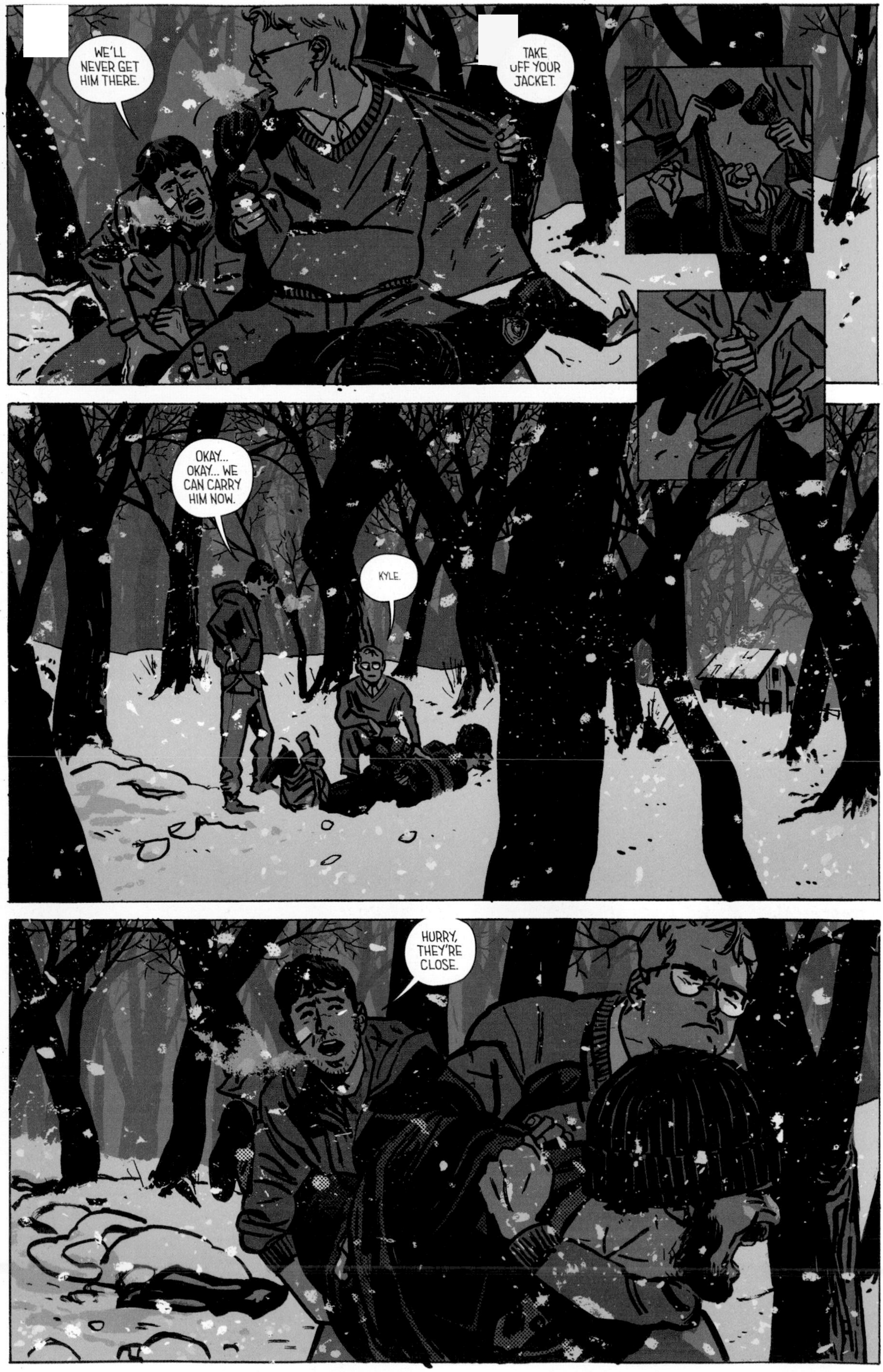
WE'LL NEVER GET HIM THERE.
TAKE OFF YOUR JACKET.
OKAY... OKAY... WE CAN CARRY HIM NOW.
KYLE.
HURRY, THEY'RE CLOSE.

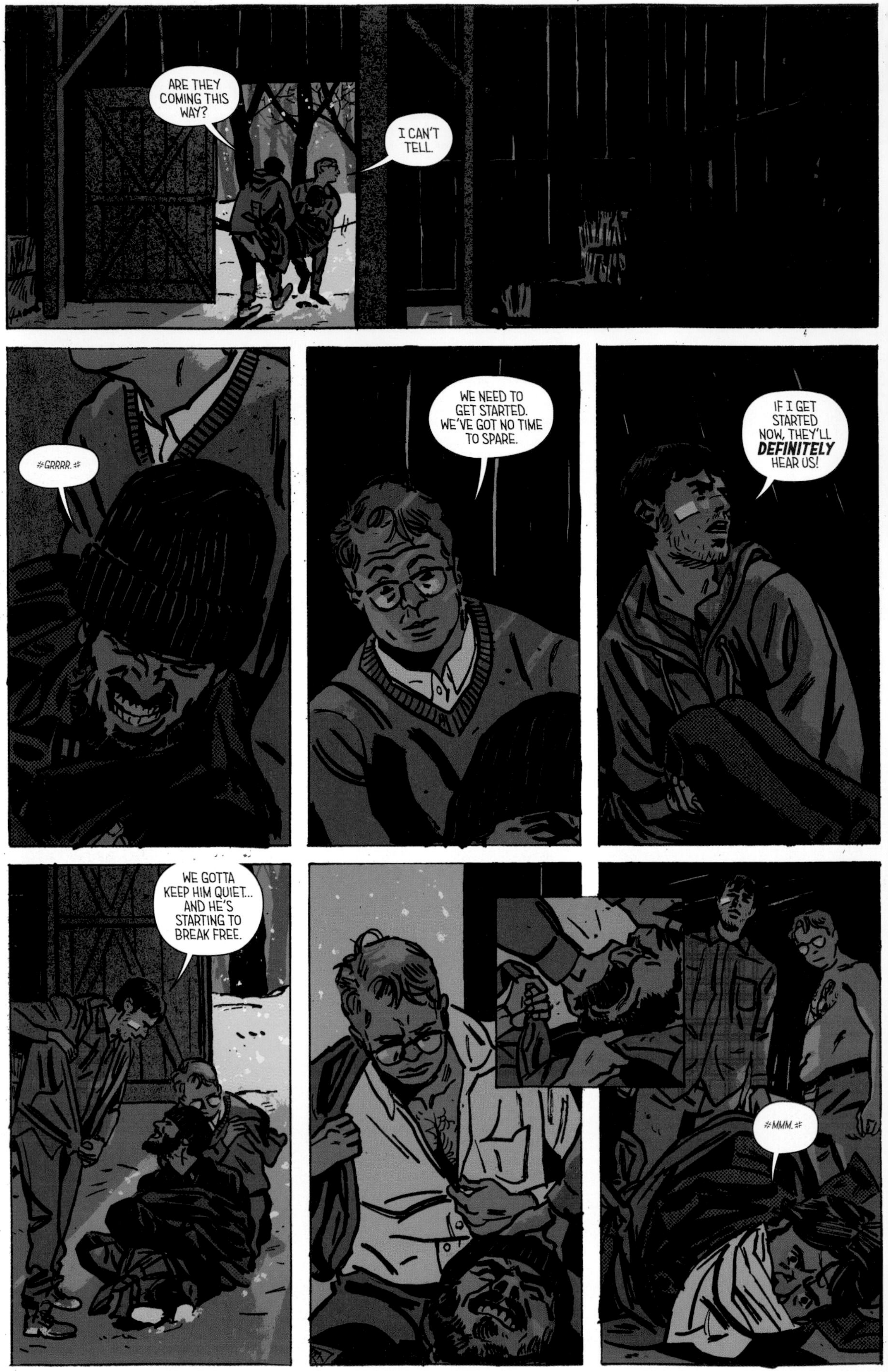
ARE THEY COMING THIS WAY?
I CAN'T TELL.
#GRRRR.#
WE NEED TO GET STARTED. WE'VE GOT NO TIME TO SPARE.
IF I GET STARTED NOW, THEY'LL DEFINITELY HEAR US!
WE GOTTA KEEP HIM QUIET... AND HE'S STARTING TO BREAK FREE.
#MMM.#

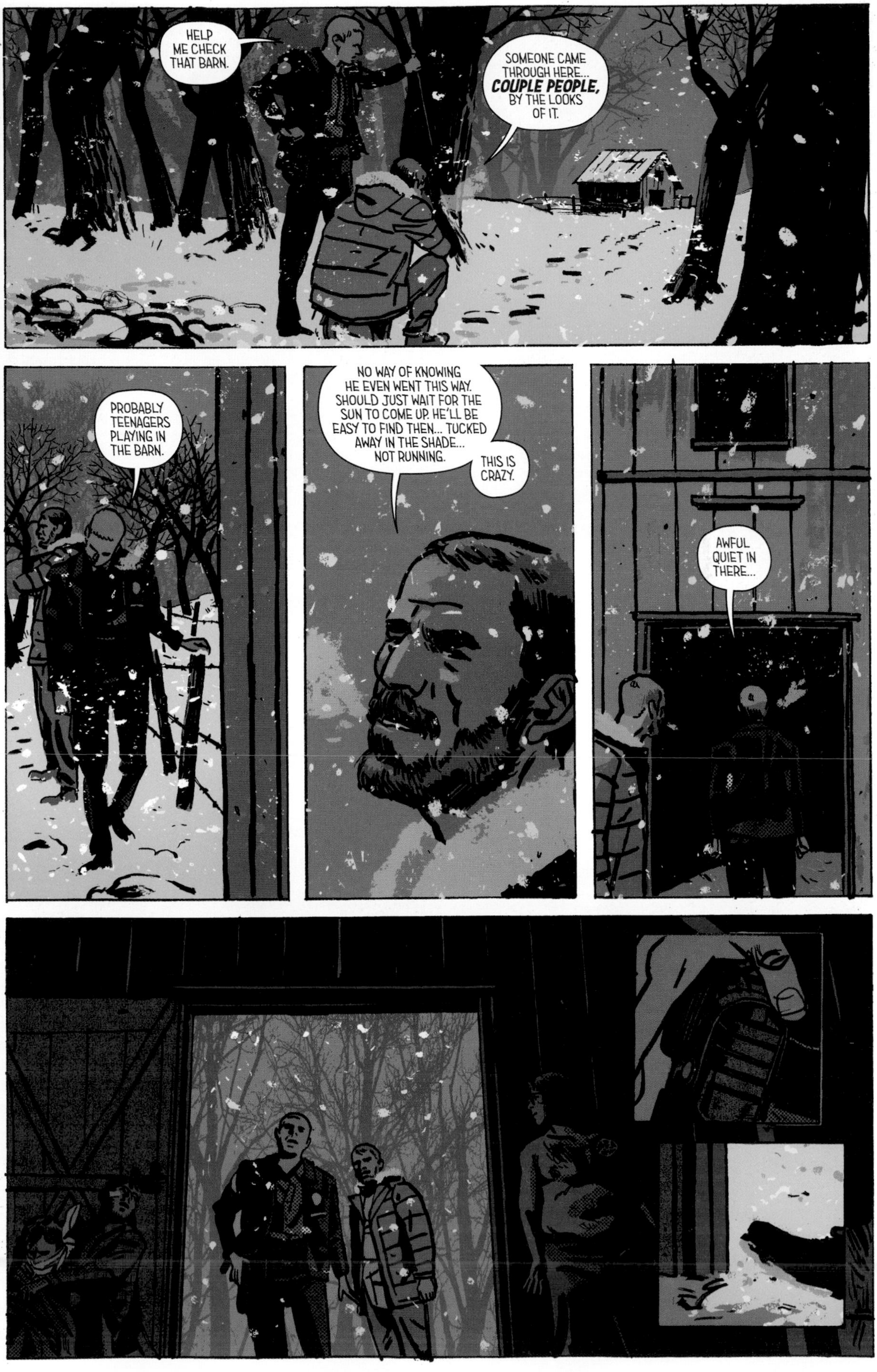
HELP ME CHECK THAT BARN.
SOMEONE CAME THROUGH HERE... **COUPLE PEOPLE,** BY THE LOOKS OF IT.
PROBABLY TEENAGERS PLAYING IN THE BARN.
NO WAY OF KNOWING HE EVEN WENT THIS WAY. SHOULD JUST WAIT FOR THE SUN TO COME UP. HE'LL BE EASY TO FIND THEN... TUCKED AWAY IN THE SHADE... NOT RUNNING.
THIS IS CRAZY.
AWFUL QUIET IN THERE...

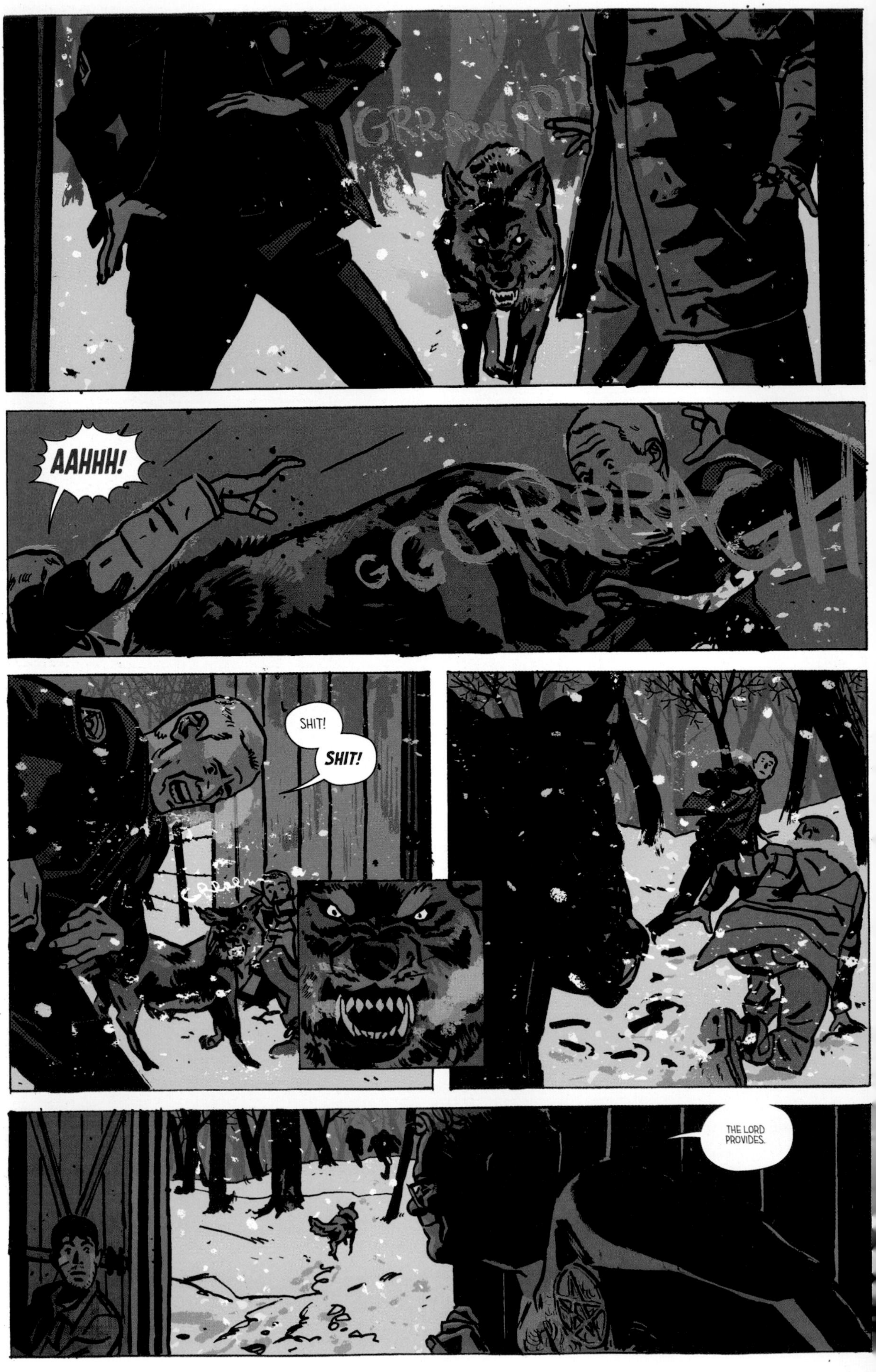

GRRRRRARRRR
AAHHH!
GGGRRRAGH
SHIT!
SHIT!
THE LORD PROVIDES.

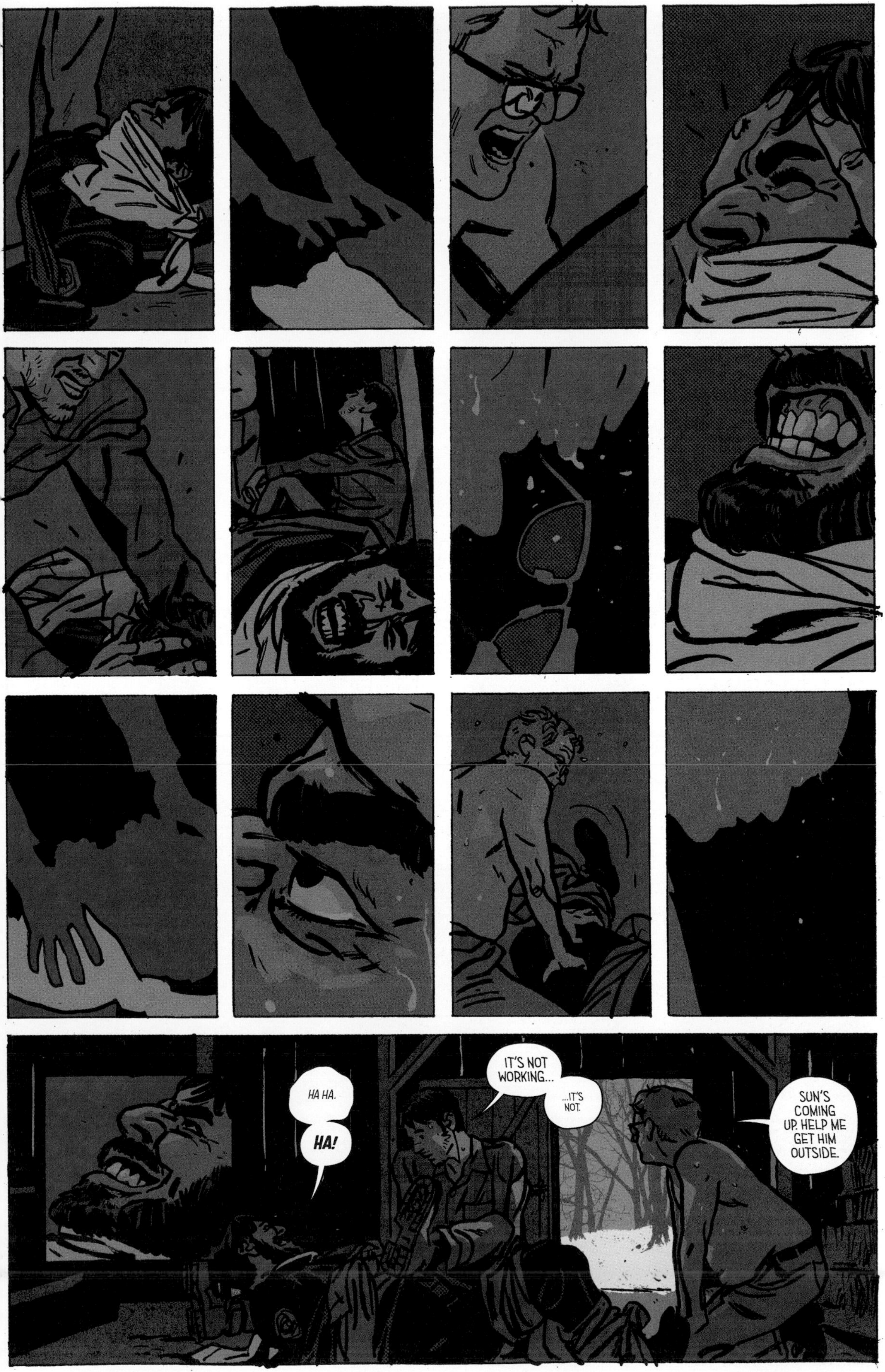
HA HA.
HA!
IT'S NOT WORKING...
...IT'S NOT.
SUN'S COMING UP. HELP ME GET HIM OUTSIDE.

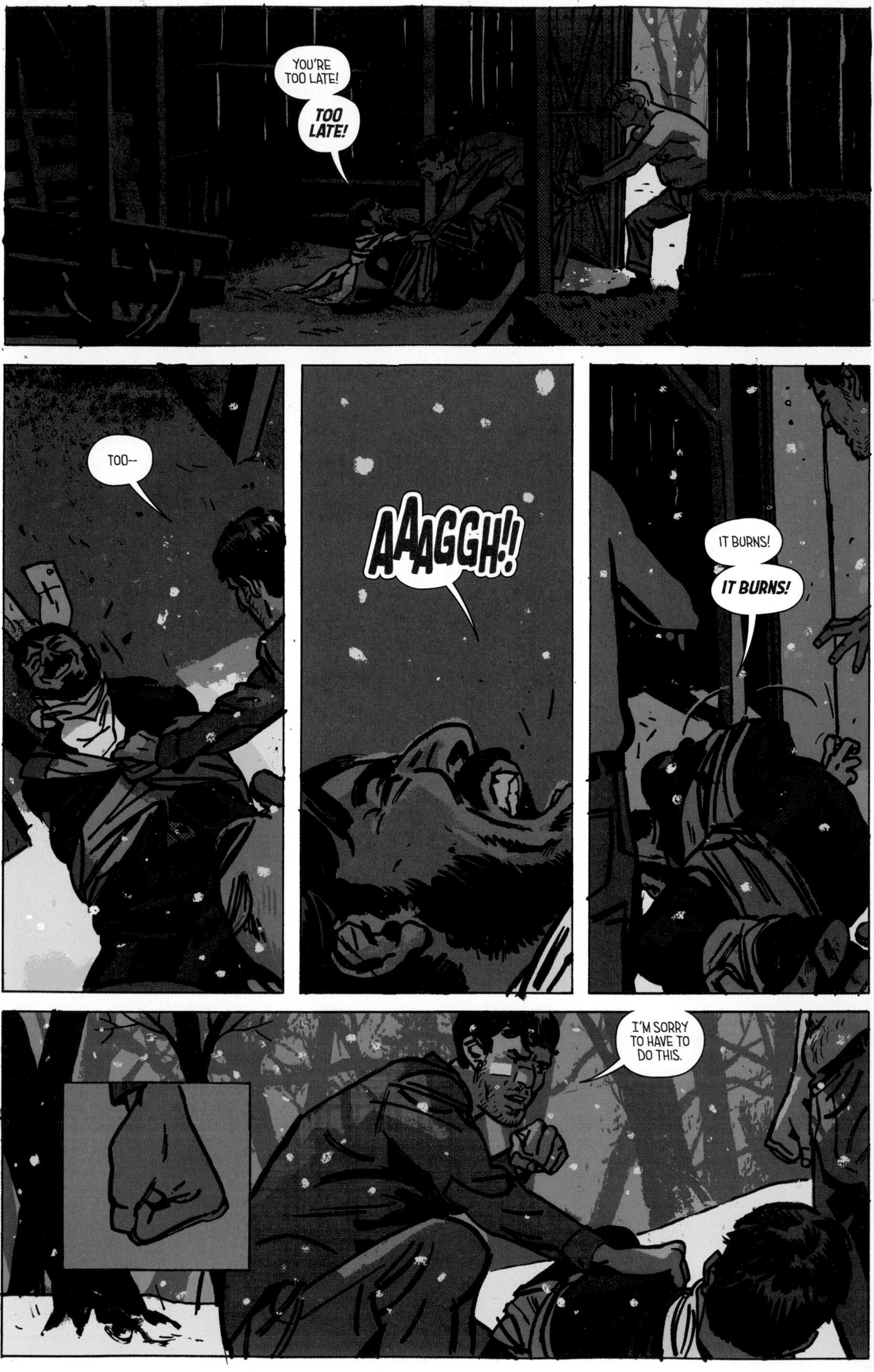

YOU'RE TOO LATE!
TOO LATE!
TOO--
AAAGGH!!
IT BURNS!
IT BURNS!
I'M SORRY TO HAVE TO DO THIS.

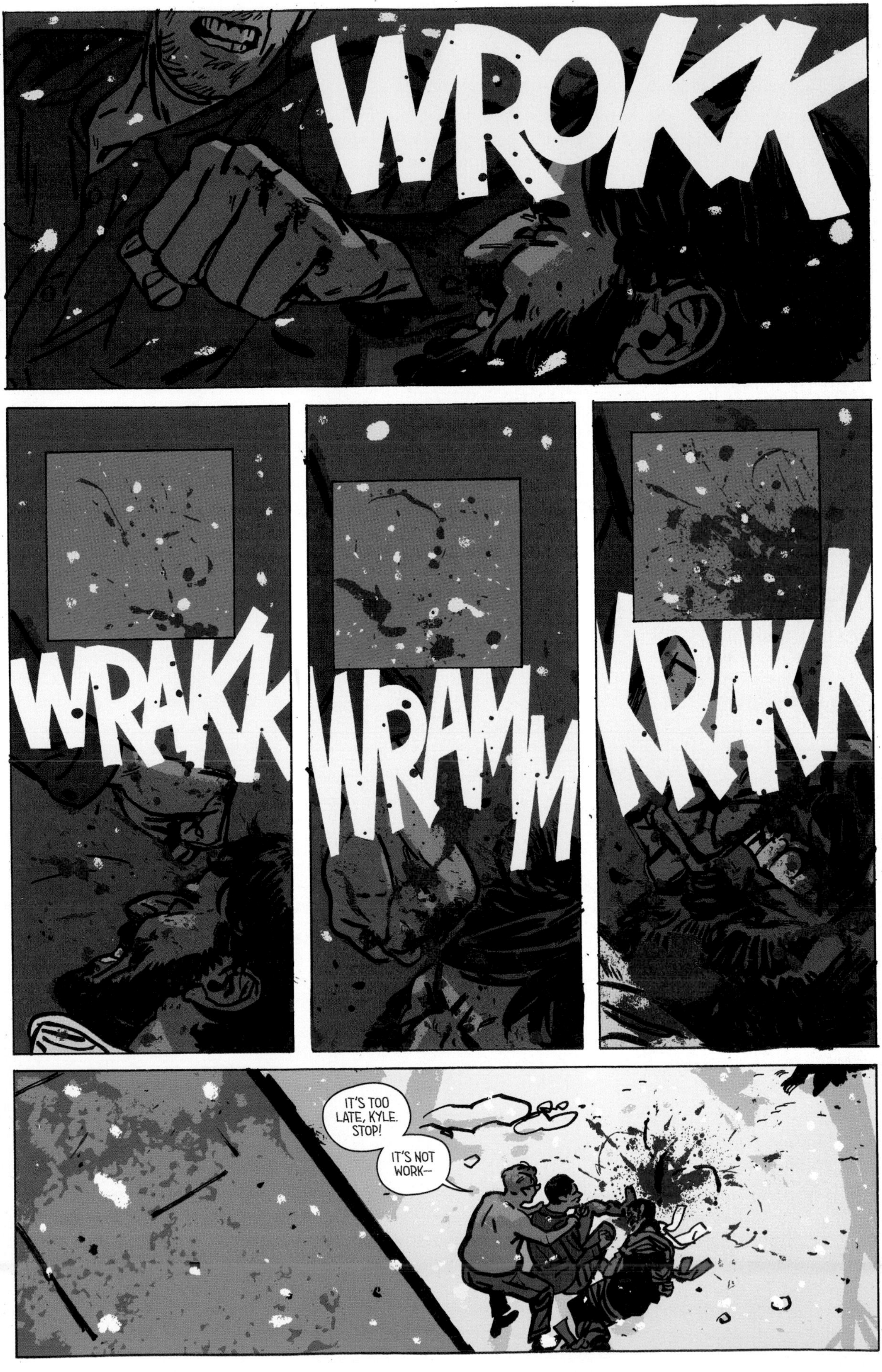
WROKK!
WRAKK
WRAMM
KRAKK
IT'S TOO LATE, KYLE. STOP!
IT'S NOT WORK--

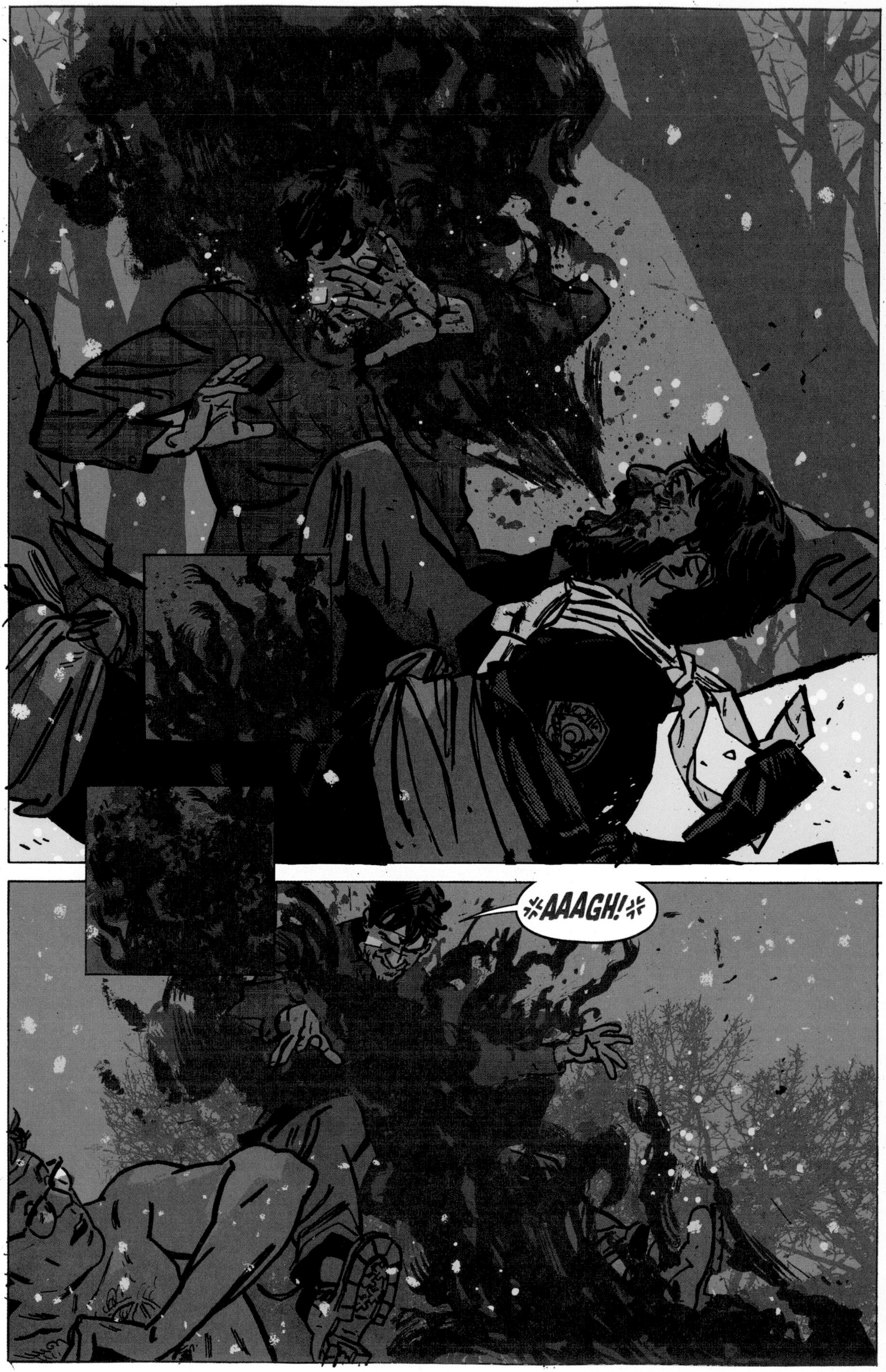
AAAGH!

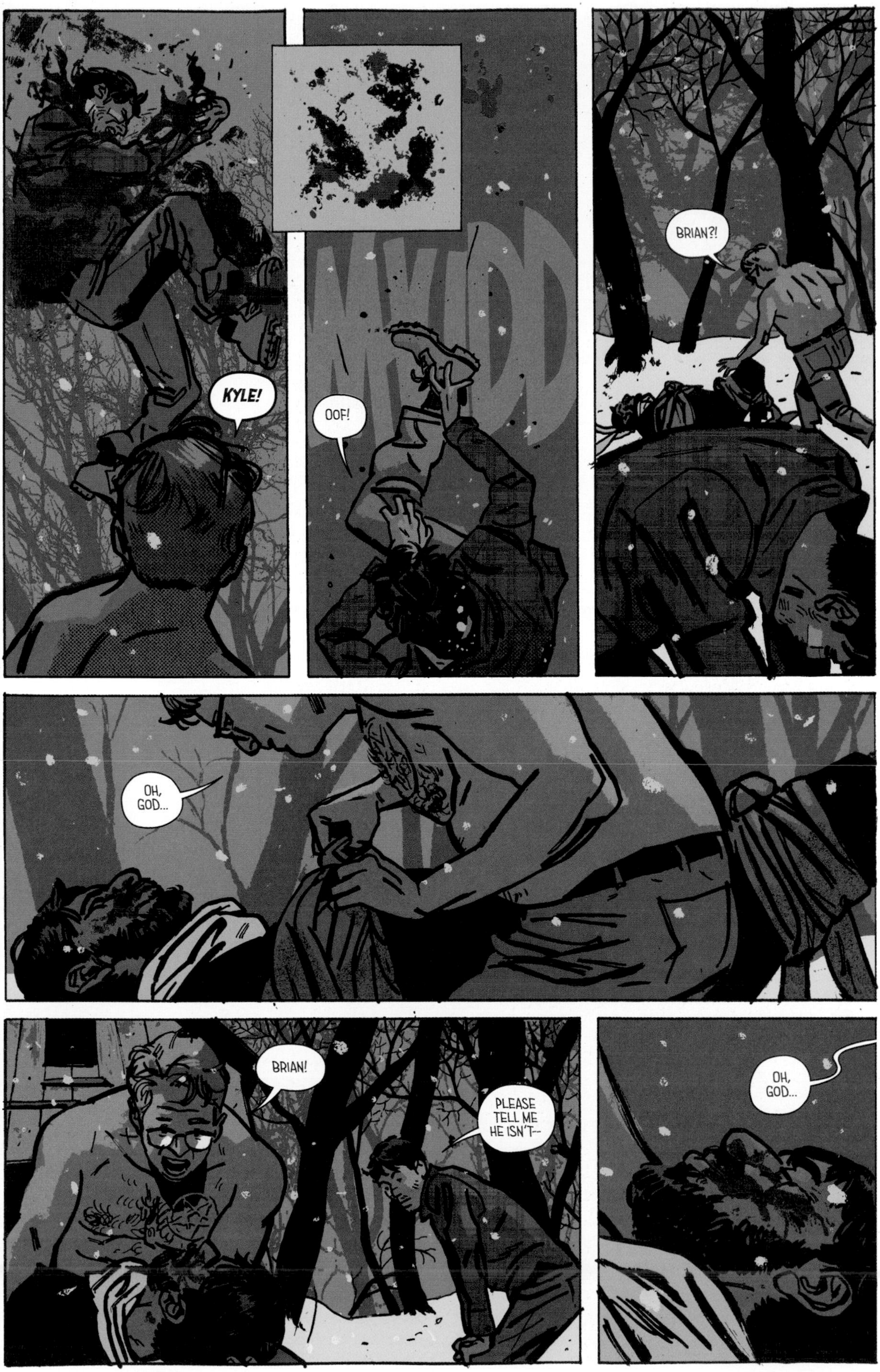
KYLE!
MVDD
OOF!
BRIAN?!
OH, GOD...
BRIAN!
PLEASE TELL ME HE ISN'T--
OH, GOD...

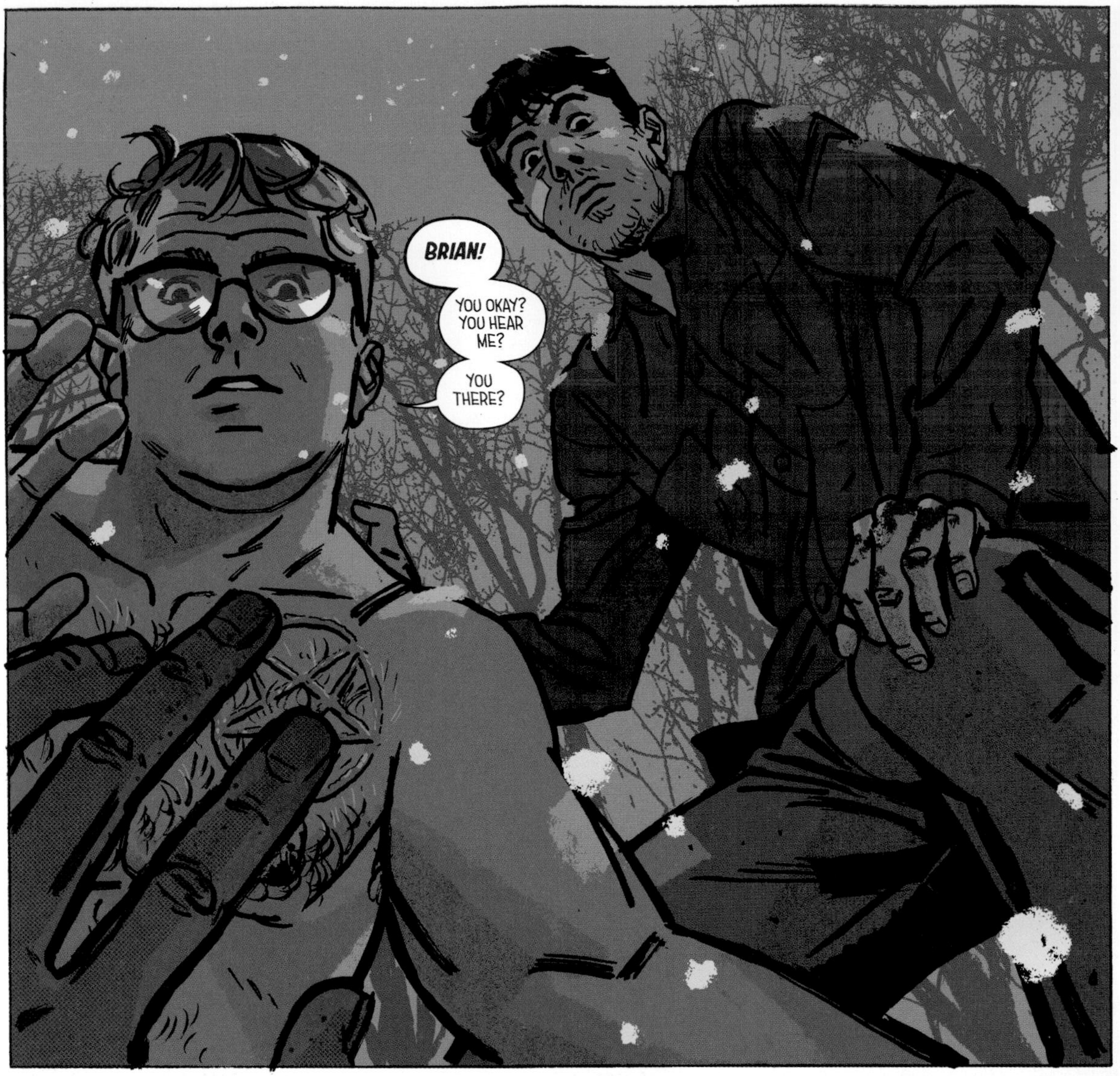
BRIAN!
YOU OKAY? YOU HEAR ME?
YOU THERE?

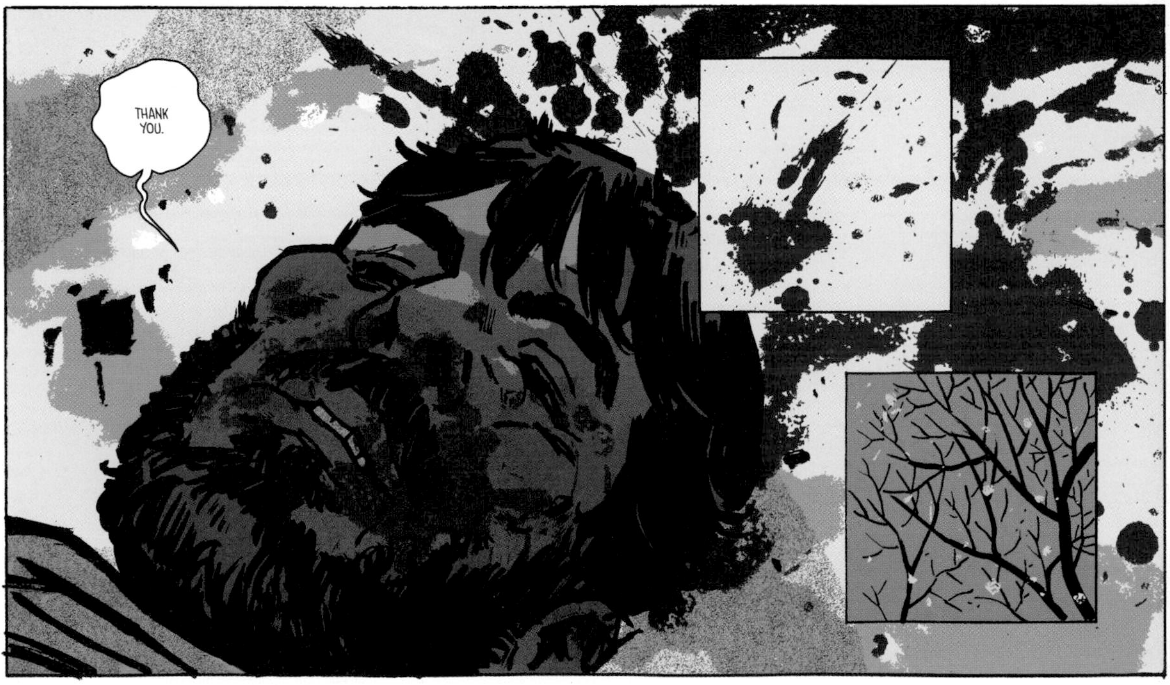
THANK YOU.

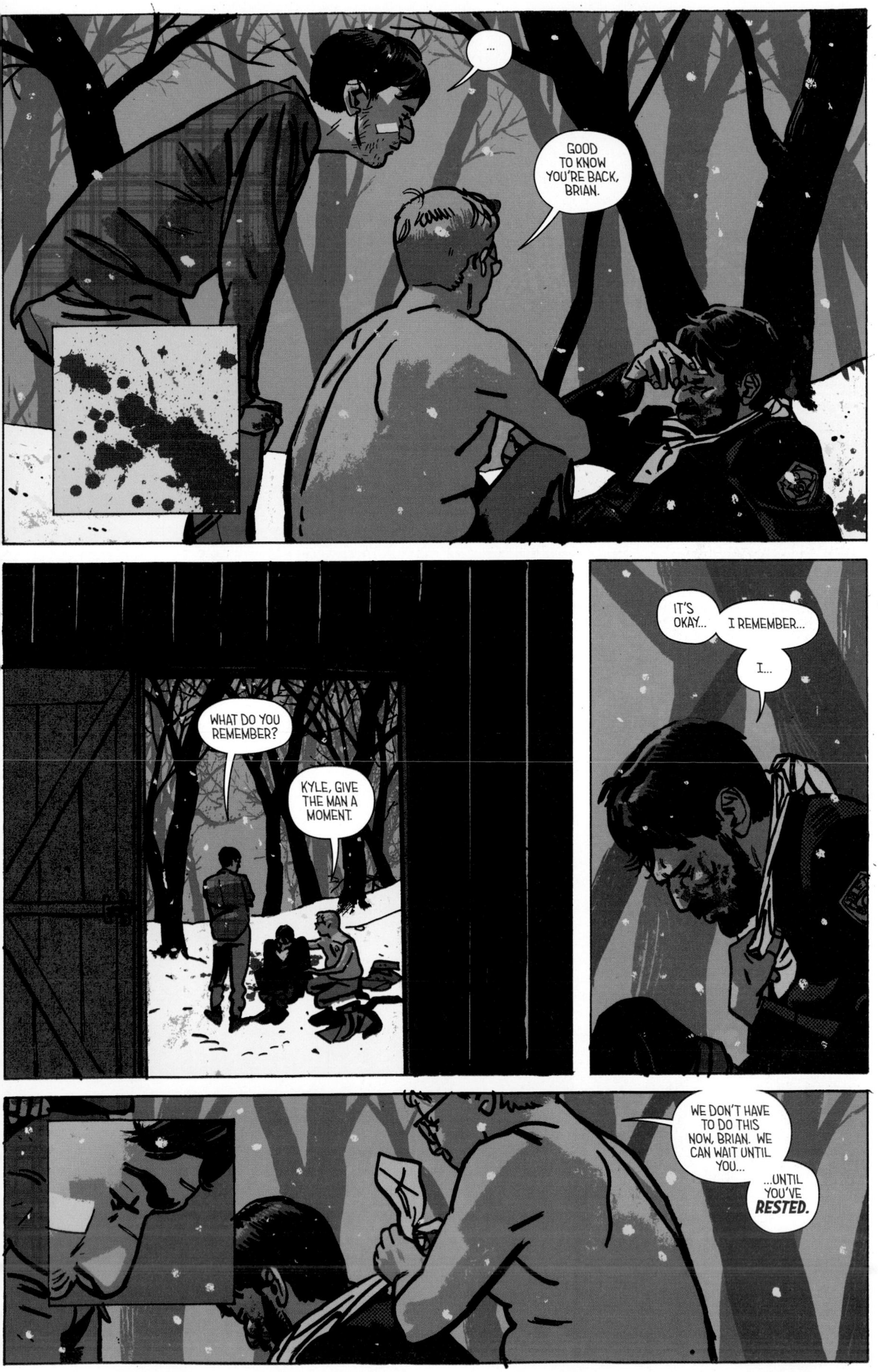
...
GOOD TO KNOW YOU'RE BACK, BRIAN.
WHAT DO YOU REMEMBER?
KYLE, GIVE THE MAN A MOMENT.
IT'S OKAY...
I REMEMBER...
I...
WE DON'T HAVE TO DO THIS NOW, BRIAN. WE CAN WAIT UNTIL YOU...
...UNTIL YOU'VE RESTED.

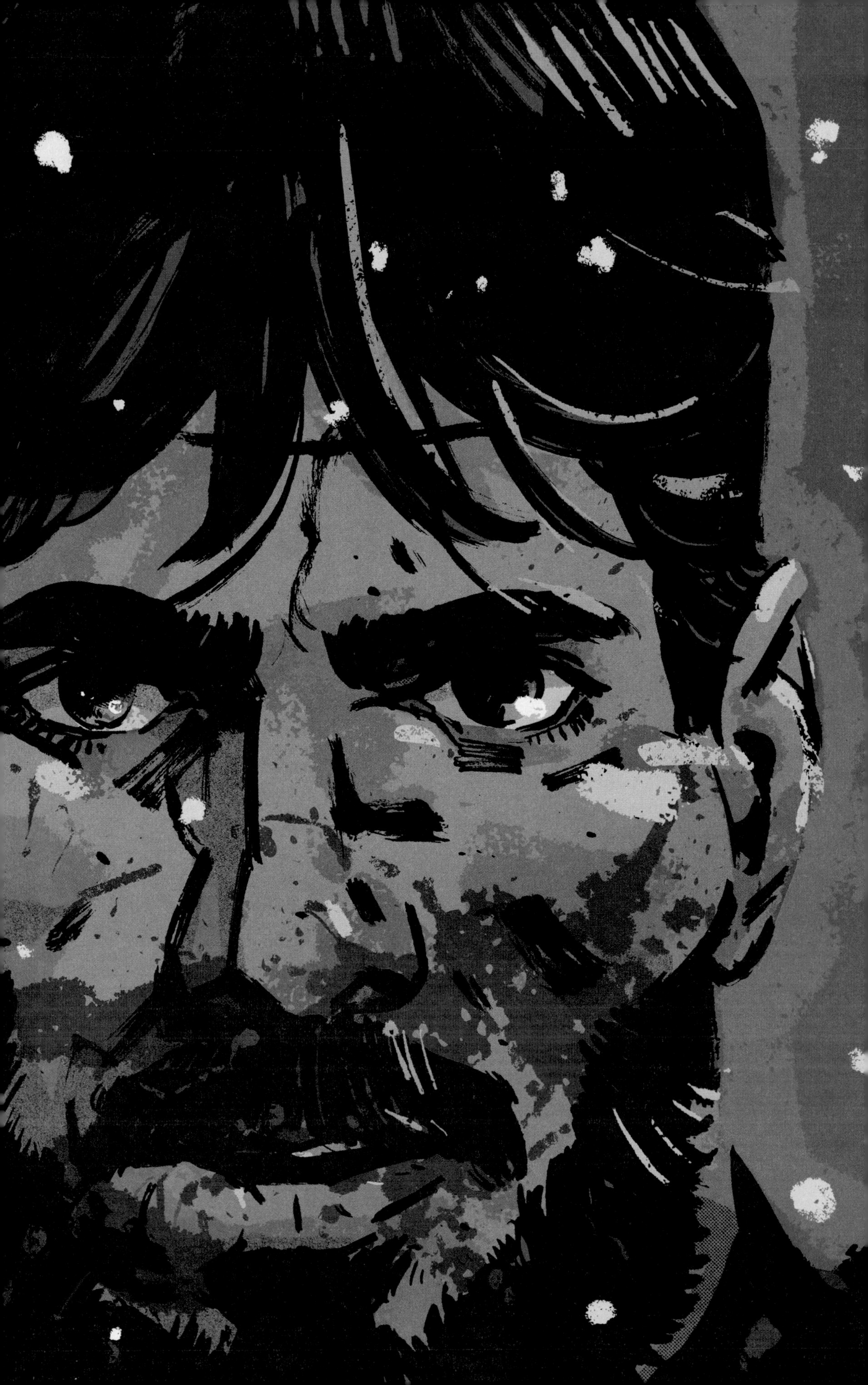

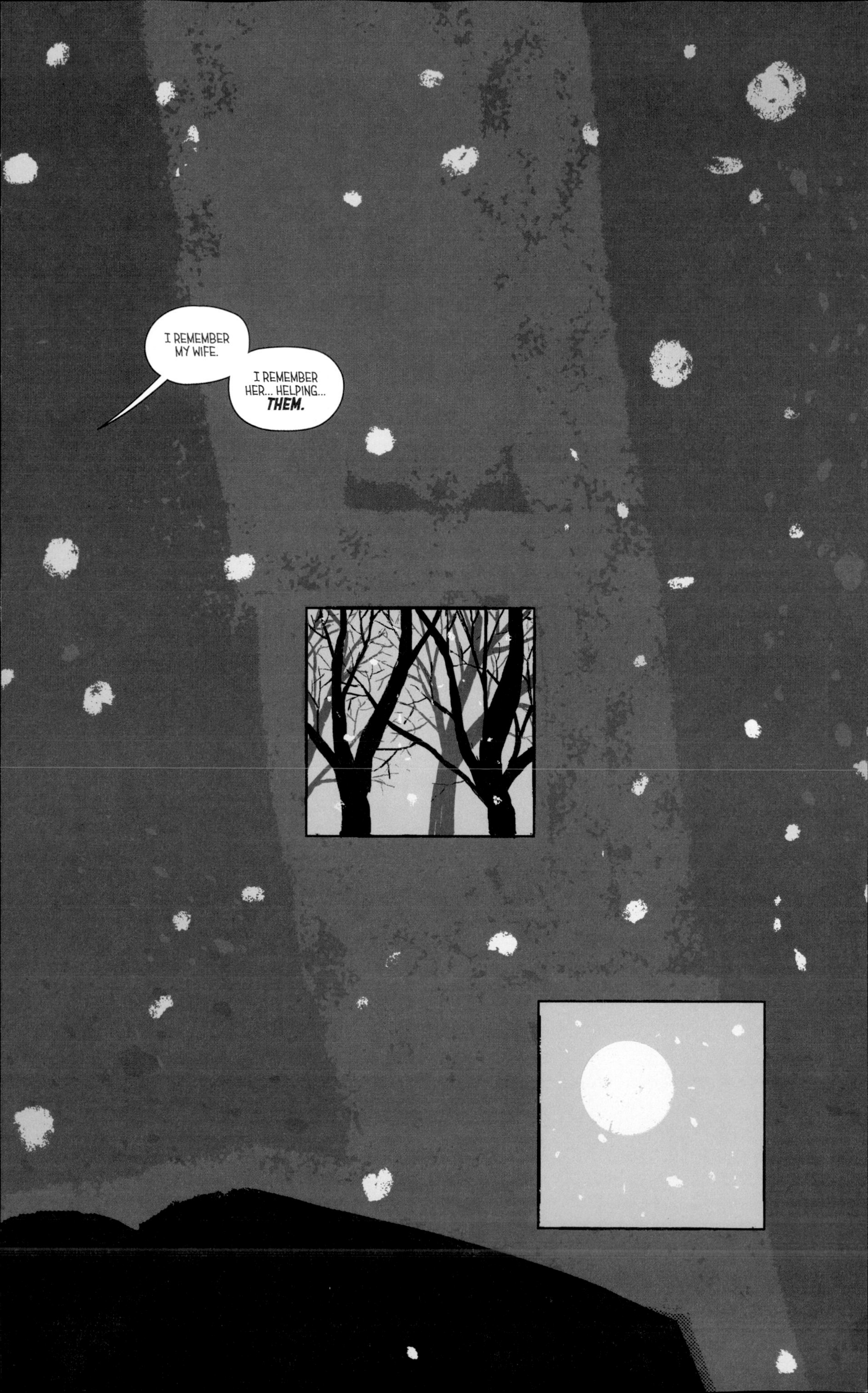
I REMEMBER MY WIFE.
I REMEMBER HER... HELPING... **THEM.**

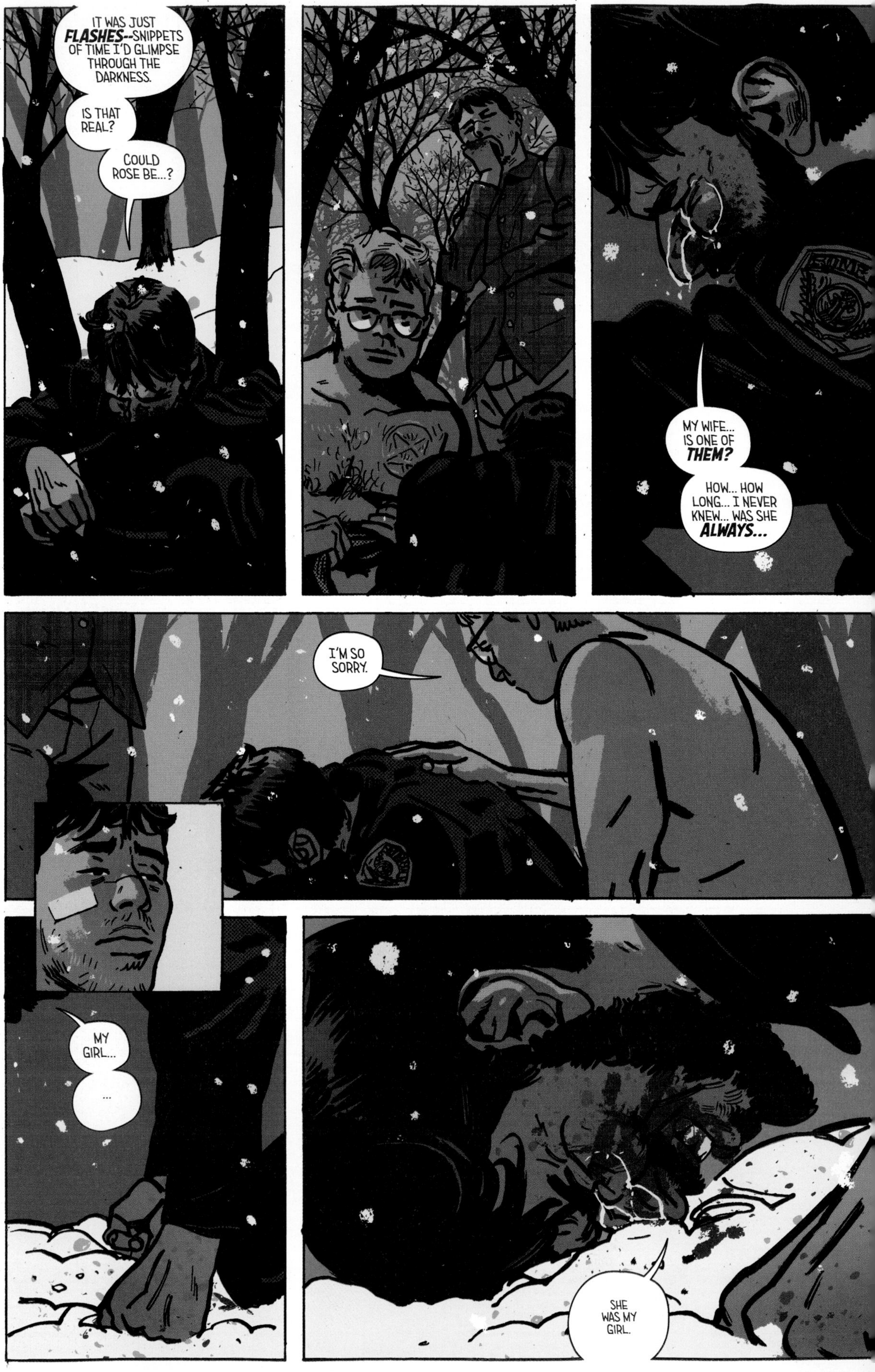
IT WAS JUST FLASHES--SNIPPETS OF TIME I'D GLIMPSE THROUGH THE DARKNESS.
IS THAT REAL?
COULD ROSE BE...?
MY WIFE... IS ONE OF THEM?
HOW... HOW LONG... I NEVER KNEW... WAS SHE ALWAYS...
I'M SO SORRY.
MY GIRL...
...
SHE WAS MY GIRL.

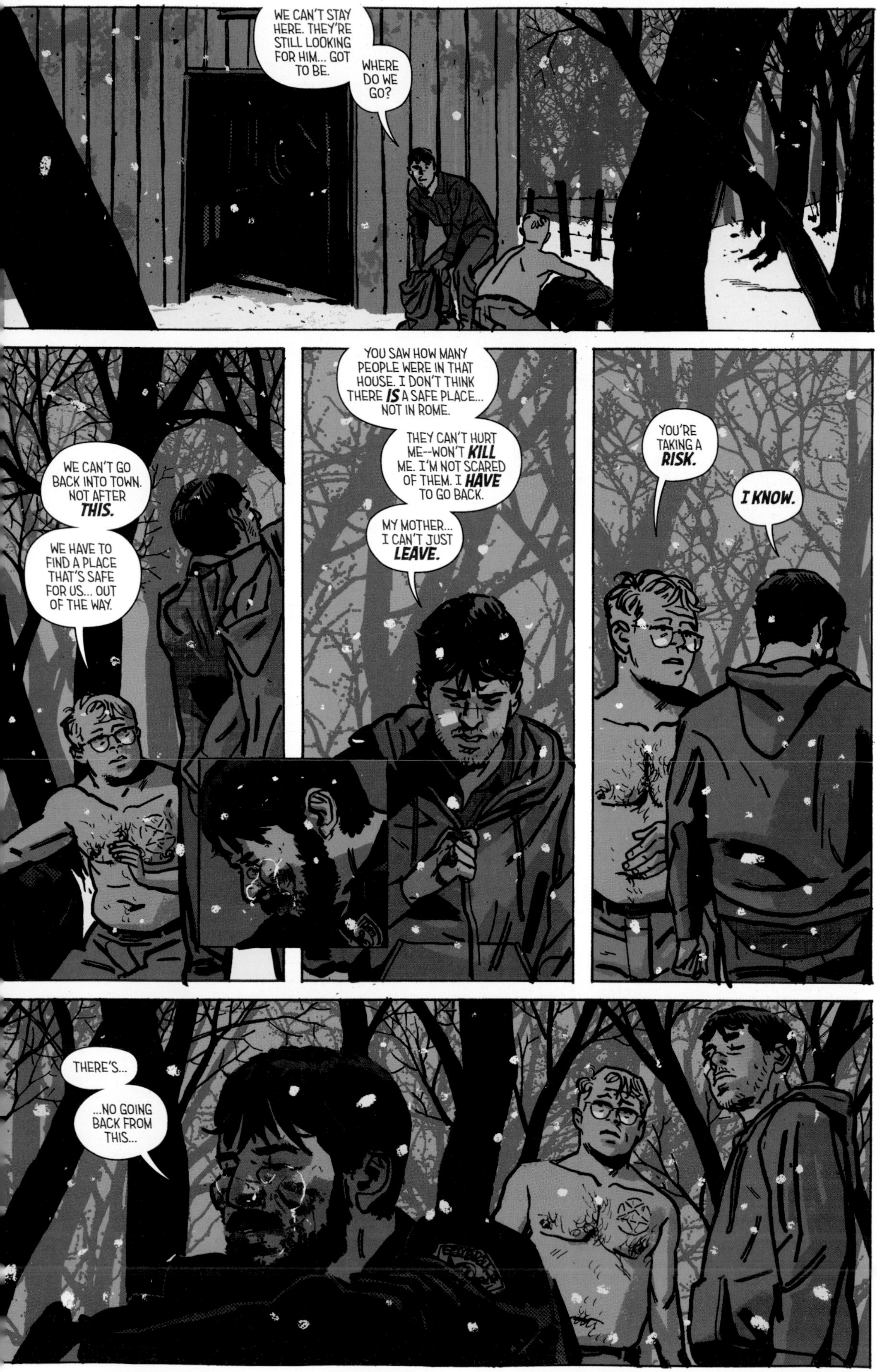
WE CAN'T STAY HERE. THEY'RE STILL LOOKING FOR HIM... GOT TO BE.
WHERE DO WE GO?
WE CAN'T GO BACK INTO TOWN. NOT AFTER THIS.
WE HAVE TO FIND A PLACE THAT'S SAFE FOR US... OUT OF THE WAY.
YOU SAW HOW MANY PEOPLE WERE IN THAT HOUSE. I DON'T THINK THERE IS A SAFE PLACE... NOT IN ROME.
THEY CAN'T HURT ME--WON'T KILL ME. I'M NOT SCARED OF THEM. I HAVE TO GO BACK.
MY MOTHER... I CAN'T JUST LEAVE.
YOU'RE TAKING A RISK.
I KNOW.
THERE'S...
...NO GOING BACK FROM THIS...

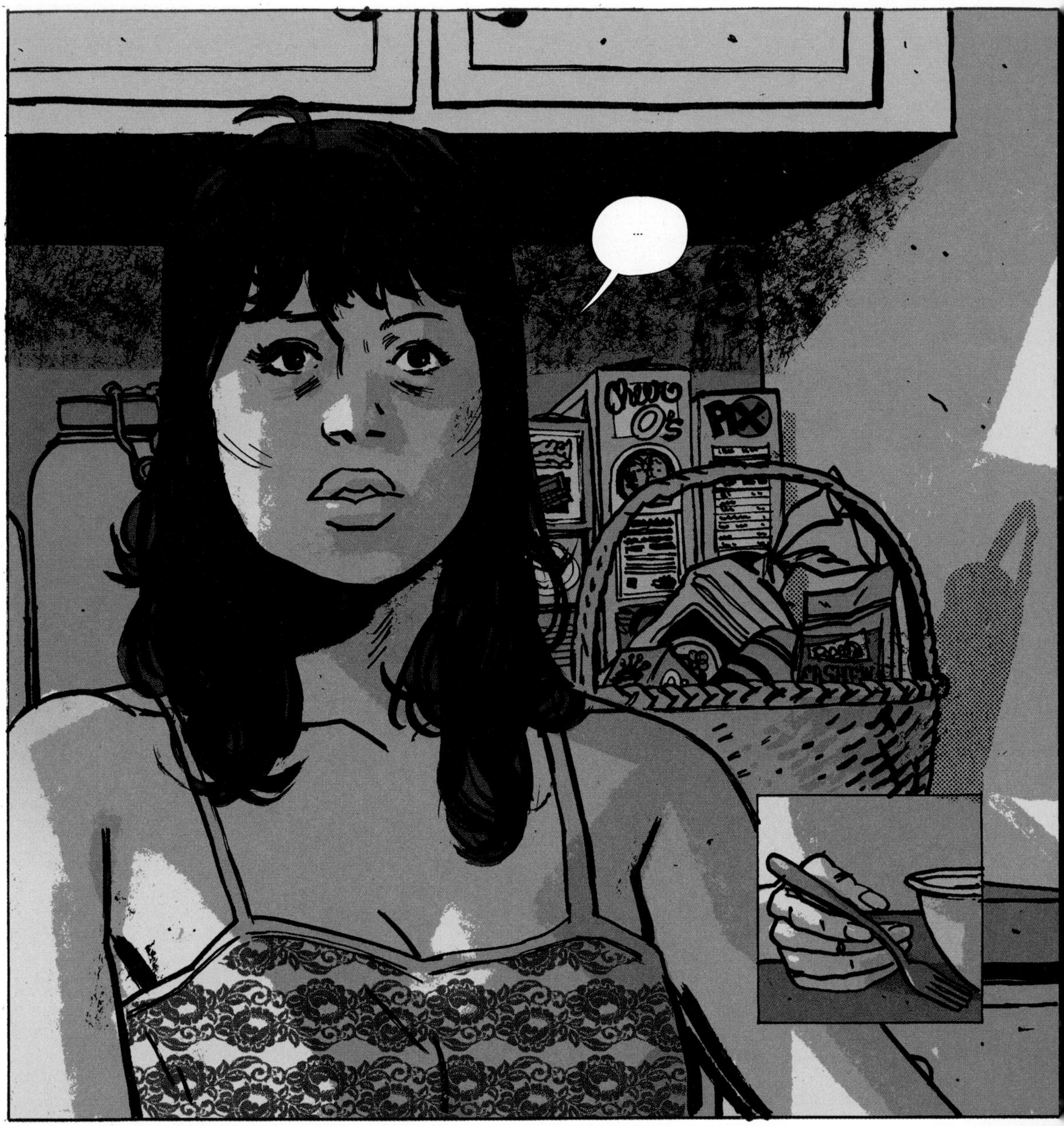
...

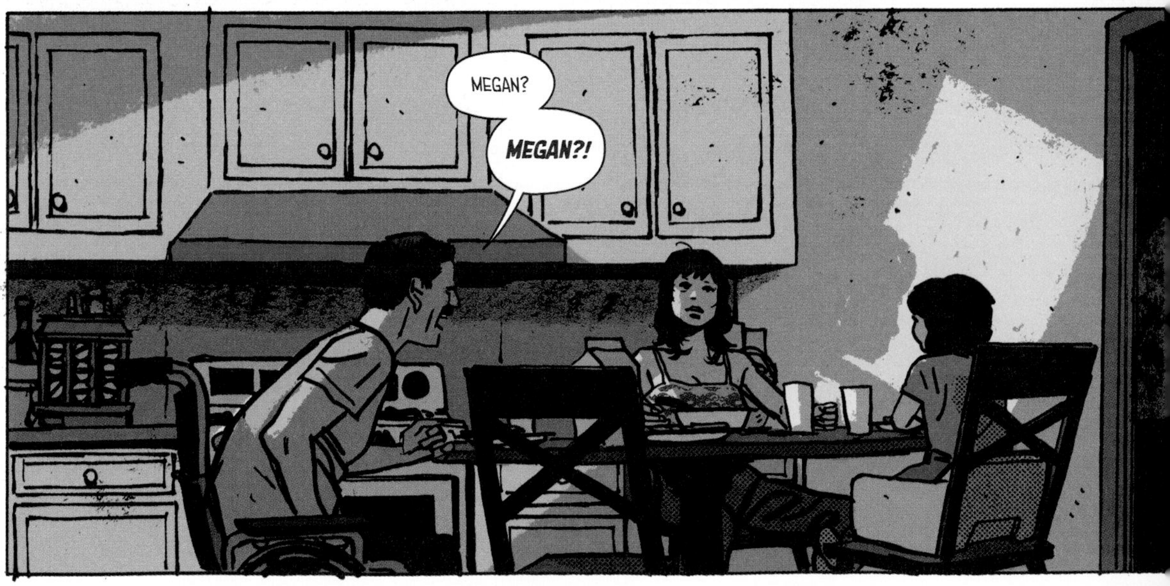
MEGAN?
MEGAN?!

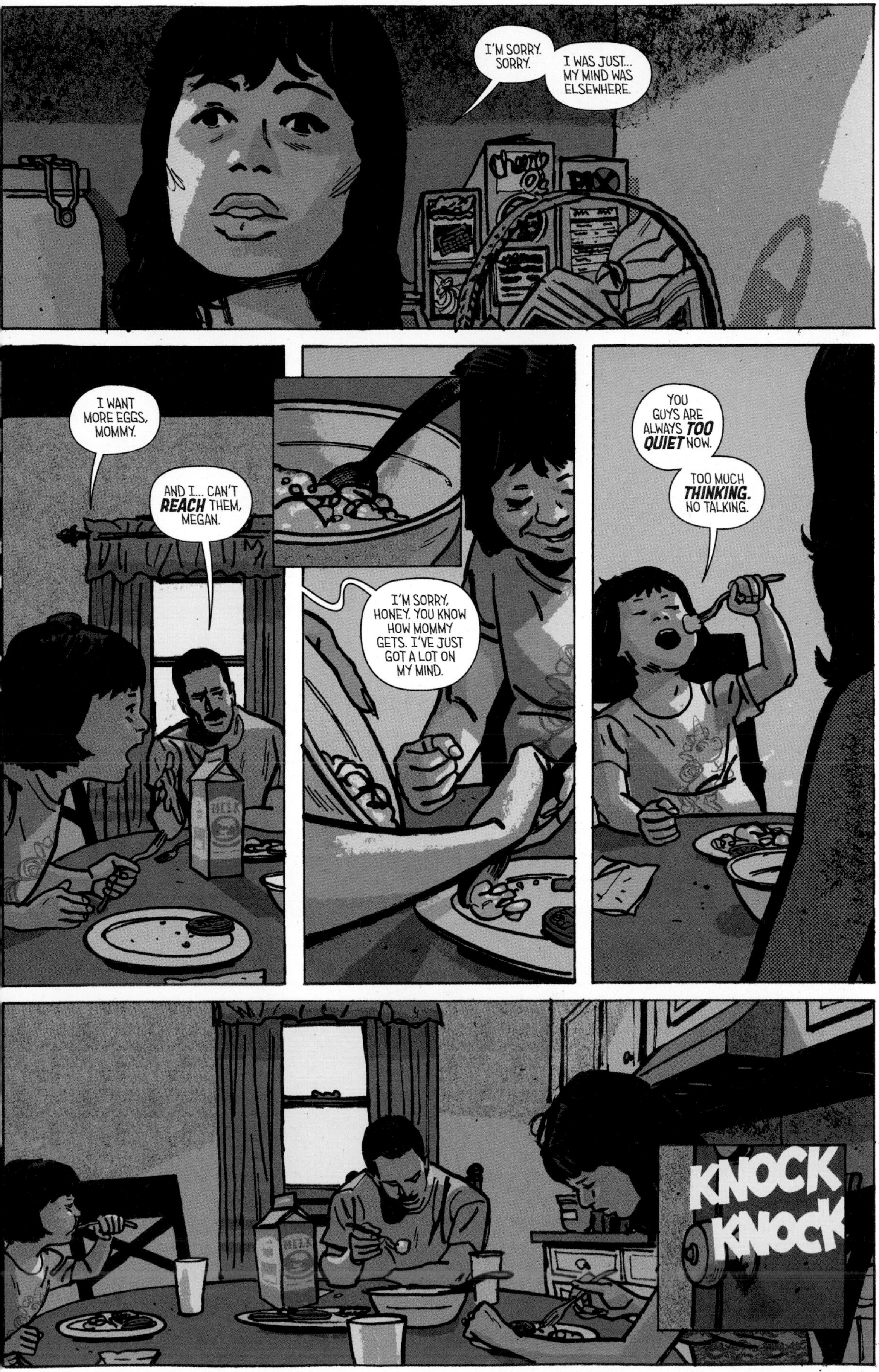
I'M SORRY. SORRY.
I WAS JUST... MY MIND WAS ELSEWHERE.
I WANT MORE EGGS, MOMMY.
AND I... CAN'T **REACH** THEM, MEGAN.
I'M SORRY, HONEY. YOU KNOW HOW MOMMY GETS. I'VE JUST GOT A LOT ON MY MIND.
YOU GUYS ARE ALWAYS **TOO QUIET** NOW.
TOO MUCH **THINKING.** NO TALKING.
KNOCK KNOCK

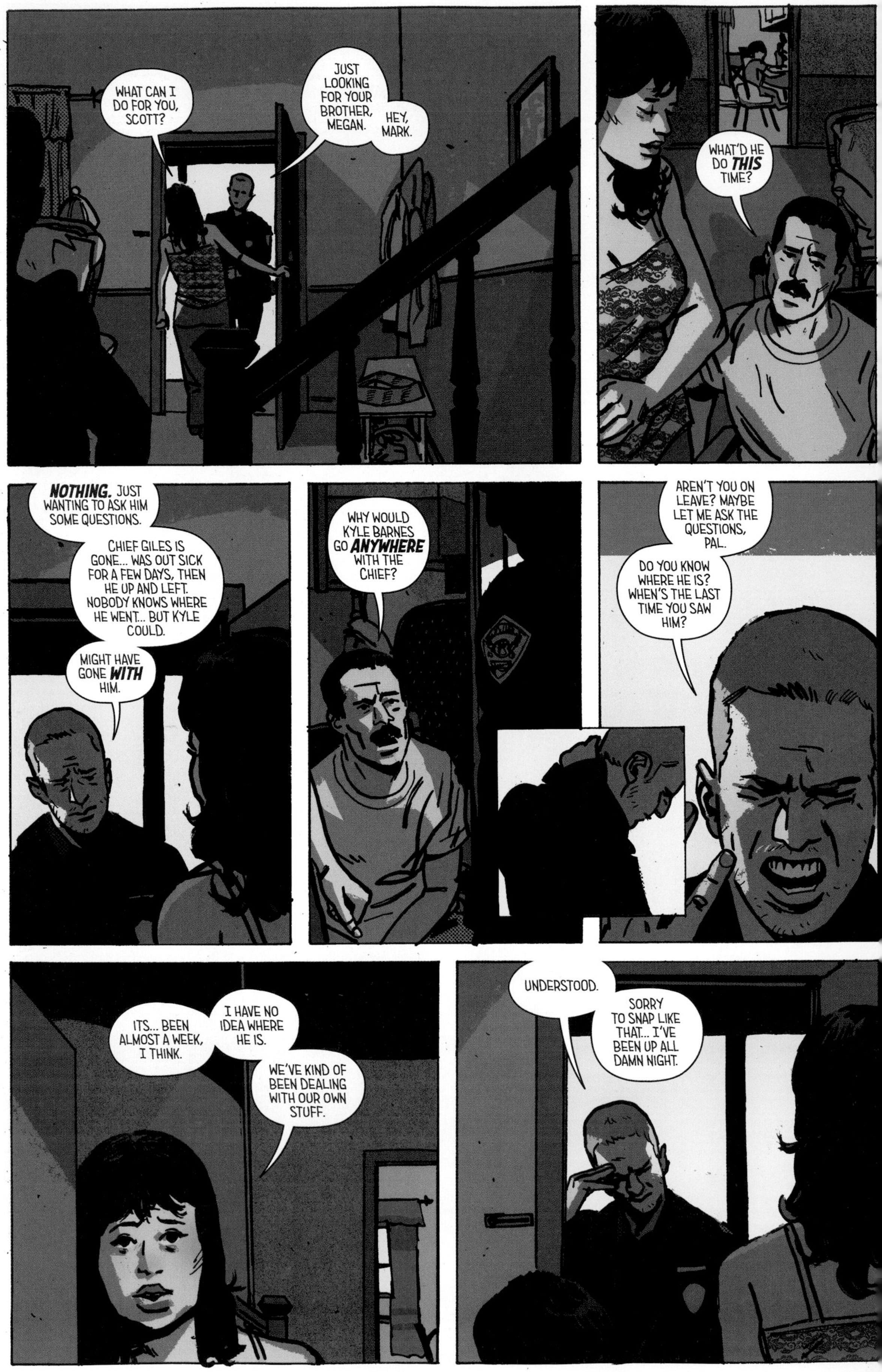
WHAT CAN I DO FOR YOU, SCOTT?
JUST LOOKING FOR YOUR BROTHER, MEGAN.
HEY, MARK.
WHAT'D HE DO THIS TIME?
NOTHING. JUST WANTING TO ASK HIM SOME QUESTIONS.
CHIEF GILES IS GONE... WAS OUT SICK FOR A FEW DAYS, THEN HE UP AND LEFT. NOBODY KNOWS WHERE HE WENT... BUT KYLE COULD.
MIGHT HAVE GONE WITH HIM.
WHY WOULD KYLE BARNES GO ANYWHERE WITH THE CHIEF?
AREN'T YOU ON LEAVE? MAYBE LET ME ASK THE QUESTIONS, PAL.
DO YOU KNOW WHERE HE IS? WHEN'S THE LAST TIME YOU SAW HIM?
ITS... BEEN ALMOST A WEEK, I THINK.
I HAVE NO IDEA WHERE HE IS.
WE'VE KIND OF BEEN DEALING WITH OUR OWN STUFF.
UNDERSTOOD.
SORRY TO SNAP LIKE THAT... I'VE BEEN UP ALL DAMN NIGHT.

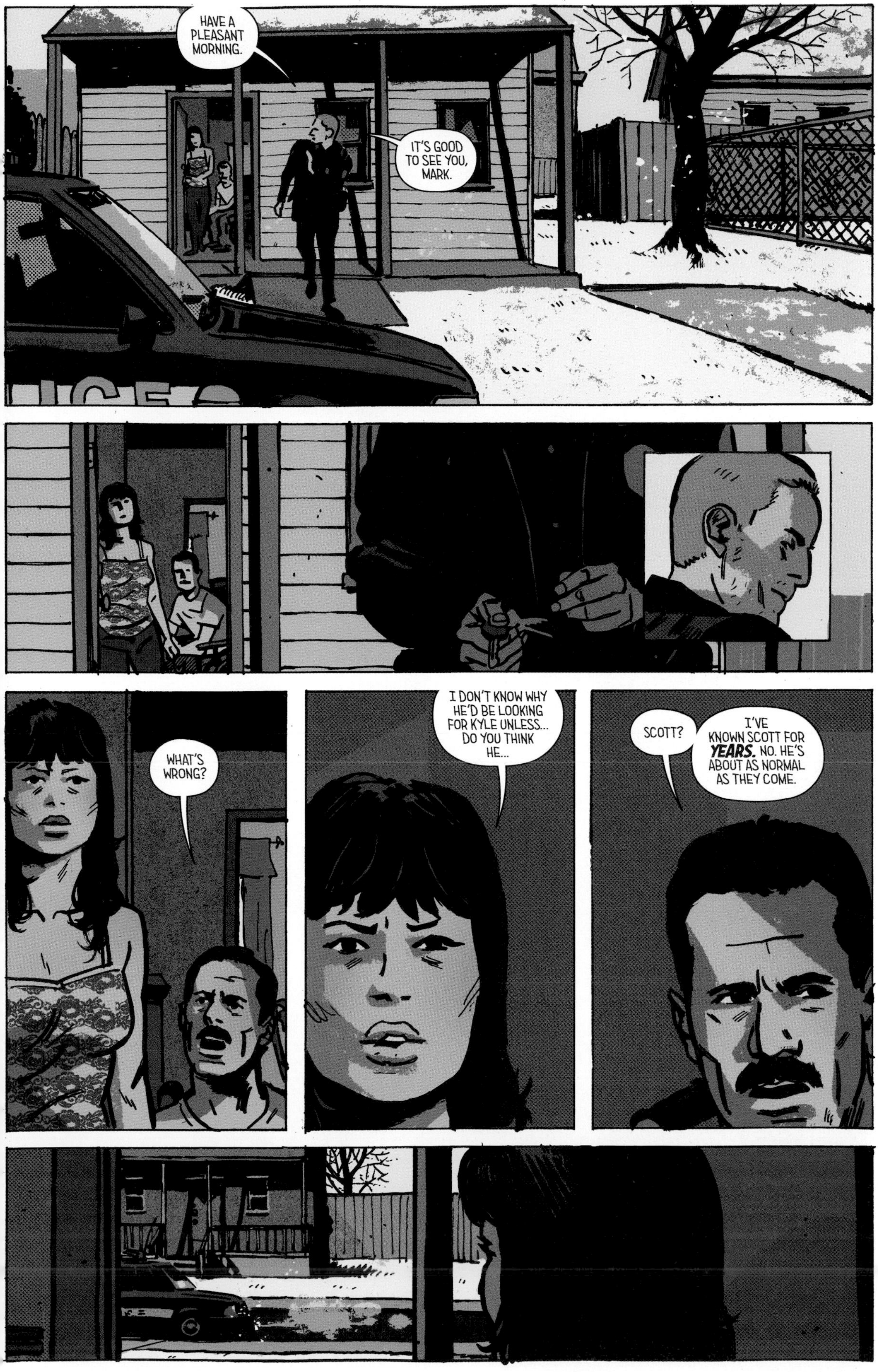
HAVE A PLEASANT MORNING.
IT'S GOOD TO SEE YOU, MARK.
WHAT'S WRONG?
I DON'T KNOW WHY HE'D BE LOOKING FOR KYLE UNLESS... DO YOU THINK HE...
SCOTT?
I'VE KNOWN SCOTT FOR YEARS. NO. HE'S ABOUT AS NORMAL AS THEY COME.

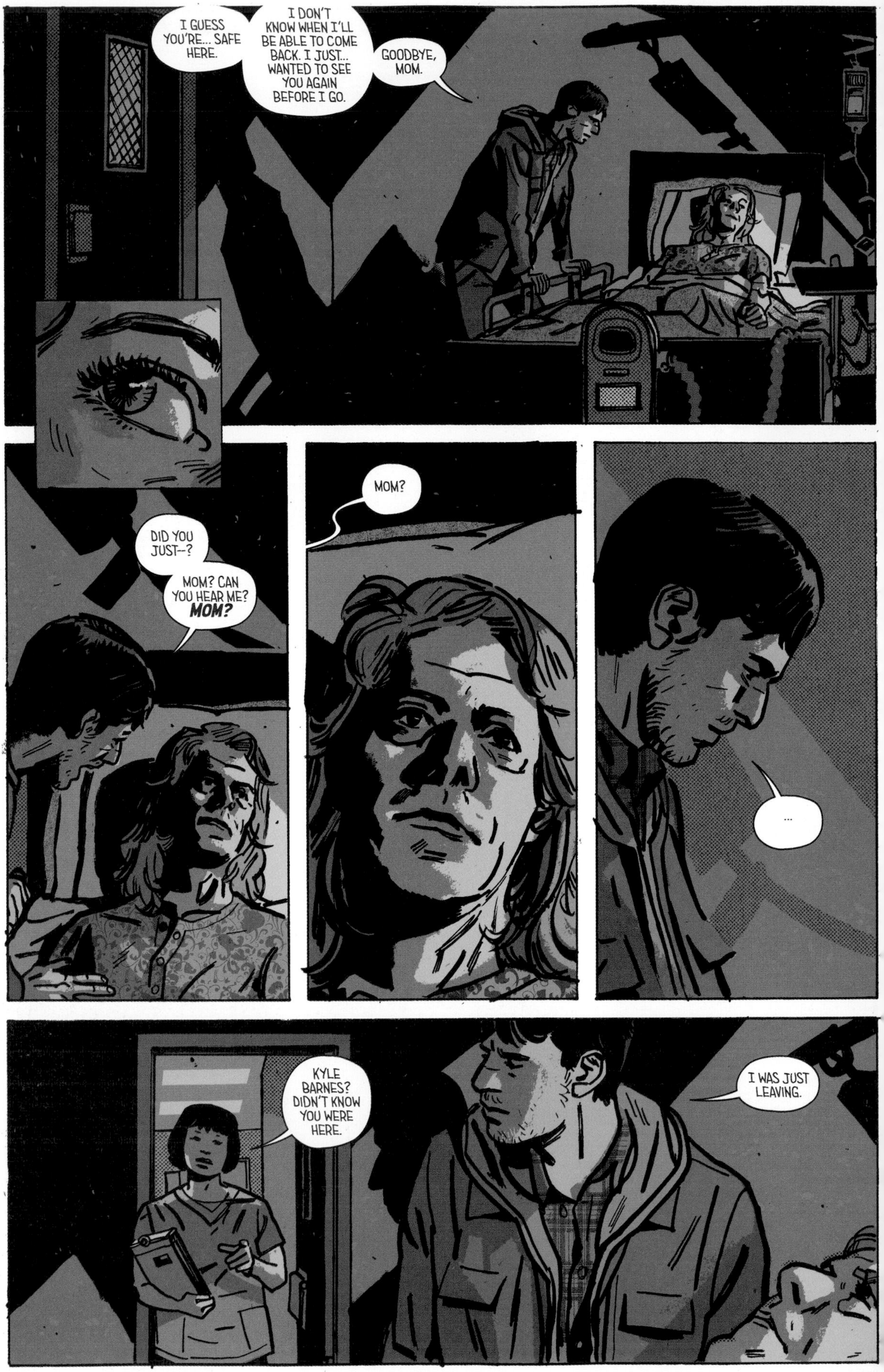
I GUESS YOU'RE... SAFE HERE.
I DON'T KNOW WHEN I'LL BE ABLE TO COME BACK. I JUST... WANTED TO SEE YOU AGAIN BEFORE I GO.
GOODBYE, MOM.
DID YOU JUST--?
MOM? CAN YOU HEAR ME? ***MOM?***
MOM?
...
KYLE BARNES? DIDN'T KNOW YOU WERE HERE.
I WAS JUST LEAVING.

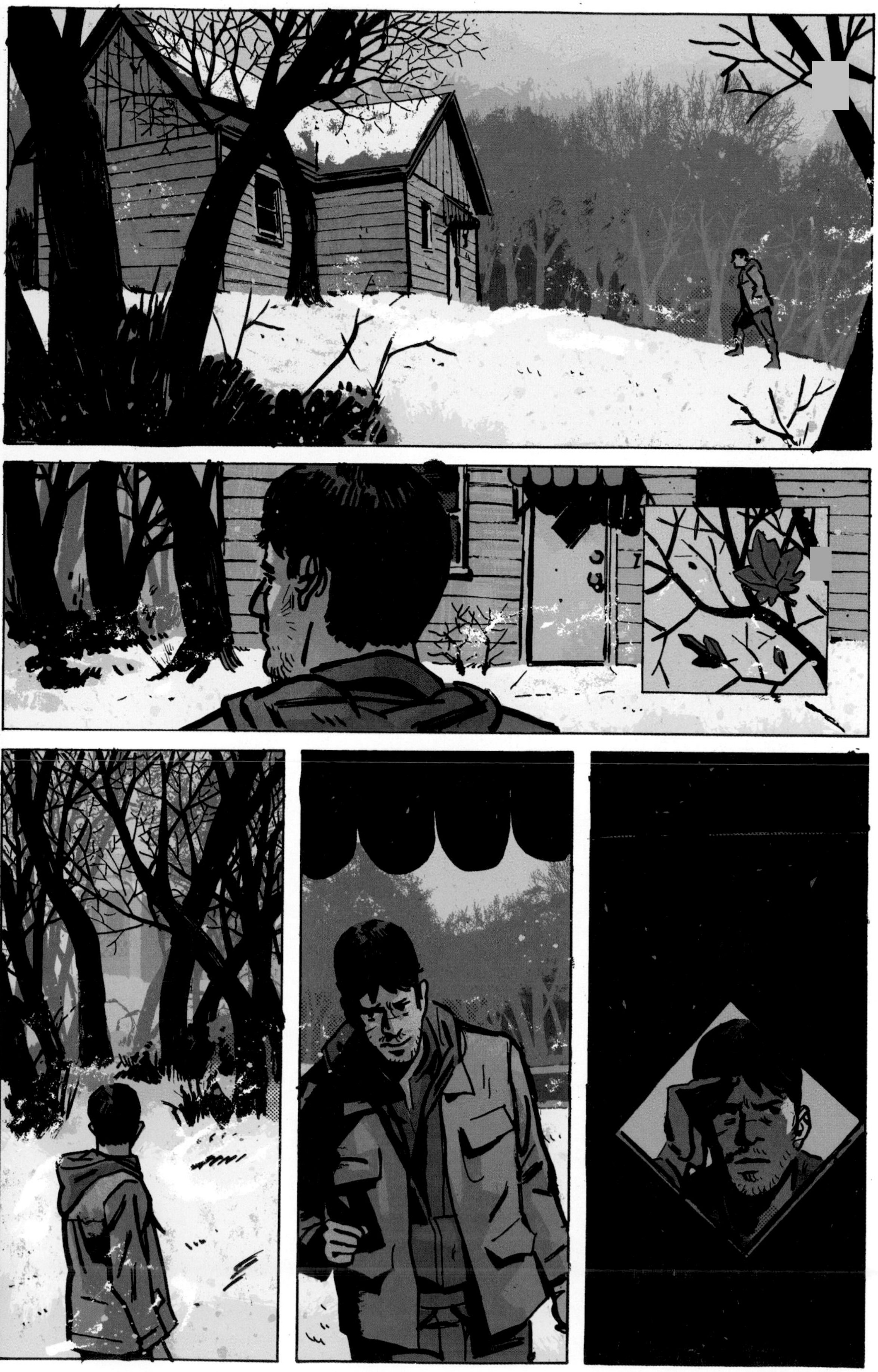

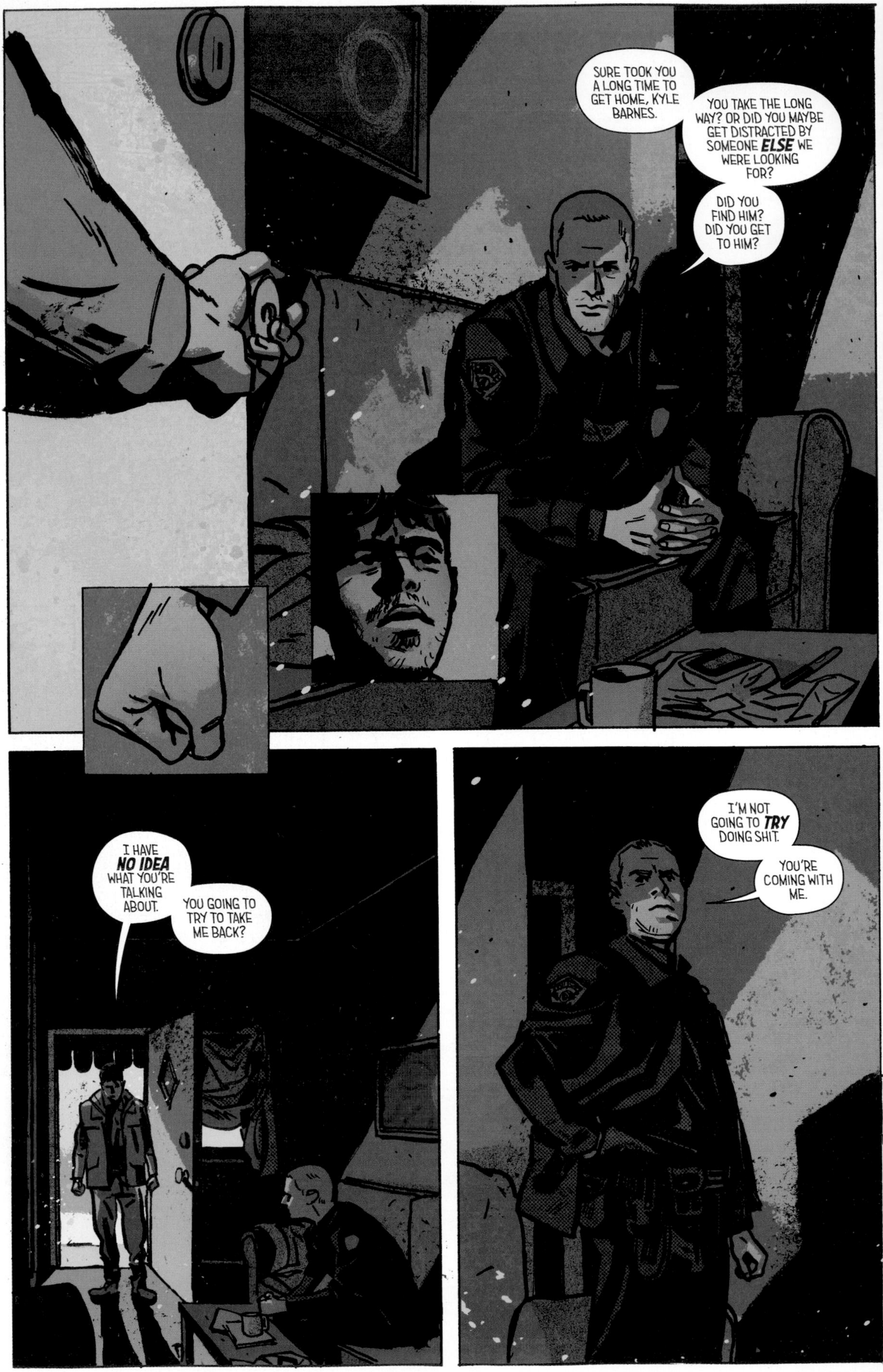
SURE TOOK YOU A LONG TIME TO GET HOME, KYLE BARNES.
YOU TAKE THE LONG WAY? OR DID YOU MAYBE GET DISTRACTED BY SOMEONE ELSE WE WERE LOOKING FOR?
DID YOU FIND HIM? DID YOU GET TO HIM?
I HAVE NO IDEA WHAT YOU'RE TALKING ABOUT.
YOU GOING TO TRY TO TAKE ME BACK?
I'M NOT GOING TO TRY DOING SHIT.
YOU'RE COMING WITH ME.

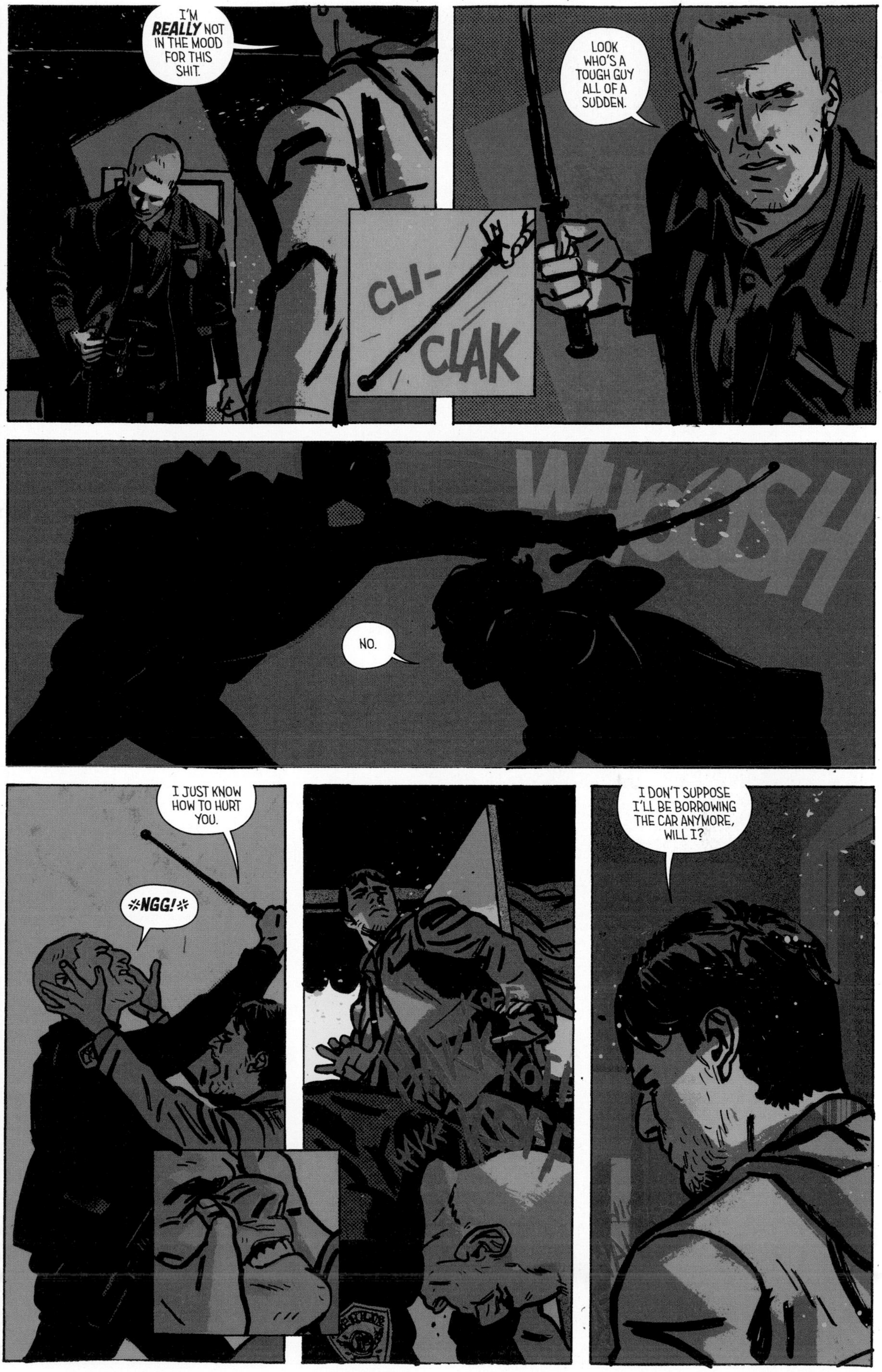
I'M **REALLY** NOT IN THE MOOD FOR THIS SHIT.
LOOK WHO'S A TOUGH GUY ALL OF A SUDDEN.
CLI- CLAK
WHOOSH
NO.
I JUST KNOW HOW TO HURT YOU.
NGG!
I DON'T SUPPOSE I'LL BE BORROWING THE CAR ANYMORE, WILL I?

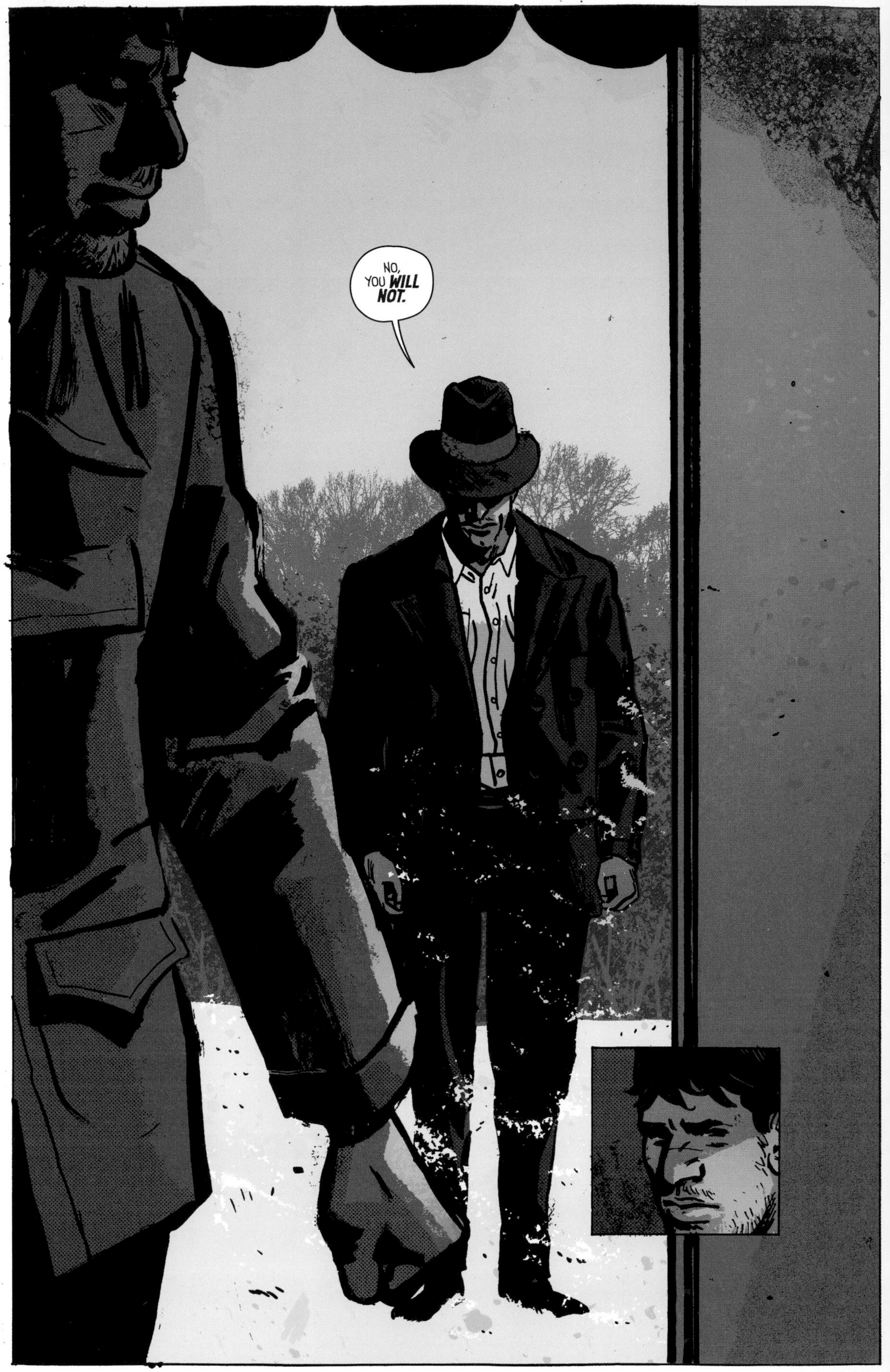
NO, YOU **WILL NOT.**

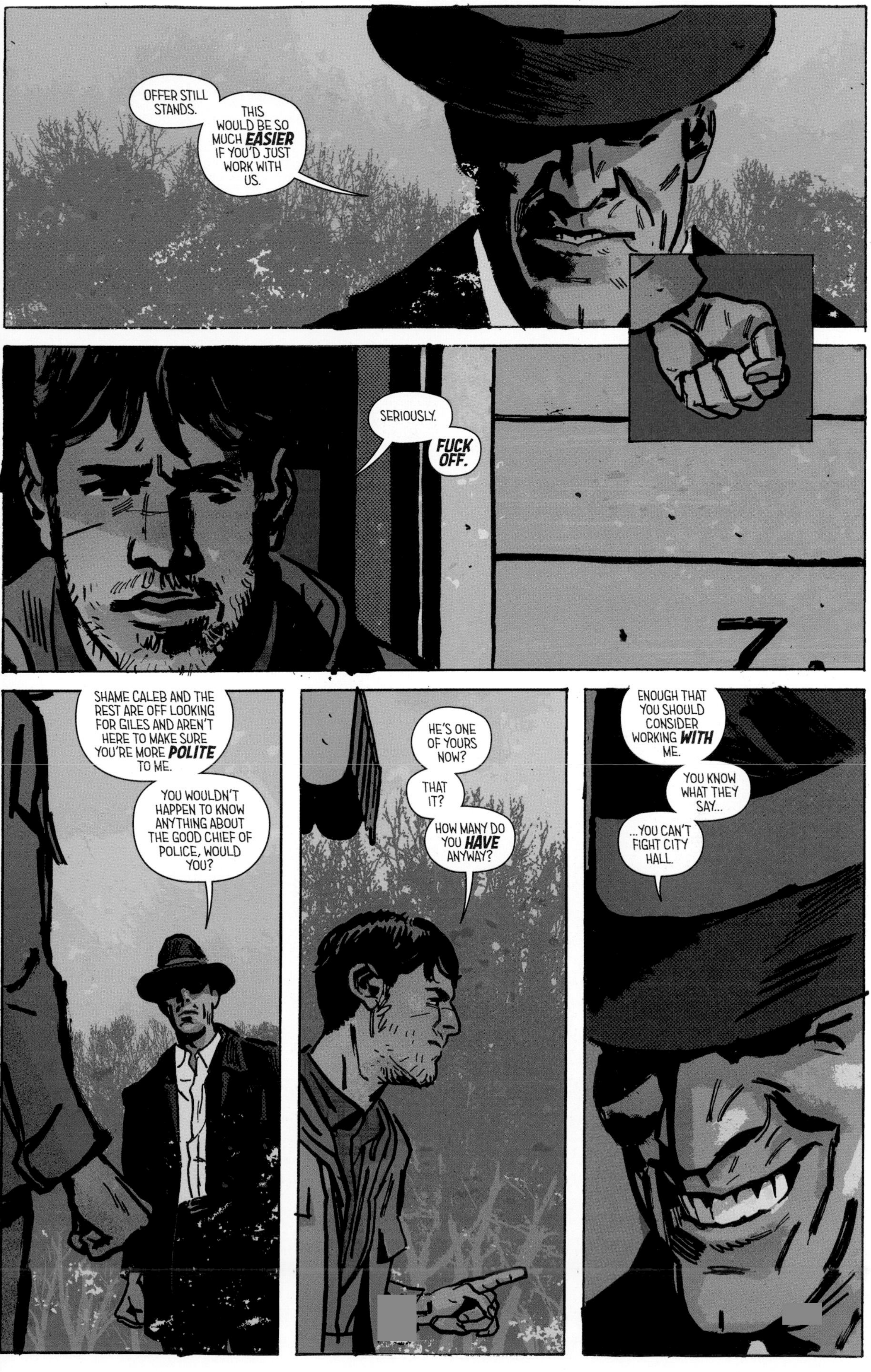
OFFER STILL STANDS.
THIS WOULD BE SO MUCH EASIER IF YOU'D JUST WORK WITH US.
SERIOUSLY.
FUCK OFF.
SHAME CALEB AND THE REST ARE OFF LOOKING FOR GILES AND AREN'T HERE TO MAKE SURE YOU'RE MORE POLITE TO ME.
YOU WOULDN'T HAPPEN TO KNOW ANYTHING ABOUT THE GOOD CHIEF OF POLICE, WOULD YOU?
HE'S ONE OF YOURS NOW?
THAT IT?
HOW MANY DO YOU HAVE ANYWAY?
ENOUGH THAT YOU SHOULD CONSIDER WORKING WITH ME.
YOU KNOW WHAT THEY SAY...
...YOU CAN'T FIGHT CITY HALL.

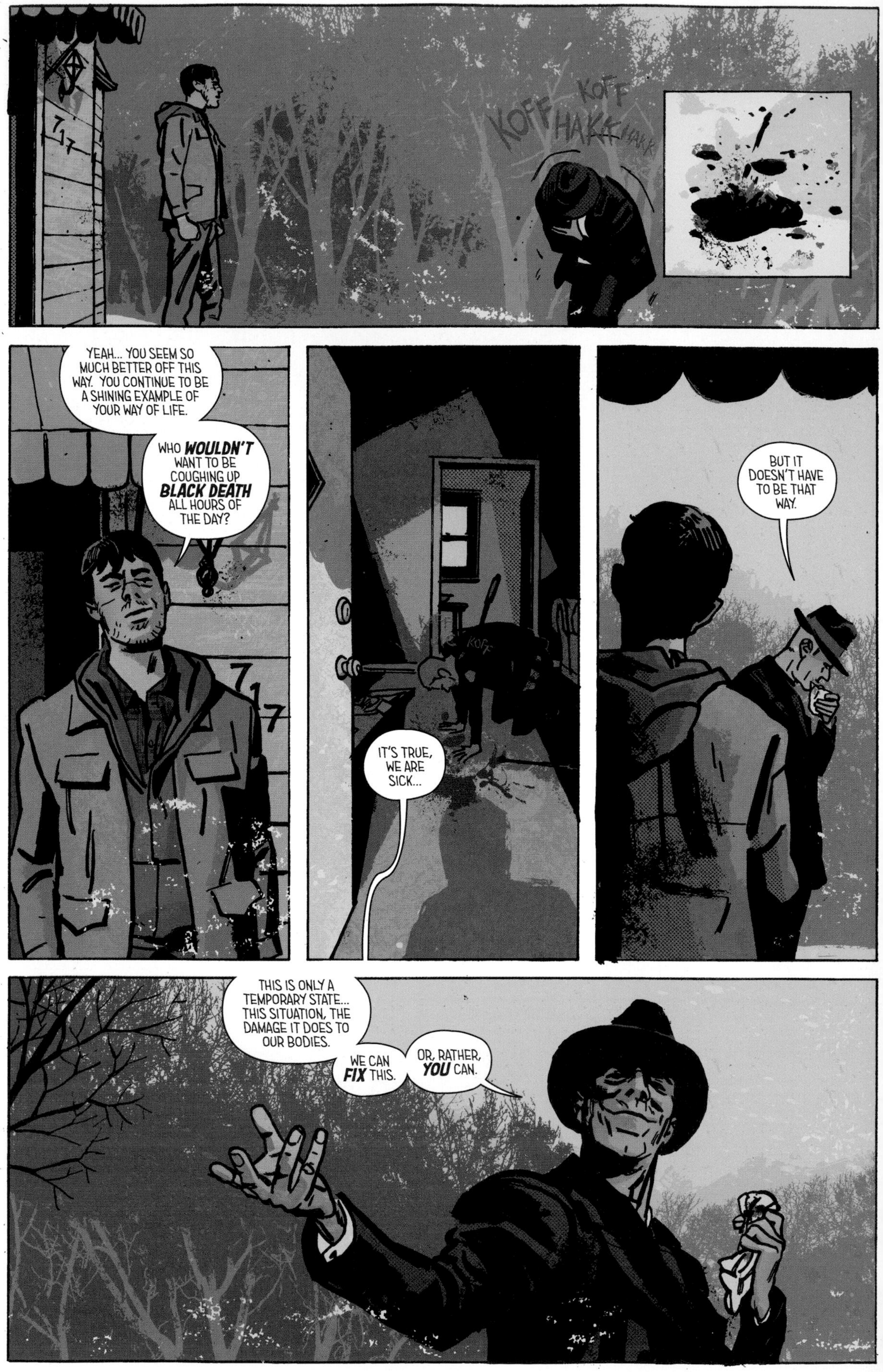
KOFF
KOFF
HAKK HAKK
YEAH... YOU SEEM SO MUCH BETTER OFF THIS WAY. YOU CONTINUE TO BE A SHINING EXAMPLE OF YOUR WAY OF LIFE.
WHO **WOULDN'T** WANT TO BE COUGHING UP **BLACK DEATH** ALL HOURS OF THE DAY?
KOFF
IT'S TRUE, WE ARE SICK...
BUT IT DOESN'T HAVE TO BE THAT WAY.
THIS IS ONLY A TEMPORARY STATE... THIS SITUATION, THE DAMAGE IT DOES TO OUR BODIES.
WE CAN **FIX** THIS.
OR, RATHER, **YOU** CAN.

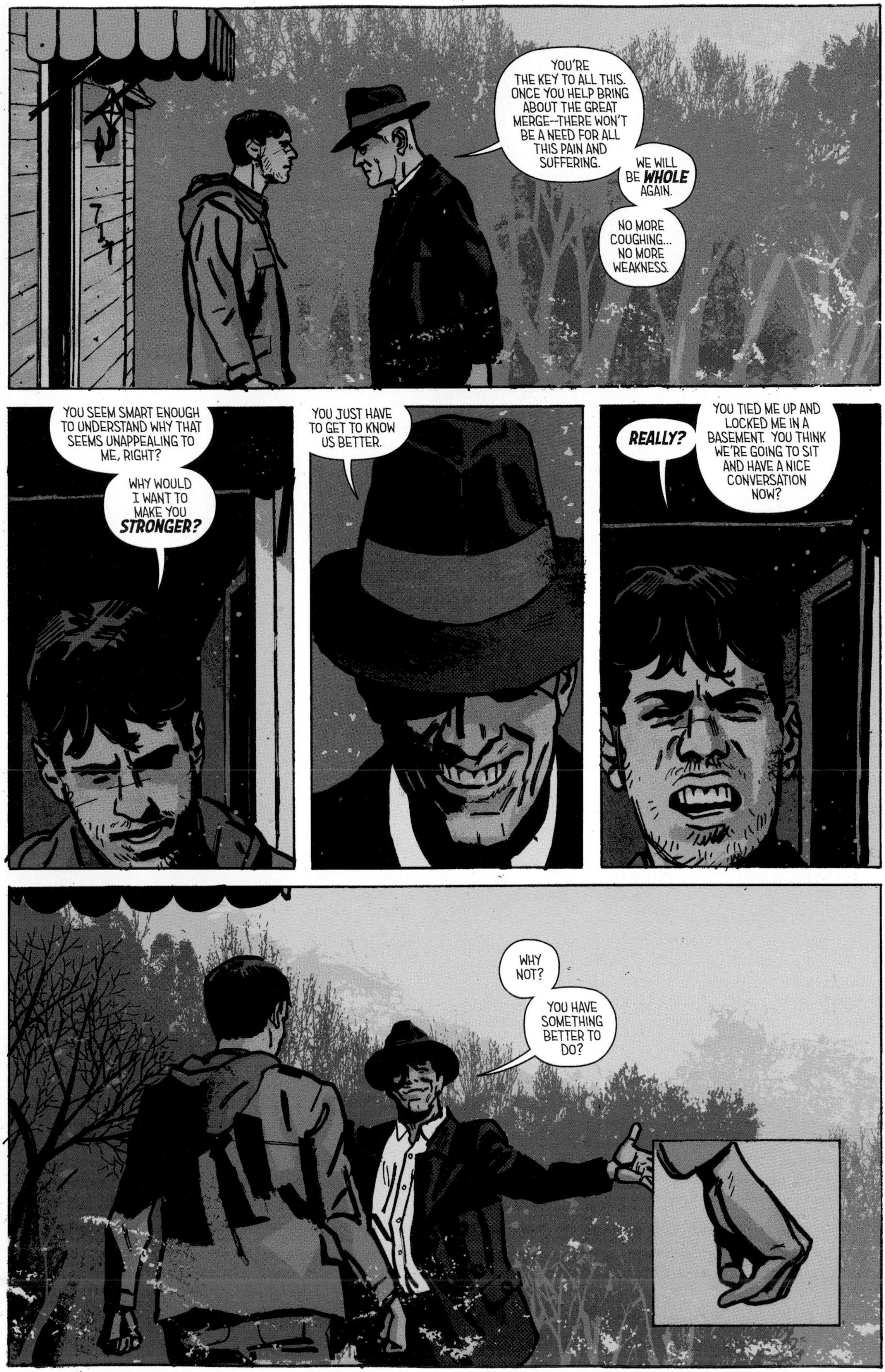
YOU'RE THE KEY TO ALL THIS. ONCE YOU HELP BRING ABOUT THE GREAT MERGE--THERE WON'T BE A NEED FOR ALL THIS PAIN AND SUFFERING.
WE WILL BE **WHOLE** AGAIN.
NO MORE COUGHING... NO MORE WEAKNESS.
YOU SEEM SMART ENOUGH TO UNDERSTAND WHY THAT SEEMS UNAPPEALING TO ME, RIGHT?
WHY WOULD I WANT TO MAKE YOU ***STRONGER?***
YOU JUST HAVE TO GET TO KNOW US BETTER.
REALLY?
YOU TIED ME UP AND LOCKED ME IN A BASEMENT. YOU THINK WE'RE GOING TO SIT AND HAVE A NICE CONVERSATION NOW?
WHY NOT?
YOU HAVE SOMETHING BETTER TO DO?

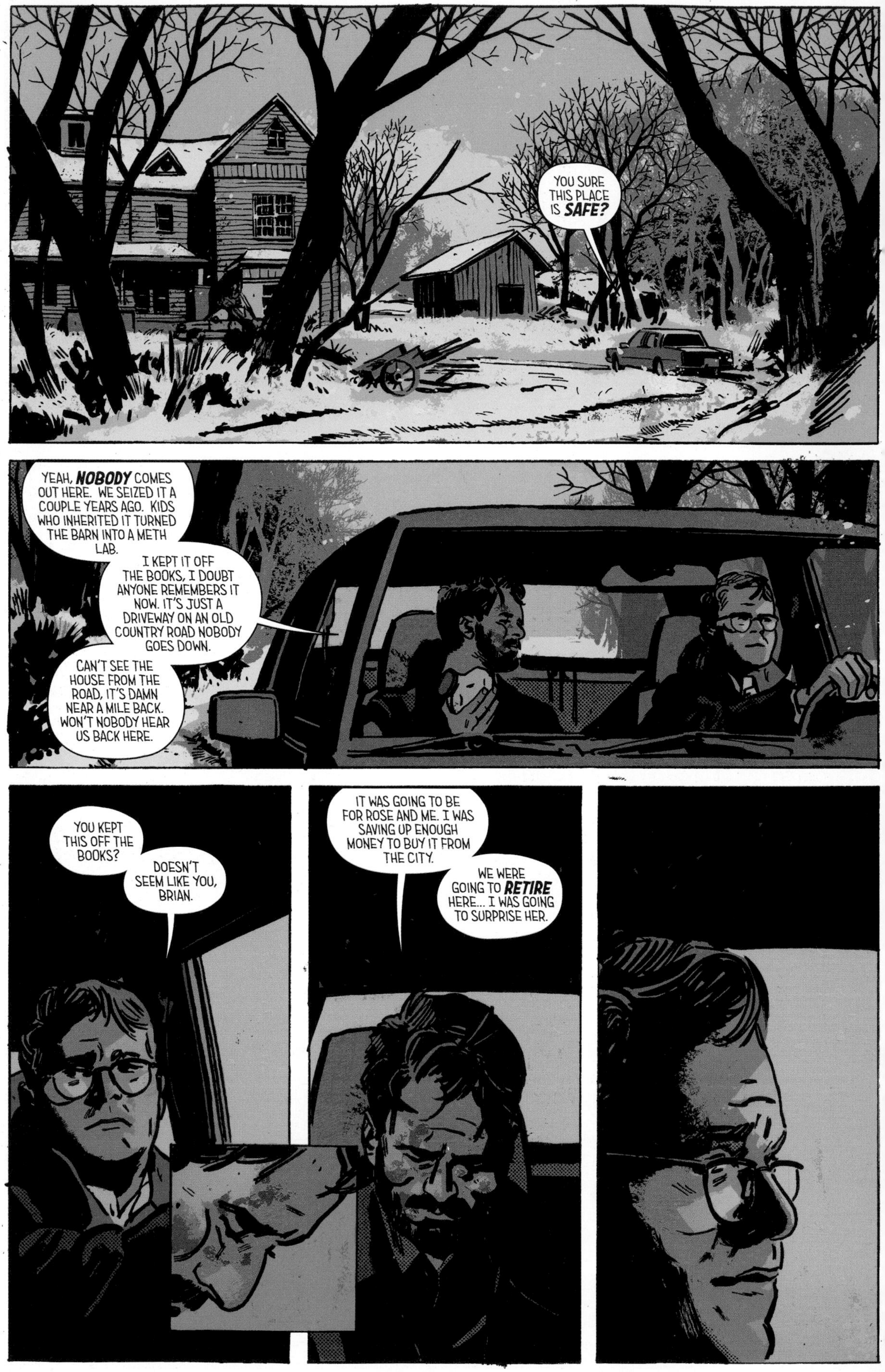
YOU SURE THIS PLACE IS SAFE?
YEAH, NOBODY COMES OUT HERE. WE SEIZED IT A COUPLE YEARS AGO. KIDS WHO INHERITED IT TURNED THE BARN INTO A METH LAB.
I KEPT IT OFF THE BOOKS, I DOUBT ANYONE REMEMBERS IT NOW. IT'S JUST A DRIVEWAY ON AN OLD COUNTRY ROAD NOBODY GOES DOWN.
CAN'T SEE THE HOUSE FROM THE ROAD, IT'S DAMN NEAR A MILE BACK. WON'T NOBODY HEAR US BACK HERE.
YOU KEPT THIS OFF THE BOOKS?
DOESN'T SEEM LIKE YOU, BRIAN.
IT WAS GOING TO BE FOR ROSE AND ME. I WAS SAVING UP ENOUGH MONEY TO BUY IT FROM THE CITY.
WE WERE GOING TO RETIRE HERE... I WAS GOING TO SURPRISE HER.

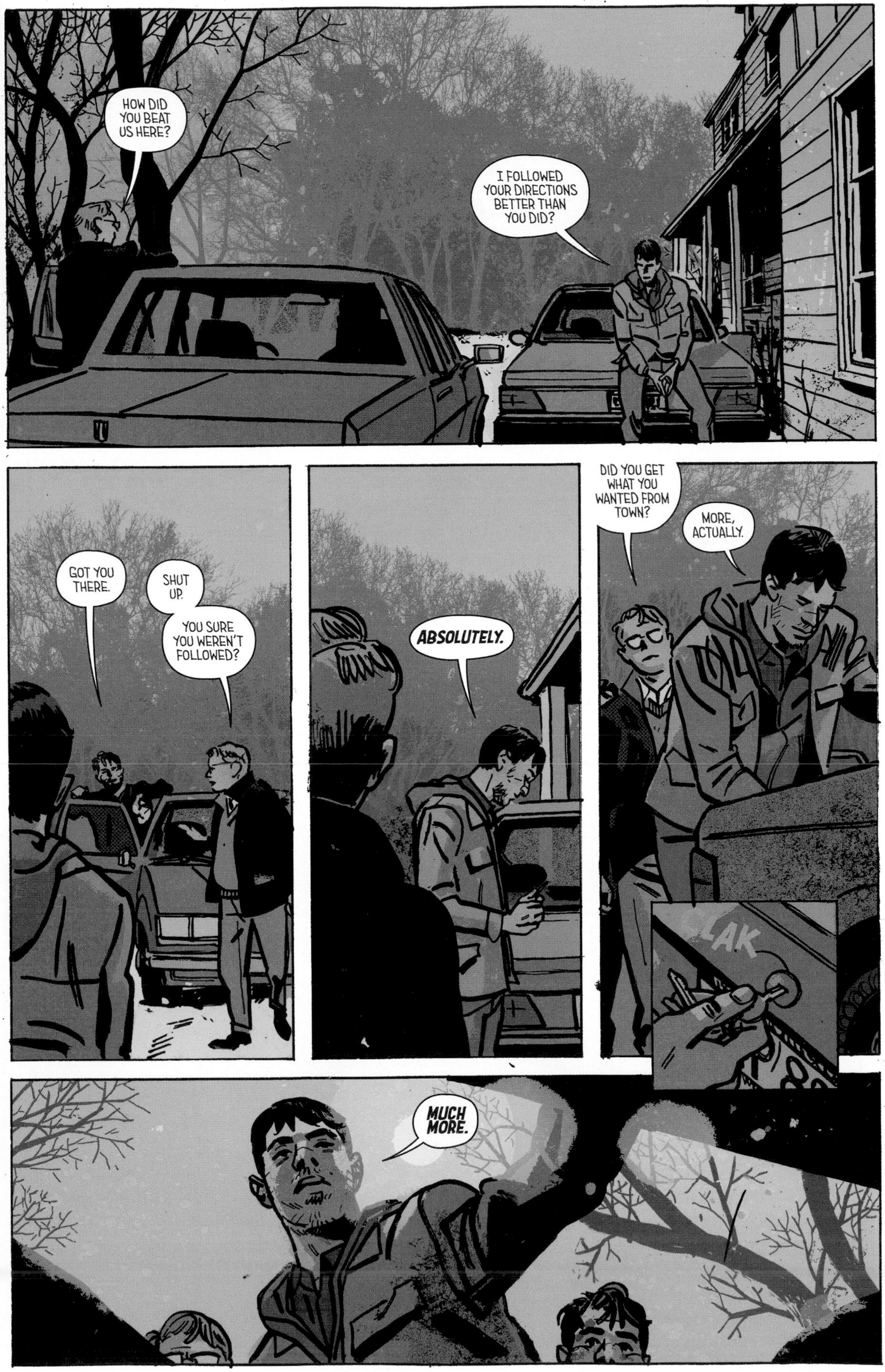
HOW DID YOU BEAT US HERE?
I FOLLOWED YOUR DIRECTIONS BETTER THAN YOU DID?
GOT YOU THERE.
SHUT UP.
YOU SURE YOU WEREN'T FOLLOWED?
ABSOLUTELY.
DID YOU GET WHAT YOU WANTED FROM TOWN?
MORE, ACTUALLY.
CLAK
MUCH MORE.

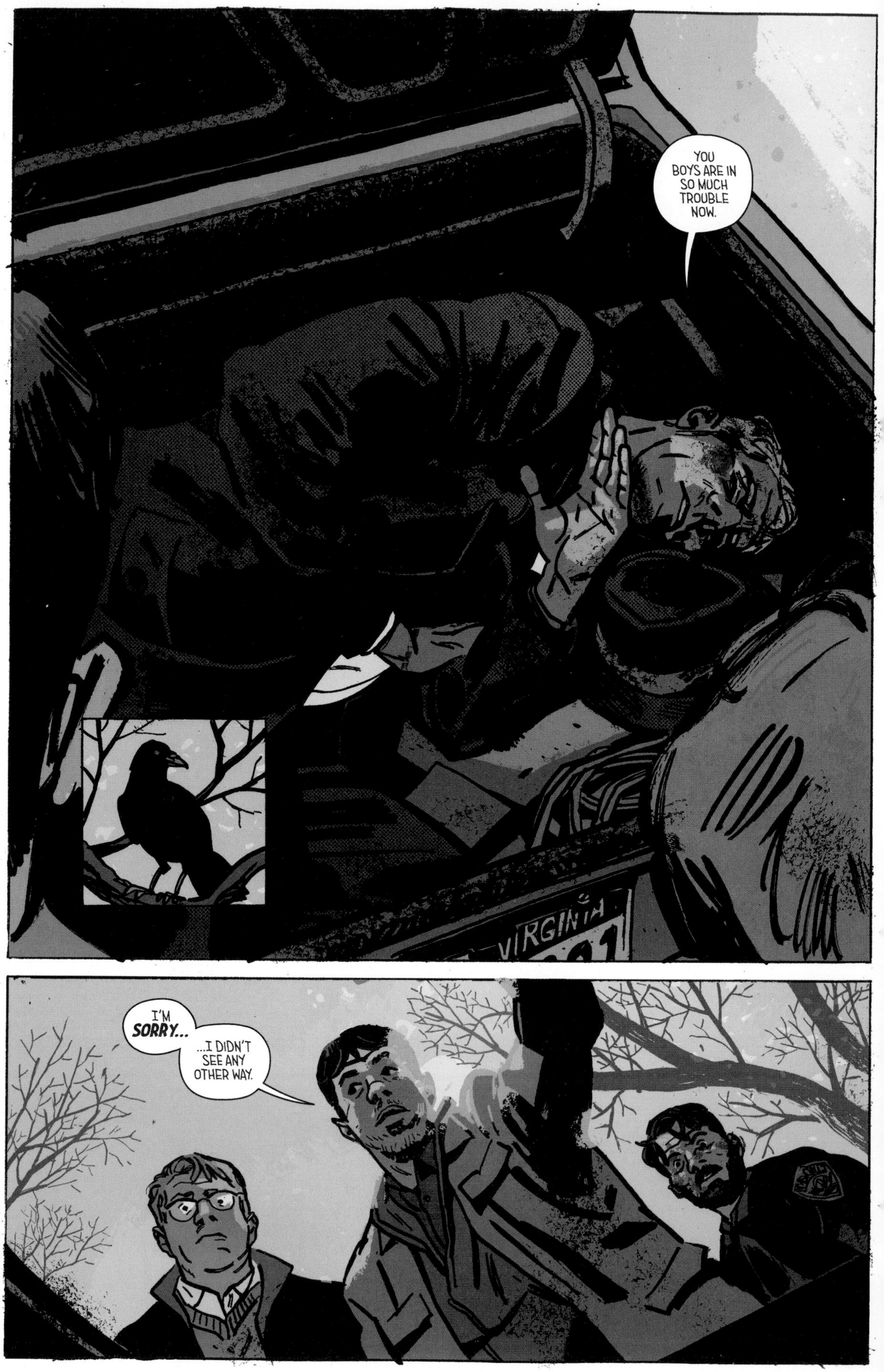
YOU BOYS ARE IN SO MUCH TROUBLE NOW.
VIRGINIA
I'M **SORRY...**
...I DIDN'T SEE ANY OTHER WAY.

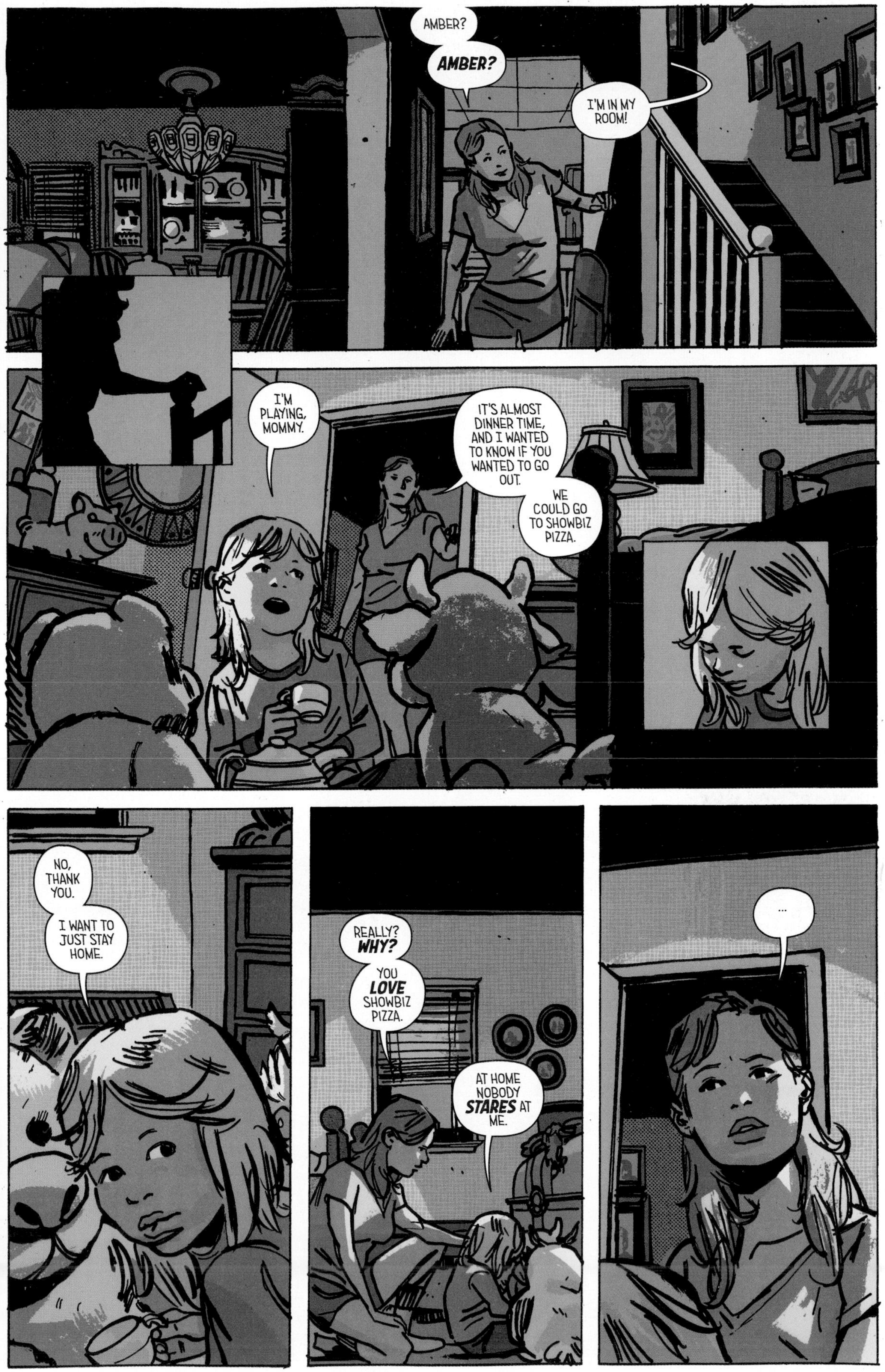
AMBER?
AMBER?
I'M IN MY ROOM!
I'M PLAYING, MOMMY.
IT'S ALMOST DINNER TIME, AND I WANTED TO KNOW IF YOU WANTED TO GO OUT.
WE COULD GO TO SHOWBIZ PIZZA.
NO, THANK YOU.
I WANT TO JUST STAY HOME.
REALLY? WHY?
YOU LOVE SHOWBIZ PIZZA.
AT HOME NOBODY STARES AT ME.
...

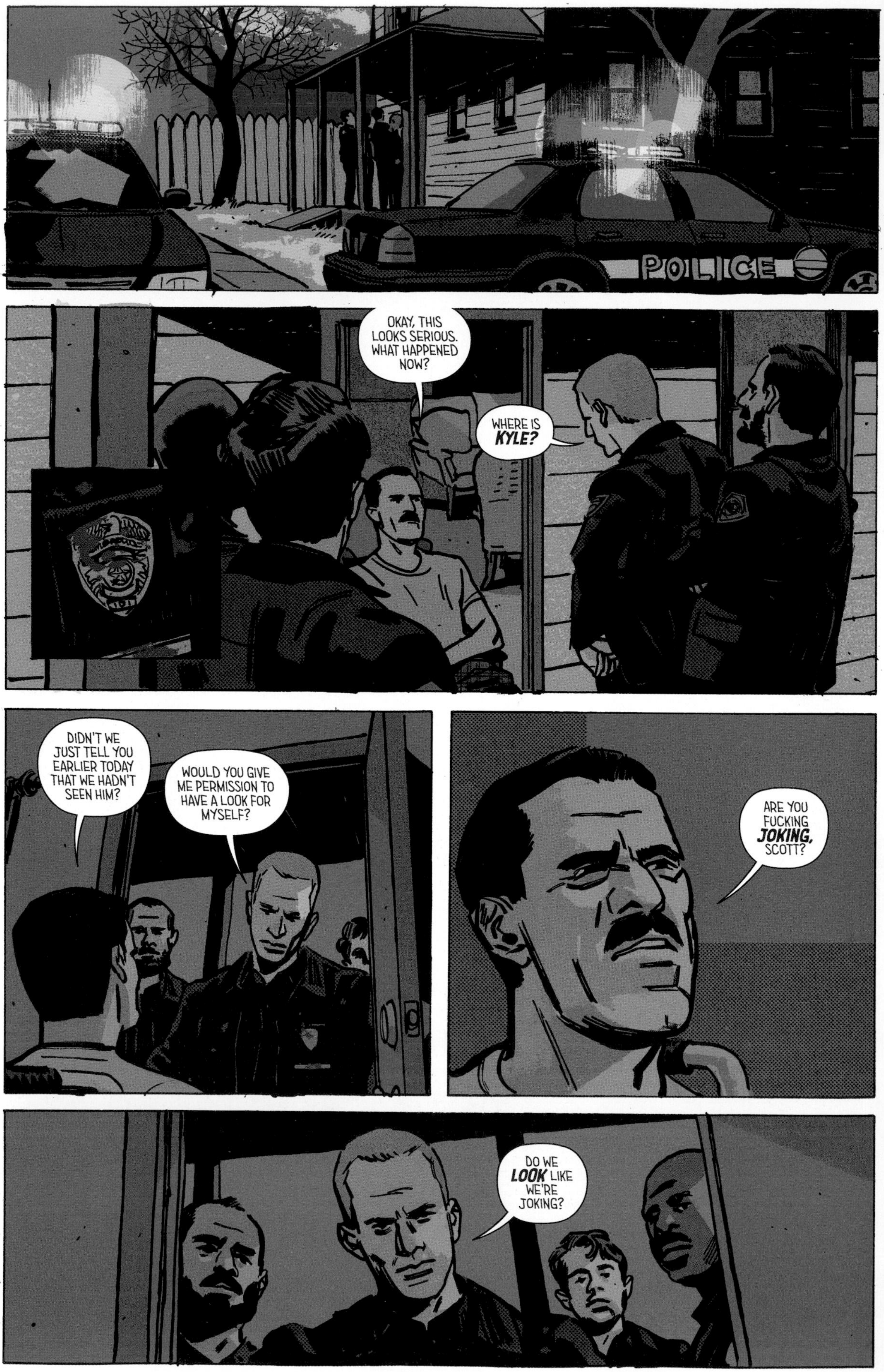
POLICE
OKAY, THIS LOOKS SERIOUS. WHAT HAPPENED NOW?
WHERE IS KYLE?
DIDN'T WE JUST TELL YOU EARLIER TODAY THAT WE HADN'T SEEN HIM?
WOULD YOU GIVE ME PERMISSION TO HAVE A LOOK FOR MYSELF?
ARE YOU FUCKING JOKING, SCOTT?
DO WE LOOK LIKE WE'RE JOKING?

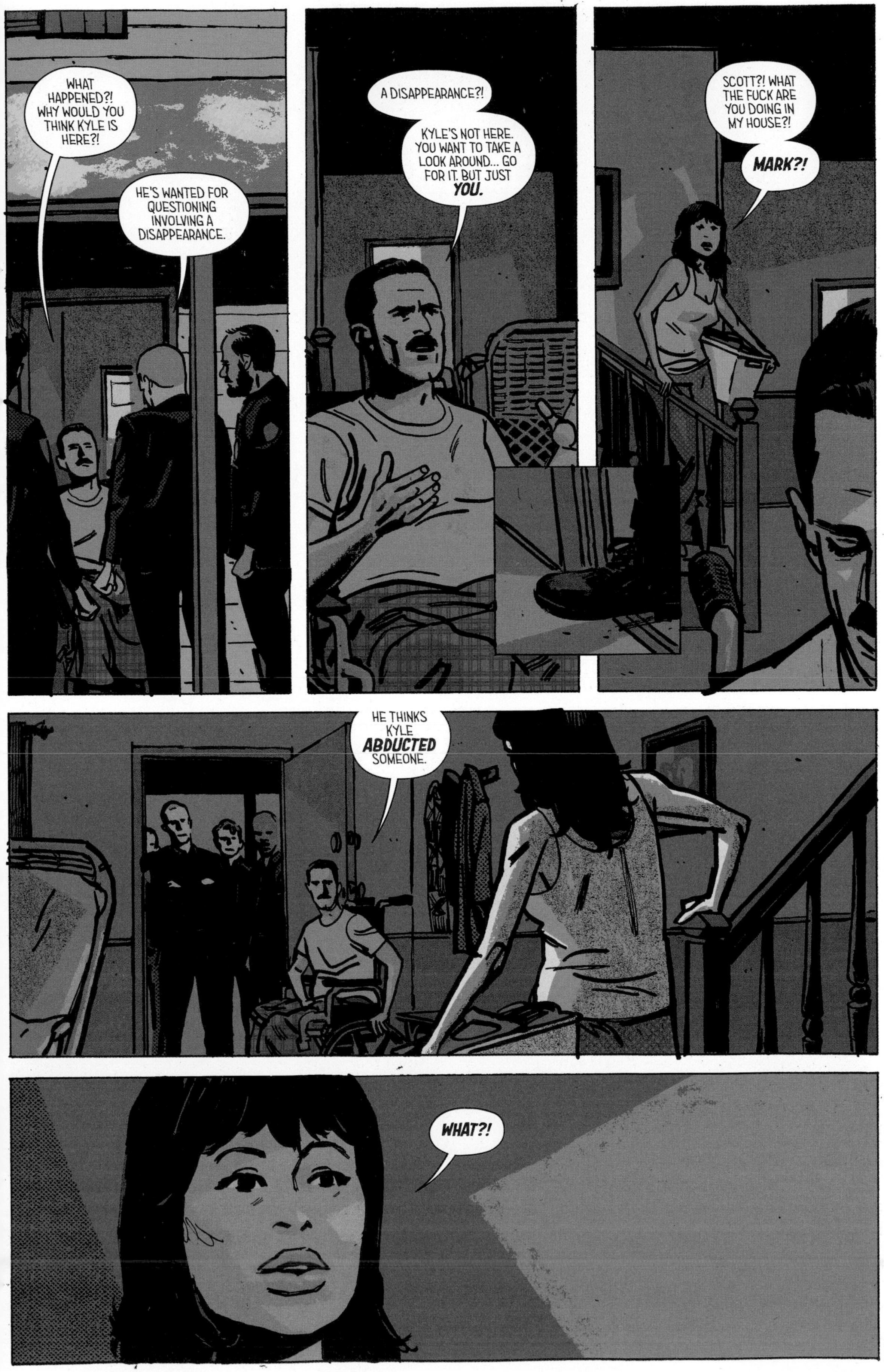
WHAT HAPPENED?! WHY WOULD YOU THINK KYLE IS HERE?!
HE'S WANTED FOR QUESTIONING INVOLVING A DISAPPEARANCE.
A DISAPPEARANCE?!
KYLE'S NOT HERE. YOU WANT TO TAKE A LOOK AROUND... GO FOR IT. BUT JUST YOU.
SCOTT?! WHAT THE FUCK ARE YOU DOING IN MY HOUSE?!
MARK?!
HE THINKS KYLE ABDUCTED SOMEONE.
WHAT?!

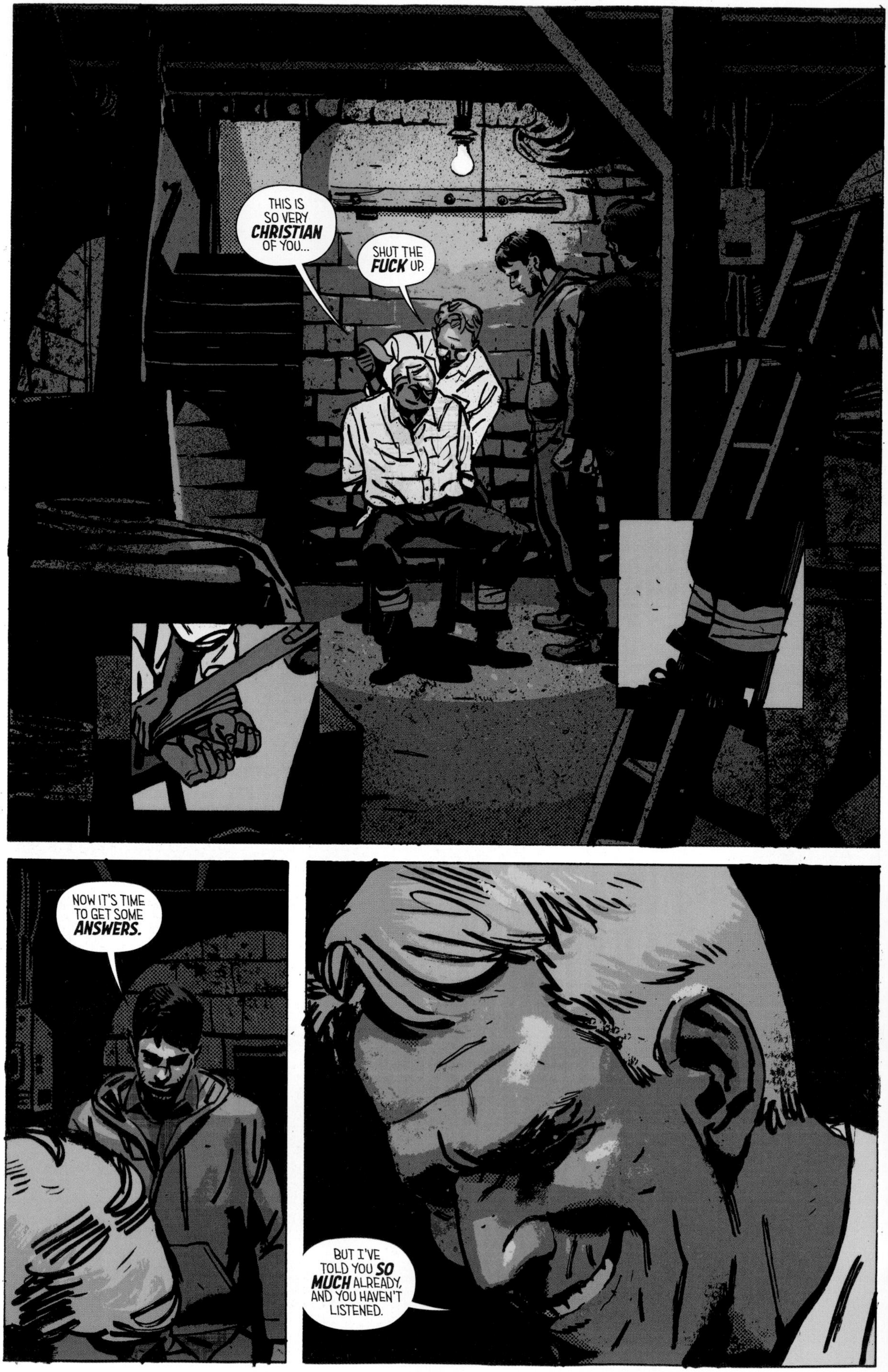
THIS IS SO VERY CHRISTIAN OF YOU...
SHUT THE FUCK UP.
NOW IT'S TIME TO GET SOME ANSWERS.
BUT I'VE TOLD YOU SO MUCH ALREADY, AND YOU HAVEN'T LISTENED.

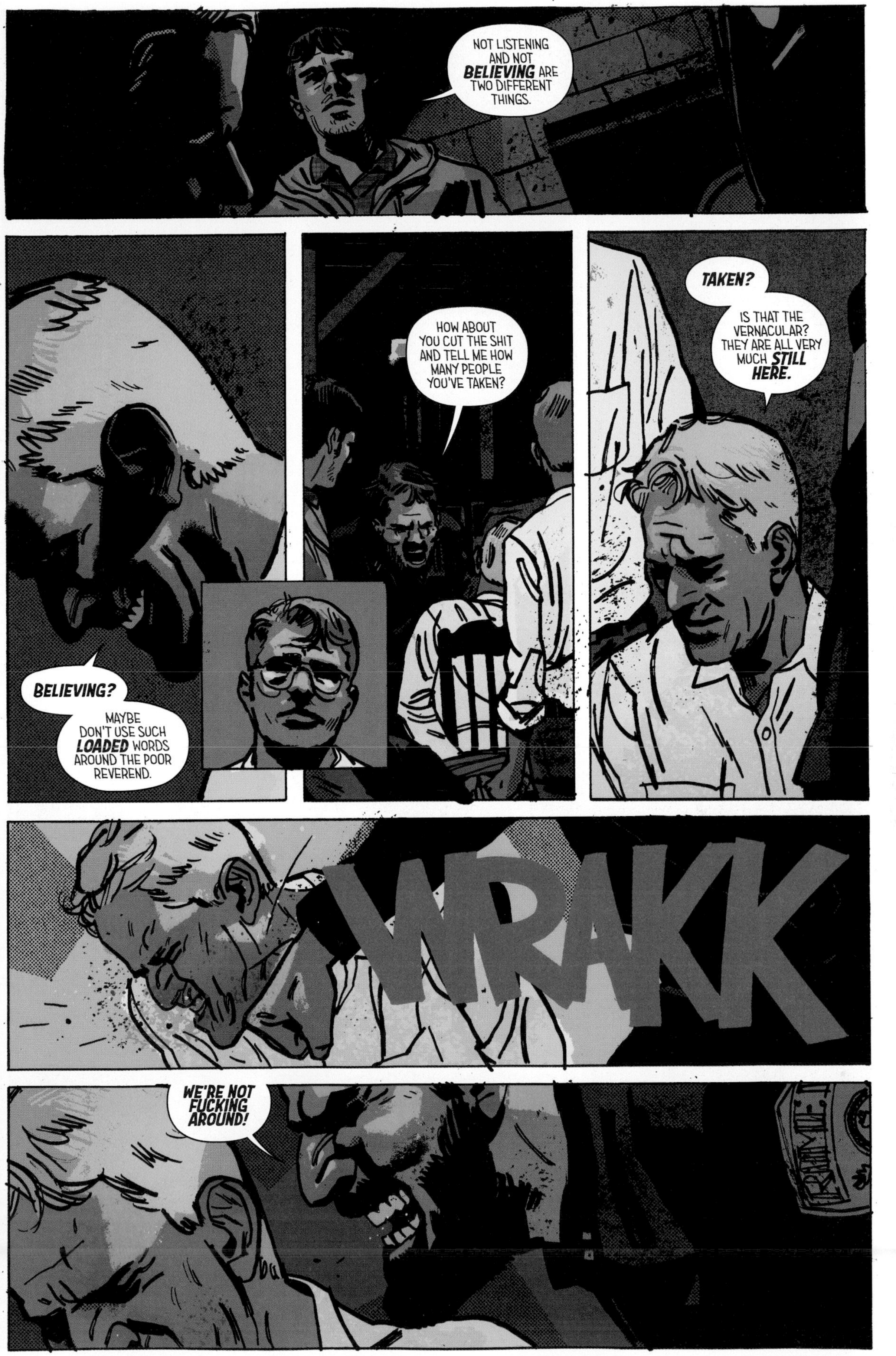
NOT LISTENING AND NOT BELIEVING ARE TWO DIFFERENT THINGS.
BELIEVING?
MAYBE DON'T USE SUCH LOADED WORDS AROUND THE POOR REVEREND.
HOW ABOUT YOU CUT THE SHIT AND TELL ME HOW MANY PEOPLE YOU'VE TAKEN?
TAKEN?
IS THAT THE VERNACULAR? THEY ARE ALL VERY MUCH STILL HERE.
WRAKK
WE'RE NOT FUCKING AROUND!

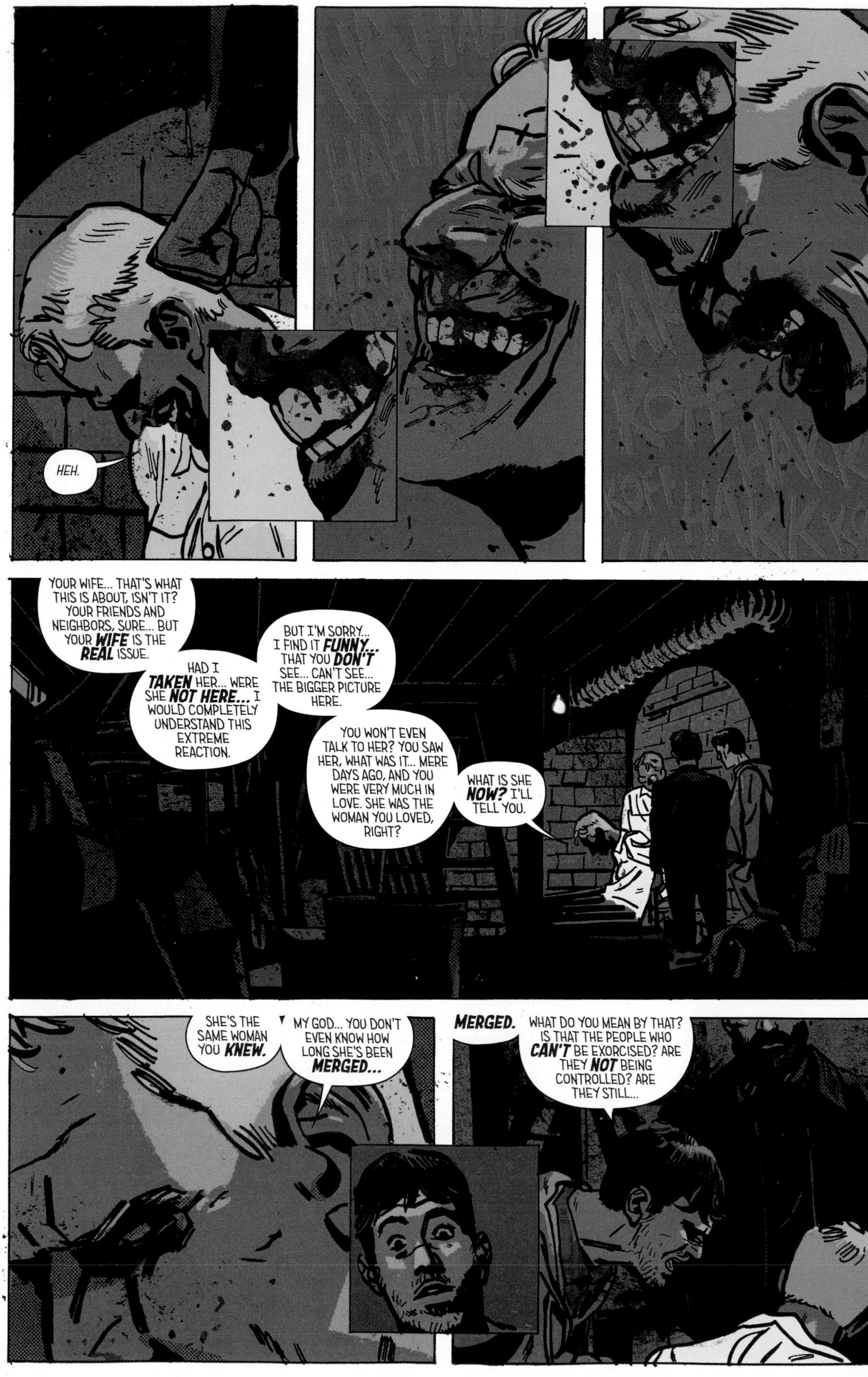
HEH.
HAH HAH
KOFF HAKK KOFF HAKK HAKK KOFF
YOUR WIFE... THAT'S WHAT THIS IS ABOUT, ISN'T IT? YOUR FRIENDS AND NEIGHBORS, SURE... BUT YOUR **WIFE** IS THE **REAL** ISSUE.
HAD I **TAKEN** HER... WERE SHE **NOT HERE...** I WOULD COMPLETELY UNDERSTAND THIS EXTREME REACTION.
BUT I'M SORRY... I FIND IT **FUNNY...** THAT YOU **DON'T** SEE... CAN'T SEE... THE BIGGER PICTURE HERE.
YOU WON'T EVEN TALK TO HER? YOU SAW HER, WHAT WAS IT... MERE DAYS AGO, AND YOU WERE VERY MUCH IN LOVE. SHE WAS THE WOMAN YOU LOVED, RIGHT?
WHAT IS SHE **NOW?** I'LL TELL YOU.
SHE'S THE SAME WOMAN YOU **KNEW.**
MY GOD... YOU DON'T EVEN KNOW HOW LONG SHE'S BEEN **MERGED...**
MERGED.
WHAT DO YOU MEAN BY THAT? IS THAT THE PEOPLE WHO **CAN'T** BE EXORCISED? ARE THEY **NOT** BEING CONTROLLED? ARE THEY STILL...

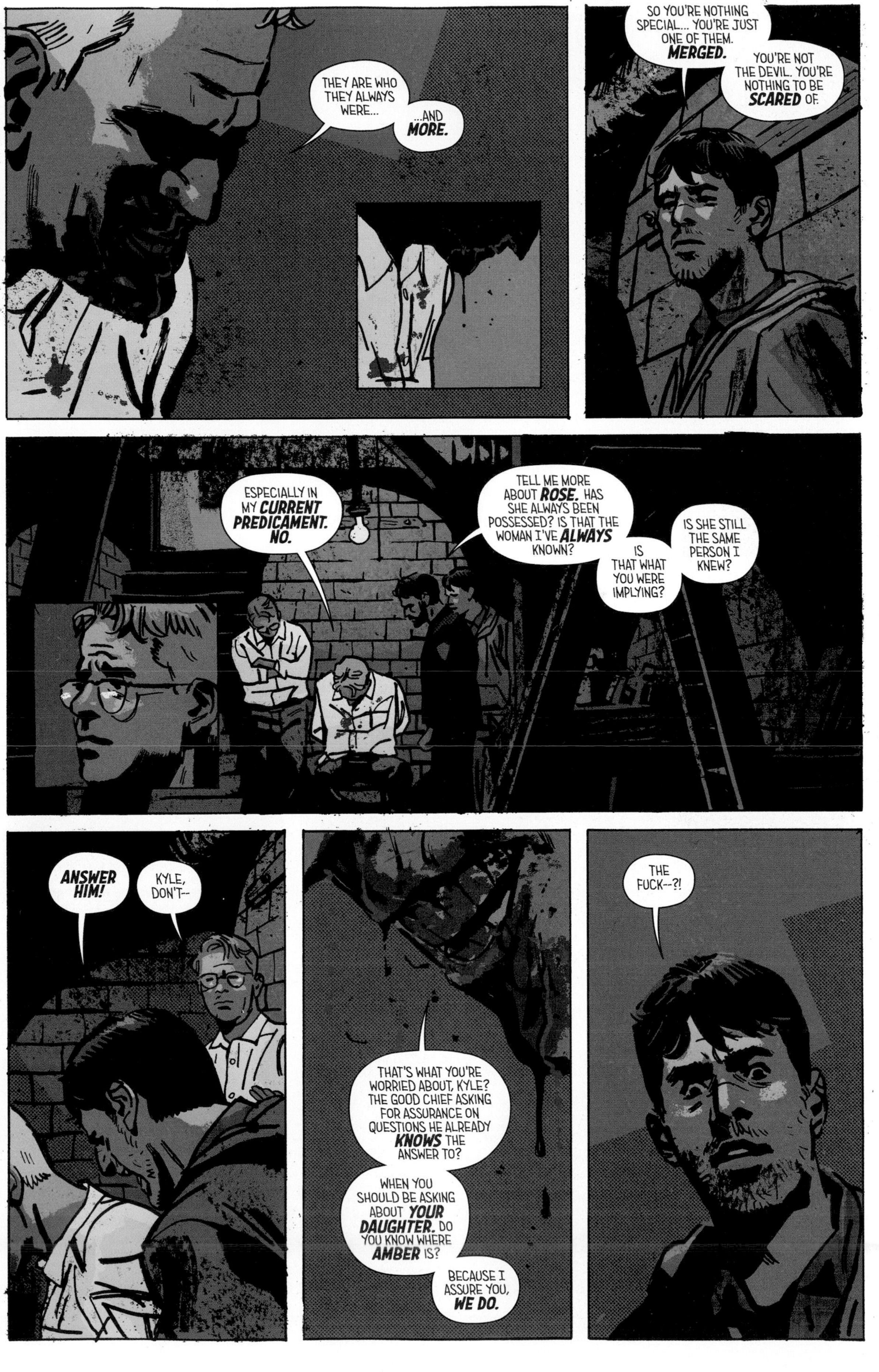
THEY ARE WHO THEY ALWAYS WERE...
...AND MORE.
SO YOU'RE NOTHING SPECIAL... YOU'RE JUST ONE OF THEM. MERGED.
YOU'RE NOT THE DEVIL. YOU'RE NOTHING TO BE SCARED OF.
ESPECIALLY IN MY CURRENT PREDICAMENT. NO.
TELL ME MORE ABOUT ROSE. HAS SHE ALWAYS BEEN POSSESSED? IS THAT THE WOMAN I'VE ALWAYS KNOWN?
IS THAT WHAT YOU WERE IMPLYING?
IS SHE STILL THE SAME PERSON I KNEW?
ANSWER HIM!
KYLE, DON'T--
THAT'S WHAT YOU'RE WORRIED ABOUT, KYLE? THE GOOD CHIEF ASKING FOR ASSURANCE ON QUESTIONS HE ALREADY KNOWS THE ANSWER TO?
WHEN YOU SHOULD BE ASKING ABOUT YOUR DAUGHTER. DO YOU KNOW WHERE AMBER IS?
BECAUSE I ASSURE YOU, WE DO.
THE FUCK--?!

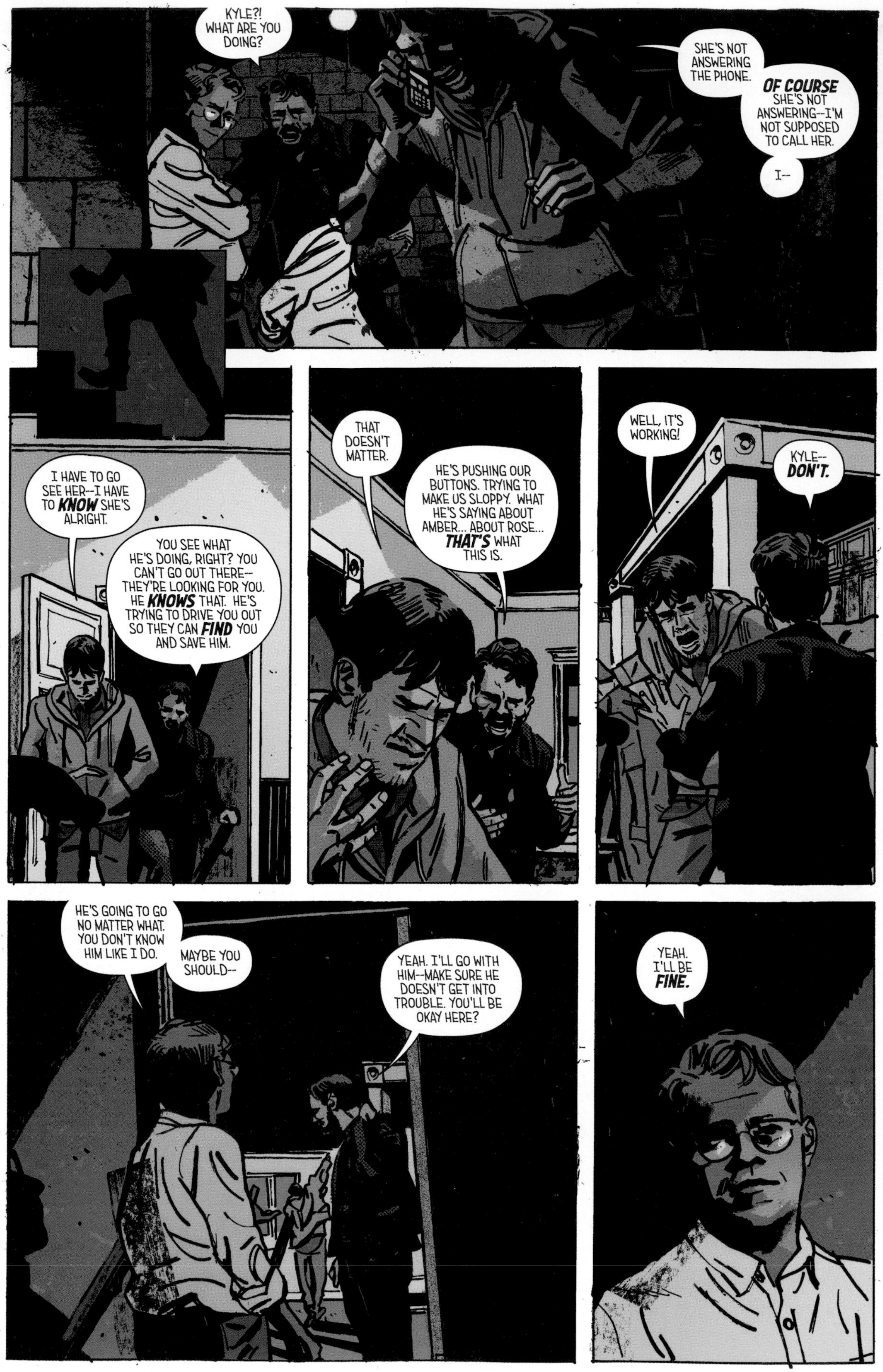
KYLE?! WHAT ARE YOU DOING?
SHE'S NOT ANSWERING THE PHONE.
OF COURSE SHE'S NOT ANSWERING--I'M NOT SUPPOSED TO CALL HER.
I--
I HAVE TO GO SEE HER--I HAVE TO KNOW SHE'S ALRIGHT.
YOU SEE WHAT HE'S DOING, RIGHT? YOU CAN'T GO OUT THERE--THEY'RE LOOKING FOR YOU. HE KNOWS THAT. HE'S TRYING TO DRIVE YOU OUT SO THEY CAN FIND YOU AND SAVE HIM.
THAT DOESN'T MATTER.
HE'S PUSHING OUR BUTTONS. TRYING TO MAKE US SLOPPY. WHAT HE'S SAYING ABOUT AMBER... ABOUT ROSE... THAT'S WHAT THIS IS.
WELL, IT'S WORKING!
KYLE-- DON'T.
HE'S GOING TO GO NO MATTER WHAT. YOU DON'T KNOW HIM LIKE I DO.
MAYBE YOU SHOULD--
YEAH. I'LL GO WITH HIM--MAKE SURE HE DOESN'T GET INTO TROUBLE. YOU'LL BE OKAY HERE?
YEAH. I'LL BE FINE.

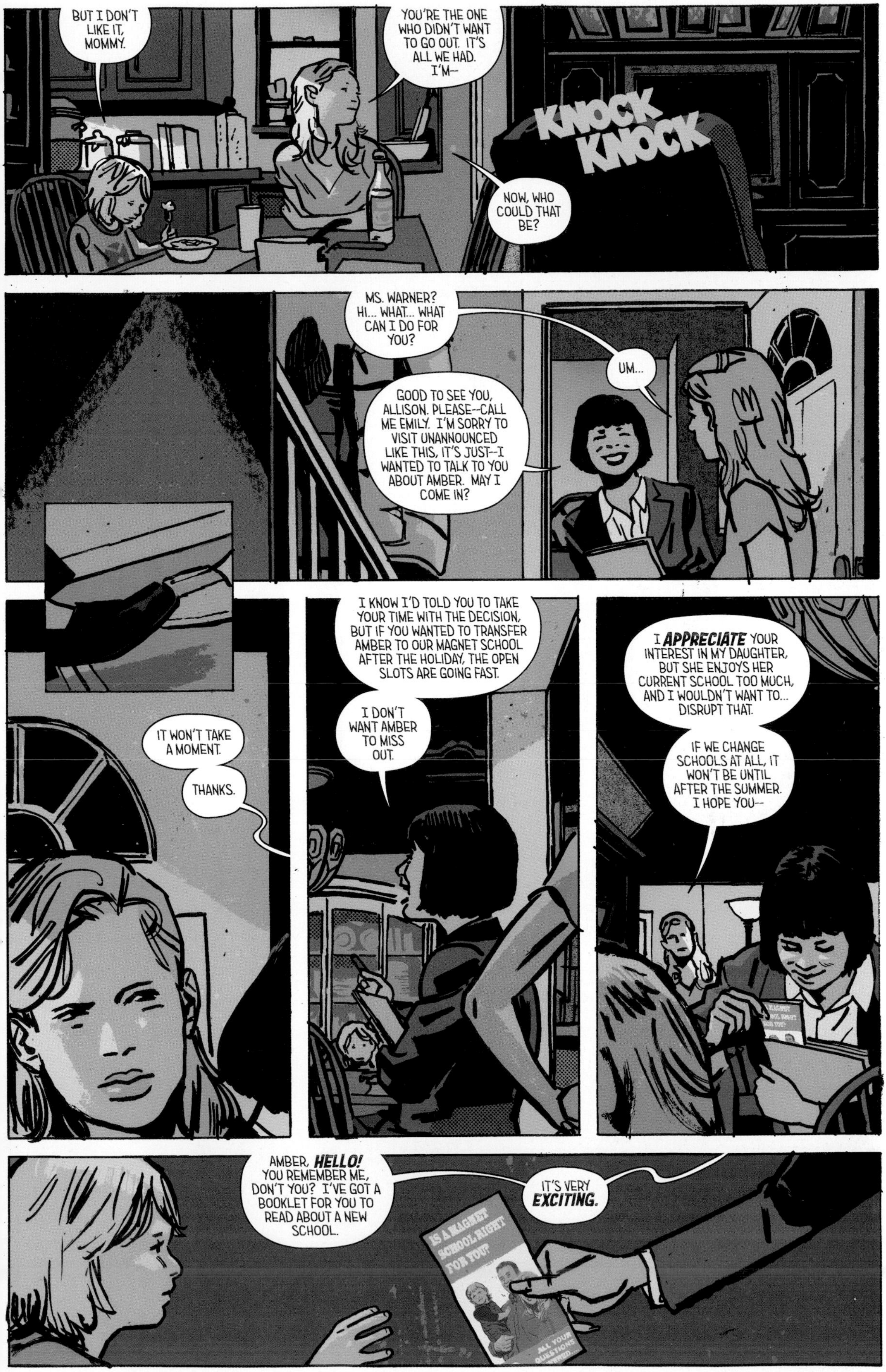
BUT I DON'T LIKE IT, MOMMY.
YOU'RE THE ONE WHO DIDN'T WANT TO GO OUT. IT'S ALL WE HAD. I'M--
KNOCK KNOCK
NOW, WHO COULD THAT BE?
MS. WARNER? HI... WHAT... WHAT CAN I DO FOR YOU?
UM...
GOOD TO SEE YOU, ALLISON. PLEASE--CALL ME EMILY. I'M SORRY TO VISIT UNANNOUNCED LIKE THIS, IT'S JUST--I WANTED TO TALK TO YOU ABOUT AMBER. MAY I COME IN?
IT WON'T TAKE A MOMENT.
THANKS.
I KNOW I'D TOLD YOU TO TAKE YOUR TIME WITH THE DECISION, BUT IF YOU WANTED TO TRANSFER AMBER TO OUR MAGNET SCHOOL AFTER THE HOLIDAY, THE OPEN SLOTS ARE GOING FAST.
I DON'T WANT AMBER TO MISS OUT.
I APPRECIATE YOUR INTEREST IN MY DAUGHTER, BUT SHE ENJOYS HER CURRENT SCHOOL TOO MUCH, AND I WOULDN'T WANT TO... DISRUPT THAT.
IF WE CHANGE SCHOOLS AT ALL, IT WON'T BE UNTIL AFTER THE SUMMER. I HOPE YOU--
AMBER, HELLO! YOU REMEMBER ME, DON'T YOU? I'VE GOT A BOOKLET FOR YOU TO READ ABOUT A NEW SCHOOL.
IT'S VERY EXCITING.
IS A MAGNET SCHOOL RIGHT FOR YOU?
ALL YOUR QUESTIONS

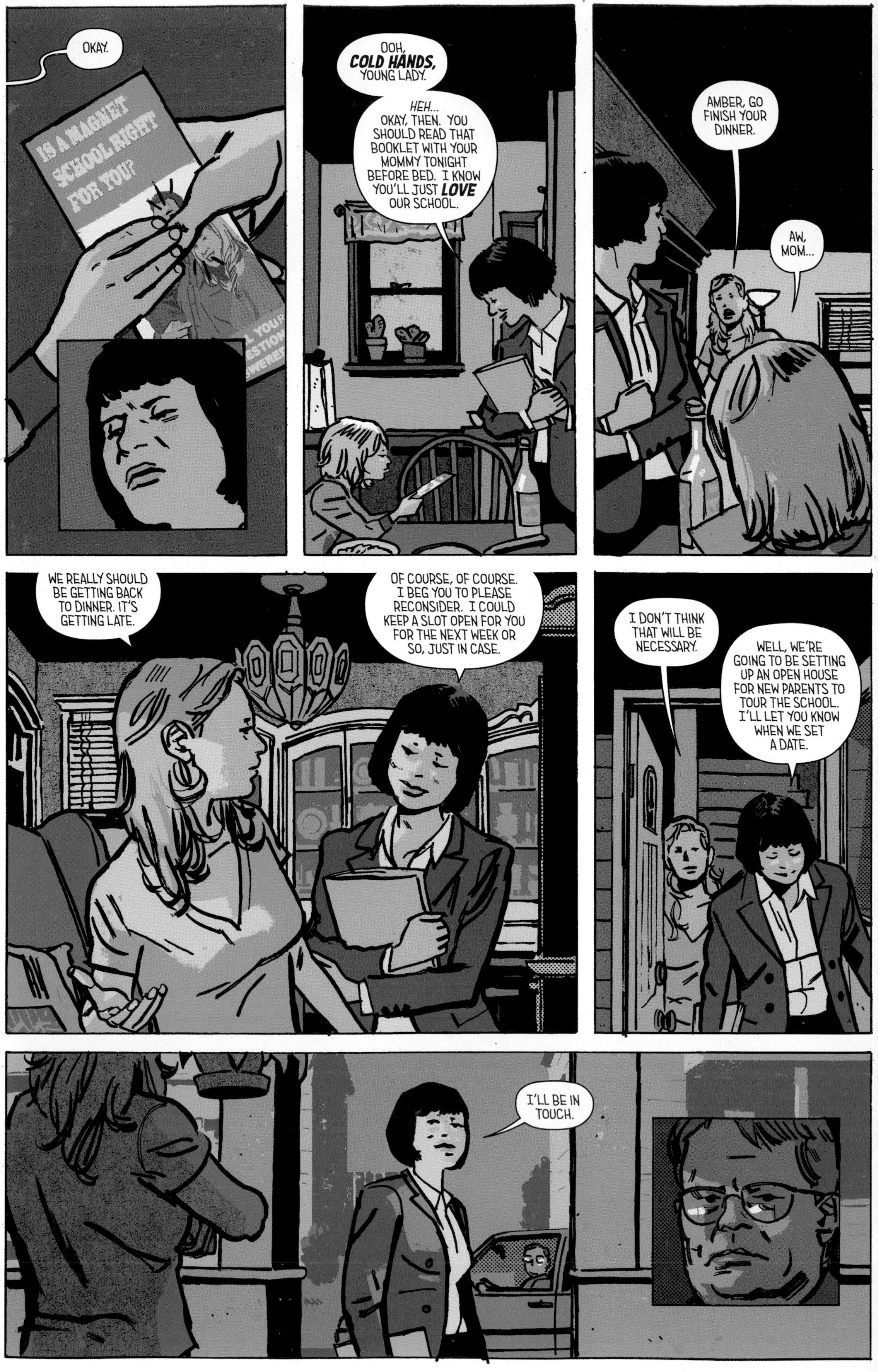

OKAY.
IS A MAGNET SCHOOL RIGHT FOR YOU?
OOH, **COLD HANDS,** YOUNG LADY.
HEH... OKAY, THEN. YOU SHOULD READ THAT BOOKLET WITH YOUR MOMMY TONIGHT BEFORE BED. I KNOW YOU'LL JUST **LOVE** OUR SCHOOL.
AMBER, GO FINISH YOUR DINNER.
AW, MOM...
WE REALLY SHOULD BE GETTING BACK TO DINNER. IT'S GETTING LATE.
OF COURSE, OF COURSE. I BEG YOU TO PLEASE RECONSIDER. I COULD KEEP A SLOT OPEN FOR YOU FOR THE NEXT WEEK OR SO, JUST IN CASE.
I DON'T THINK THAT WILL BE NECESSARY.
WELL, WE'RE GOING TO BE SETTING UP AN OPEN HOUSE FOR NEW PARENTS TO TOUR THE SCHOOL. I'LL LET YOU KNOW WHEN WE SET A DATE.
I'LL BE IN TOUCH.

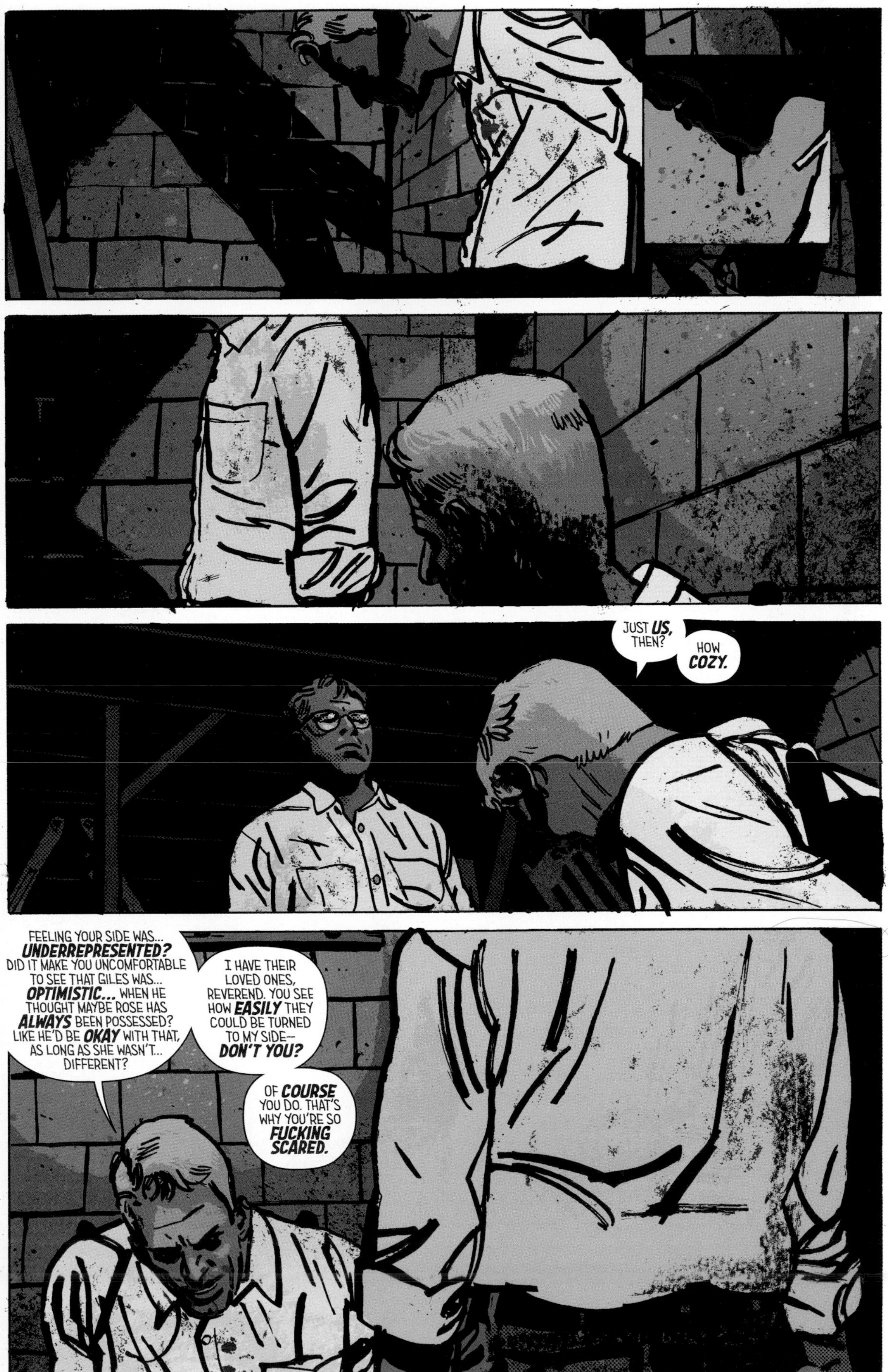
JUST US, THEN?
HOW COZY.
FEELING YOUR SIDE WAS... UNDERREPRESENTED? DID IT MAKE YOU UNCOMFORTABLE TO SEE THAT GILES WAS... OPTIMISTIC... WHEN HE THOUGHT MAYBE ROSE HAS ALWAYS BEEN POSSESSED? LIKE HE'D BE OKAY WITH THAT, AS LONG AS SHE WASN'T... DIFFERENT?
I HAVE THEIR LOVED ONES, REVEREND. YOU SEE HOW EASILY THEY COULD BE TURNED TO MY SIDE-- DON'T YOU?
OF COURSE YOU DO. THAT'S WHY YOU'RE SO FUCKING SCARED.

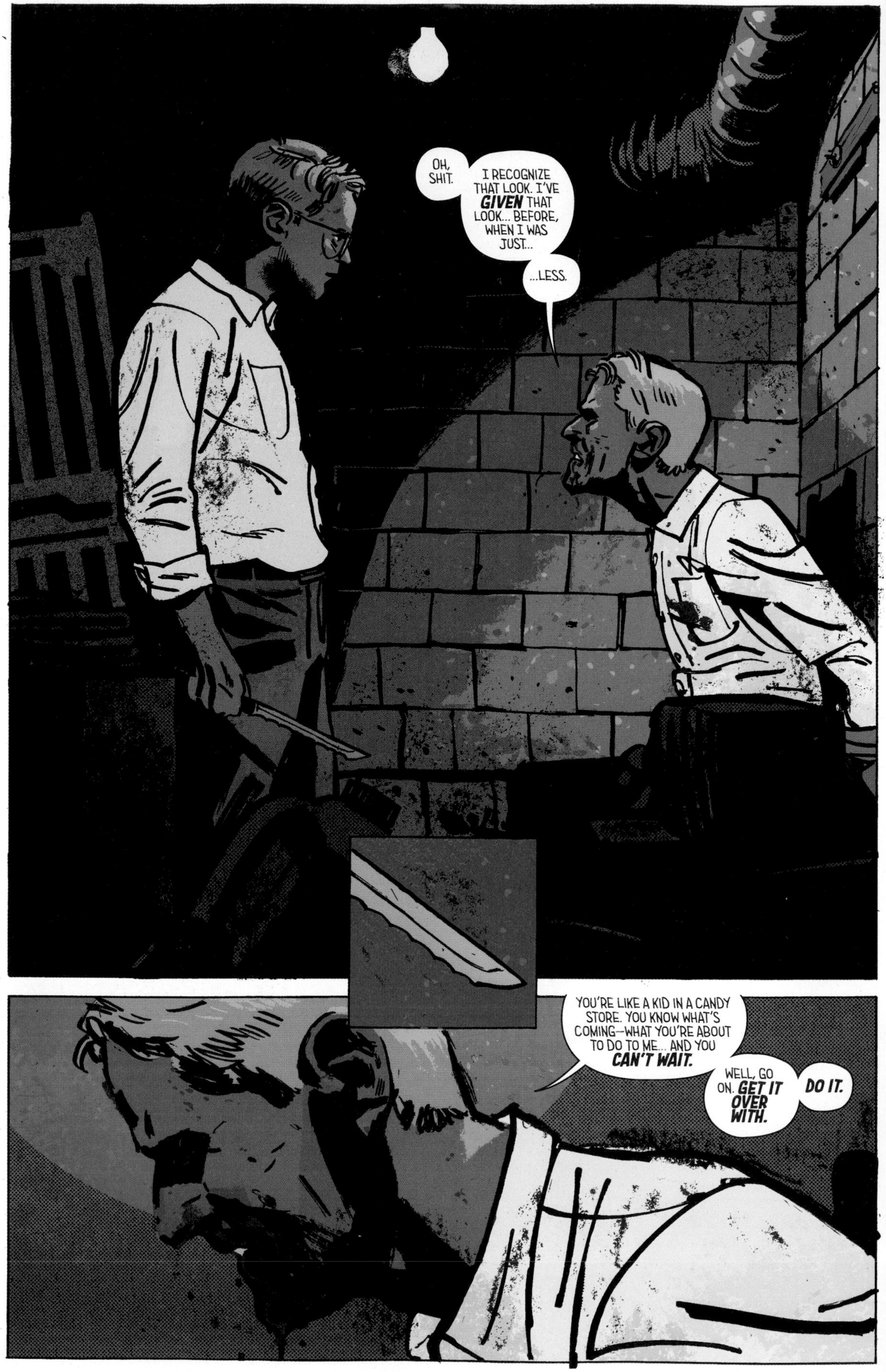
OH, SHIT.
I RECOGNIZE THAT LOOK. I'VE **GIVEN** THAT LOOK... BEFORE, WHEN I WAS JUST...
...LESS.
YOU'RE LIKE A KID IN A CANDY STORE. YOU KNOW WHAT'S COMING--WHAT YOU'RE ABOUT TO DO TO ME... AND YOU **CAN'T WAIT.**
WELL, GO ON. **GET IT OVER WITH.**
DO IT.

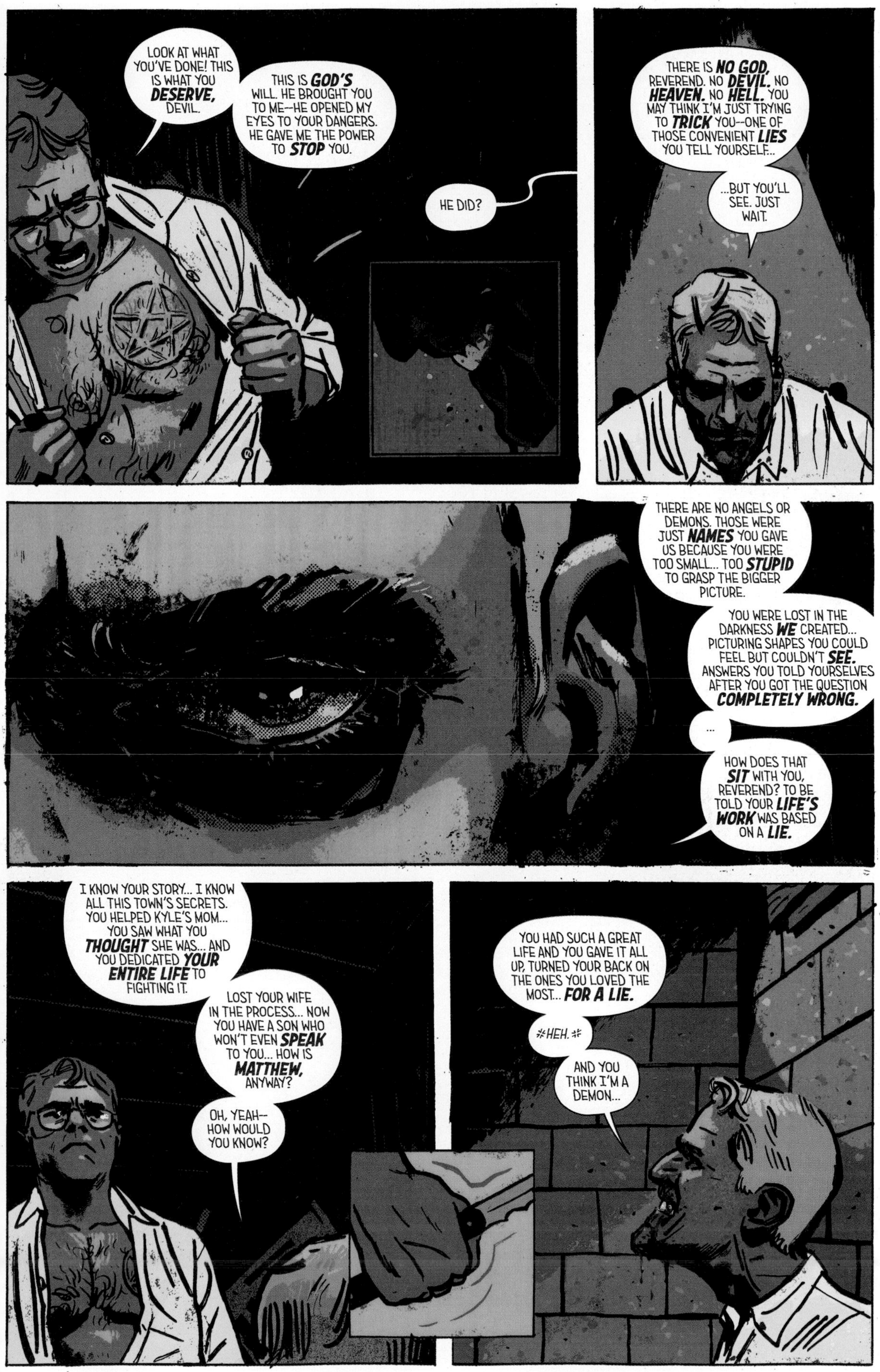
LOOK AT WHAT YOU'VE DONE! THIS IS WHAT YOU DESERVE, DEVIL.
THIS IS GOD'S WILL. HE BROUGHT YOU TO ME--HE OPENED MY EYES TO YOUR DANGERS. HE GAVE ME THE POWER TO STOP YOU.
HE DID?
THERE IS NO GOD, REVEREND. NO DEVIL. NO HEAVEN. NO HELL. YOU MAY THINK I'M JUST TRYING TO TRICK YOU--ONE OF THOSE CONVENIENT LIES YOU TELL YOURSELF...
...BUT YOU'LL SEE. JUST WAIT.
THERE ARE NO ANGELS OR DEMONS. THOSE WERE JUST NAMES YOU GAVE US BECAUSE YOU WERE TOO SMALL... TOO STUPID TO GRASP THE BIGGER PICTURE.
YOU WERE LOST IN THE DARKNESS WE CREATED... PICTURING SHAPES YOU COULD FEEL BUT COULDN'T SEE. ANSWERS YOU TOLD YOURSELVES AFTER YOU GOT THE QUESTION COMPLETELY WRONG.
...
HOW DOES THAT SIT WITH YOU, REVEREND? TO BE TOLD YOUR LIFE'S WORK WAS BASED ON A LIE.
I KNOW YOUR STORY... I KNOW ALL THIS TOWN'S SECRETS. YOU HELPED KYLE'S MOM... YOU SAW WHAT YOU THOUGHT SHE WAS... AND YOU DEDICATED YOUR ENTIRE LIFE TO FIGHTING IT.
LOST YOUR WIFE IN THE PROCESS... NOW YOU HAVE A SON WHO WON'T EVEN SPEAK TO YOU... HOW IS MATTHEW, ANYWAY?
OH, YEAH-- HOW WOULD YOU KNOW?
YOU HAD SUCH A GREAT LIFE AND YOU GAVE IT ALL UP, TURNED YOUR BACK ON THE ONES YOU LOVED THE MOST... FOR A LIE.
HEH.
AND YOU THINK I'M A DEMON...

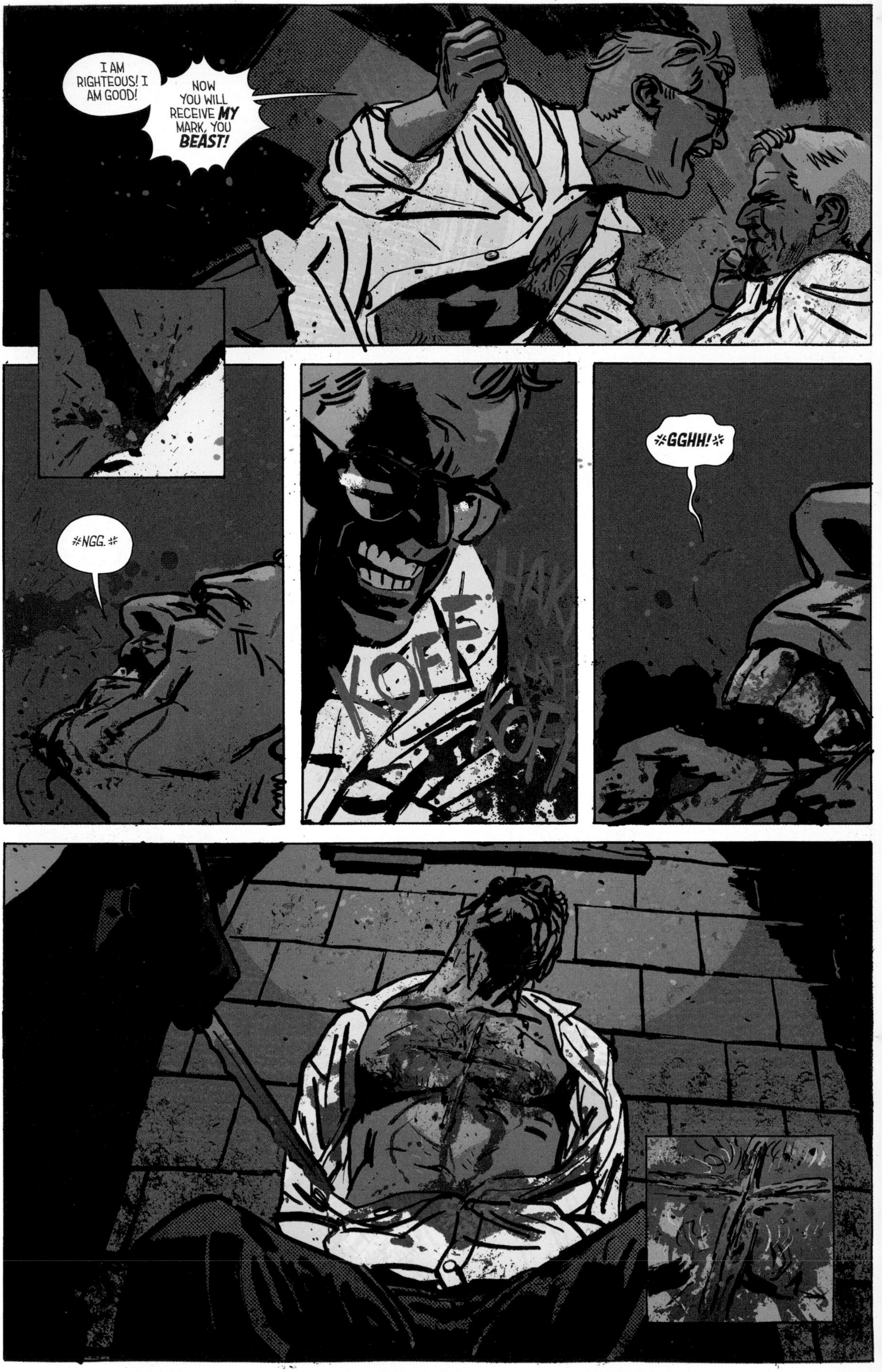
I AM RIGHTEOUS! I AM GOOD!
NOW YOU WILL RECEIVE **MY** MARK, YOU **BEAST!**
#NGG.#
KOFF
KOFF
#GGHH!#

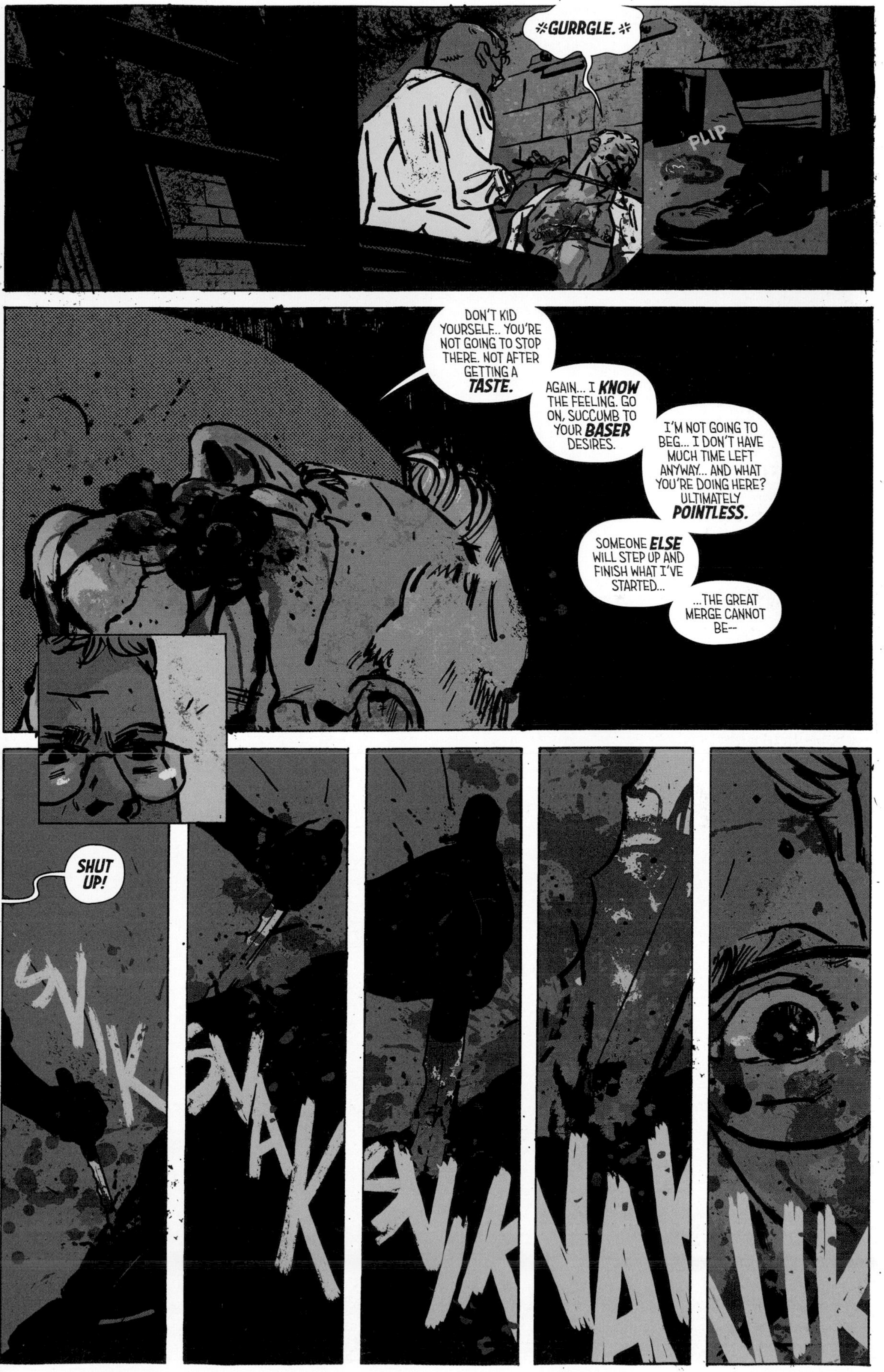
GURRGLE.
PLIP
DON'T KID YOURSELF... YOU'RE NOT GOING TO STOP THERE. NOT AFTER GETTING A TASTE.
AGAIN... I KNOW THE FEELING. GO ON, SUCCUMB TO YOUR BASER DESIRES.
I'M NOT GOING TO BEG... I DON'T HAVE MUCH TIME LEFT ANYWAY... AND WHAT YOU'RE DOING HERE? ULTIMATELY POINTLESS.
SOMEONE ELSE WILL STEP UP AND FINISH WHAT I'VE STARTED...
...THE GREAT MERGE CANNOT BE--
SHUT UP!
SNIK
SNAK
SNAK
SNAK
SNIK

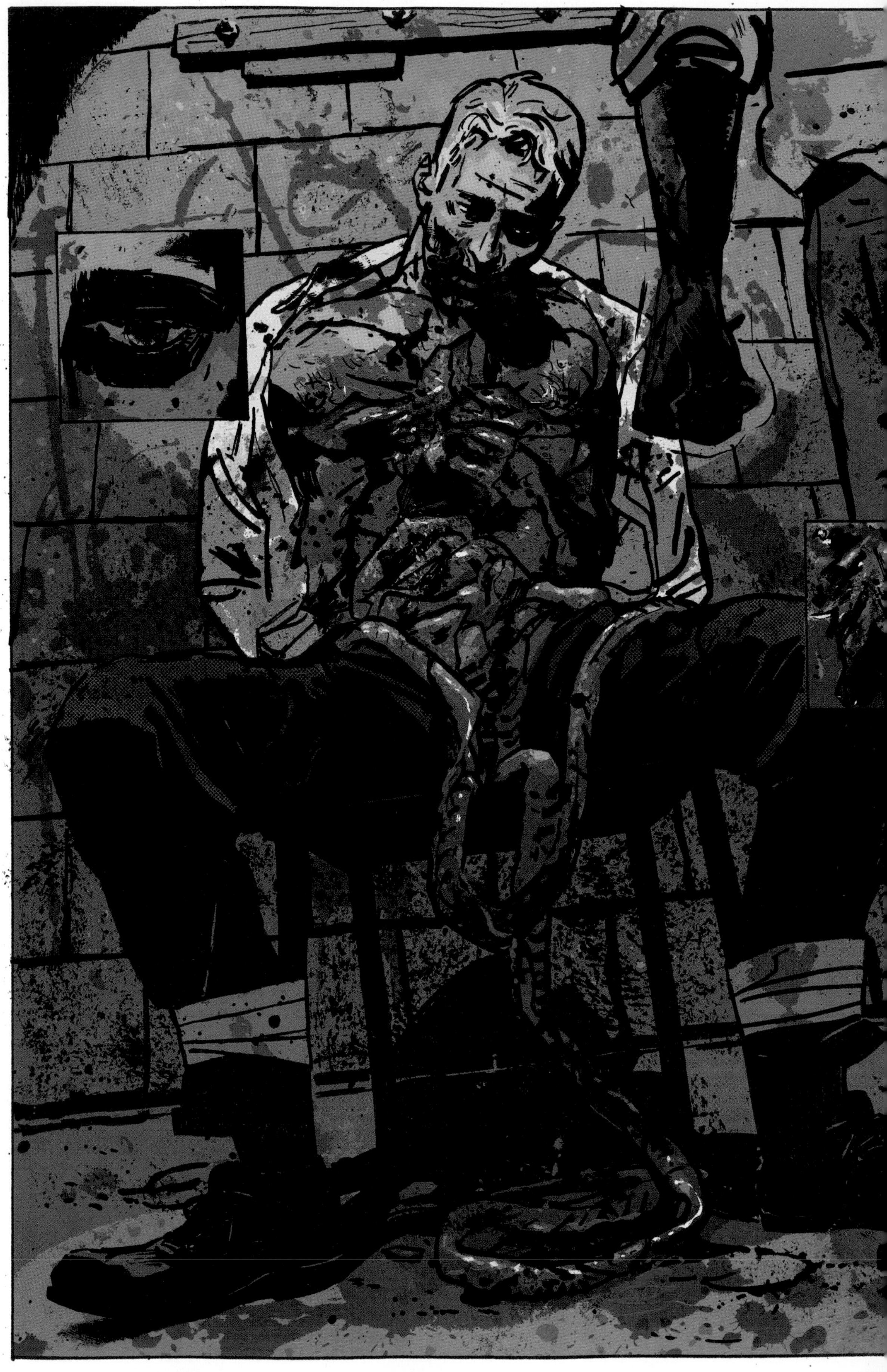

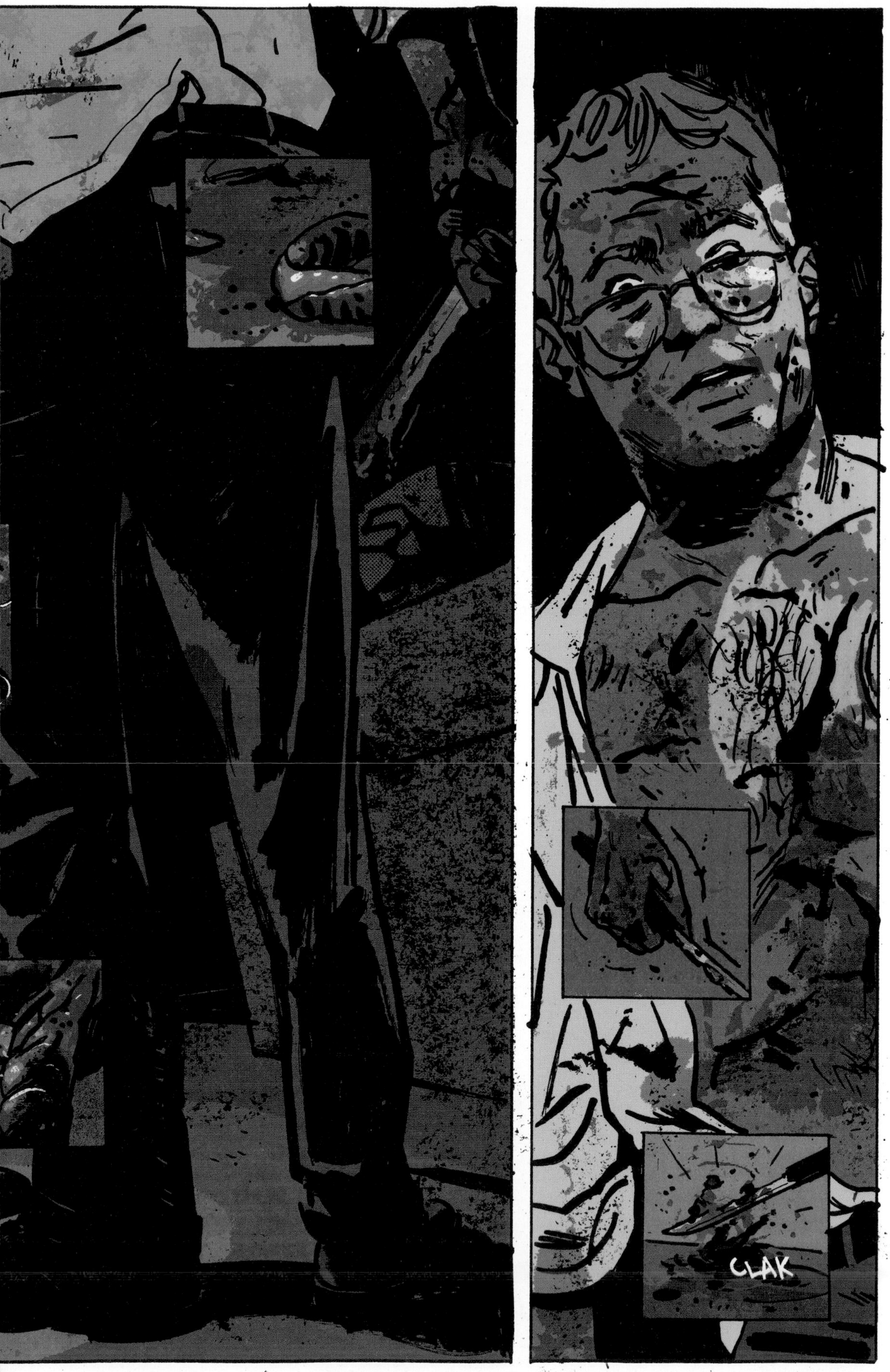
CLAK

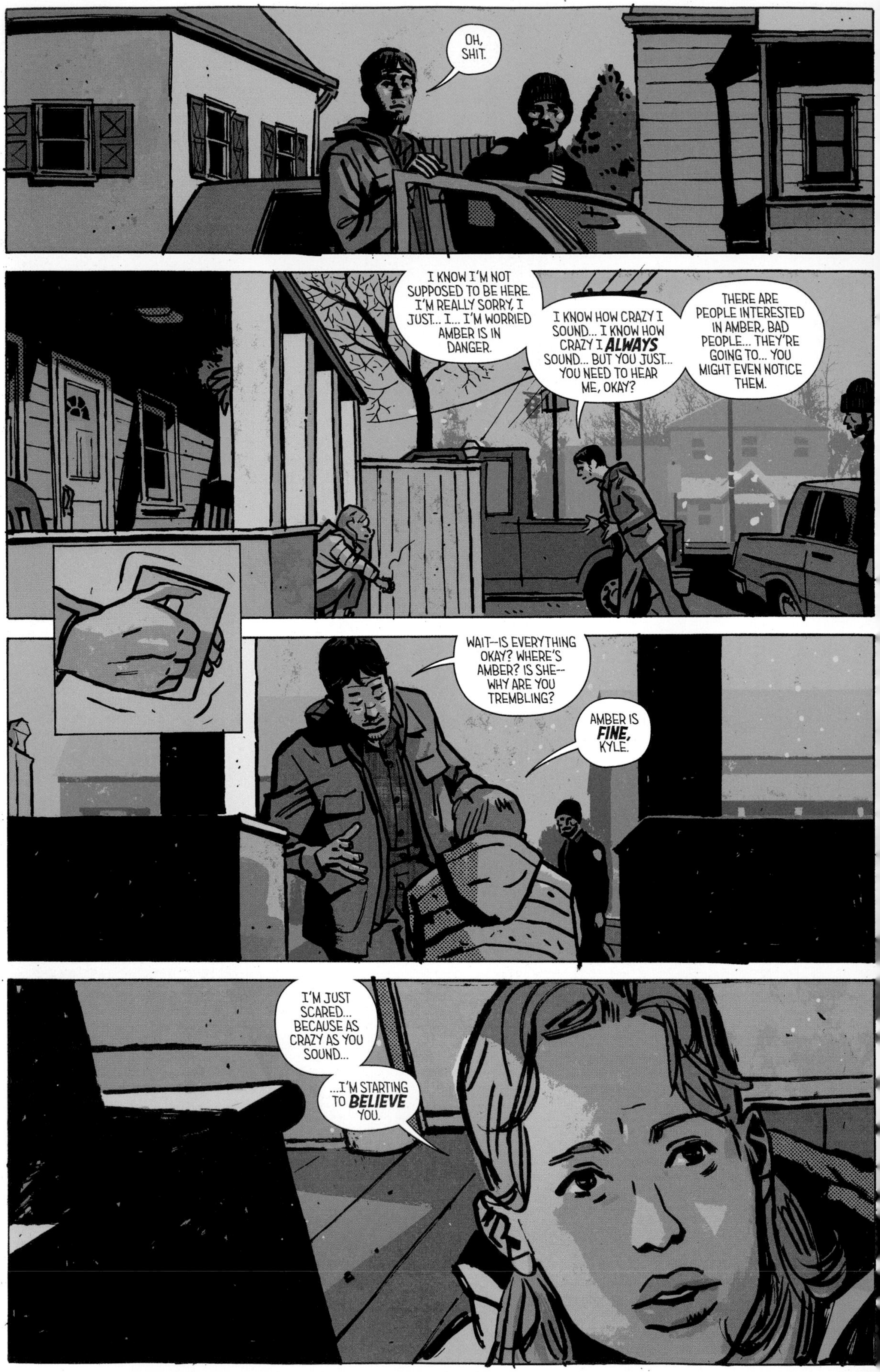
OH, SHIT.
I KNOW I'M NOT SUPPOSED TO BE HERE. I'M REALLY SORRY, I JUST... I... I'M WORRIED AMBER IS IN DANGER.
I KNOW HOW CRAZY I SOUND... I KNOW HOW CRAZY I ALWAYS SOUND... BUT YOU JUST... YOU NEED TO HEAR ME, OKAY?
THERE ARE PEOPLE INTERESTED IN AMBER, BAD PEOPLE... THEY'RE GOING TO... YOU MIGHT EVEN NOTICE THEM.
WAIT--IS EVERYTHING OKAY? WHERE'S AMBER? IS SHE--WHY ARE YOU TREMBLING?
AMBER IS FINE, KYLE.
I'M JUST SCARED... BECAUSE AS CRAZY AS YOU SOUND...
...I'M STARTING TO BELIEVE YOU.

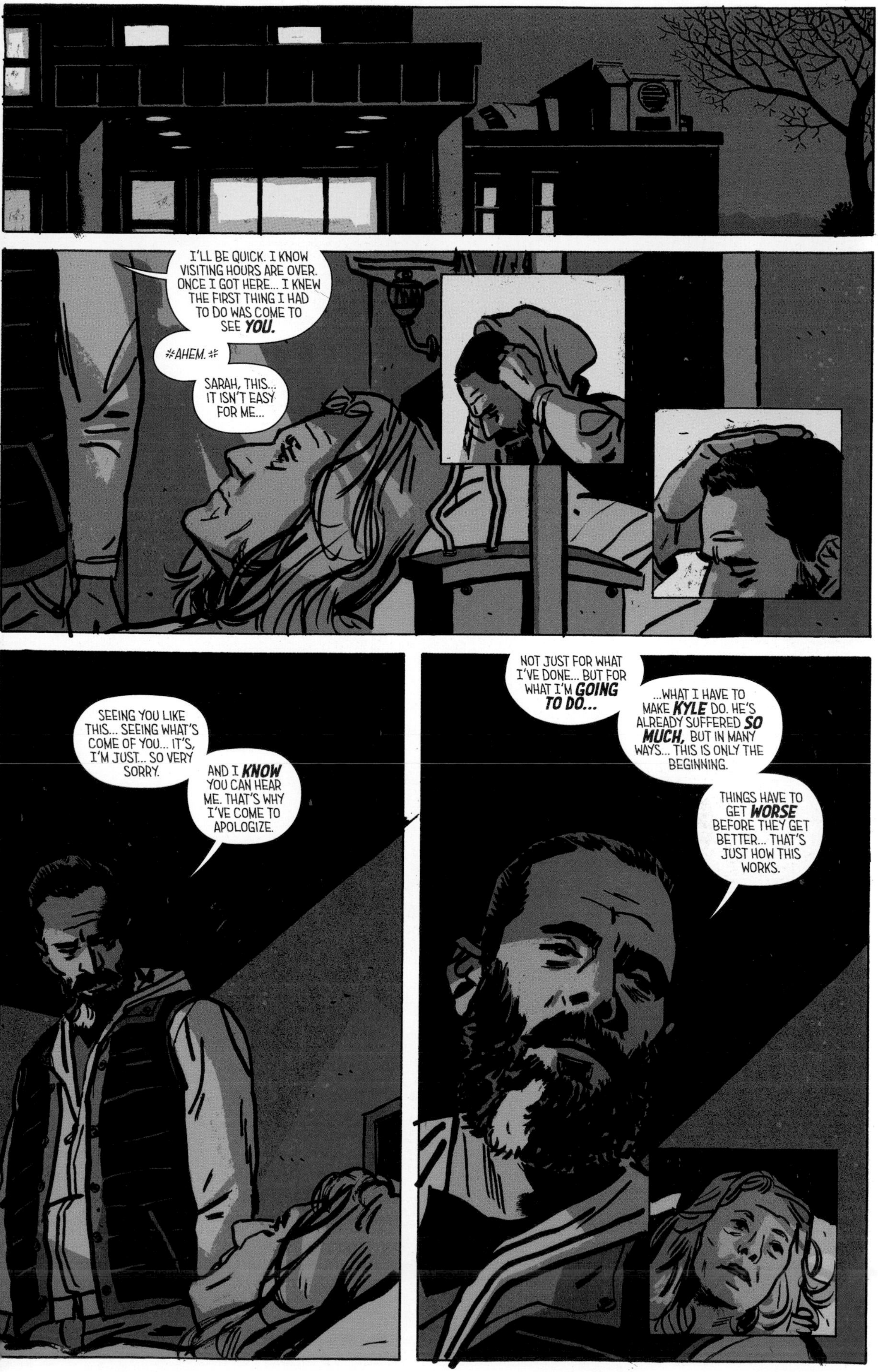
I'LL BE QUICK. I KNOW VISITING HOURS ARE OVER. ONCE I GOT HERE... I KNEW THE FIRST THING I HAD TO DO WAS COME TO SEE YOU.
#AHEM.#
SARAH, THIS... IT ISN'T EASY FOR ME...
SEEING YOU LIKE THIS... SEEING WHAT'S COME OF YOU... IT'S, I'M JUST... SO VERY SORRY.
AND I KNOW YOU CAN HEAR ME. THAT'S WHY I'VE COME TO APOLOGIZE.
NOT JUST FOR WHAT I'VE DONE... BUT FOR WHAT I'M GOING TO DO...
...WHAT I HAVE TO MAKE KYLE DO. HE'S ALREADY SUFFERED SO MUCH, BUT IN MANY WAYS... THIS IS ONLY THE BEGINNING.
THINGS HAVE TO GET WORSE BEFORE THEY GET BETTER... THAT'S JUST HOW THIS WORKS.

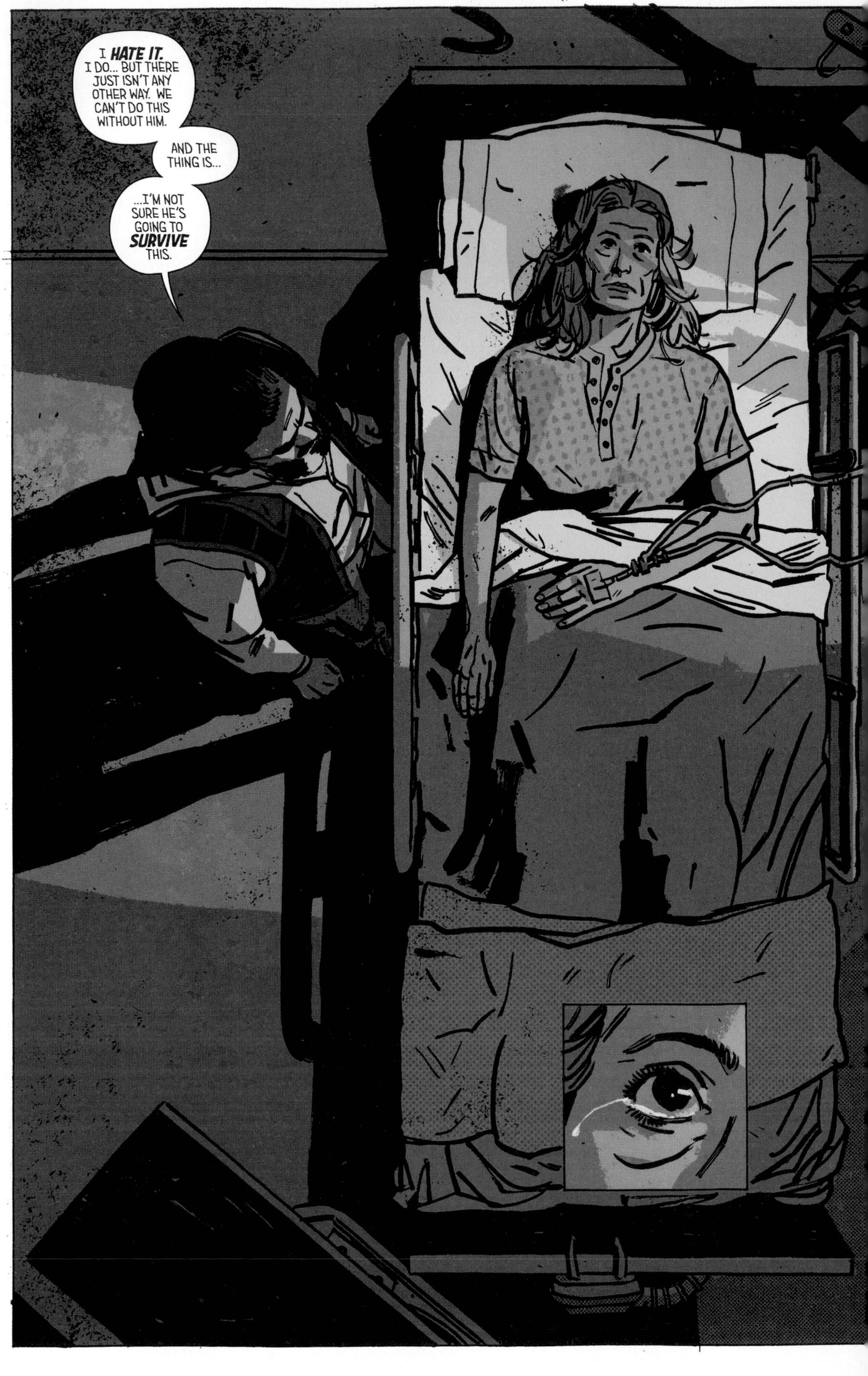
I **HATE IT.** I DO... BUT THERE JUST ISN'T ANY OTHER WAY. WE CAN'T DO THIS WITHOUT HIM.
AND THE THING IS...
...I'M NOT SURE HE'S GOING TO **SURVIVE** THIS.

TO BE CONTINUED

"What would you do for your people?

What line would you cross?"

FOR MORE TALES FROM **ROBERT KIRKMAN** AND **SKYBOUND**

ROBERT KIRKMAN CHARLIE ADLARD STEFANO GAUDIANO CLIFF RATHBURN
THE WALKING DEAD
VOLUME 27
THE WHISPERER WAR

VOL. 1: DAYS GONE BYE TP
ISBN: 978-1-58240-672-5
$14.99

VOL. 2: MILES BEHIND US TP
ISBN: 978-1-58240-775-3
$14.99

VOL. 3: SAFETY BEHIND BARS TP
ISBN: 978-1-58240-805-7
$14.99

VOL. 4: THE HEART'S DESIRE TP
ISBN: 978-1-58240-530-8
$14.99

VOL. 5: THE BEST DEFENSE TP
ISBN: 978-1-58240-612-1
$14.99

VOL. 6: THIS SORROWFUL LIFE TP
ISBN: 978-1-58240-684-8
$14.99

VOL. 7: THE CALM BEFORE TP
ISBN: 978-1-58240-828-6
$14.99

VOL. 8: MADE TO SUFFER TP
ISBN: 978-1-58240-883-5
$14.99

VOL. 9: HERE WE REMAIN TP
ISBN: 978-1-60706-022-2
$14.99

VOL. 10: WHAT WE BECOME TP
ISBN: 978-1-60706-075-8
$14.99

VOL. 11: FEAR THE HUNTERS TP
ISBN: 978-1-60706-181-6
$14.99

VOL. 12: LIFE AMONG THEM TP
ISBN: 978-1-60706-254-7
$14.99

VOL. 13: TOO FAR GONE TP
ISBN: 978-1-60706-329-2
$14.99

VOL. 14: NO WAY OUT TP
ISBN: 978-1-60706-392-6
$14.99

VOL. 15: WE FIND OURSELVES TP
ISBN: 978-1-60706-440-4
$14.99

VOL. 16: A LARGER WORLD TP
ISBN: 978-1-60706-559-3
$14.99

VOL. 17: SOMETHING TO FEAR TP
ISBN: 978-1-60706-615-6
$14.99

VOL. 18: WHAT COMES AFTER TP
ISBN: 978-1-60706-687-3
$14.99

VOL. 19: MARCH TO WAR TP
ISBN: 978-1-60706-818-1
$14.99

VOL. 20: ALL OUT WAR PART ONE TP
ISBN: 978-1-60706-882-2
$14.99

VOL. 21: ALL OUT WAR PART TWO TP
ISBN: 978-1-63215-030-1
$14.99

VOL. 22: A NEW BEGINNING TP
ISBN: 978-1-63215-041-7
$14.99

VOL. 23: WHISPERS INTO SCREAMS TP
ISBN: 978-1-63215-258-9
$14.99

VOL. 24: LIFE AND DEATH TP
ISBN: 978-1-63215-402-6
$14.99

VOL. 25: NO TURNING BACK TP
ISBN: 978-1-63215-659-4
$14.99

VOL. 26: CALL TO ARMS TP
ISBN: 978-1-63215-917-5
$14.99

VOL. 27: THE WHISPERER WAR TP
ISBN: 978-1-5343-0052-1
$14.99

VOL. 1: SPANISH EDITION TP
ISBN: 978-1-60706-797-9
$14.99

VOL. 2: SPANISH EDITION TP
ISBN: 978-1-60706-845-7
$14.99

VOL. 3: SPANISH EDITION TP
ISBN: 978-1-60706-883-9
$14.99

VOL. 4: SPANISH EDITION TP
ISBN: 978-1-63215-035-6
$14.99

COMPENDIUM TP, VOL. 1
ISBN: 978-1-60706-076-5
$59.99

COMPENDIUM TP, VOL. 2
ISBN: 978-1-60706-596-8
$59.99

COMPENDIUM TP, VOL. 3
ISBN: 978-1-63215-456-9
$59.99

BOOK ONE HC
ISBN: 978-1-58240-619-0
$34.99

BOOK TWO HC
ISBN: 978-1-58240-698-5
$34.99

BOOK THREE HC
ISBN: 978-1-58240-825-5
$34.99

BOOK FOUR HC
ISBN: 978-1-60706-000-0
$34.99

BOOK FIVE HC
ISBN: 978-1-60706-171-7
$34.99

BOOK SIX HC
ISBN: 978-1-60706-327-8
$34.99

BOOK SEVEN HC
ISBN: 978-1-60706-439-8
$34.99

BOOK EIGHT HC
ISBN: 978-1-60706-593-7
$34.99

BOOK NINE HC
ISBN: 978-1-60706-798-6
$34.99

BOOK TEN HC
ISBN: 978-1-63215-034-9
$34.99

BOOK ELEVEN HC
ISBN: 978-1-63215-271-8
$34.99

BOOK TWELVE HC
ISBN: 978-1-63215-451-4
$34.99

BOOK THIRTEEN HC
ISBN: 978-1-63215-916-8
$34.99

BIRTHRIGHT
WILLIAMSON BRESSAN LUCAS
VOLUME FOUR
FAMILY HISTORY

VOL. 1: HOMECOMING TP
ISBN: 978-1-63215-231-2
$9.99

VOL. 2: CALL TO ADVENTURE TP
ISBN: 978-1-63215-446-0
$12.99

VOL. 3: ALLIES AND ENEMIES TP
ISBN: 978-1-63215-683-9
$12.99

VOL. 4: FAMILY HISTORY TP
ISBN: 978-1-63215-871-0
$12.99

WILLIAMSON · LACI · RYP · MRVA
GHOSTED
VOLUME FOUR · GHOST TOWN

VOL. 1: HAUNTED HEIST TP
ISBN: 978-1-60706-836-5
$9.99

VOL. 2: BOOKS OF THE DEAD TP
ISBN: 978-1-63215-046-2
$12.99

VOL. 3: DEATH WISH TP
ISBN: 978-1-63215-051-6
$12.99

VOL. 4: GHOST TOWN TP
ISBN: 978-1-63215-317-3
$12.99

CHRIS DINGESS MATTHEW ROBERTS OWEN GIENI
MANIFEST DESTINY
VOLUME 4 · SASQUATCH

VOL. 1: FLORA & FAUNA TP
ISBN: 978-1-60706-982-9
$9.99

VOL. 2: AMPHIBIA & INSECTA TP
ISBN: 978-1-63215-052-3
$14.99

VOL. 3: CHIROPTERA & CARNIFORMAVES TP
ISBN: 978-1-63215-397-5
$14.99

VOL. 4: SASQUATCH TP
ISBN: 978-1-63215-890-1
$14.99

THIEF OF THIEVES
VOLUME 6
"GOLD RUSH."

VOL. 1: "I QUIT."
ISBN: 978-1-60706-592-0
$14.99

VOL. 2: "HELP ME."
ISBN: 978-1-60706-676-7
$14.99

VOL. 3: "VENICE."
ISBN: 978-1-60706-844-0
$14.99

VOL. 4: "THE HIT LIST."
ISBN: 978-1-63215-037-0
$14.99

VOL. 5: "TAKE ME."
ISBN: 978-1-63215-401-9
$14.99

VOL. 6: "GOLD RUSH."
ISBN: 978-1-53430-037-8
$14.99

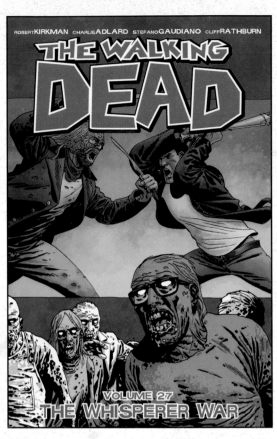

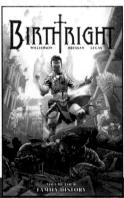

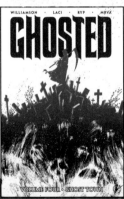

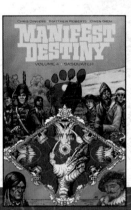

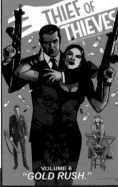